# DRAGONS, DEMONS & DEMIGODS

## DAVID H. MILLAR

# TITLES BY DAVID H. MILLAR

DRAGONS, DEMONS & DEMIGODS
THE TUATHA DÉ CHRONICLES
DAVID H. MILLAR

David H. Millar, LLC, Houston, TX
http://david-h-millar.com/

Paperback ISBN: 979-8-9940184-0-8
Hardback ISBN: 979-8-9940184-1-5
eBook ISBN: 979-8-9865756-9-8

Library of Congress Control Number: 2025924953

# CONTENT WARNING

*Dragons, Demons & Demigods* contains language, scenes of sex, and fantasy violence, which may not be suitable to those under the age of 14 without the parent's permission.

*To Jim, Linda, and the great people of East Belfast where
I spent many happy years and made many friends.
And, of course, to my great-grandfather Lazarus.*

# ACKNOWLEDGEMENTS

The process of writing, publishing, and marketing novels is a team sport. I have always appreciated the international cast that comprises Team Millar. Thanks to my editors, Kahina Necaise and Naomi Muntz from The Fabled Planet, my cover designer and internal formatter, Ida Jansson, Amygdala Design, my cartographer, Dewi Hargreaves, and artist Irene Adam.

Thanks to my beta readers: authors Judith Fullerton, Brendan Sullivan, Lauren Millar, and Jolie Reynolds. Lauren also doubles as PA, roadie, and proofreader.

A big thanks to the many readers I meet at author events and book signings and to those who organise such events.

# CONTENTS

# PRONUNCIATIONS

The following is a guide to the pronunciations
of the Gaelic names used in the story.

Áine (**AWN**-jah)

An-Ársa (Un-**AWHR**-sah)

Anúna (ah-**NOO**-nah)

Aodh (**AWD)**

Badhbh (**BOVE)**

Baoth (**BEE)**

Bráchthine (**BRA**-tin)

Ceara (**KYAR**-a)

Ciarán (**KEE**-a-rawn)

Clíodhna (**KLEE**-uh-na)

Conn (**KUN)**

Daghdha (**DAG**-da)

Eochaidh (**OH**-hee)

Ériu (**AIR**-ee-oo)

Ide (**EE**-deh)

Lugh (**LOO)**

Macha (**MAH**-ha)

Manannán mac Lir (Man-uh-**NAWN** mak **)**

Meadhbh (**MAE**-ve)

Midhir (**MEE**-dur)

Neasán (**NYAS**-awn)

Nuadha (**NOO**-a)

Scáthach (**SKAW**-hokh)

The Mórrígan (**Moe**-rig-**gAHn)**

Tuatha Dé Danann (**TOO**-a day Du-non)

Tuirill (**TOO**-ril)

Uathach (**OO**-hokh)

Ultán (**UL**-tawn)

# CHAPTER 1

*Island of Dragons*

Bráchthine's growl was muted, but her sob could not be contained. Even the formidable Queen of the Dragons was not immune to pain during childbirth, and hers had been difficult. Wisps of white smoke curled from broad nostrils. She shifted her position for comfort and to maintain an even warmth around her warmlings.

She smiled. *Hardly warmlings yet.* Her daughter and son were encased in shells whose size dwarfed an ostrich's egg. Bráchthine had no fear of crushing her progeny. Their temporary homes were stronger than diamonds. They would need a little help to crack the shell, but she would know when.

Dragons were powerful creatures and the only beings feared by their neighbours, the demigods of the Tuatha Dé. The two societies made strange bedfellows. They shared a common root in their mother, Anúna, and each guarded the borders of their homelands jealously. Apart from this, their cultures, governance, and philosophy were vastly different.

The Tuatha Dé resided in the *Land of Immensity* in grand palaces. Their cities were built of marble and crystal, and embellished with gold, silver, and precious stones. The serpents resided in the inhospitable, sun-scorched, red mountains of the *Island of Dragons*. They valued solitude and most lived in humble caves with a single mate. Their monogamy was a singular achievement for beings whose lifetime was measured in millennia. Still, the dragons shared one quality with the Tuatha Dé—a

1

partiality for promiscuity.

The two kingdoms were connected by a single bridge on the northern coast of the Land of Immensity. It was a narrow, rickety, wooden edifice rather than gold or crystal. That was Bráchthine's choice. The link marked the symbiotic relationship between the races. Nevertheless, the queen saw no benefit in a gaudy structure. Who would use it? Neither dragons nor the Tuatha Dé needed a bridge to travel to each other's lands.

* * *

Nuadha, *Ard-Rígh*—High King—of the Tuatha Dé, was ten feet tall like most of the Tuatha Dé. He ducked reflexively, if unnecessarily, as he entered Bráchthine's home. The dwelling's walls were scorched and smelled of brimstone and dragon breath. *The birth must have been difficult. Why did she not ask me for help?* That Bráchthine had not called for him pained Nuadha. There was no light in the cavern, but *Claímh Solais*—the Blade of Light—shone and the area was bathed in daylight.

"This is my home, Nuadha, and the darkness is restful for me. Put away your bloody sword and use your eyes. You can see perfectly well in the dark, and you are in no danger unless *you* come as an assassin." The dragon snorted and a wisp of white smoke curled from her nostrils. "You are too honourable for that, and besides, murder is more your sister The Mórrígan's style. Put the Blade away." Nuadha dipped his head and banished the light.

Bráchthine's mood was better than Nuadha expected. Childbirth is notoriously difficult for a serpent. Perhaps it was the Goddess's blessing they could only birth two eggs in a lifetime. Nuadha looked around the cave. The dragon's laugh echoed around the massive cavern's walls. "You're getting old, Nuadha, or maybe my magic is stronger than yours. We should test our strengths in the Arena." Bráchthine's challenge was one no Tuatha Dé ruler would ever take up and a none-too-subtle reminder of the balance of power. That said, Bráchthine knew of another reason Nuadha would always decline her challenge.

The sound of a long tail pushing aside the dirt as it unfolded echoed through the cave. Nuadha looked at the earth adjacent to Bráchthine's scaled belly and chuckled. In the Land of the Humans, many believed a dragon's weakest point was its belly. *Fools and their myths!* One opalescent and one black egg awaited their mother's warm embrace and the fires that rumbled within her. The warmlings would hatch in a cycle of the moon.

"You know the prophecy, Nuadha. 'A male will challenge his sister for the Dragon Throne.' I cannot permit it to be fulfilled. The dragons are a matriarchal society and have been for aeons. Male serpents are unstable and violent creatures. They are brave and fierce warriors, but few have brains." Bráchthine looked at the black egg and huffed. "Especially the Black Clann. To challenge the status quo will mean endless wars and the inevitable demise of the dragons. There are too few of us as it is. We will not survive a civil war."

Brimstone filled the cave as Bráchthine exhaled. "The foolish wars of the Tuatha Dé have created many enemies, some within their ranks." She ignored the growl from Nuadha. The Tuatha Dé did not like their dirty linen revealed, even in an intimate setting. "Do they want to add the dragons ruled by a tyrannical king to that list? More to the point, I will not allow my daughter to be a pawn for amoral politicians or the target of assassins and bounty killers. You know your duty. Promise me, that when I die, you will take Clíodhna as your ward, educate her on her legacy, and deliver a queen who is fit to reign to the Arena."

Clíodhna was an ominous name chosen by Bráchthine for her daughter. Privately, Nuadha found it amusing. The hackles on his neck stiffened. "Obligation be dammed, Bráchthine. I love you and need no call to duty to help you. I am honoured to be Clíodhna's mentor and protector." Incensed and hurt, Nuadha turned to exit the cave.

"Please, don't be angry with me, Nuadha. I fear for Clíodhna. I know I have chosen wisely but needed to be assured one more time. Forgive me and put it down to post-birth hormones." Bráchthine's voice sounded strangely fragile.

"I could never be mad at you for long."

"I know." Bráchthine's long eyelashes fluttered. "Why couldn't you have been a dragon?"

"Or you a Tuatha Dé?"

The serpent snorted. "That would be a sacrifice too far... even for love."

Nuadha chuckled. "We could have been happy in the Land of the Humans."

"Yes, were it not for duty."

"Damn duty." Silence filled the cave. "When?" It was a question Nuadha dreaded asking and Bráchthine did not want to answer.

"As you observed, the birth was difficult, so shorter than I had hoped," said Bráchthine.

"No," said Nuadha softly. A golden tear rolled down his cheek. "Goodbye, my love."

The dragon shook her massive head, and the plumes of her great crest rustled. "Silly man, my strength will recover. I said shorter, not to-morrow. Like all serpents, I can see that my death draws closer. Thus, my life is now measured in centuries, not millennia. The Womb-Born and the Wind-Born are long-lived, not immortal, Nuadha, although dragons may be reborn, if they wish and the Goddess consents."

The leader of the Womb-Born dipped his head. He could not en-visage life without Bráchthine, even for a brief period, let alone many centuries. And there was no guarantee the Bráchthine he loved would re-turn. Anguish overwhelmed him and he turned to hide his sorrow from his lover.

"What about the boy?" Nuadha suddenly felt ashamed of his lack of concern for the black egg.

"Aodh will take Ciarán to Clann Dubh..."

"That nest of vipers. Do you trust them?"

"No, but he should be with his father's family, if not his father." A grunt was Nuadha's response.

"If the Goddess wills it, we will love again." whispered Bráchthine as Nuadha retraced his steps. A beam of sunlight caught Bráchthine's tears, turning them into tiny rainbows as they trickled down her massive face. They splashed Clíodhna's egg. For a fleeting moment, the egg breathed, and the tears were gone.

"Look after him, Clíodhna. He will need you as much as you will need him."

# CHAPTER 2

*1940—Autumn—Belfast, Northern Ireland*

The demons appeared from nowhere. The huge, black-skinned creatures unfurled leathery wings, blotting out the sun. Frozen to the spot, Clío stared into their malevolent red eyes. Her heart thumped impossibly fast in a chest that seemed much too small to contain it. Sweat poured from pores suddenly flung open, staining the clothes she wore. Only a dogged determination helped her avoid the embarrassment of pissing and shitting herself. She snorted—small victories.

Four creatures, each positioned at the cardinal compass points, moved steadily and claustrophobically closer to her. Clío could make out the rows of incisors when they opened their maws and the long, black talons sprouting from their paws and feet. *How do they walk with those?* She swore. *They fucking retract them, eejit!*

They called out her given name, "Clíodhna." She wondered how such monsters could speak, but, most of all, she was surprised that they knew her name. *Why do they hate me?* She had no avenue of retreat and no means of defence, so she forced a defiant mien. Refusing to be cowed, Clío closed her eyes, listening only to the thud of the demons' heavy footfall.

When she finally opened her eyes, she gazed down into the demons' fiery red eyes. *How?* Her limbs were transformed and her torso covered in opalescent scales. Her jaws opened, her tail swatted the demon behind her, and she bellowed. Yet it was not just a roar. Fire spouted from her maw, and she heard the demons shriek as they were incinerated.

\*\*\*

"Fuck!"

Clío flung bedding sodden with sweat onto the floor and instantly regretted it. It was six o'clock in the morning, late autumn, and the chill of winter did not refuse the invitation. Naked and covered in a film of cold perspiration, she shivered, reached for the woollen blanket at the foot of the bed, and wrapped it around herself.

She gagged on the taste of ashes in her mouth and reeled at the smell of brimstone in her nostrils. *How? It was just a dream… wasn't it?* Clío poured a glass of cold water from the jug on her bedside table. It washed away the aftertaste, but the scent lingered. She swore to stay away from horror movies.

Where did these nightmares come from, and what was their purpose? Why had their frequency and intensity increased? She had asked the same questions for centuries, which, given her age, was a short time. *Who or what am I? Will I ever find out? When?* That was another subject to ponder. "I need answers," she muttered for the thousandth time, but why had it suddenly become so urgent?

She ground her teeth at the thought of another of those talks with Lazarus. She would rant and scream; he would be calm and reasonable. Dissatisfied, she would storm from the house to her haven and the ducks in Victoria Park. After millennia with Lazarus, mistrust slipped into her mind. *What is he hiding from me and why?*

*He needs you as much as you need him. Be patient.*

The voice in her head was female and strangely familiar. Clío sensed a smile and tears, which were both loving and deeply sad. *I'm going mad.*

\*\*\*

The cold, damp sheets forced Clío from her musing. She swore and grumbled. It felt as if she had pissed the bed and she sniffed the air to make sure that was not the case. She tried to reclaim her sleep, but anxiety made her sit up straight. "Shite! I must get ready. My girlfriends will be banging on the front door soon."

Lazarus would be furious. *He's not a morning person.* "We'll miss the bus, be late for work at the linen mill, and they'll dock our pay." Her not-particularly-attractive feet missed the bedside mat, instead landing on well-polished, cold linoleum. An innate sense of balance narrowly saved Clío from landing on her arse.

Clío cursed again. She did not agree with those who believed frequent swearing indicated a lack of education and a poor vocabulary. The benefits of being millennia old included the mastery of a hundred languages and a deep knowledge of history and anthropology. She and Lazarus had participated in or observed every major historical event in human history. To Clío, academic tomes were for ignorant university professors who relied on propaganda written by victorious kings or religious zealots.

She brushed her teeth and spat into the porcelain basin. The start to Clío's day worsened when it dawned on her that it was Saturday and she was fully awake. *This is just not my day.* Then her face broke into a broad smile. She did not have an overtime shift, and she and her girlfriends had tickets to attend the dinner dance at the Grand Central Hotel. She finger-combed her mass of long, blonde hair. A look in the dressing table mirror elicited a loud moan. It would take hours of brushing and combing to make herself presentable.

Optimism shattered the gloom of an autumn dawn. Thoughts of free drinks, calloused hands groping her, and hard sex by multiple men, individually or in a group, overtook her complaining. "There is a God!" shouted Clío. She began to sing loudly, ignoring the banging on the wall from Lazarus' room. So what if the cats on the yard wall held a tune better than she?

On another plane, an ancient entity smiled. "No, Clíodhna. There is a Goddess."

\* \* \*

It was a typical Belfast October—cold, wet, and miserable. Pregnant clouds lumbered across broody grey skies. Occasionally, a sheepish sun peeked from behind layers of cumulus, apologized, and slipped back under the fluffy blankets. In every home, fires burned in cast-iron grates. The air smelled of wood smoke, sulphurous coal, and the sweet fragrance of peat. Their only competition was the sharp odour of ozone from the trams that trundled up and down the Newtownards Road.

The weekend had arrived, and the brave souls of the communities on either side of the road refused to be intimidated by inclement weather. With woollen outer coats buttoned from calf to neck and laden down with the week's shopping, women battled the rain while holding onto children, umbrellas, and hats.

Their partners and sons, many of them the "hard men" from the Harland and Wolff Shipyard, "The Yard", would not be seen dead with a shopping bag. Instead, the men stuffed what remained of their pay into deep trouser pockets, buttoned their jackets, turned up their collars, and stepped outside. Mothers and wives had taken their due—a tradition honoured by all but a few drunken reprobates. A cast-iron skillet on the skull soon sorted out the rebellious. The "wee" working-class women of East Belfast could face down and put the fear of God into brawny men twice their size, if the wage packet was not handed over—unopened.

Still, the men's curses were never for the women—they were wiser than that. It was for the storm that tried to dislodge dunchers from closely cropped heads as, en masse, they forged a path to the bars and bookies. In the betting shops, thick fingers ingrained with dirt used pencil stubs to mark betting slips. They gazed at black-and-white television screens and swore at their poor choice of dog, horse, or football team.

In the bars, the real venom was reserved for the elements that delayed their first pint of Guinness and the whiskey chaser. If another world existed, it never occurred to them. Why was it their business? They had their own problems. Still, the local newspapers were filled with news of the war in continental Europe, which threatened to spread and set fire to the world. Belfast's young men would be among the first to volunteer to fight… and die.

Yet, how different was it to previous generations and millennia? Celts and Gaels loved to drink, fight, and rut. Was it not better to have a common enemy than to kill each other?

# CHAPTER 3

*Belfast, Northern Ireland*

In a corner of McHugh's Bar, Lazarus savoured the cigarette smoke and caressed his whiskey. A pint of Guinness sat on the table before him. It would remain there when he left the pub as he did not care for its taste. Maybe one day, he would. Until then he would admire the barman's talent for pouring the perfect stout, time after time. No one joined him at the table, yet he was not unfriendly. Those around him sensed he preferred his own company and let him be.

In the Land of Immensity, he was known as Nuadha, the High King. In the Land of the Humans, his name was Lazarus. He appeared to be about seventy years of age, but when he stood, his posture was erect. Tall and slim. Gaunt yet not skeletal. His hair, black as ravens' feathers, was slicked back from a high forehead with Brylcreem. Deep, sapphire-blue eyes held a twinkle of mischief and the threat of menace. Sallow skin and the blue tone from an illusory six o'clock shadow made the colour of his eyes more intense.

He had pale, thin lips. His teeth were yellowish and rarely seen, even when he smiled, which was deceptively often. Deep dimples in his cheeks testified to that. His breath smelled of tobacco—unfiltered Woodbines—and whiskey. Eschewing modern fragrances, his skin smelled of coal tar soap.

Outside the sanctuary of the bar, a flash of lightning was quickly followed by the drumming of rain on the bar's windows. The bar manager swore. The windows had just been cleaned. "Wasted money," he grumbled.

Lazarus took a gold pocket watch from his vest and gazed absently at its face. He had no need for the watch. He naturally knew the time, date, and year. The timepiece made him look normal, if a little eccentric. The front case contained no image of a loved one or lock of hair. *How could I have an image of Bráchthine?* His love had no hair to clip, and cameras came millennia after her death. A stolen snippet of her feathery crest would have hurt... him. His memory was as sharp as it was painful and every time he looked at Clíodhna, he saw Bráchthine.

He grimaced and growled. Assuming they had infringed on his personal space, those nearest to his table apologised and moved away. The waiting staff glared at those they held responsible. Lazarus was a regular customer, and, unlike most, a generous tipper. He shook his head. "Painful memories." They understood and shortly after, three Bushmills whiskies were set on the table. He raised a glass. "*Sláinte mhaith*—Good health."

***

It was an anniversary of sorts, and each year the memory of a sharp pain in his right arm reminded him of it. Aeons ago, when he was Nuadha, Womb-Born of Anúna, he lost the arm in the First Battle of Mag Tuired against the Fir Bolg. Iron and arrogance were the weaknesses of the Tuatha Dé. Armed with the Blade of Light, Nuadha thought he was invincible.

The Goddess showed him he was wrong. The severed arm lying at his feet underlined her disapproval. Worse, Tuatha Dé law ruled that no imperfect man or woman could be High King or Queen. Hubris meant none of the Womb-Born foresaw the possibility of such an event. They were demigods with ambitions to be gods. Angry at their haughtiness, the Goddess refused their pleadings to revise the rules. They were stuck with the law and Nuadha was forced to abdicate.

"Pathetic bastards." Lazarus grunted his judgment of his siblings.

His replacement was not a Womb-Born. His brothers and sisters had pleaded their shoulders were overburdened with responsibility. Thus, a minor king, of mixed Tuatha Dé and Fomorian heritage, whose main attributes were his good looks and silver tongue, became High King. He was a traitor and provoked a war with Fomoria. Without Nuadha's experience and strategic mind the Tuatha Dé barely won the Second Battle of Mag Tuired.

The Goddess, however, deemed them not suitably humbled. Soon after, the demigods were defeated by the progenitors of man, the Sons of Mil. An appeal to Nuadha to negotiate a peace treaty resulted in the Tuatha Dé's banishment to the underground Mounds, which became known as the Land of Immensity.

Embittered, but restored to full health and given a new arm through *Coire Ansic*—Daghdha's Undry Cauldron, Nuadha considered rebellion and civil war to get his throne back. Yet, by nature, Nuadha was honourable not treasonous. His response was, "The Hag take them!" He took Clíodhna and left the Land of Immensity for the Lands of the Humans. On this day and every year since, he mourned his loss and pondered whether he had made the right decision… and under what circumstances it could be reversed.

He continued to grieve for Bráchthine and hoped she approved of his guidance of Clíodhna. In his heart, he knew she would not. How would he answer why he had not informed his ward of her heritage or trained her for battle in the Arena? No matter how detailed, dreams were an imperfect preparation to inform her about potential enemies, the dragon culture, and her role in it. "Soon," he promised Bráchthine. "Very soon." He imagined puffs of white smoke and snorts of disbelief.

Lazarus' brow furrowed and he sighed. During his travels with Clíodhna he had discovered clues of An-Ársa—the Ancient One—an evil from the dark, chaotic days before the Tuatha Dé became civilised. The violent entity had violated his mother, Anúna. Thus the Womb-Born were a family brought to life by violence.

"To weak-kneed siblings and a meddling Goddess," snarled Lazarus. He lifted his Bushmills in a mock salute. The discovery of An-Ársa gave him an excuse to delay a permanent return to the Land of Immensity. *Yet how long can I prevaricate? Clíodhna has a destiny to fulfil.*

# CHAPTER 4

*Bryson Street, Belfast*

Clío sat with her leg hooked over the arm of a worn leather armchair. She looked at Lazarus and sighed. She had intended to confront him, but that would have insulted the tradition of the parlour. The room was a haven of peace and good manners in the working-class homes of Belfast. Who knew what god guarded that sacrament? So, Clío held her temper and took stock of what she knew. It was a cop-out, and she knew it.

After aeons, Clío had no definitive proof of her origin, just persistent murmurings in her head and colourful dreams. Lazarus never revealed who or what type of beings they were and studiously avoided or deflected the topic when raised. Given their longevity, this was a remarkable accomplishment. Veiled or cryptic hints and increasingly detailed dreams increased Clío's frustration. In a contemplative moment brought on by a gnawing desire to know her origin, Clío listed what she knew.

They were warm-blooded, with beating hearts, and crimson blood coursing through arteries and veins. Clío bled if she nicked her legs when shaving. She was not so sure about Lazarus. She had never seen his skin broken or even bruised, unless he wanted it to appear so, and never a cut from the straight razor he shaved with.

Philosophically, Clío defined them by what they were not and excluded predators living on blood and flesh. Although, given her passion for blue-rare steak, and how she hoovered up beef carpaccio as if there were no tomorrow, she wondered. However, she was reasonably confident that neither of them was ghoul, vampire, or zombie.

Blood-drinking revenants are common to most cultures and mythologies, including the Celts and Gaels. In the Land of the Humans, Clío suspected most were fakes or mentally disturbed. Currently, true vampires basked in the limelight of twentieth-century revisionism. And why not? It made hunting much more straightforward. Bela Lugosi's Dracula was an easier sell to impressionable young women than Max Schreck's Orlok.

She ruled out golem and gargoyle. Such creatures tend to be the preserve of the religious. Neither she nor Lazarus had wings or tails, which should rule out angels and demons—yes, some stereotypes have a factual basis. Clío tried a few times to shapeshift when there was a full moon. *I love Lon Chaney Jr.'s "The Wolf Man."* All she achieved for her effort was a vague tingling in her fingers and toes and a debilitating headache worse than a hangover. Therefore, she eliminated werewolf or were-anything from her list.

Thus, the jury was out on whether Lazarus and she were Brothers Grimm or Walt Disney.

***

In one of his rare forthcoming moments, Lazarus had told her she was named after Clíodhna, Queen of the Mná Sídhe—banshees in the modern lexicon. Contrary to her deathly responsibilities, Queen Clíodhna was a beautiful, charming young woman, loved by all. She was also as promiscuous as Queen Meadhbh, a demigoddess renowned for her insatiable sexual desire. Clío blushed at the latter. *Was my mother an Oracle who divined how I would grow up?* Clío's eyebrows knit at another thought. *Is Lazarus' intimate knowledge of the Tuatha Dé a clue to his and my origin?*

Known as Clío to those she counted as friends, she appeared to be in her early twenties. In public, Lazarus assumed the role of her grandpa. The honorific suited him, and she often used it in private, assuming he was comfortable with it. That said, the title was many generations inaccurate and their bloodlines had never suffered the scrutiny of deep conversations. *Honestly, after several millennia, would that not piss you off, too?*

Their relationship made sense to their working-class neighbours, whose generosity and tolerance would only go so far. She loved to reel off alternative roles they might play and delighted in suggesting novel ones to shock Lazarus. Rich, dirty, old man and his arm candy; pimp and whore; adulterer and mistress; dominant and submissive. In this, Clío was spectacularly unsuccessful. At his most demonstrative, Lazarus usually sighed, shook his head, and returned to his newspaper. It is incredibly hard to shock someone many millennia old.

Clío's eyes were hazel-gold and appeared to change colour frequently. She called her hair ash blonde, because that sounded fashionable. At times, she considered adding pink highlights. Maybe in a future time. This was conservative Belfast during the war years. Clío was tall and stunning, yet her beauty did not faze the men of East Belfast. They could bring any diva down to earth with a single look, phrase, or slap.

She believed Lazarus chose their current home to keep her grounded. They lived an unremarkable lifestyle in an average, terraced house. The strategy worked because Clío rarely took herself seriously. Working men and pimply-faced adolescents made backhanded compliments, ranging from the quaint and somewhat humorous "Nice arse," to the honest brutishness of "She's a good fuck." Clío wore rouge. Her admirers thought it concealed her embarrassment. She tittered. *Some hope!*

Clío tended to gravitate to men and women who wanted to screw her rather than be bosom friends. Admirers described her as a "long drink of water," but her skin tone suggested milk was more accurate. She blossomed. *How? Who controls my growth?* She glanced askance at Lazarus. She had strong suspicions but no proof. To Clío's chagrin, her breasts refused to be anything other than perky. A handful rather than full and heavy like those of Jane Mansfield or Russell, movie actresses she admired.

Glamours are the fae's first line of defence and are an invaluable tool for avoiding conflict with or simply staying hidden from mankind. They appear and feel solid, but are detailed, subtly laid defences. Lazarus and she chose human forms, ages, and appearances with which they were comfortable. *When did I choose mine?* Clío's brow wrinkled. *Have I ever chosen my glamour? Who did?* Her expressions cycled through a range from perplexity to consternation. Finally, she stared at Lazarus who ignored her. *Perhaps it comes naturally to me.*

Lazarus' glamour was the wiser and more acceptable option to a remarkably incurious, "It's none of our business" public. Youthful narcissism guided Clío's preference. By choice, she no longer grew older and remained a female in her early twenties who delighted in wanton shamelessness. *Why not? I can't get pregnant.* At infrequent times she longed for a son or daughter, but nothing transpired. *Am I infertile?* The thought made her sad.

They had few friends. From their perspective, all human relationships were fleeting. Clío sniffed and Lazarus looked up in time to see a tear tumble down Clío's cheek. He knew she remembered centuries of standing at the gravesides of those she had loved. He shook his head. He adored her for her compassion and worried about her sanity.

Clío perpetually had a small group of girlfriends and confidants she socialised with. In Belfast, they were from her job at the linen mill. She loved them but knew they would inevitably marry, settle down, have kids, and disappear from her social circle. Another cycle would begin, and she would find another set of playmates.

On balance, Clío and Lazarus' existence appeared sad and lonely, yet was not so. Did a chemical imbalance in their brains enable their acceptance of isolation as a social benefit and protection from insanity? Or perhaps, they denied knowledge of the loneliness. Sex was Clío's diversion. She often wondered how Lazarus coped.

\*\*\*

After another evening of fruitless contemplation, Clío stood up and stamped her feet. It was an ineffective protest. The parlour was the only room in the house with a deep, luxurious pile carpet. She would have slammed the door but that would have breached the room's etiquette. Before exiting, she paused briefly, noticing a fleeting shadow thrown by a flickering gaslight. "We need a new mantle," she muttered before closing the door.

Lazarus smiled and waited for the inevitable bang of Clío's bedroom door. His behaviour was deplorable. He knew what Clío wanted to talk about and once again had avoided the conversation. *How much longer can I prevaricate?* He snorted. *Probably millennia.* One of the sins of demigods is procrastination. To the long-lived, there was always another decade, century, or millennium to address the problem. The room's flickering gaslight caught his attention, and he rose to examine the mantle. At that moment, the shadow detached itself from the wall.

"Good evening, brother."

He dipped his head. "It has been millennia, sister." Hurt infused his voice. Lazarus had been sure The Mórrígan would have his back, but he was wrong.

"Has it? Or perhaps you have not seen what was in front of your regal nose."

"You have been here all this time?"

"At your side? Of course I have. Among other things, I am the Queen of Whispers and Shadows." Lazarus sensed exasperation in his sister's voice and bearing. He opened his mouth to protest but was cut off. "Every day? No, I have not. I have other duties, some of which should be yours. I have been with you too many times to count, but you ignore me.

"Do you hate me so much? Or are your powers so weak you are unable to see or feel the presence of another of the Womb-Born? Or to sense your sister? We were very close, once." The tear that rolled down The Mórrígan's cheek shocked Lazarus. He had never seen his sister cry, not a solitary tear.

"Why are you here?"

"At this time? Bráchthine was my friend as well as yours. She is disappointed and angry."

"How do you know? Have you seen her?" The hope and anguish in her brother's voice prompted a second tear to escape her eye.

"Don't be ridiculous. You would not be the first she would appear to, especially not now." The Mórrígan's words were a brutal slap to Lazarus' face, and he flinched. "The child is clueless about who or what she is or is about to become. She does not know about her destiny or the prophesy. You were supposed to be her teacher and protector, not a doting grandpa. You have left her defenceless, Nuadha." The Mórrígan reached out and took Lazarus' hands. It was the second shock of the night. The Womb-Born stopped sharing affectionate embraces aeons ago.

"Why now? Why reveal yourself now?"

"One word, brother. *Puberty!*" Lazarus' mouth flopped open like a fish stranded on a riverbank. "All your procrastination and waiting for the right time; all your clever glamours and planted dreams. Soon they will be smashed into a million pieces by biology, when dragon hormones rampage through her pretty body. She is unprepared... and so are you."

"Shite!" Lazarus fell back into his chair. Long fingers combed his hair as he grappled with The Mórrígan's words. Moments later, he looked up, but his sister was gone, although he could still hear the strains of her laughter. "*Bitseach!*" His problems had tripled. He had pissed off Bráchthine, Clío, and The Mórrígan.

"What else? What else?"

\* \* \*

Outside the room, The Mórrígan paused. "What else?" she repeated. "I made a grave error once, brother, and intend to correct it. I will restore you to the position given to you by Anúna or I will destroy the Tuatha Dé."

# CHAPTER 5

Clío and Lazarus resided in a modest, gable-end, terraced house on the corner of Duke and Bryson Streets. It comprised two bedrooms, a kitchen with a porcelain jawbox sink, a living room, and the parlour. Clío constantly moaned at Lazarus to replace the outside toilet. In winter, the wooden seat, a luxury in these times, gave no protection for her bare arse. Lazarus' retort was always, why should they be more privileged than their neighbours?

In retaliation, Clío insisted the cleaning and maintenance of the "bogs" was his chore—eternally. That included tearing old newspapers into square toilet wipes. Ink-smeared arses were nothing to be ashamed of when you were fucking because everybody used the same type of cleaning sheets. Beyond the lavatory was a door to an alleyway that ran the length of the street. She avoided it as much as possible. It smelled of cat pee, dog shite, and spilt garbage. On Fridays and Saturdays, vomit and stale beer were added to the perfume.

Neighbours would rarely intrude but were always at hand if needed. No one would dare try to raise another's offspring. That only led to fist fights between the men… and the women. Yet there was mutual agreement that all could cuff the ears of any child who stepped out of line.

A gaslit streetlamp dominated the pavement corner to the right of their home. The mantle's soft glow reflected off the high-gloss, black-painted entrance door with its polished brass kick-plate and doorknocker furnishings. The streetlight made them extremely popular with the neighbours' children, who threw ropes over the iron crossbars to make swings.

The local Catholic church and grounds were located behind a high, red brick wall on the opposite side of the street. The dark, gothic St. Matthew's Roman Catholic Church had an adjoining convent and school. The lack of respect shown by the Catholic children of the street towards the nuns shocked Clío. While not religious, except in a vague ancient way, it struck Clío that disparaging any god's servants was a recipe for a short and painful life and an unpleasant afterlife.

The less imposing Pitt Street Mission Hall, which turned no one away but catered mainly to Protestants, sat on the opposite side of the Newtownards Road to Clío's street. For those of that persuasion who preferred ritual and a more impressive edifice in which to worship, St. Patrick's Church of Ireland was a short walk up the road.

Homes had no refrigerators, and the food was free of chemical additives and colourings. It tasted and smelled real. Cool pantries contained fresh and slightly stale groceries and victuals wrapped up in newspapers or brown paper. Milk and groceries—and even coal, peat, and firewood—were delivered to the doorstep: fresh bread and buns, fish and meat, vegetables with farm dirt still clinging to them, and bottles of lemonade in a multitude of delicious, tooth-decaying flavours. Knives were sharpened at the doorstep. Gipsies brought a variety shop to the door and would read palms or the tea leaves for a modest amount.

Fragrances always brought memories rushing back to Clío, filling her heart with joy and her eyes with tears. The comforting scents of wood, sulphurous coal, and peat fires soothed her. They combined seamlessly with old leather couches, linoleum floors, and the smell of Mansion Guard Shine floor polish to make their house into a home.

One fragrance, above all, wore the crown. The aroma of hot fat and batter from the local chippy, The Star, on a Friday night. Battered fish, sausages, and thick potato scallops partnered with chips—crisp on the outside and soft on the inside. All were well-dusted with salt and splashed with malt vinegar. Clío's preferred appetizer was a cup of cooked, but not mushy, peas in vinegar. Centuries in the future, the smell of malt vinegar would make her eyes tear up, and she would yearn for the times when a fish supper was only a short walk away.

The memories evoked were powerful. Life was hard and humdrum, but Clío was happy… mostly.

\*\*\*

Living in a close community brought with it the shared sorrows of the neighbourhood as well as the pleasures. Demigods are not immune to personal tragedy. Lazarus and Clío lived through the Titanic disaster. They wept alongside the kin of the shipyard's tradesmen lost to the icy seas. They stood with the crowds thronging the Newtownards Road when news of the Ulster Regiment's dead from the Battle of the Somme headlined the *Belfast Telegraph*. Brave men—foolish leaders.

Often, they shook their heads at humanity's innumerable wars, which began with the first tribe coveting its neighbour's wealth. Tens of millions had died since then. Clío continued to hope mankind would learn its lesson, which only proves that longevity does not necessarily come with foresight. Perhaps if, like dragons, humans could only procreate a limited number of times, they would value life more.

\*\*\*

The strangeness began in the late autumn of 1940, a year after the Second World War commenced but before the German Luftwaffe flattened most of East Belfast during the 1941 Blitzes. Until that time, the good folk of Belfast had been relatively untouched by the conflict engulfing the rest of Europe.

# CHAPTER 6

Clío was awake, enjoying the warmth of her bed and knowing she had an hour before she had to rise and get ready for work. An hour earlier, the pre-dawn clinking of glass bottles heralded the daily delivery of two pints of milk and a pint of orange juice.

The frantic pounding of fists and the metallic hammering of the front door's heavy brass knocker were impossible to ignore. Clío grabbed her robe and hurried downstairs. She opened the door to find a small group of nuns, frantically crossing themselves and reciting, "*In nomine Patris, et Filii, et Spiritus Sancti,*" over and over. Across the doorstep, on the cold, grey pavement, lay the bodies of two naked girls.

They looked no more than thirteen years of age and could have been twins. Hands crossed over pubescent breasts, their limbs and features were frozen by the rigour of death. Two pairs of blue-grey eyes stared heavenward and seemed to ask, "Why?" There was no clue as to how they met their fate and no visible marks on their bodies—except a small sigil—a thorny, red rose imprinted on each child's inner right thigh. It seemed an odd choice. Female tattoos were uncommon, certainly in girls of their age.

Clío's silk night robe put up a token defence against the dawn chill of the October morning. She shivered and rubbed at the rash of goosebumps on her arms. Her reaction was not due to the cold morning as she was immune to changes in temperature—hence the scanty attire.

The girls looked as if they had been left as sacrifices. But by whom, to whom, and for what? Clío would not have been surprised to discover that they were virgins.

The blare of bells and an ambulance's siren shattered what little remained of Bryson Street's early morning calm. Further up the street, a pair of uniformed Royal Ulster Constabulary constables from the nearby Mountpottinger Station passed Beechfield Primary School's gates and strode purposefully towards the house.

Involuntarily, Clío reached out to touch the bodies. Lazarus, standing behind her, instantly clamped her hand and jerked it back. Still, it was not the force of the grip that surprised Clío but Lazarus' command. "*Do not touch their bodies.*" His tone negated any possibility of disobedience or dissent. Usually, Lazarus' rich baritone was a pleasure to hear. Now it vibrated with rage. The slight shaking of his hands and tremor in his voice, which Clío knew to be affectations, were gone. In their place was the strength of a man used to being obeyed.

With a snarl, Clío turned, ran down the hallway, and returned with a heavy woollen blanket. "I'm not letting them lie exposed for the world to gawk at." She laid the cover over the girls.

In a display of remarkable coordination, the constables arrived at the doorway, the police car's brakes squealed and two men in plain clothes stepped onto the pavement, and the ambulance doors slammed open. With a quick nod to the officers, the nuns turned to Lazarus and Clío, crossed themselves, and hurried across the street to the safety of St. Matthews and a day of prayers for the children.

One look at Lazarus and the detectives abandoned any thoughts of intimidation, adopted a conciliatory tone, and suggested they talk inside. The constables were disappointed. Most of their daily work was a monotonous routine. On this morning, they were treated to the sight of Clío's prominent nipples attempting to poke their way through her robe's fabric.

Clío considered her breasts nothing to write home about, but her nipples and areolae were genuinely magnificent and extremely sensitive. At times such as this, their response to stimulation was painful and unhelpful.

*** 

In Belfast, nothing happens without a cup of well-brewed, milky tea and a biscuit. Whether the biscuit is plain or chocolate-covered generally signifies the importance of the guest or the conversation's friendliness. In this instance, the digestives were plain, although they were McVitie's and served on the best Royal Doulton china.

The conversation proved unproductive for both parties. What could Lazarus and Clío tell the detectives that could be useful? They did not know the girls. They had no idea why they had been left on their doorstep, they were not responsible for their deaths, and no, they did not know what the small tattoos might signify. If they remembered anything that might be of help, they would, of course, call the more senior of the investigators.

In turn, the detectives promised to keep Lazarus informed of the girls' identities when known and any progress in their investigation. They also thanked Clío for the tea and digestives. As the door closed behind the officers, Clío turned to Lazarus.

"Well?"

His visage told her he was more than aware of what she meant. Clío's responses to the police had been honest. Of Lazarus's answers, the only one that had been utterly truthful was that he did not know the girls.

"Well?"

Lazarus's response sent shivers along Clío's spine. Turning his back on her, he climbed the stairs and slammed the door of his bedroom shut. She had not seen that much emotion from Lazarus since the Black Death in the fourteenth century. "Fuck! Can it be that bad?" Clío should have known better than to tempt Fate.

# CHAPTER 7

## *The Land of Immensity*

"The Tuatha Dé Danann—the People of the Goddess Danu—are a race of demigods and the progeny of the nine Womb-Born," said Lazarus. "I am one of the Womb-Born." Clío and he sat in the parlour, she in open-mouthed amazement that Lazarus had decided to share his history. *Why now?* She was enthralled and yet certain this was not her legacy. *Why? Whose voice had she heard?*

"The name is often abbreviated to Tuatha Dé. We number precisely forty-four thousand four hundred and forty-four. Punished by the Goddess with infertility, there will be no more pure-blood Tuatha Dé." Lazarus chuckled. "Perhaps in a fit of perverse humour, the Goddess allowed interracial fertility. This and interspecies relationships are an ongoing subject of discussion by Tuatha Dé philosophers and others seeking to expand or re-establish the race's influence." Clío wondered at the relevance of that snippet of information but filed the knowledge.

"In a war with the Sons of Mil, the Tuatha Dé were defeated and banished to the Mounds. Centuries later, the Sons of Mil realised, albeit too late, that they had been duped by the negotiating skills of Nuadha, the former High King of the Tuatha Dé. A clause in the fine print of the Treaty gave the demigods full access through portals to the Land of the Humans." Lazarus coughed and looked embarrassed. "I was called Nuadha in my previous life."

"Shite! My grandpa was the High King of the Tuatha Dé. What

does that make me?"

"That is a conversation for another day." The statement cut off Clío's train of thought, but only momentarily.

Lazarus' synopsis of his heritage was a skeleton without flesh. Still, he left Clío with the impression that the Tuatha Dé, and even their battle-hungry queen, The Mórrígan, had become tired of endless conflict and wars. Hence, they perceived the Treaty as a means of retiring on their own terms.

"The Tuatha Dé's passion is art in all its forms," said Lazarus. "If you were not an artist or artisan, you are of lesser worth. High office or any position of note is not in your future. Added to this, sibling in-fighting between the four Tuatha Dé cities and punishing the treasonous exiled families mean the Womb-Born have enough to occupy them.

"Below the earth in the Mounds, which is collectively known as the Land of Immensity to the Tuatha Dé, life is not all darkness. We are demigods, after all. Indeed, there is a school of thought that the Land of Immensity is not below ground at all but on a different plane or dimension. I think the argument has merit." Lazarus described the individual Mounds as equivalent to huge human cities. They are a paradise beyond human comprehension or imagination. This is hardly surprising, given the Tuatha Dé were skilled artists and unconstrained by finite resources.

Lazarus refilled his crystal glass with whiskey and drained half of the contents. Clío braced herself for more revelations. "Paradise needs darkness to define it. In the Land of Immensity, the Womb-Born and their sons and daughters could swiftly revert to their dark, violent origins." Clío speculated that perhaps this was their way of overcoming the boredom of being long-lived.

"Demigods, supernatural pre-humans, and the demon races hold the capacity to ravage the earth, creating bloody mayhem on a global scale, and causing irreparable damage to land, sea, and peoples. This is countered by humanity's numbers and their feverish passion for procreation." Clío's eyes threatened to burst from their sockets.

"Since the Treaty, conflict avoidance became a priority for the former antagonists. Both races arrived at the same conclusion. An eternal war between the Sons of Mil and the Tuatha Dé played straight into the hands of their common enemies—the Fomorians, the Nemed, and the Fir Bolg. These nations had, and still have, no scruples about interfering in any race's affairs." According to Lazarus, the Fomorians had an unquenchable hostility to just about anyone. Compounding this, the demons of Fomoria, banished by the Tuatha Dé to the ocean depths after the Battle of Mag Tuired, had a huge chip on their collective armour-plated shoulders.

# CHAPTER 8

*Fomoria*

The chamber's windows were small and round, with glass the thickness of Balora's longest claw when fully extended. Beyond that there was neither land nor sun nor sky—just endless water, a sandy bottom, colourful reefs, and fantastic sea creatures. It was a beautiful landscape to all but the Fomorians, who hated their underwater prison.

Balora, named after her father, Balor, the late Fomorian king and battle commander, loathed and trembled at the mere thought of the oceans. Like most of her race, she had developed a fear for waters deeper than her knee joints. Unlike the many, she respected the seas and its currents and became an excellent swimmer. Like all Fomorians, Balora had gills and webbed feet and paws. She saw them as a curse from the sea god, Manannán mac Lir. *Why didn't he show mercy and drown us?*

The constant marauding of Manannán and his clann made the Fomorians' exile worse. He had never forgiven his brother, Nuadha, for despoiling his domain with Fomorian vermin. Yet it was the Fomorians, not the Tuatha Dé, who suffered the brunt of Manannán's displeasure.

Perhaps that was always Nuadha's intent: a never-ending punishment for the Fomorians' audacity to confront the insufferable Womb-Born. Millennia passed and few Fomorians argued against the urgent and vociferous calls to war; to conquer a land that was not submerged. The Land of Immensity was only a beach away.

Unlike her previous sojourn among the Tuatha Dé, Balora intended her next to be profitable. Nuadha killed Balora's father in battle, which had unintended consequences for her. The daughter of the Fomorians' greatest general and hero instantly became the queen of a dynasty. However, unlike the dragons, Fomorian society was patriarchal. Women were accepted into the army, but only on the rationale it was better for them to die than their male counterparts. Generally, females had two roles: breeding and sexual slavery.

Hence, Balora's elevation achieved little more than invitations to the best balls and boring committee meetings. It took many decades of humiliating herself in the nests of Fomorian kings, queens, princes, and princesses to arrive at her current situation—a queen feared for her ruthlessness and owed favours by many. More importantly, she had gained access to the High King and his council. Centuries of assassination, bribery, and sexual favours finally resulted in her receiving the council's blessing on her foray to Northern Ireland. Her goal was to search for her grail—Daghdha's Cauldron—and its associated artefacts: the Staff and the Harp.

Balora huffed. A talkative council member, mesmerised by her beauty, libido, and appetite for extreme sex, confessed that the Fomorian hierarchy considered her out of control and wanted her out of the way. No one believed her stories about the artefacts or that the Cauldron could be used to incubate an endless supply of deadly bacteria and viruses. She was an unwanted distraction while they concentrated on a more important matter—the invasion of the Land of Immensity.

The Council's attitude explained the low-level talent and intelligence of the Fomorians assigned to her "army". Of the four hundred warriors she was assigned, only half were veterans from her clann. The remainder were barely competent. Balora sighed. At least they were huge. She had a use for brawn as well as brains.

Nothing dampened Balora's excitement. Her former lover and partner, Nuadha, resided in Northern Ireland with his ward. Willingly or not, she needed his help to enter the Land of Immensity. The thought of pitting her wits against Nuadha, and the possibility of rekindling their stormy relationship, retrieved a flood of pleasant memories of better days. Balora purred like a feral cat. She had not experienced the warm feelings between her legs in many centuries—certainly never when she had to whore herself out for political gain.

# CHAPTER 9

*Belfast, Northern Ireland*


Clío's and Lazarus' combined glamours were holding but wearing thin. It was Saturday afternoon, one week after the incident with the girls, and the duo were guests of the Royal Ulster Constabulary. They perched on rickety, wooden chairs in a claustrophobically small room, which badly needed a fresh coat of paint and new air fresheners. The chairs rocked, with one leg intentionally shorter than the others. Clío reached for her perfume to dab her wrists and ameliorate the smell of decay and body odour. It was a waste of her favourite jasmine and violets scent.

Lazarus yawned, bored with the obvious nature of the interview tactic. Clío threatened to make his life miserable if he did not fix the annoying furniture. The room's flickering fluorescent lights irritated her eyes and did nothing to improve her mood. Air trapped in the building's ancient steam pipes and radiators caused them to rattle incessantly with maddeningly irregular patterns.

Two cracked mugs of tea sat on the battered metal table. The colour suggested a paucity of milk or a well stewed brew, perhaps both. A teaspoon, encrusted with the previous occupants' endeavours, sat in a cheap ceramic bowl amid a corona of spilt crystals. Clío surrendered, sighed, and reached for the left mug, grumbling at the lack of originality. Lazarus ignored his beverage and removed a cigarette from the silver case he carried in his inner jacket pocket. He lit up just as the room's door opened.

Clío rolled her eyes. *They think we've simmered enough.* Given the state of the room's disrepair, she expected to hear the grinding protest of hinges and the door shuddering as it fought against years of grime. In fact, the movement proved noiseless and struggle free. Had Clío been in the mood for philosophy, she was sure there was a life lesson to be drawn.

Two men entered, one old and one young. They sat down on chairs which had some, if not much, padding and did not rock with every movement. Both gripped mugs of tea, the contents of which looked a fraction less toxic than Clío's.

The dour, younger man looked in his mid-thirties. His demeanour was not solely because of the incident. Most men of his age had volunteered for service—army, navy, or air force. His current profession ruled out the option for death, glory, and the unrestricted opportunities to seduce foolish women of all ages, which a military uniform offers. He had short, black hair, dark half-moons under blue eyes, and a deepening six o'clock shadow.

Clío observed that his wedding finger had the mark of a ring but no band. *Newly divorced, separated, or philanderer?* Something about his demeanour irked Clío, although it was quite possible that she was simply pissed off. She had better things to do on a Saturday afternoon. Clío detested the taste of cigarettes, so she chewed gum—strawberry flavour—and constantly blew and cracked bubbles as loudly as she could.

The older man held the weary air of someone who neared retirement. Likely, he wished for a quiet life until he received his gold watch, pension, and garden allotment. His red nose and cheeks, spider veins from too much alcohol, and a heavily lined and pockmarked visage accentuated the man's intense annoyance with life. He coughed as if preparing his throat for speech, scratched a head of salt-and-pepper hair, and addressed Lazarus. "This is a mess. Isn't it?"

Lazarus nodded and took another drag on his cigarette. Clío sniggered. Her grandpa could be infuriating at times.

"Two girls murdered, although the coroner and senior medical staff at the Royal Victoria Hospital are mystified as to the means. There is no evidence of a sexual assault, which is a mercy for the girls and their parents."

"Thank the Goddess," whispered Clío.

"However, they were left dead and naked on *your* doorstep. That's good and bad. If you were responsible for their deaths, I doubt you would have left the evidence at your front door." The detective took a sip of his tea and grimaced. "That conclusion may change; we have no other suspects. I think it is a message, but from whom, and what is its meaning or purpose?"

The man's eyes narrowed and the lines around them tightened up. He opened the repurposed manila folder before him and lifted a single page of paper. It was blank on both sides. "This is the sum of what we know about either of you. Nothing. No birth certificates. No work history. No passports. No drivers' licences. No National Insurance numbers. No medical history. No fingerprints. No criminal records. In short, you do not exist, yet you are sitting in front of me."

Clío cleared her throat, not to provide an explanation but to voice umbrage. A fan of Humphrey Bogart movies, she had always pictured herself slapping an unwelcome cop's face or saying the immortal words, "I want a lawyer."

The detective raised a hand, forestalling any diversions or fabrications. He sighed and closed the file as if to emphasise he was done. He looked to Lazarus again and, for a brief time, was able to pierce the cloud of cigarette smoke and meet the blue stare. Placing both hands on the table, he rose slowly. "We are at war with Germany. Thankfully, it has not touched us yet. But people are increasingly more nervous, more observant, and less forgiving of anything strange."

The detective stopped and exhaled. "I will be forwarding your case to Special Branch. They will, almost certainly, be in touch. My partner will escort you out."

\*\*\*

The advantage of being aeons old is having the experience to maintain a poker face in almost any situation. Once past the station's guard post, Clío inhaled the damp morning air. Except for a few weeks in the summer, the rain never entirely goes away in Belfast. It simply diminishes to a drizzle. She turned to Lazarus. "Shite! They think we're spies."

"Someone had better not taken my seat at McHugh's," said Lazarus, before a taxi appeared and whisked him away. Clío chose to think he knew she wanted to walk home.

# CHAPTER 10

The day after the interrogation, Clío needed a quiet sanctuary to ponder recent events. Suitably attired, she approached the parlour. The parlour sits ageless and often unused, unless for special occasions—births, deaths, and marriages. It is a haven, a refuge for those wanting a wee bit of peace, but there is a cost, an entrance fee—you must wear "Sunday-go-to-church" clothes.

Winter and summer, the fire was always prepared but rarely lit. In Clío and Lazarus' parlour, an array of bronze statuettes graced the black marble mantelpiece. Original paintings hung on walls lined with faded burgundy-red flock wallpaper. The fragrances of leather, tobacco, whiskey, and furniture polish permeated the space.

From the clamour within, it sounded as if her haven was a war zone. With the doubtful wisdom of a horror movie heroine, Clío grasped and turned the doorknob, pushed the door open, and stepped across the threshold. The parlour was gone, and before her stretched a sea of lush green meadows and forests. In the distance the ruby-red towers of a huge city glistened. The sun sat high in a cloudless, impossibly blue sky.

Amid the pastures, two fierce creatures faced off. The Mórrígan—the Tuatha Dé's unholy Trinity, Queen of Desolation, and Queen of Whispers and Shadows—was beautiful with unblemished, porcelain-white skin. A mane of lush, raven-black tresses crowned her head and slapped a perfectly rounded arse. Pale green eyes, which could turn black in an instant, and ruby-red lips completed the flawless, yet awful, visage.

Clío knew most articles, books, and theses written about the Tuatha Dé and the Womb-Born were fantasy because the Tuatha Dé wanted it that way. Between the more reliable papers and Lazarus' recent talk, she gleaned The Mórrígan's strength was not her gift for slaughter. Rather, her true talent was whispering words in the ears of kings and those who stood behind the throne. On her behalf, they committed violence and mayhem. With few exceptions, this was the way of the Tuatha Dé. The heroes wielded magical weapons, and the women honeyed words.

In the arena before Clío, The Mórrígan hurled wrath at Nuadha. Clío's mind grappled with the impossibility of his striking resemblance to Lazarus. *What are they doing in my parlour?* The object of The Mórrígan's ire did not flinch at his sister's ferocity. With patience and a brother's understanding, Nuadha swatted the blows away. They were little more than annoying gnats to him.

Occasionally, when The Mórrígan came too close, Nuadha changed into a great Irish wolfhound, the size of which dwarfed normal-sized hounds—and they are big enough. *So much for my theory on shapeshifters.* Canine teeth nipped and snapped at The Mórrígan's heels, forcing the demigoddess to retreat or seamlessly change into a massive black raven.

Nuadha was ten feet tall, wrapped in solid muscle, and impressively naked. A golden aura, likely contributed by the Blade of Light grasped in his right hand, softened his appearance and contour. Clío shook her head. She had thought the sword a fanciful story of a long-dead *seanchaí*—storyteller. The implication of her being able to look the demigod in the eyes had not dawned on Clío.

The faux battle between brother and sister faded when The Mórrígan stopped circling Nuadha and thundered, "You may be the true High King of the Tuatha Dé, but Fate and iron do not owe you any favours. What if the Fomorians take possession of Daghdha's Cauldron? How will you grow cleaved limbs back again?"

"That will never happen," bellowed Nuadha. There was a rare note of uncertainty in his voice.

The Mórrígan seized on the hesitation. "Are you so sure? The Fomorians were always quite persuasive and, as *you* know, their women are exotic and cunning. Give Daghdha a hundred Fomorian virgins, a score barrels of ale, and a feast and he will grant anything they request. His royal fatness is and has always been ruled by crude appetites and that monstrous erection between his legs."

"As I recall, there was a time our brother, Daghdha, took you—and not forcibly. The fruit of your union was Midhir." The Mórrígan made to slap him, but Nuadha stepped aside. "At least Midhir had the sense to put distance between him and his father. Can *you* say the same?"

Wrongfooted and a little deflated, but with her anger still simmering, The Mórrígan countered, "We have all done foolish, if necessary, things, the memory of which brings regrets. The Cauldron can be used for evil as well as good and you know it. Do you want to see it in the hands of our enemies? You always keep the Blade of Light with you. Lugh does the same with his spear. Can you speak with confidence of our brother's care of the Cauldron and the artefacts—the Staff of Life and Death and the mysterious Harp—which accompany it?"

"You know as well as I the Cauldron only reveals itself in the presence of a Womb-Born. That is our insurance." Nuadha's tone was conciliatory, hoping to draw the fire from his sister's temper.

The Mórrígan snorted. "A pair of heavy breasts will convince Daghdha to expose himself… and the Cauldron." The Mórrígan paused, weighing her next words. She rarely gave quarter in a fight. "Look me in the eyes and tell me Balora could not beguile or trick you into revealing the Cauldron."

"You cross the line, sister. Go now or it will be another millennium before we speak again."

The Mórrígan bit her tongue. Still, she had always been a poor loser, and one arrow languished in her quiver. The temptation was irresistible.

"Have you told Clíodhna about her family and heritage since our last meeting? Bráchthine must be sorely disappointed in you. Dreams will never replace physical training, Nuadha. She is not battle-tested. How will she fare against her arsehole twin brother in the Arena? What will you do when puberty destroys your plans?"

"My twin? *Puberty?*"

*** 

The combatants were startled into an embarrassed silence at Clío's intrusion into their quarrel. The Mórrígan looked at Clío with eyes that were coal-black. Clío discerned anger, consternation, and fear in them. *Why on earth is the Queen of Desolation afraid of me?* Clío had no idea.

The Mórrígan gave a half-snarl, half-squawk, transformed into a magnificent black raven, and swooped upwards. Clío flinched, half expecting to feel a spiteful splash of bird-shite splatter her head. She turned from the diminishing black shape to stare at Nuadha. Like mist on a hot summer's day, the rolling green meadows disappeared. The parlour resumed its original appearance—and so did Lazarus.

# CHAPTER 11

The smell of age, leather, and lilac-scented polish flooded Clío's senses. It was as if the parlour were sentient and wished to calm her down. The man across the room was once more the Lazarus she knew. Yet who was he? "You have a lot of explaining to do. Start with my brother." Clío's outward calm belied her inner turmoil.

Lazarus looked at her awkwardly. It was the look of an adolescent boy caught ogling the centrefold of one of the racier, under-the-counter magazines—the ones that corner newsagents claim they never sell to the young and impressionable. The gaze was quickly replaced by exasperation. Long fingers swept a few rebellious hairs from his face to rejoin the Brylcreemed masses. Lazarus' composure returned, but Clío's eyes told him that he could no longer postpone a conversation he had avoided for millennia. Clío barred the doorway, and he was not getting out of the room until she had answers.

"Your twin, Ciarán, is a black dragon from Clann Dubh. He is the guardian of the Island of Scáth and its queen, Scáthach. She used to be one of the more sensible Tuatha Dé and a great role model. Something changed her, and now she's a real bitseach."

Clío held up a hand. "My brother is a *dragon*." She shook her head. "No, no, no. They don't exist—even in the land of fanciful things. They are not real." A horrible understanding began to form in Clío's mind.

There was a look of genuine sympathy in Lazarus' eyes, followed by mild surprise. "Surely you saw your transformation when you entered the room. The golden eyes, opalescent scales, increased height, and muscle tend to be giveaways. Possibly you missed the eye colour, but not the scales or the change in body anatomy—or your tail."

Clío's incredulous look gave Lazarus his answer. Lazarus dropped his hands to his sides. "I guess my sister and my confrontation held your attention."

"Your sister."

"Yes, The Mórrígan is my sister. She called on me recently to upbraid me on my neglect of educating you on your heritage. Today's quarrel was partly a continuation of that conversation." Lazarus sighed. "I am sorry, I have failed you, and your mother. Yes, Clíodhna, you are a dragon. They exist, and are beautiful and terrible creatures, but are exceedingly rare."

Lazarus snorted. "The incident with Eve and a randy dragon in the Garden of Eden did not make your race popular. Eve was, and still is, a beautiful woman but has no more common sense today than when life was breathed into her lungs. In the modern parlance, she's a bimbo." With a wry smile, he added, "On the other hand, she has mitigating circumstances. Adam was a disappointment, not a great companion, and had a temper, which Cain inherited."

A pour from his whiskey decanter drew Lazarus' focus back to the main topic. "A dragon, or serpent, is a guardian or gatekeeper. Most protect the royal cities or high-value individuals like the Womb-Born. They can be very generous or mean bastards." Lazarus reluctantly added, "Your brother is the latter. Sorry."

"Do you have a guardian dragon?" asked Clío.

He smiled. "Mine was your mother, Bráchthine. We were very close. When she crossed the veil, I declined the option of a replacement." The look of loss and sadness on Lazarus' face forced tears to Clío's eyes. "As with all female dragons, your mother laid two eggs. Female serpents cannot lay more than two. Bráchthine did not tell me the name of your father."

*All Tuatha Dé choose their words carefully, Clíodhna. Lazarus is no exception.*

The voice in Clío's head sounded familiar, but she was at a loss to put a name or face to it. She tilted her head to rejoin the discussion.

"Female dragons are annoyingly secretive and promiscuous. However, given Ciarán's shell colour, he is from Clann Dubh. Your mother is long dead, Clíodhna, although death does not have the same finality for dragons—or the Tuatha Dé. She will remain in that state for as long as she chooses or until the Goddess commands her return."

In truth, uppermost in Clío's mind was the thought that Lazarus had spoilt her enjoyment of her traditional Sunday morning Ulster Fry. How could she, being from an egg, enjoy her usual two "over-easy"?

"Why did you stop me from touching the dead child?"

Lazarus had expected a torrent of questions but not this one. "To be a dragon is to be an avenger. One touch of the child and no one could have stopped you from hunting down her murderer. It is in your blood and part of your nature. That said, you must be trained and taught how to bring the powers under control. Not all wrongs need to be punished." Lazarus chuckled. "Besides, I do not think the good folk of East Belfast are ready for a marauding dragon in the skies."

"So, I have wings."

"Ummm… no. That's a fallacy, like vampires not being able to walk in daylight. Too many medieval priests, authors, and modern movie directors with rampant imaginations." Clío's disappointment was obvious. "You will learn an absence of wings is not an impediment to flight."

Clío got the message. Given the latest comic hero, Superman, did not have wings, she figured she was not totally deprived. *Would a cape look good on me?*

Lazarus shook his head. It was as if he had lost something—or failed in a task. "You and I have so much to do and not much time. As my sister brutally pointed out, that is my fault. It is time for me to make amends."

"Why? Why did you not tell me?"

Lazarus took a step forward and held Clío in his arms. Strangely, it was the first time, and yet she had never missed out on affection. It both comforted and alarmed her. "Your mother was a powerful and wonderful lady. When she discovered I was leaving the Land of Immensity, she asked me to take you with me and tasked me to look out for you. She wanted you to have a life outside of the Land of Immensity and the Island of Dragons for as long as possible. I neglected to carry out her wishes to teach you about your heritage and prepare you for your future. For that, one day I will pay."

He watched a question form on Clío's lips. "Go ahead, ask."

"There was fear in The Mórrígan's eyes. Why?" Clío also wondered how on earth she knew The Mórrígan. Until today, she had never met the Trinity known as The Mórrígan! *Gaelic deities are complex.*

"Few things can kill a member of the Tuatha Dé, and even fewer a Womb-Born. Iron, and blades forged by the Tuatha Dé, can hurt and cleave body parts. Human-forged weapons are even more potent. To a human's perception, they bring death. Daghdha's Cauldron or a centuries-long sleep in *recapithe* usually sets things to right." He smiled, remembering, and lifted his right arm. "In this, The Mórrígan was right. I used the cleaving of my arm to escape my responsibilities as High King of the Tuatha Dé. In hindsight, it was a mistake, but I was young—only a few centuries old.

"To answer your question. Only a dragon can put a Womb-Born or any Tuatha Dé beyond the veil, beyond recapithe, and beyond the healing of Daghdha's Cauldron. Every powerful tribe needs a counterbalance. The dragons are our friends until they become our executioners."

"Hell's teeth!"

"Oh, and you knew The Mórrígan because instinctively all dragons know the names of the Womb-Born, as you are now aware of my birth name. Most times, you will know where we are, unless we do not wish it."

Clío's lips pursed. Hands held up in apology, Lazarus spoke quietly, "Yes, the Womb-Born can read and communicate by thought—so can dragon royalty. No, I do not continually rummage around in your thoughts. At my age, they are much too pornographic! And yes, I can teach you how to veil your mind."

"Nuadha or Lazarus?"

"Nuadha has been dead for millennia. He was too reasonable, too compassionate, and that was his… my downfall. I prefer Lazarus."

"My dreams?"

"Not all were *your* imagination." At Clío's stern look, he added, "In my defence, I needed to get your training started. Even humans acknowledge that learning while asleep is useful. You will find the recall of your dreams is both easier and sharper."

"Who controls my glamours?"

"Until now, I did. It was not too difficult. You are a very open young woman, Clíodhna. From today, your glamour is your responsibility. I will provide advice or support, if asked." A boyish slice of devilment twinkled in Lazarus' blue eyes.

"What?"

"My sister reminded me that all my excuses and plans would crash and burn in the flames of one thing—puberty. I advise you to make a trip to the bank in the next few days. You will need to shop for a new wardrobe. By accident, you have discovered that you are a serpent. That cannot be reversed and once awakened, dragon puberty comes swiftly and with surprising outcomes."

"Shite! I must go through puberty again?"

"You never went through it before, Clíodhna."

"Bastard!"

As she turned to leave the room, Clío asked one final question. "You said you neglected to prepare me. What for? What have you not told me?"

"Your mother was the Queen of the Dragons."

"So, I'm a princess. My friends will delight in making fun of that."

The parlour door closed behind Clío as Lazarus said, "No, Clíodhna. You are the Queen-in-Waiting."

***

Clío left shortly after, having donned suitable shoes and a heavy winter coat. It was a long walk up the Newtownards Road, along the neat red-brick terraced houses of Dee Street, and across the construction works on the new Sydenham Bypass to finally enter Victoria Park.

She needed green space to think, and the only interruptions she would entertain were the demands of the ducks for stale bread. Thankfully, the only other person about, a man wearing a fedora and a heavy outer coat, was not in a mood for talking. He kept his distance and sat on a nearby bench.

# CHAPTER 12

Several weeks had passed since Clío discovered she was a dragon. Unsurprisingly, she awoke most days with a flurry of questions, which Lazarus, after millennia of evasion, was delighted to answer. Most of the time, she coped well with the torrent of surprises forcing permanent changes on her life. Each day gave birth to new revelations. Some were pleasant and thus acceptable. Others were more challenging to assimilate.

Clío was pleased with many of the changes. Her body had "filled out" in a manner movie stars paid plastic surgeons a fortune to achieve. Under the softness that emphasized her upgraded curves, there was a solid foundation of hard muscle. Her bones were stronger—more rebar than calcium and collagen. A furnace replaced her stomach, allowing her to indulge—perhaps binge would be a better word—all her food fantasies with negligible impact on her shape.

Her wish for better breasts was granted, and she developed a pair that put Hollywood movie star Jane Russell's 38 Ds in the shade. She now had a figure that prompted admiring wolf-whistles, causing Clío no end of delight. Still, she took the occasional opportunity to complain.

"Fuck!"

Lazarus looked up. "What?"

"My breasts have always been smallish and perky, so I've never needed a bra. With the size of these, I'll need custom-made lingerie. That will be bloody expensive, and they'll be sweaty at the end of the day. I'll have a mountain of washing to do. We'll need to hire a part-time maid."

"No, we will not. You are a supernatural being, Clíodhna. Use your abilities to lessen the burden."

Clío rolled her eyes. "And what will my girlfriends say when we're in the common changing room at Templemore Avenue Swimming Baths? A few of them are natural DDs. Their tits will be flopping about but my bigger ones will be firm and perky. My friends are neither geniuses nor stupid, Lazarus. They'll know I'm not human."

Another wail escaped Clío, "*Nooo!*"

"What now?" asked Lazarus.

"My fancy basques won't fit and those things are outrageously expensive."

Initially, Clío wondered at her admirers' lack of curiosity at the changes in her shape. Then she rolled her new amber-gold eyes and giggled. Men see everything through their cocks. Her girlfriends, however, were more jealous of than happy for her and made catty remarks for several weeks. That ended in a bar one night when, to the applause and entertainment of the men, Clío punched the offender. She sent her friend skidding through the sawdust, beer spills, and across the mosaic floor. After make-up sex—Clío's sexual appetites were never limited to one sex—all was forgiven, and the bitchiness ceased.

\*\*\*

Lazarus set his morning paper down at Clíodhna's scream of "This is fucking unfair!" He preferred to use Clío's full name rather than the modern short form she had adopted. He assumed a neutral mien and waited for the living room door to burst open.

Some surprises, like when her toenails suddenly extended and she tripped and fell down the stairs, took a little more time to become accustomed to or to control. On this Sunday morning, Clío whirled around, her bath towel strategically placed to expose her back. Nakedness before "Grandpa" Lazarus, unless accidental, she considered taboo.

"*I've got scales,*" wailed Clío.

A double line of tiny, opalescent laminae traced her spine from nape to arse. This morning, to dispel the built-up mugginess of life, Lazarus had cracked the downstairs windows open. In the brisk cross-breeze that wafted through their home, Clío's fragile plates, little more than the size of a fingernail, made their debut. Those with exceptionally sharp hearing could hear them strike against each other, like wind chimes.

To Lazarus' ears, the melody was beautiful. Clío's expression said she was not impressed. "You are a dragon. I have seen much worse," said Lazarus.

Hurling curses, Clío stormed back up the stairs to her sanctuary and slammed the door shut. Downstairs, Lazarus mused that centuries of neglecting his famed tact and diplomacy had conferred on him an unfortunate directness. As it turned out, that conversation was the most pleasant event of that day.

\*\*\*

The missive was served by a young constable barely able to conceal both his certainty of Clío and Lazarus' guilt of the young girls' murders and his admiration of her figure. Once again, their presence was requested at the local police station, although it was more a demand than an invitation.

Of course, ignoring the order was always an option. How would the authorities enforce it? Special Branch and their MI5 friends are powerful but set against a demigod and a dragon, they were well outmatched. Lazarus' curiosity about the meeting tilted the balance. Besides, what purpose would it serve to flaunt the authorities' impotence in their faces?

This morning's interrogation duo combined several tropes—old and cultured with young and boorish. Clío half expected the younger of the two men to pick his nose and flick the snot at one of the room's walls. There it would join the multitude of other indeterminate blemishes and spots. The elder of the pair affected an air of pained tolerance and paternal understanding. Clío mused whether, given the similarities with their previous interrogators, the authorities had a stock of similar pairs in the basement.

The scratch of a match was quickly followed by the familiar smell of sulphur and cigarette tobacco as Lazarus took a long drag on his Woodbine and exhaled. Clío was grateful for its sanitising effect on the room's unpleasant smell of body odour tinged with piss. Lazarus and Clío were immune to intimidation and a nightmare to their inquisitors. At any moment, Clío fully expected Lazarus to slip his silver hip flask from his jacket's inner pocket and take a sip of its contents—Bushmills single malt.

Sat opposite Lazarus, the older officer sighed with resignation and opened a manila file. It was much fatter than the previous one. Whispered words between the interrogators and frequent glances in Clío's direction suggested she was the subject of their confusion. Taking Lazarus' lead, Clío tamped down her smouldering anger, pushed her breasts forward, putting strain on her silk blouse, and smiled pleasantly at both men. It did not help.

"You, *miss*, do not look at all like the description I have of you or your photograph from the earlier interview. The latter was taken not long ago. Who are you?" The last question was obviously meant to be rhetorical, but Clío was in a literal mood.

"I'm a new dragon. What did you expect?" The younger detective started. Forget tales of wise, patient, and ancient dragons. Clío was young and pissed off. She looked at each of them in turn and rolled her eyes. "Just kidding."

The fluttering scales along Clío's spine, a rise in her internal temperature, and her opaline nails extending led her to a disturbing conclusion. If she had to exert this much mental fortitude to tamp down her dragon instincts, something in this ill-lit, smelly, and shabby room was awry. She focused more intently on the detectives. It was as if the room split into two and the senior detective was shunted into a world of his own, conversing with phantoms.

The young interrogator ignored Clío and focused on Lazarus. There was unexpected reverence in his tone and as much of a bow as anyone could do while seated. "Did our gift not please you, King Nuadha?" His voice was a combination of ingratiating hiss and lisp.

"Nemed!" spat Lazarus. "Are your people still in thrall to the Fomorians?" Lazarus turned to Clío. "The Nemed used to be good people—mostly farmers. They made the mistake of asking the Fomorians for help. Instead, they were made vassals and corrupted over centuries." Lazarus returned to the Nemed. "Do you have a name?"

The question was dismissed with a flick of a hand. "That is irrelevant to our conversation."

Lazarus' patience with the Nemed ceased. "I do not converse with anonymous, low-level underlings. This dialogue is over. Unlike Fomorian kings or queens, my companion and I are not appeased or bribed by the sacrifice of innocent children." He glanced at Clío. "You can be assured your future, along with whoever else took part in the children's murder, will be determined by a visit from my friend."

Clío gasped as Lazarus laid the Blade of Light on the table. Where had he been hiding the weapon? That he was also starting to glow indicated his growing anger. It foretold imminent disaster for the police station and possibly the neighbouring streets. Lazarus pointed the Blade at the Nemed. "Whatever your plan is," Lazarus looked at Clío again, "end it now. Or *I* will." By reputation, among the Tuatha Dé, Nuadha was wise, compassionate, and much more level-headed than his brothers and sisters. The Nemed had hit a raw nerve, and weaklings do not become High King of the Tuatha Dé.

Clío shook her head and rested her hand on Lazarus'. "Vengeance is my duty."

Lazarus' mind ran through multiple possible scenarios, dissipating his wrath. The Blade of Light vanished, to be replaced by a cigarette. Blue smoke curled in the direction of the Nemed, only to be consumed by the oily charcoal miasma surrounding the creature. Without his glamour, the figure's humanity rapidly receded.

"Let my friend touch you, and we can end this quickly," said Lazarus. The Nemed recoiled and sent his chair spinning across the room. "It seems you did not expect this turn of events, and your masters will not thank you for the news. They will be disturbed by the presence of a dragon, and with good cause."

The Nemed snarled and fled the room, his body changing into a slick of oily black smoke and exiting via the ceiling vent. The smell of putrefying flesh that followed made Clío gag.

"I did not think that dragons had weak stomachs," said Lazarus. "What will happen when you eat a few of the Nemed?" Clío puked into the wastepaper bin.

\*\*\*

A cough reminded Clío and Lazarus they were not alone. The older Special Branch officer finished flicking through his papers and lifted his head. "I apologise for my partner's sudden exit. Probably something he ate for breakfast in the canteen roiled his stomach. That said, with the rationing, there's not much variety to disturb anyone's eating." He rolled his eyes and grumbled, "Being the authorities, we are discouraged from availing ourselves of the range of foods smuggled across the border from the Free State."

The man paused and inhaled. "To recap. This morning's meeting was to stress that this case has not gone away. We will be monitoring *anything* related to the murders. To that end, I will update the obvious irregularities in the file."

He turned to Clío. "Perhaps, Miss, you would ask the constables at the front desk to update your pictures. I apologise in advance for the additional photos they will undoubtedly take… for personal use. They have few perks in this job." As he stood, signalling the end of the interview, the man's nostrils flared at the smell of decay and vomit. "I apologise for the stench. I think we have a rat infestation."

"Never a truer word was spoken," muttered Clío.

\*\*\*

Flurries of snow twisted and glided like mini tornadoes along the pavement as the pair exited the building. Clío inhaled a lungful of fresh air. "Why was the Nemed upset at my presence, and why will his masters be disconcerted?"

"When the Tuatha Dé banished the Fomorians, the dragons were our shock troops."

"Fuck!" Dragons are not inclined to verbosity.

# CHAPTER 13

*1940—Winter—Northern Ireland*

It was Saturday morning in mid-December. Clío lounged in a silk robe on a comfortable, well-worn armchair in the living room. Her dragon metabolism meant she could walk around naked in winter, should she choose to, but exhibitionism had never been one of her fantasies.

Having conquered her short-lived egg phobia, she mopped up the last traces of the egg yolk and tomatoes from her Ulster Fry with pieces of fried soda farl and potato bread. After washing it down with a mug of steaming hot Irish Breakfast tea, essential to keep the grease moving in the right direction, she patted her belly and burped—loudly.

She angled her head towards the door as it opened, curious to know who the guest was. Clío ruled out Lazarus. He rarely got out of bed before mid-morning on the weekend. Yet Lazarus it was, and he was dressed as if he were going to a wedding. His suit was Parisian designer haute couture, his shoes were hand stitched, made in Italy, and his tie paid homage to Picasso.

"Where are you going?" she asked. "Are you dating someone I don't know about? It can't be me because you hardly take me anywhere, these days." *The Hag! I sound like his wife!*

"*We* are going to the Island of Dragons. The time for learning from books and visions is over," said Lazarus. "You need tactical and battle training from experts and to socialize with other serpents. If you are to rule, you must become fully acquainted with all aspects of dragon society and governance." He waited for the inevitable explosion.

Clío jumped up from the leather armchair, launching the plate and china mug into the air. They descended, hit the linoleum floor, and smashed into a thousand shards. She swung around to face Lazarus. Simultaneously, the single button, hanging by a single thread on a robe which barely covered her breasts, gave up and shot across the room.

Ignoring her state of undress, she shrieked, "No! Just no! You cannot on a Saturday morning announce, 'We're going to meet the family,' with no warning. It's a land I have neither seen nor know where it is." Clío glanced at a mirror. "You bastard! Look at my face, hair, and my nails—fingers and toes. I need a day in the Culloden Hotel's spa. What will I wear? I can't go like *this*."

Lazarus nodded in agreement. "Yes, with those free, there's not a male or female who will not sense danger… or opportunity."

Too angry to be embarrassed, Clío said, "We cannot possibly travel today. I will need at least three changes of clothing—formal, casual, and fighting—and matching footwear. What season is it in the Island of Dragons?"

Clío's hand suddenly went to her mouth. "*No!* My girlfriends and I have an invitation to a New Year's Eve party in one of the big houses on Cypress Avenue. It has so many rooms and there's a prize for whoever gets laid in all of them. Odds have been set and bets placed. I'm the favourite." Clío slumped back down in the chair.

"I hate you."

"You will be fine," said Lazarus.

She indicated her breasts. "What? As your whore? Typical man!"

In response, Clío received a grandfatherly pat of assurance on her arm, immediately followed by a firm grip of her hand. "We are going, *now*, Clíodhna."

At that moment, Clío's dragon recall slipped into gear, and she assessed the morning's surprises more calmly. The composed Clío lasted no more than a few breaths. "What do you mean 'if I am to rule'?" The words were said slowly and deliberately. Delicate wisps of white smoke puffed from her nostrils, portents of impending doom.

"There will be time for explanations when you meet the Dragon Council. They are much more knowledgeable on serpent governance and lore than me."

"Balls!"

"We're going. Get used to it."

\*\*\*

The black basalt columns of the Giant's Causeway, on the north-east coast, and the structures they form are Northern Ireland's primary tourist attraction. It is claimed by many to be the Eighth Wonder of the World. Legend has it that the causeway was built by the giant, Fionn mac Cumhaill, who wanted to visit his girlfriend in Scotland.

Unfettered access to humanity was a loophole in the Treaty between the Tuatha Dé and the Sons of Mil. Lazarus continued to wonder how he pulled the wool over the eyes of the victor's negotiators. Before the Sons of Mil understood the fine print of the Treaty, portals had been built at key locations with ancient Celtic roots in Ireland, Scotland, Wales, and France.

As millennia passed, the gateways to the Land of Immensity spread worldwide following the migration paths of the Irish diaspora. They now encompassed the United States of America, South America, Canada, and Australia. Every portal had a Tuatha Dé guardian who protected access to and from the Land of Immensity.

\*\*\*

Like most of the population of Northern Ireland, Clío had visited the Giant's Causeway many times with her friends. The area's small, seaside towns with their bed and breakfast accommodations, beaches, and tall sand dunes were well-known centres of partying and promiscuity during the summer weekends. Clío never had an inkling of its ancient role or the presence of the subterranean portal to the Land of Immensity. *How did Lazarus blind me to this?*

When Lazarus informed her that glamours were even more powerful in the Land of Immensity and took less effort to maintain, Clío's curiosity eclipsed her wrath. She simply had to think of an outfit, fashion, hair colour, or make-up combination and it would instantly adorn her body. Still, Clío swore to get even with him. Surprises were for birthdays and Christmases.

In the half-light of flickering torches, Clío was glad of her enhanced dragon eyesight and sense of balance. The duo descended what seemed like a thousand steps carved in the volcanic rock. All were covered in wet, slippery seaweed and included a random scattering of stumble steps. At last, they stood before an archway carved into the rock. Though not large or terribly impressive looking, the arch hummed with magic when they approached.

Clío correctly attributed this to the hundreds of intricate runes carved into its uprights and curvature. She did not know that if the portal deemed them a threat or unworthy, splinters of bone and scraps of flesh would bear witness to their demise. All trace of their existence would be washed away on the next high and ebb tides. With a flourish of his hand, Lazarus indicated they should proceed through the archway.

"Now that's more like it," said Clío. The cavern they entered was huge and covered in a mantle of blue crystalline deposits resembling frost. Like lovers, ancient fingers of stalactites and stalagmites reached out to touch each other. Some had achieved their goal; others had centuries more to wait. Clío marvelled at the inclination of Mother Nature towards beauty. However, and unlike the Giant's Causeway on the surface, this subterranean vault would never be a place for tourists.

The duo crossed a narrow rock causeway, bordered by lakes. Without a breath of air, the great mirrors of the waters' surfaces were perfectly still, reflecting the cave's ceiling. Nausea forced Clío to stop looking when her mind failed to cope with the infinite echoes. Once across the bridge, they walked up broad semicircular steps, finally arriving at a rock platform. The gateway before them glowed with powerful runes and enough gemstones to purchase a small country.

Clío looked at Lazarus, and he dipped his head. She reached out to touch the archway and felt it throb as if alive. "Was the first archway a feint?"

Lazarus smiled and shook his head. "More triage than deception. Think of it as the outer defensive wall of an ancient hillfort."

When a single guard emerged from the shadows, Clío jumped. He bowed deeply to Lazarus. "It has been a long time, my king. Where do you wish to travel—Coria?"

Lazarus shook his head. "My companion and I travel to the Island of Dragons." Lazarus signalled for Clío to step forward.

The sentinel instantly recognised Clío and smiled. "I completely understand why." Once again, he bowed deeply. "It is my pleasure to be the first to greet you, Princess Clíodhna. Your mother was a great Queen of the Dragons, as I am sure you will be." Clío's eyebrow lifted.

Lazarus ignored Clío's unhappy look. "Contrary to what many believe is a posting for low-level Tuatha Dé nobles, each portal is and remains a high honour for its guardian. It is a vital logistic and intelligence hub. An army can be flowed to and from the gateway almost instantly, if the alarm is sounded." It was a valiant attempt at diverting Clío's train of thought, but it failed.

"How did you know my name?" asked Clío. "I have never been to the Land of Immensity or the Land of the Dragons."

The Portal Keeper smiled. "The same way that you know each of the Womb-Borns' names, without ever having seen them."

Lazarus dipped his head to the Portal Keeper. "We should go. I wish to keep this visit between trustworthy friends. I hope that does not cause you a problem."

"No one will know of your visit, but I hope it is not the last. The Land of Immensity misses its true king."

\*\*\*

The pair arrived at the portal exit in the blink of an eye. "This rickety, wooden bridge is a portal?" said Clío, disappointed at the lack of grandeur.

"Quite a clever disguise, is it not? Your mother and I conceived the idea and to this day, only she and I know its secret. To everyone else, it is a wooden bridge."

"Enough of the evasiveness, Lazarus. What did the Portal Keeper mean when he said my mother was a great queen… another fact *you* avoided telling me for millennia?" asked Clío.

"That is one of the reasons we are here and is better answered by the dragon elders. Your mother was a great queen and ruler. She was loved, respected, and feared by all. The serpents' society is matriarchal, and it works surprisingly well."

"I get it, Lazarus, I'm a princess. Do I have sisters?" said Clío with a broad smile.

Lazarus shook his head. "No, Clíodhna, just a brother. The serpent population is small and measured in hundreds. Therefore, one Dragon Queen rules over the kingdom from when she sits on the throne until she dies. The dragon crown passes to the eldest female child of the queen. You are the Queen-in-Waiting. It has been so for millennia. In turn, your daughter will become queen."

"And you waited until now to tell me this. Why?" Lazarus blanched at the question. "I assume I must fuck a dragon to get pregnant. That would explain why I've never need birth control. What happens if I don't like serpents? With a small population, there can't be much of a pool of eligible bachelors. The Hag, I hope they are not all inbred. Ewww!" Another thought occurred to her. "What happens if there are two sons and no daughter?"

"War."

"Shite!" She pointed to a group of shapes in the sky. "Who are they?"

"Your welcome party."

"Fuck! Do I look presentable?"

# CHAPTER 14

## *The Island of Dragons*

The group of three dragons landed twenty yards from Clío and Lazarus with much more control and finesse that she thought possible for such huge beasts. *Shite, will I insult them if I say "beasts" or "animals"? Will I be that big?* Instantly, the serpents transformed to their human personæ. Clío giggled as they flicked non-existent dirt from their attires. She did the same when she wanted to collect her thoughts.

"The tallest, the one built like a *broch* and with a ramrod for a spine, is Aodh Dearg, your general and battle commander. He commands the dragon armies and the intelligence resources. I like him. He is blunt and will try to bully his way to accomplish what he wants. His assertiveness is common to all dragons, which explains your attitude issues." Lazarus ignored Clío's hiss.

"There are five clanns: Clann Dearg (red), Clann Dubh (black), Clann Foruaine (green), Clann Ór (gold), and Clann Umhaí (copper-bronze). The dragons' custom, wherever possible, is to combine a chosen name with the clann's colour."

"If that's the case, I will stick out like a sore thumb," said Clío.

Lazarus laughed. "You have your mother's lustrous, opalescent colour and yes, it is unique. No other dragon has the same colouring. Bear your scales with pride, Clíodhna. Your mother, Bráchthine, was a great queen."

"My brother?"

"His scales are black. Likely, there were two fathers or Serendipity wanted to set the gossip tongues wagging." Lazarus coughed to clear his throat. "The second, slightly shorter male is Neasán Ór, the Leader of the Dragon Council. He is a politician and as trustworthy as any of that breed can be. That said, he was loyal to your mother. She always took note of his counsel—and then did what she thought was best for her people."

Clío laughed and looked closely at Lazarus. Every time he mentioned Bráchthine, even if it was a single word, it was filled with…. she searched for the right term. When it hit her, she was rocked back on her heels. "Adoration." *Lazarus loved my ma. Could he be my da?* It was unlikely. They were two species as well as races. Yet he was a demigod. Who knew what was possible for him? And she was aware of ancient texts about the dragons and the Tuatha Dé being from the same root—Anúna. She met Lazarus' gaze and swore. His eyes twinkled. *The bastard's not going to tell me.*

"I am not sure who the young female is, but she bears a resemblance to the general. Possibly she is a companion for you." Clío growled at the suggestion anyone would choose her companions. However, the group was a few paces away from her and had stopped.

The group bowed deeply. "Welcome to the Island of Dragons, Lady Clíodhna. My name is Neasán Ór, and I am the Leader of the Dragon Council. I am delighted to greet you on your first visit to your birthplace, which we hope will become your home. My friend is Aodh Dearg. He is the General of the Dragon Army and Head of Intelligence."

Lazarus murmured in Clío's ear, "This is your first lesson in diplomacy and politics, Clíodhna. Tread carefully; you need both men on your side. Treat them fairly but never allow them to dominate or bully you. Dragons will always be assertive. It is your nature."

Clío smiled. "Thank you for your kind words. I am told my mother valued your loyalty, service, and counsel. I am also informed she was a wise judge of men and dragons." She then startled the men by walking between and past them. "Thank the Goddess, a woman. For a moment,

I thought there was a scarcity of females in this land." Clío winked at the young female dragon. "Although, it would be fun to watch the men compete for our attention, wouldn't it?"

The young serpent's mouth opened wide in shock at Clío's lack of formality and the wink that accompanied Clío's words. "I have been introduced. Who are you?" Clío stretched out her hand. "I am sure I am breaking all sorts of protocols. However, for the moment, I prefer to keep things informal."

"I am Ceara Dearg, my lady. I am the General's daughter." Caught between a handshake, a curtsy, and a deep bow, Ceara looked as if she might topple over.

Clío took her by the elbow. "This is new to me and I'm as nervous as you are. How about we bluff this out?" whispered Clío.

Ceara smiled broadly, dipped her head, and took a deep breath to calm her racing heartbeat. "I hope to earn your trust as a friend, my queen. However, it is also my honour to be your shield-maiden and the captain of your personal guard. As well as me, you have a wing of ten serpents assigned as your protectors. Our first duty will be to oversee your fighting training. My father, the General, will instruct you in tactics and strategy. There are other tutors for history and culture, if we require them."

\*\*\*

Aodh took advantage of Ceara and Clío's interlude to draw Lazarus aside. The expression on his face was not promising. "You bring her to us *now*. She should have been here a millennium ago. Bráchthine would be furious at your neglect. What panicked your Tuatha Dé serenity? Surely, you know the deadline to her coronation fast approaches. She must meet her brother in the Arena, and that's only the first hurdle before she can ascend the throne."

Lazarus was shocked, not at Aodh's bluntness or his criticism, but at the length of his speech. He had never heard the dragon speak more than one or two short sentences. He dipped his head to Aodh, which set the older serpent back on his heels. No Womb-Born conceded fault, even when deserved.

"I am sorry, old friend. As to why now, my sister, The Mórrígan, has already chastised me. You have her to thank for our visit." He looked at Clío and Ceara chatting and smiled. "I suggest we set our sights on getting Clíodhna ready for the Arena challenge. Once we have passed that test, we can inform her of the second. Agreed? It should be a formality, shouldn't it?" The grunted acquiescence from Aodh and avoidance of eye contact from Neasán were not encouraging.

*** 

"I accept you have an agenda and likely there are formal procedures and events that require my presence. That is fine with me, but first I would like to visit my mother's home and my birthplace." Clío addressed Neasán. "I believe Lazarus, sorry, Nuadha, knows where it is. There is no reason for everyone to accompany us, although I would like to get to know Ceara better."

"Nuadha has informed us about his change of name. It is not unusual for long-lived beings to update glamours and names." Aodh scratched his chin. He and Neasán appeared to be delighted at Clío's request but also perturbed. "Your birthplace is in the tallest mountains." He looked at Lazarus. "Can Lady Clíodhna fly?"

"*I* can answer for myself, General. Lazarus should know better," retorted Clío. She felt the scales on her spine clash angrily, and so did the other dragons.

"I apologise, my lady. Forgive an old man, who is used to herding grandchildren. To reach your mother's home, apart from Lazarus who has his own means of transportation, we will need to fly. It is deliberately inaccessible."

"You could carry me between you," said Clío, disappointed at the hitch. "Or Lazarus could transport me as usual." The General nodded to Ceara. Both grinned. Clío was instantly wary, and her scales fluttered madly.

"We could, but it would be remiss of us not to grasp an opportunity, especially as you will have the strongest of incentives to succeed."

"Opportunity for what?"

"Your first flying lesson. It was programmed in the agenda, although not for a few days. I see no reason to postpone it… unless you are not feeling up to the challenge. Perhaps you are tired after your travels. We will understand if you choose not to." Under no circumstance was Clío about to decline the obvious challenge. By the grin on the General's face, he had measured Clío well.

"Let's do this," snapped Clío.

"Do you remember the 'platform'?" Aodh asked Lazarus. He nodded. "We will meet you there."

*　*　*

The platform was a flat, rocky outcrop jutting from a red sandstone cliff. Clío's stomach did several flips when she cautiously peered over its edge. There seemed to be no bottom to the chasm. Worse, her body swayed in the breezes that swirled around the cliff.

She stepped back. "You are out of your mind," she gasped in between measured breaths to prevent her nausea from advancing to projectile vomiting. Clío glared at Lazarus. "Do you agree with this 'jump and die' training method?"

"Birds push their offspring out of the nest all the time. It is a well-known and tested method for creatures who can fly."

"I am not a bird. Have you never noticed the numerous tiny bodies spattered on the pavements? Only cats support that training approach."

"There is no pressure on you, Lady Clíodhna," said the General. His tone was conciliatory and as false as the fatherly smile on his weather-beaten face. Concentrating on not being swept off the platform by a stronger gust of wind, Clío missed Aodh's signal to Ceara.

"Of course there's pressure on me. I'm the fucking…" The word "queen" became "bitseach!" when Ceara firmly locked her fingers with Clío's and jumped off the platform. The torrent of curses released as the bodies plummeted would have caused the hard men of the Yard to blush.

Lazarus laughed and Aodh hid an admiring smile.

Neasán blanched. "You cannot do this to a future Queen of the Dragons," he spluttered. He also prayed Clío did not have a vengeful nature. *If she's anything like her mother, we are all dead.*

\* \* \*

The red sides of the cliff were a blur as Clío fell gathering increasing speed. Conversations on physics and philosophy with Archimedes, Galileo, and Newton to which she wished she had paid more attention flashed through her mind.

Clío quickly passed the stage of outright panic and emerged into a calm analytical phase. *I'm in shock.* Unaware her eyes had turned from amber to red-gold, Clío knew only that she could see every crack and sedimentary line that rushed past her. *With death comes heightened senses!* She noticed with a start that Ceara still gripped her hand. *Let go, Ceara. Leave me. You can fly. I refuse to be responsible for your death.* Clío became aware of her ability to hold a conversation without needing speech.

*You misunderstand my role, my lady. I am your shield-maiden. It is my duty to die protecting you. When we hit the bottom of this chasm, I will be underneath you. Any other action will bring disgrace on my family and clann.*

Anger at the situation and a determination not to cause Ceara's death took priority over Clío's emotions. *How, Ceara?*

*You are a dragon, my lady. Your eyes and the scales on your spine witness it. King Lazarus told me you changed when you saw The Mórrígan and him fight. Give in to the ridiculous knowledge. You are a serpent and there is no turning back for you.* Ceara giggled nervously. *As soon as possible, please. The fall will not kill us, but we will spend many cycles of the moon in the healing beds and waters. We may even need Daghdha's Cauldron.*

One moment, Clío was looking at individual grains of sand on the rocky bottom of the gorge, the next she stared wide-eyed at a beautiful blue sky. She screamed with pleasure at the sensation. *Fuck! I think I had an orgasm.* Ceara laughed, relieved she had not lost the future queen.

*We should return, my lady. You will have plenty of time to enjoy flying later. I promise.*

*How do I land, Ceara?*

*I'm sorry, my lady. Flying is easy. Landing takes longer to master. You can expect a lot of bruises.*

*One thing, Ceara.*

*Yes, my lady.*

*It's Clío, unless we are at a formal or official occasion. If anyone questions that, send them to me.*

*Yes... Clío.*

***

Bráchthine's home was at the tip of the highest peak in the Land of the Dragons. The view of the kingdom was breathtaking and desolate. "It's not exactly a vacation destination," muttered Clío. "How do you feed the population? Airlifts of food? There's not a blade of grass to be seen and I have yet to see any rivers."

"You are very observant, my lady," said Neasán, relieved that Clío had not converted Aodh and him to ash. "The springs, lakes, and rivers are underground. There are also fields with livestock in huge caverns. We bring them out and feed them on alfalfa when the sun is not so stifling."

The Council Leader spread his hands. "Being dragons, we can be anywhere in an instant. Therefore, food and other supplies are not a major issue. In fact, often the gathering of food becomes a social occasion for the clanns." At Clío's sceptical look, he said, "Yes, my lady, we may prefer solitude, but serpents also enjoy the occasional *céilí*.

"Shall we enter your mother's, or should I say *your* home?" asked Aodh, pointing to an entranceway. "Please, mind your head."

Clío was surprised at how rapidly her eyes adjusted to the change in light from bright sunshine to the gloom inside. She could see how the ability could be a significant advantage in perilous situations. "It's a cave, Lazarus," she whispered. "My mother lived in a cave... and she was the queen." Catching herself, Clío felt embarrassed and ashamed. *I've insulted my future subjects.*

Aodh guffawed. "She is as honest and plainspoken as Bráchthine." The General gestured with flourish of his hand. "Our land is beautiful but hostile. Most of the population live in the high mountains where the winds are cooler."

Clío felt a breeze on her face and her scales chime. She felt the dwelling become sentient. It was as if her mother's essence had been released and wanted to join with hers. The compulsion was irresistible. Clío padded barefoot around the cave, touching the walls. She wanted to imbibe everything with which Bráchthine had infused her home.

The remains of two eggs glistened in a shaft of sunlight on the dirt floor. She pointed and glanced at a smiling Lazarus. "I was born here, wasn't I?" He nodded. "This is my home."

Lazarus watched as Clío knelt before the pearlescent remains of her egg. She looked at him and the others for guidance. She could neither believe nor understand what her body wanted her to do. It was irrational. Again, she looked helplessly at the others, but they had faded to shimmering ghosts.

*Eat, my daughter. Claim your birthright. Eat your birth shell.*

Clío had often wondered how her mother's voice sounded and cried golden tears when she finally heard it. Her imaginings were pale shadows of its rich, loving tone. *Hold me, Ma*, pleaded Clío. Ethereal arms enclosed Clío. She felt the warmth of Bráchthine's breasts and the steady beat of her heart. *I don't want to be queen, Ma.*

Bráchthine smiled. *Neither did I at your age.* A sterner maternal note crept into Bráchthine's voice. *It was not Lazarus' role to become an indulgent 'Grandpa', and that displeases me. You have led a long life without duty and responsibility. That must cease. The Dragon People await their queen… they need you. Do not disappoint them… or me.* Once again, Clío felt Bráchthine's arms enclose her.

*It's not fair to lay this burden on my shoulders, Ma.* Clío sniffed and wished she had a handkerchief.

*I know, my love. I told my ma the same thing, but she had confidence in me, as*

*I have faith in you to become a remarkable queen.* Bráchthine sighed long and mournfully. *My baby, I have longed for this day, but I must go, Clíodhna. I am weak and the Goddess only allows me infrequent and brief visits.*

Bráchthine wept at Clíodhna's soft, "No," and Clío felt her hair and face wet with golden tears. *Please do as I say. Eat the shell. Know that I am watching over you, as I have always done.* As Clío reached for the first piece of her shell, Bráchthine pleaded, *Take care of my Lazarus.*

Clío slowly ground each shell fragment in her mouth and swallowed. They tasted nothing like the bits of shell that sometimes adulterated her scrambled eggs. Indeed, she was quite disappointed at the lack of taste or reaction. She sighed and placed the last piece in her mouth.

That was the moment when the world shifted.

\*\*\*

"This is some dream," whispered Clío. The contradictions confused her. Her head throbbed like a weekend hangover but lay on soft, plump pillows. She opened her eyes briefly, enough to glimpse the matching linen sheets, before the light forced them shut. The bed was so soft, it was as if she lay on clouds. Suddenly she sat up and screamed, "Where's my cave? What bastard took me from my home… from my ma? I want to be in my ma's arms again."

Lazarus and Aodh looked at each other. "She's delirious," said Aodh.

"I would not be so sure, Aodh. Who knows the powers Bráchthine amassed during her long reign."

"She has fallen asleep again," said Ceara, rising from a chair beside the head of the bed. "I will stay with the Lady Clíodhna and send for you when she awakens." The men did not contest the challenge in Ceara's eyes.

\*\*\*

"Will this headache ever go away?" lamented Clío. She turned her head to look at the tousled head of copper-red hair sharing one of her pillows. "If I look as bad as you, then we're both in trouble." Ceara smiled as she raised herself onto one elbow. "Ceara, how long have I been comatose and how long have you been in my bed?"

"A half-cycle of the moon… and a half-cycle of the moon," said Ceara. She yawned and stretched. "I should call Lazarus, Neasán, and my father. Everyone is distressed about your long sleep."

Clío sniffed the air, and her nostrils recoiled. "If I smell as bad as you… and I do…" Clío's stomach growled loudly. "And am as hungry, we have more pressing priorities. I badly need to piss. Can we take a bath and have some food and refreshments without the men knowing? Also, the bed linen needs to be changed. I'm hoping the dampness on my arse is just sweat."

Ceara nodded. "The staff are loyal to you and there's more than one way into or out of this bedchamber." She laughed. "My father and Lazarus have been warned not to enter unless I give them permission."

"Good. We will bathe each other, eat, and then go to bed." At Ceara's raised eyebrow, Clío chuckled. "You and I need to get to know each other… in much greater depth. What better way than a day and night, naked, in bed together?"

"I'm a dragon and quite domineering," said Ceara.

"So am I. This will be a very informative session. However, you should know I am a poor loser and will invoke rank."

\* \* \*

"You told me everyone lived in caves." Clío sat up in bed, looking much healthier, and with a mountain of pillows supporting her. She indicated the room with a regal flourish. "*This* does not resemble a hole in the mountain." She looked accusingly at all three men. "You lied to me, which is not a good way to start a productive relationship with the future Queen of the Dragons."

Neasán looked at Aodh and Lazarus for support. They passed. "I prefer to view it, not as a falsehood, but as not having reached that specific item on the agenda. You did pass out after eating your shell." He was relieved at Clío's smile.

"Ceara has been very helpful and explained to me that while dragons prefer caves, they do have several locations with accommodations of which a five-star hotel would be envious. Apparently, this includes my palace." Clío looked sternly at the men and was gratified to see Aodh and Neasán avert their eyes. Lazarus stood with a broad grin on his face.

"Ask me any question," said Clío.

"*What?*" came the joint response from all three men.

"Ask me any question about dragons, dragon government, history, culture, and society," said Clío. "I went into my mother's cave knowing nothing about my race. Now, I defy you to ask me a question I cannot answer."

She looked at Lazarus. "It is like one of those science-fiction movies we watched where electrodes are attached to a mechanical thinking cap on someone's head. Suddenly, they know everything. Between this and my powers of recall, I could make a fortune on radio quiz shows or in casinos. *How?*"

"It must be your shell. Crudely, human placentas provide nourishment for the growing baby. Some cultures even eat the placenta after the birth." Lazarus ignored the "Ewwws" from Clío and Ceara. "I can only conclude your birth was incomplete until you consumed your birth shell." Lazarus looked at Aodh and Neasán. "It appears we do not need the tutors."

# CHAPTER 15

The Mórrígan stood on the wooden bridge and chuckled at what she felt but could not see. "Very clever, brother. A portal only you and Clíodhna can use. I am not surprised. Of the Womb-Born, you always saw the long game. Why am I here? What part in your game do I play? Certainly not the fool, because that would not end well for you."

Lazarus feigned offence. "This is a short visit. Can I not build on our reunion after many millennia? Are you not glad that we have become brother and sister once more?"

"I am very pleased but also wary, *Lazarus*. You have changed your name, which will take a while before it sounds normal on my lips. What else is different? If I utter a whisper about your clandestine visit to the Island of Dragons or that a young Queen-in-Waiting accompanies you, will the serpents who watch and guard her incinerate me?"

The Mórrígan paused and smiled. Of her siblings, Lazarus was the least duplicitous. To find him playing a game of shadows intrigued her. She would not admit it to his face, but The Mórrígan was immeasurably pleased he chose her to disclose he had returned to an active role. She had much to atone for, for not having his back when he lost his arm and throne.

"How is Clíodhna progressing? Will she make a good Queen of the Dragons? Will Bráchthine be proud of her? *Is she yours?*"

Lazarus' eyebrow arched and he laughed. "Clíodhna has also

quizzed me on the topic of fatherhood." The Mórrígan knew her brother would not give a definitive response. *Was that an answer in itself?* The Mórrígan's eyes widened, and Lazarus maintained the same enigmatic smile.

"When will you return to the Land of Immensity... 'officially'?"

"Clíodhna needs to be better prepared for the Arena. When she has completed the battle training plan Aodh and Ceara designed for her, we will return to Belfast." Lazarus' demeanour became grim. "We have a Nemed problem."

"No!" exclaimed The Mórrígan. "The Nemed are never allowed out of their Fomorian masters' sight. You may need my talents." The scent of imminent battle made The Mórrígan's nostrils quiver, and she barely restrained herself from begging Lazarus to let her join his band.

"We have not seen any demons, but, as you say, the Nemed are never allowed to travel unsupervised. After a thousand generations, the Fomorians still do not trust their thralls. The timing of our next visit to the Island of Dragons or the Land of Immensity may depend on the Fomorians' strategy."

The Mórrígan shook her head. "You cannot allow them to take the initiative, Lazarus. As much as I dislike the demons, they are not stupid and play the long game as well as, if not better than, the Tuatha Dé. Do you think *she* is involved?"

"I hope not."

"Before I leave, brother, I have some unwelcome news for you."

"What?" asked Lazarus.

"Your attempt at a clandestine visit was well-meaning but unsuccessful. Clíodhna's brother, Ciarán, has friends in the Clann Dubh. He, and more importantly, Lady Scáthach, know Clíodhna and you are here." The Mórrígan could not hide her amusement. "She is furious. Scáthach has plans for Ciarán. She sees herself as the power behind the throne and him as the tool to achieve her ambitions. Mother and daughter will ruthlessly pursue them."

The smirk on Lazarus' face told its story. "You bastard, you knew your visit would leak." The Mórrígan bowed. "A clever first strike, brother. It is worthy of me."

Lazarus dipped his head. He thought about embracing his sister before returning to Clíodhna's camp but his was not a hugging or sociable family, with the exceptions being Daghdha and Meadhbh who added a whole new dimension to intimacy. Instead, he said, "We should meet much more often in the future."

It was enough for The Mórrígan. Perhaps a hug the next time? "I'm getting soft," she muttered and transformed into a raven.

*** 

Clío gasped for air. Her lungs felt as if they had exploded. That being insufficient, someone had removed them, kicked them around the field, and put them back… in the wrong position. She had a permanent stitch in her right side and her head reeled from the lack of oxygen. Pigheaded, she refused to faint and shunned showing any weakness in front of Aodh, Ceara, and her flight of bodyguards.

Still, this was only the second of ten laps around the field, twenty miles in all. She was in dragon form—the size of a small mansion—and forbidden from flying. Bent over double, Clío held her hand up. "Enough, Aodh. What is the need for all this? We're dragons. We have abilities. When will I ever have to run at the enemy?"

"You will do what you are asked, which includes ten laps of this field. More if I deem it necessary." Aodh had no sympathy.

Emboldened by the chorus of groans from her guards, Clío assumed she held the high ground. "No, I won't. I am the Queen-in-Waiting. You can't tell me what to do." Her moment was sweet but brief.

"On this field, you have no rank and are equal with the others… except me," replied Aodh. "Perhaps the traditions of the training arena have slipped your mind. Frankly, I'm disappointed you chose a coward's way to excuse yourself. When your mother drilled with her personal protectors, she accepted the need for discipline and following orders. How can I expect you to fight in formation? How can your comrades expect you to stand firm and protect their backs?"

Embarrassed, Clío stood before Aodh and those she thought of as her friends. The ground trembled beneath her paws as she stomped to and fro. She breathed deeply, attempting to control her pounding heart and roiling emotions. Instead, her lungs filled until they pushed painfully against her rib cage. She glared at Aodh, and her eyes took on a red tint. On the periphery of her vision, she saw fear in Ceara's eyes.

Rage engulfed her. A great roar grew from deep in the pit of her stomach and emerged from her cavernous maw. In the distance, she heard Ceara scream, "Da!" Too late she realised it was not a bellow of anger that spouted from her mouth but her first gush of dragon breath. For one hundred yards in front of her, anything that lived, whether animal or plant, was ash. Sand became glass. The smell of brimstone clogged her nostrils. Her throat burned. She had literally screamed fire.

"What have I done?" shrieked Clío.

Transforming to her human form, Clío beat her hands on the dirt. Gradually, she became aware of the absence of communal cries and condemnation, especially from Ceara, whose father she had incinerated. Suspicions germinated in Clío's brain. She looked up at Ceara, whose face had transformed from dread to where she was trying hard not to smile. "Bitseach! Where is he?" asked Clío.

She whirled around at the sound of dragon's paws touching the dirt. About to launch into a rant of how inappropriate his actions were, she noticed the blistering on his forearm. "You stupid man!" she shouted. "I could have turned you to ash. How would I ever have looked myself in a mirror or Ceara in the face? Who would command my army?"

Aodh looked slightly guilty, but that mien disappeared quickly. "It worked for your mother, and it worked for you. You are two of a kind, Clíodhna. Can you see why we must work on control and focus before I let a powerful dragon loose on either of our worlds?"

"*Tuilí*—bastard!" muttered Clío and stormed from the arena.

*✷✷*

"You were rough on her, Da," said Ceara.

"Yes, I was, Ceara but she has very little time to learn even the basics of dragon abilities and fighting. Clíodhna and Lazarus return to the Land of the Humans in two sunsets." Ceara looked crestfallen at the news. "I know you have grown close to our future queen, but you cannot go easy on her, unless you wish to see her die in combat."

Aodh rubbed his whiskered chin as Ceara strode after Clío. "The security of the Dragon Throne rests in your hands, my daughter."

*✷✷*

Curses flew. Bruises, cuts, and abrasions multiplied as Clío's *caomhnóirí*—personal guard—subjected her to their training plan on the ground and in the air. Clío hoped in the air, she could use her speed to avoid her "enemies". That hope disintegrated under Ceara's tactics and shifting formations. For the hundredth time her "protectors" ganged up on her and used their massive heads, bodies, and tails to force her into a spin.

Clío tumbled, rolled, and hit the earth, roaring, "*Bitseacha!*" Their response of cheers and taunts reminded her of the children of Bryson Street, playing "chicken-in-the-run" against the gable wall. She was the unfortunate hen unsuccessfully dodging their missiles. Yet, the experience in the air was exhilarating, and Clío knew she was getting better. She became less a beautiful, floundering seahorse and more a sleek, deadly predator.

For all her misgivings and love of flying, Clío discovered standing shoulder to shoulder with her comrades in the dragon equivalent of the human shield-wall gave her the most sense of purpose. The camaraderie brought tears to her eyes. Paradoxically, it also made her homesick for Belfast and her girlfriends. She knew it was time to return, and so did Lazarus.

*✷✷*

"Thank the Goddess dragons are not big on goodbyes," muttered Clío. The small party gathered one hundred yards from the wooden bridge, awkwardly searching for the right words. "Shite!" said Clío. "It's not that you'll never see me again. If the Goddess wills it, I will be your future queen." She looked at Aodh and Neasán. "You've always known there were hurdles to overcome before I can ascend the throne, but I trust you to prepare my path as you see fit." Both men smiled and dipped their heads. It was a good first speech for the Queen-in-Waiting.

Clío turned to Ceara and hugged her. Tears streamed down Clío's face as she took a pace backwards. Ceara stood smiling, even grinning. "Of all those I have met and become friends with, I had hoped our parting would be less of a celebration. Will you not miss me at all?"

"Have you forgotten my duties, my queen? I am your shield-maiden, and my place is at your side… always and wherever you are. I am coming with you."

Clío glared at Aodh, Lazarus, and Neasán. "None of you thought to inform me of this. Enjoy your moment, gentlemen. My retribution is certain and will be at a time of *my* choosing."

# CHAPTER 16

*1941—Winter—Belfast, Northern Ireland*

Clío's screams of joy could be heard half-way down Bryson Street. She discovered time moved differently beyond the portal and she had returned in time for her New Year's Eve party. "It's the perfect way to introduce 'cousin' Ceara to my girlfriends, Grandpa," Clío said, slipping seamlessly back into her human role. "For appearances, I should get Ceara a job in the mill. They're always looking for workers so that shouldn't be a problem, and I think our team is missing at least one person. Everyone will love you, Ceara."

The look of trepidation on Ceara's face stopped Clío's flow of exuberance. It had not crossed her mind that Ceara had never been beyond the borders of the Island of Dragons or the Land of Immensity. "Shite! I'm so stupid. This must be scary for you." Clío put an arm around her friend. "Don't worry. You are my shield-maiden, and I will be yours. I will be at your side… and my friends are very friendly."

Ceara's lips quivered. "I'll be fine. It just hit me that I'm not just in a different country but in a different world and time. I'm homesick, but I'll get over it." Clío sensed her apprehension, but then Ceara brightened. "So, when do I get to try the famous Ulster Fry and fish suppers you have missed so much?"

\*\*\*

Clío's unqueenly burp drew a snort from Ceara and a frown from

Lazarus. All three had finished mopping up the last traces of egg yolk, tomato juice, and grease with fried bread. Such was their efficiency, the dishes would require only a cursory wash. The young women rested back in their seats and patted bellies swollen with food and beer.

Lazarus leaned back and folded his arms. His expression took on a troubled look. At Clío's raised eyebrow, he said, "This is a small house, Clío. Where will Ceara sleep? Dragons like their own space. We may need to move to a larger home." Lazarus' deadpan delivery gave Clío no inkling whether he was serious.

"Let Ceara and me worry about that. We'll figure something out." Ceara returned Clío's wink with a smile.

\*\*\*

In the Island of Dragons, Clío had not been aware of her tail. Everybody had one. It seemed natural and was very useful when she flew. The tail had many practical applications, including maintaining her balance when she transformed. In Belfast, the appendage made an impromptu appearance while Clío slept.

Her mind befuddled from the dragon equivalent of jet lag and the over-indulgence of the previous evening, Clío awoke convinced it was a dream. She smiled at Ceara. It was awkward getting out of bed and the erection in her arse just kept growing. Swearing filled the air as she descended the stairs. Her tail caught on the final step, and she face-planted. At least the hallway was carpeted. Ceara and Lazarus were doubled over laughing at her expense. She stumbled back to the bedroom and, with Ceara's help, bent the appendage to her will.

Clío's tail usually disappeared when she took human form, unlike her line of spinal scales. *What will happen when I am fucking, and my partner stimulates me to orgasm?* She snorted. *As if that ever happens.* The hard men of the Yard were not known for prolonged foreplay. Clío sighed. At least they had stamina and could hold an erection. Plus, their enthusiasm was guaranteed, especially the married ones. Compared to their wives who knew one position, she was a living Kamasutra.

Ceara's finger traced the scales on Clío's spine, playing a sensual melody. *I will teach you how to control rebellious body parts… and show you how useful the tip of your tail can be.*

\*\*\*

Days later, Lazarus issued an order to capture a Nemed. Immediately after that, he sought sanctuary in the warmth of McHugh's bar and comfort in several single malts.

Clío and Ceara took up positions on the corners of the street opposite Mountpottinger Police Station. The dragons' chameleon-like ability for camouflage proved to be a major advantage in stakeouts. Also, cold or hot, wet or dry weather did not bother dragons in their natural form. For five days, from dawn to dusk and sometimes into the night, the pair faithfully reported to their post. Clío's tail swished the pavement. Although her lineage was known for its great patience, the waiting was tedious for Clío.

To amuse herself, she pondered the pluses and minuses of her "condition". Examining her clawed extremities, she noted that dragons never have cracked, hang, or ingrown nails. *That's a plus.* On this occasion, her extremely sensitive sense of smell was a disadvantage. Clío's location was close to a family-owned home bakery and the smells of baked bread continually wafted in her direction. Thoughts of a freshly baked soda farl split, spread liberally with butter, and filled with several slices of fresh elder made her drool. The possibility of discovery due to a rumbling belly was considerable.

\*\*\*

On Saturday evening, Clío stood alone. She leaned against the red-brick corner terrace house and observed this small part of humanity. A protesting Ceara had been ordered to take the night off. A stray thought popped into Clío's head, and she chuckled. She had become every Belfast mother's nightmare—a corner girl. Clío half expected an irate father to appear and drag her away, promising to "tan her hide" when they got home. It saddened her when it did not happen. *Who is my father? Is it Lazarus?* As for the arse smacking, Ceara would take care of that later when she returned home. *She'll probably spank me extra hard tonight.*

After a week of surveillance, Clío's dedication was rewarded. She observed a small group of Nemed exit the police station at dusk. Ribbons of oily darkness slithering around them like the Gorgon's snakes gave them away. Agitated, they surrounded a much taller, dark entity.

Apart from a few almost imperceptible lapses, the Fomorian maintained her superb glamour. Clío was impressed. Glamours did not come naturally to Fomorians. Those who mastered the ability were often suspected of being half-bloods or spies of the Tuatha Dé. From the body language and obeisance, there was no doubt who was in command and that the Fomorian was furious with the Nemed who stood before her.

"Who authorised you to bribe Nuadha with child sacrifices? I want him unbalanced and off his game, not hunting us down to avenge dead children." Even at a distance, Clío had no problem in listening to the conversation or in sensing the demon's displeasure.

Clío recognized the obnoxious young Special Branch officer. Gone was any trace of haughtiness. She saw terror on his face, and heard it in his unending grovelling and pleas for mercy. He knew an unpleasant and painful demise awaited him. Clío's had wondered how Fomorians disciplined or punished their thralls. She did not wait long to find out.

Cloaked by the evening gloom, the Fomorian transformed to her native state. The root of the name "Fomorian" is *"fó"*—female—and *"mahr"*—demon. The creature Clío observed fulfilled both criteria. She plucked the detective effortlessly from the ground and dismembered him. Like a sadistic schoolboy with a fly, the Fomorian removed and ate his limbs, one at a time. However, most flies do not, at least to human ears, scream in pain as the last morsel—the head—is eaten.

Clío heard the crunching of the Nemed's skull as if the Fomorian stood next to her. "Fuck!" She had much to learn about demons and stakeouts. Demons have excellent hearing and the involuntary expletive was Clío's undoing. A look in her direction brought a screech from the demon, who unfurled leathery black wings and disappeared into the descending darkness of the night. The Nemed scattered to all points of the compass.

One ran directly into Clío. Unlike his mistress, or dragons, the Nemed had no night vision and no ability to reveal Clío's presence. Snatched abruptly off the ground, horror appeared in the Nemed's smoky eyes as his captor was revealed. Clío briefly wondered what she looked like to him. His fear echoed that of the young detective before the demon ate him. *I must look terrifying.*

The Nemed shrieked continuously. Clío briefly wondered what she should do with him. Her dragon nature removed the decision from her, and she opened her jaws. Disappointed and a bit startled, Clío watched as the last flake of ash drifted away. Only the unpleasant smell of toasted Nemed remained. *What will Lazarus say at my failure? I was supposed to capture the Nemed?*

* * *

Back at the house, Ceara was furious at Clío. She took being omitted from the night's stakeout as a personal slight. "You deserved the night off," said Clío, annoyed at Ceara's reaction to her generosity.

"I am your shield-maiden. I do not get nights off. How did you intend to fight the Fomorian if she chose to attack? They are powerful creatures. You are not ready for that fight." Ceara saw the hurt in Clío's eyes, and her anger subsided. She pulled her into her arms. "We have become more than friends and that was poor judgment on both of our parts. I serve the Queen of the Dragons. Please let me do my job, my queen."

The tense atmosphere did not last long. Lazarus roared with laughter when Clío confessed to the Nemed's immolation. *Perhaps, in times of great danger and high emotions, people grasp at anything humorous.* Finally, he brought himself under control and resumed his sage persona. "What did you see? I want to know every detail."

About to demonstrate the length of her middle finger and how far she could shove it up his high-kingly arse, Clío stood slack-mouthed and eyes wide at the movie of the Nemed's thoughts that played in her head. Amazed, she recited every detail to Lazarus. *I have a promising career as a court reporter if the dragon gig doesn't work out.*

"Shite, Lazarus! There are an awful lot of Fomorians and Nemed scattered around, and not just in Belfast and the North. How do we fight them?" Full of youthful confidence, Clío looked at Ceara, smiled, and declared, "We defeated them once. We can do it again."

"You need to listen more carefully to the words the Tuatha Dé use and be more discerning." Clío's arched eyebrow demanded an explanation. "I stated that we 'banished' the Fomorians, and we did. But only after *they* decided the battle was not looking favourable and sent ambassadors to negotiate a truce.

"The Fomorian generals' priority was to preserve their army before the Tuatha Dé and dragons reduced it to a size from which they could never recover. We were killing tens of thousands of them and their Nemed thralls but were making little impact on the nest of vipers. Indeed, our only advantage was the ferocity of the dragons." Clío and Ceara smiled smugly as ancient pride warmed their hearts.

"The leaders of both sides met. I proposed banishment to the sea, which upset my brother, Manannán. He has not spoken to me since. The Fomorians accepted my offer with alacrity. In hindsight, that should have set alarm bells ringing loudly in my head, but at the time, I doubted the Tuatha Dé's ability to break the Fomorian flanks, even with the dragons. The Mórrígan was furious. She wanted to eradicate the Fomorians." Lazarus smiled wanly. "My sister was right." He looked at Clío. "Bráchthine was not overjoyed with my decision either."

"Well, at least they're ugly bastards and bitches. With their locations in my head and endless re-runs, it should be easy for us to track them down," said Clío.

Lazarus studied his long fingers for a moment and shook his head. "Life is never that simple. The images will fade, so start making notes.

Ceara will help." Clío scowled. "It makes sense. No dragon wants to have thousands of other beings' memories clogging up his or her mind. That is the path to insanity." What could Clío say? Lazarus was right.

"What are you not telling me?" Clío's spinal scales played a discordant melody.

*  *  *

The trio retired to the parlour's comfortable embrace. "In the beginning, the Tuatha Dé had excellent relations with the Fomorians," began Lazarus. "They were exotic, and many had relationships with them. Like humans, Fomorians are exceptionally fertile. Some bore children, which we could not have with our Tuatha Dé partners.

"We realized too late the race was dark, malicious, and patient. One of the mixed children—a young man called Bres—convinced the Womb-Born to crown him High King in my absence. It was around the time I lost my arm. According to Tuatha Dé rules, only someone 'whole' could sit on the high king's throne. None of my Womb-Born siblings wanted the job. They were content with the kingdoms and cities they ruled. Their apathy almost doomed the Tuatha Dé."

Lazarus observed Clío's "How could you be so stupid" look. He held his hands up. "It was not as if Bres did not have providence. He was the son of Ériu, a princess of the Tuatha Dé, and a Fomorian prince called Elatha. Bres was very handsome, personable, and charming. He was a decent artist, which helped, too."

Clío rolled golden eyes. "Even I could have predicted that would end badly."

Lazarus ignored her and continued. "Ériu was the daughter of my brother, Daghdha, and our sister, Meadhbh." At this, Clío's eyes threatened to escape their sockets, but she refrained from commenting. "Once crowned, Bres set about methodically undermining the Tuatha Dé." Lazarus exhaled a mournful sigh. "It transpired that Fomorian blood is more potent than Tuatha Dé. Had Bres been as patient as a pureblood Fomorian, he would have succeeded. In the end, he incited the war between the two races, which led to the Fomorians' exile."

"You recognized *her* from my description." Clío's eyes widened in sudden realization. "You fucked her, didn't you? You betrayed my mother. *The Hag!* I hope you're not my father."

Lazarus' eyes reflected the pain of remembrance. "It was a long time ago, Clíodhna, and before Bráchthine ascended the Dragon Throne." He breathed deeply and exhaled. "The creature you saw was Balora, the daughter of Balor, and a queen of the Fomorians. He was the commander of the Fomorian army and an evil bastard. She was beautiful and intoxicating." There was a wistful look in Lazarus' eyes. "I cut off his head at the Battle of Mag Tuired. The tattoo on the sacrificed children is the central image from Balora's ancestral coat of arms."

Silence descended on the room. It was followed by the chink of a crystal tumbler on a silver platter and the soft, wooden clunk of Lazarus closing the parlour door.

*** 

A distressed Lazarus kept to his room for the next week. Over the millennia, his custom was to sequester himself when he had a great problem to mull over.

In this, he and Clío took widely contrasting approaches to troubles. Clío screamed frequently, got drunk, and copulated like an oversexed rabbit. Her newly improved shape had extended the number and quality of potential partners and in Ceara she had a willing hunting mate. Clío discovered that female dragons and Tuatha Dé queens had one thing in common—they were raving nymphomaniacs. To Ceara, humans were exotic rutting partners. Clío valiantly maintained she was not jealous, but she was.

When Lazarus finally emerged from his isolation, he spoke to a bemused Clío as if their conversation had never been interrupted. "I'm puzzled why the Fomorians are taking such an interest in Belfast or me. Their preferred tools of mischief are usually demonstrated on a much larger scale using war and plague. They were largely responsible for the world's major plagues, which killed almost half of its population. As for wars, the litany goes on and on. Humans are quite susceptible and often led by fools with Fomorian demons perched on their shoulders."

Clío gazed at Lazarus and shook her head. "Your vision has a blind spot, Grandpa." Anger flashed in Lazarus' eyes until she touched his hand. "It's personal." Grief filled him.

"Then that is their weakness. We will find, and *you* will end the bitseach. Once Balora is dead, the rest will flee."

As Lazarus left the room, Clío muttered, "And she is your Achilles heel." The bile of future duplicity rose in her gorge.

# CHAPTER 17

The Sons of Mil conquered the Tuatha Dé and at that moment their good fortune ended. Only the Goddess chastised her people. Thus, while the numbers of the Tuatha Dé stabilised, albeit under duress from the Goddess, the population of the Sons of Mil shrank. They intermarried with the more numerous humans who evolved from that branch. Hence, the Sons of Mil became diluted and declined until they became a footnote in history.

Many scholars thought the Sons of Mil had disappeared. However, facing extinction, desperate leaders drew the remnant of pure-blood Sons of Mil together. The emergent society was governed by a privileged and strict social hierarchy. In modern times, the race numbered five hundred families for a total population of about two thousand people. Their once vaunted army could, at best, field five hundred warriors. Inter-race relationships were forbidden. Thus, inbreeding would likely doom the Sons of Mil to final extinction.

The remnant of the Sons of Mil needed an edge and a strategy for survival. They rejected their gods, replacing them with science, and committed themselves to gaining expertise in genetics, genetic modifications, and the creation of an elite force—the Watchers. The Watchers were experts in assassination, concealment, and hand-to-hand combat.

The Watchers' lofty ideals quickly fell victim to avarice and politics. They became mercenaries for hire, not an elite force formed to protect the people. As to who the Sons of Mil considered friends or enemies, it was a question that went unanswered. Considered too few to be a threat by the demigods of the Tuatha Dé, the dragons, or the demon hordes of the Fomorians, the hierarchy of the Sons of Mil continually searched for the relevance their egos demanded.

* * *

Ultán was the best of the Watchers and one of the few who held to the unit's original philosophy. He was eight feet tall, physically unattractive, and had a bold demeanour. His access to glamours—a misguided gift from the Tuatha Dé to seal the Treaty—mitigated his outward appearance.

Few could match Ultán's ability as a tracker and his skills were best carried out in perilous solitude. He considered himself to be personable, yet found the idea of teamwork, relying on the trust and synergies created by its diverse talents, uncomfortable. Even the pretence of cooperation was challenging to maintain. Thus, his talents were put to better use when he worked alone.

An innate sense of distrust meant Ultán had no one he could call a comrade. The Watcher found comfort in weapons, not people. He wore a broad, ancient leather belt etched with runes. Hung on the belt were ornately inscribed sheaths protecting two knives. The pieces of metal were closer than friends. They had saved his life on many occasions and no one of flesh and blood could claim or better that.

The ever-watchful glyphs offered comforting assurance yet were an anathema to the science that made him. Both knives were made of steel with edges honed wickedly sharp. Ultán was never convinced of the need to carry more. He had two hands, and if he needed another blade, death approached. One weapon was a large knife with a broad blade, cross-guard, and clip point. The length of a short sword, it was designed for slashing. The second was shorter, slimmer, and tapered to a needle point. It was a blade designed to punch through protection, penetrate flesh, and ruin vital organs. Ultán coated its edges with a pernicious venom. Unfortunately, this advantage disappeared after its first thrust into flesh.

The weapons and belt were a gift from his mother and father. Immensely proud of Ultán, his parents were spiritual and not in harmony with either the ruling caste or their son's career choice. In the highly structured society of the Sons of Mil, Ultán and his parents' concerns and preferences were unimportant and subservient to the greater good.

Ultán's enhanced vision gave him an advantage in that he could position himself beyond the range of a normal human's sightline while observing his quarry. On this cold, wet January dusk, he stood under a porch, ostensibly to shelter from the rain. He congratulated himself on his tracking skills. They had delivered an unexpected bounty and a major problem. He had not anticipated the presence of a Fomorian queen, the Nemed, and two dragons. *What is going on and why on this tiny island?* Ultán cursed the major gaps in the intelligence provided to him. *Was it deliberate or incompetence?*

His mission was clear: assassinate Nuadha's companion, Clíodhna. He did not ask why. He never did, assuming it must be for the betterment of the Sons of Mil. Yet he could not prevent a worm of doubt from slithering into his mind as he watched her walk to her stakeout position and saw her transform into her dragon form. *Why was I not told this?* Even if it were possible to kill the dragon, its clann and race would exact brutal revenge not just on him but on the citizens of the Sons of Mil. His next thought was both disquieting and a logical deduction. *Have I been set up? Why?* He shook his head.

The Watcher unbuttoned and adjusted his heavy greatcoat, allowing quick access to the blades. The long coat was as much a part of his armoury as his knives. He smiled at the approving glances from passers-by. January, in Belfast, was undoubtedly the weather for such a garment. Through all seasons, Ultán wore the overcoat and a black fedora. Suffering a few drops of perspiration was a fair trade for the protection it provided. The thick material with its inner sleeve of chainmail had turned away knives and claws. Thankfully, the quality of the mail and its weight had substantially improved with more modern materials and better machinery.

He grinned at the fedora. It was an affectation, which gave no advantage but looked good on him. Such individualism was frowned on by the hierarchy of the Sons of Mil.

\*\*\*

Ceara's laugh was silent. *The fool thinks he is unseen. Give the command and I will end him.*

*No, I want to know more about him. Why is he here? I saw him once before in the park and thought nothing of it. This cannot be a coincidence. Watch him. Don't get caught. We'll discuss his presence with Lazarus over breakfast.*

*If his cock is as big as his ego, then we might have some fun before incinerating him.* This time Clío grinned.

# CHAPTER 18

A thin sprinkling of fresh, powdery snow accented the roads, pavements, and cobblestones. The sky was pitch black, apart from a scattering of twinkling stars and a few planets. Soft, diffuse light backlit a solitary cloud betraying the presence of a timid moon. There were no streetlights. Slivers of yellowish light escaped windows covered by blackout blinds and drapes. In the blackness, the runes on the back yard's door glowed silver—but only to those who might prove to be a threat.

"You are a fast learner, Clíodhna."

The "old" Clío would have been surprised, but heightened senses had alerted her to another's presence in the yard. Clío waited. The Mórrígan knew the question in Clío's head since the younger woman had permitted entrance to her thoughts. She inclined her head, pleased that Clío trusted her to abide within the constraints of her access. She would not disappoint the young dragon. "I am here to see my brother. We have mutual concerns and problems to discuss." Clío did not drop the veils quick enough to disguise her scepticism.

"Do not misinterpret our behaviour, Clíodhna. I have known Lazarus since Anúna birthed us. We may fight and disagree on many matters, but we are brother and sister. If needed, we will defend each other to the death… against *anyone*. Even the ward of whom he is much too fond and overly protective. May I pass?" The queen's tone was stern.

"Small children know that 'please' opens doors. Did the Womb-Born miss that lesson?" Clío tilted her head towards the home's back door.

"Dragons! Never ones for obeisance or humility. It amazes me humans consider your race to be wise."

To allow The Mórrígan to pass, Clío moved to her left, clockwise. It was an ancient custom. The ballet ceased when The Mórrígan placed a hand on Clío's arm. It was a strangely maternal touch. Still, Clío knew she was not going anywhere until The Mórrígan released her.

"Are you aware of the Nemed and their Fomorian mistress in the alleyway?" Clío could not resist a roll of her eyes.

"Curb your arrogance, Clíodhna, or it will be your downfall." The tone was sharp and Clío had the grace to blush. "Do not underestimate the Nemed… or Balora, although she is not among them tonight. An underling commands the Nemed." The Mórrígan laughed. "They will give you *and* your shield-maiden some exercise."

In a dark corner of the yard, a shadow grunted her displeasure at being revealed.

"Please step out from the darkness, Ceara Dearg, daughter of my friend, Aodh. We have not been formally introduced, and it would be a tragedy if I mistook you for an enemy in a future battle. The apology to your father would be embarrassing."

"Bitseach," muttered Ceara. She stepped into the half-light and bowed respectfully to The Mórrígan. "I am indeed Ceara Dearg and also the Lady Clíodhna's shield-maiden." She smiled pleasantly. "I agree, it would be unfortunate *for you* if we did not recognise each other in battle. The effects of dragon breath are painful and disfiguring. I am sure you would not want an extended soak in Daghdha's Cauldron."

The Mórrígan hissed her annoyance and her hand gripped Clío's arm tighter. Had Clío been human, the bones would have shattered. "Lazarus is the best of us and should never have been forced to abdicate the throne of the High King. It was and remains his birthright. I will forever regret not supporting him and will not make the same mistake again. Protect my brother, Dragon." The threat was implicit. She was the Queen of Desolation and would exact revenge… even on a dragon.

Clío dipped her head in acquiescence and took a pace forward.

The long, artistic fingers looked fragile but gripped Clío's forearm as the jaws of a vice. "I have a message from your brother." The clipped tones and understated disgust in The Mórrígan's voice confirmed she held as low an opinion of Clío's kin as Lazarus. "More likely it is from his mistress, the Lady Scáthach. He has waited a long time for your awakening and wishes to meet with you. He expressed his deep disappointment that you did not introduce yourself during your recent visit to the Island of Dragons."

This time, Clío chuckled and shook her head. "Not yet, my lady. My mother passed on her knowledge of dragon laws and traditions. I know what Ciarán has in mind for our first meeting, but we are long past poison or a sharp blade to put him on the throne. First, I must train for battle. That is one of the reasons Ceara accompanies me. She is a hard taskmaster, and my goal is to be as proficient in fighting as she.

"In the end, Ciarán will have no option but to challenge me in the Arena to prove he is the better choice to rule the dragons." Clío snorted. "Men and their dick-waving." It was the first time she heard The Mórrígan laugh. The sound was unrestrained and joyful. It was a glimpse below the surface and of what, in other circumstances, The Mórrígan might have become. "I am young, my lady, but wise enough to know my talents are not fully developed. For me to accept the duel at this time would be foolish. He would beat me. Like you, I never like to lose."

\*\*\*

*Why are the Nemed here? What message do they bring?* Despite The Mórrígan's plea for caution, a group of twenty Nemed, even with a Fomorian leader, were no match for a dragon. With two serpents, they were well outmatched, even if one was still learning her skills. The Mórrígan watched Clío and Ceara transform and slip serpent-like over the yard wall.

Dragon laminae are flexible and impervious to most barriers. Clío and Ceara ignored the shards of beer- and milk-bottle glass embedded in the roughly laid concrete that capped the bricks. It was a common and inexpensive way of discouraging unwelcome visitors. In the streets and dark alleyways of Belfast, thieves earned their plunder.

Most times, dragons prefer the balance and comfort of standing on all four paws, but their tails and the strength of their rear limbs also permitted them to stand upright. Clío stood with her back to the wall, and twice her human height. To all eyes, she was no more than a patch of inky blackness. She listened and watched. The Nemed had divided into two groups, one on either side of the doorway. It was a foolish strategy, and not because they faced two dragons. The squad who drew the short straw were only a few paces to Clío's left. Since theirs was an end-house and the alleyway's exit to Duke Street was only ten steps from the back door, the Nemed had little choice. The remainder milled around twenty paces further down the entry.

A few paces beyond them, the Fomorian's talons tightened. Was she anxious, bored, or fearful? Glass crunched as she perched gargoyle-like on the yard wall. The creature's eyes glowed red like a cigarette after a deep draw. Clío heard the rustle of wings stretching as if in preparation for flight. *Be careful, Ceara.* Clío instantly felt a warm, ethereal embrace. *Wow! You must teach me that one, although I prefer the real thing.*

Clío assumed the Nemed knew nothing about the home's occupants, but how aware was the Fomorian? Did she know a Womb-Born and two dragons were the residents? *Surely not. Who or what compels them to ignore any sense of self-preservation? Does it matter?* Clío's goal was straightforward: kill all but one without destroying the neighbourhood in the process.

Dragon breath was out of the question. The combination of fire and corrosive mist would destroy most of the neighbours' walls and a good portion of their backyards. Clío smiled. With Aodh's and Ceara's guidance, she had learned to control her dragon breath and had avoided singeing anyone recently. Over the past month, Ceara and she had taken several trips to the Cavehill—a small mountain to the north of

Belfast—to practice. At this time of the year, there were few tourists or locals, so they had the hill to themselves. Only scorch marks marked their visits. New growth of heather and gorse would conceal those in the spring.

Clío's senses were on high alert, filtering out the yowling of amorous cats, the episodic barking of dogs unhappy to be left outside in kennels of rough wood, and the soft cooing of racing pigeons. A persistent hissing rose and fell from the Nemed. The Fomorian's wings rustled with impatience and irritation at the low-value task Balora had assigned to her.

For the life of her, Clío could not understand why the Fomorians and Nemed were here, but she concluded she was overthinking their motives. What good would it do to get inside their heads? Her patience and faux philosophising exhausted, Clío dropped her camouflage and broke from the wall.

Iridescent scales glowed in the night as Clío turned to the ten on her left. *"Child-killers!"* Their fear was palpable, and their demise was quicker and much less cruel than afforded to the obnoxious detective eaten by Balora. Dragon talons reduced Nemed flesh to a putrid, black ash that clung to her scales. *I'll need a hot antiseptic bath after this.* The Nemed on her right discovered freedom of thought and ran for the alleyway's far exit.

Serpents are exceptionally fast on land and air, and Clío would have had no problem in catching them, but Ceara had already blocked that avenue of retreat. The level of nightmarish shrieking from the Nemed rose to headache level. Thankfully, Ceara's fight, an exaggerated description of the confrontation, lasted less than a minute.

Clío gagged on the stink of corrupted flesh and grumbled about her dull throbbing headache. *What is it about these creatures that turns my stomach? Is my reaction emotional, imaginary, or physical?* No matter, it was something she must overcome. Barked commands from the Fomorian made no impact. Her warband were destroyed and once the outcome of the fight was evident, the demon took wing. *Good sense, cowardice, or orders?*

"I could have caught her," said Ceara.

"The Nemed were sacrificed, Ceara. Likely, the Fomorian's goal was to confirm who occupied the house. I see no harm in letting whoever leads this warband know who they face." She looked at the Nemed struggling in her fist. "We can get any other information we need from this one."

Suddenly Clío 's senses tingled, and her spinal scales fluttered. There was not a breath of air, and both dragons instantly became cautious. "I will go into the house. Reconnoitre the immediate area and make sure there are no more surprises." Ceara nodded and disappeared.

* * *

"Our cat has brought a mouse home to play with, Lazarus."

The last of the Nemed struggled feebly in Clío's grasp. It was the first female Nemed Clío had encountered, and only the wraith's voice pointed to her sex. The swirling black tendrils that shrouded what remained of a corporeal body made it difficult to ascertain what set her apart from a Nemed male.

The creature's eyes opened wide in terror; she knew there was no good end for her, either from the dragon or her Fomorian masters. The best she could hope for was a quick disintegration. At worst, who knew what torture the serpent who held her and the two Womb-Born who flanked her could inflict?

Lazarus scratched a non-existent beard. He had been impressed at Clío's fine control. The night's activities added reality to her previous battle practices on the Island of Dragons. "Have you elicited any information from this one or her former comrades?" he asked.

Clío shook her head. "Nothing new. Only better details on the locations of the Nemed bands. We should remove those pieces from the board. No intelligence on where Princess Balora has gone to ground. Next time, Ceara and I will focus on securing a Fomorian to interrogate."

At the sound of Balora's name, the Nemed hissed defiantly. "Queen, not a princess."

"A Fomorian queen has more abilities than a princess," said Lazarus. "She may even be using this one like a crude walkie-talkie." The Nemed hissed once more but this time with an undertone of despair. She had divulged information, and her queen, if listening, would be furious. Lazarus laughed. "The queen will never know." He nodded to Clío. In an instant, the Nemed was ash.

"Do the Nemed have an afterlife?" asked Clío.

"What?"

"I was just wondering if the Nemed had an afterlife and what it was like. Does death release them from their Fomorian shackles?" Clío was unsure whether the silence from Lazarus and The Mórrígan was due to her foray into philosophy or incredulity at the question. She suspected it was the latter.

Lazarus was unsympathetic. "They were disposable. Their mission was to confirm our location and assess our defences, and it was successful. The only surprises were the presence of The Mórrígan and a second dragon. It is to our advantage that they know our strength."

# CHAPTER 19

Ultán pulled the tip of his fedora down. The action was unnecessary; in the pitch blackness, no human could see his face. A predator, his footsteps made no sound, and he left no prints in the snow as he walked away from his observation nook.

Hidden by the shadows, Ultán had observed the confrontation. There was no benefit to him taking an active part since the dragons were both in control and controlled. The latter was a relief. Serpents tended to be so focused on their mission that they destroyed everything and anyone who got in the way. What complicated matters was that one of the combatants was his target.

He had arrived in the area several weeks past, which meant he did not fully comprehend the true situation. His mission necessitated a period of observing Lazarus and Clíodhna. Intelligence had filtered back to the Sons of Mil's council, likely from the Nemed, of the duo's presence in Belfast. *Why are the Council dealing with the Fomorians?*

Ultán's instincts screamed, "Beware!" Yet who should he be wary of? Duplicity was part of a Watcher's armoury. He had standing orders to kill any who threatened the future of the Sons of Mil and Clíodhna had risen to the top of that list. Yet no Watcher had ever assassinated a dragon or a Womb-Born. *Is it even possible? Should I be pleased at the honour or horrified?* His knives could never hope to penetrate a serpent's scales and certainly not before he was turned into ash. The uncomfortable thought that he was the target, not the arrow, soured Ultán's belly. *I must return to the Land of Immensity.*

The presence of Fomorians and their thralls, the Nemed, was always ominous, especially in a time of human war. The dragons could be a threat, a curse, or an unexpected blessing. According to the members on the Council of Elders, serpents and the Womb-Born should not be considered as potential allies. Ultán thought that was a short-sighted and potentially terminal policy.

The Watcher imagined the conversation at the small terrace house. The dragon had sharp eyes, and he had felt them. He shrugged in disappointment at his unmasking, yet it was unlikely they had identified him. His glamour was excellent. Still, it left him with fewer cards to play than he would have liked. He turned right at the corner and entered Bryson Street and thence to the Newtownards Road.

Ultán would have been humiliated to know a second dragon had followed him unseen until he reached the city centre. He was fortunate. Instead of him sleeping in his bed that night, Ceara could have buried him in an unmarked grave on the Cavehill.

\*\*\*

Ceara's report, supported by Clío's park experience, confirmed the house and its members were under observation. Rather than fostering alarm, the information aroused Lazarus and The Mórrígan's curiosity. They were more intrigued by the presence of the Watcher than the Fomorians and Nemed. Who was his target? A litany of possible identities was tossed into the conversation. Most were discarded, some contemptuously.

Like cream rising to the top of the milk bottle, one theme began to dominate. Now was not the time for the good people of East Belfast or Ulster to become aware of the reality of the Tuatha Dé. Mythology and faerie tales provided comfort and safety—for the natural and the supernatural. Facts were dangerous.

Clío turned to The Mórrígan. "How did he evade you?"

"He is a Son of Mil. Some well-meaning eejit permitted them the use of glamours." The Mórrígan's piercing eyes gripped Lazarus' gaze. "Genetic modifications made it impossible to take the gift back and now they can use it against us."

"There are non-interference agreements in place," said Lazarus.

"And yet, here we are… interfering. Albeit with good intentions." The Mórrígan looked at her brother. "At least on the surface."

"Bloody Tuatha Dé!" a frustrated Clío shouted. "Enough of your family intrigues. Explain."

\*\*\*

Clío had some measure of confidence in the narrative's veracity since both brother and sister added complementary pieces to the jigsaw puzzle. In the long battle between the Sons of Mil and the Tuatha Dé, traitors surfaced among the ranks of the Tuatha Dé and their progeny. Full of hubris and envy, two males, Eochaidh Breas and Tuirill, who were both well down the pecking order of the Tuatha Dé's nobility, thought they deserved to be ranked as highly as the Womb-Born. Both were power-hungry narcissists but exceptionally cunning.

Their designs achieved nothing but discovery, ridicule, and scorn—the latter being an extremely effective weapon against the Tuatha Dé's massive egos. Eochaidh and Tuirill turned to the Tuatha Dé's enemy—the Sons of Mil. In exchange for promises of mercenaries, they offered wealth, lands, and influence. However, few actions remain unknown when the Womb-Born can read minds. Eochaidh and Tuirill's clanns were banished for sedition. That said, exile did little to cause a change of the rebels' heart or stop their plottings.

Clío weighed Lazarus and The Mórrígan's words. "I understand the Sons of Mil are the ancestors of the people of this island, but that was millennia ago. Surely breeding with other clanns and peoples, even in an island as small as Ireland, has diluted the bloodline beyond the point of existence." Clío laughed. "Otherwise, people would greet Lazarus and me with 'Hi King Nuadha' or 'Hi Dragon Clíodhna.'" Clío shook her head. "It doesn't make sense."

"It does if there is a remnant of pure-born Sons of Mil," said The Mórrígan. She scowled at her brother. "The Trinity—Badhbh, Macha, and I—could have sown enough strife among the Sons of Mil that they would have destroyed themselves. *You* stopped us." It was the ultimate "I told you so." Clío read The Mórrígan's pale green eyes and knew she was holding something back.

"It strikes me that humanity took to mass killing zealously and without any help from the Tuatha Dé, Fomorians, or these super-humans," said Clío. She took the silence from Lazarus and The Mórrígan as agreement. Interceding before Lazarus and The Mórrígan's conversation turned acrimonious, Clío asked, "Is Ultán an ally or an enemy?"

"He is an assassin," said Ceara, drawing a grunt from Lazarus. "The important question is 'who is Ultán's target?' Clío, Lazarus, The Mórrígan, or someone else? I doubt it is me."

Clío interpreted The Mórrígan transforming into a raven and flying off as a, "You deal with him, or I will," response.

***

Lazarus sat in his favourite worn leather armchair reading the *Belfast News Letter*. The living room was dark since neither he, Ceara, nor Clío needed light to see. Sprawled across the matching sofa, Clío flicked a nail at one of the many cracks in the material and watched a sliver float to the floor. She ignored Lazarus' scowl and rumble of disapproval. He was very protective over the furniture.

Clío's stomach continued to roil from the disintegration of the Nemed, and she felt distinctly queasy. Her head pounded as if she were in the grip of a severe flu and she had a fever, which was unusual for a dragon. *Surely, I should be developing some immunity to this. There are many more Nemed to kill.* A fit of trembling rippled through her body.

Lazarus glanced at Ceara and then Clío. "Are you feeling well, Clíodhna?"

She shook her head uncertainly, coughed up blood into her hand,

and threw up. Mercifully avoiding the puke, she slipped off the couch and onto the floor. Her last memory, before delirium eclipsed her ability to think logically, was of the revolting grin on the female Nemed's face.

\*\*\*

Lazarus blanched. "I have seen these symptoms during the Black Death and Bubonic Plagues. The Nemed must have been a carrier for one of the Fomorians' favourite bacteria. Carry her to your bedroom. Strip her and lay her on the bed. Then undress and lie with her." Lazarus took a shaking Ceara by the shoulders. "You know what must be done?"

Ceara nodded. "It will destroy the room, if not the house and part of the street. There will be casualties."

"Leave that to me. Just follow my instructions. I will be back shortly with the antibiotic injections I keep for emergencies. Medicine has improved immeasurably between the seventh century and today. Still, we must hurry before the bacteria gets a deep hold on her. Neither of us want to lose her."

# CHAPTER 20

Sunlight streamed through the bedroom window, forcing Clío's reluctant eyelids open. For a few moments, she lay on the bed, pondering horrific dreams of fire and pestilence. *How long have I been asleep?* Her skin felt prickly where a light cotton sheet touched it. Curiosity got the better of Clío, and she peeked under the cover.

"No!"

It was meant to be a scream but limped from cracked lips as a painful croak. She attempted to sit up, but severe stomach pains drove her back onto the charred bedding. She winced, tentatively feeling the tender, swollen lumps under her arms and groin. *What happened to me?* A wave of nausea conspired with the worst headache of Clío's life. She threw up.

"The Hag's arse, Clío. Not on me, *again!*" Ceara's cry held a combination of disgust and deep concern.

"Sorry."

Clío's throat felt full of sharp-edged gravel. For the first time, she inspected the naked form lying beside her and the state of her bedroom. She contemplated the scorched remnants of her bed, ceiling, and furniture. Indescribably weak, a wail of "What happened to my beautiful bedroom?" never made it past her lips. She flopped back onto the ashy remains of her bed.

Clío's nostrils shrank from the melange of smells assaulting them. *How long have I been sick?* The air was tainted with body odour, pee, vomit, and a scent that at first eluded identification, mainly because it should not have been in the bedroom: smoke. She noted the top sheet was pristine, apparently untouched by the flames.

Ceara's voice was weak as water. "After the worst passed, Lazarus changed as much of the bedding as possible." Only then did Clío notice Ceara's drawn features and the skin hanging on her bones. Black spots, like tiny bruises, covered Ceara's once unblemished and slender body. Many had pink overlays. Tears flowed down Clío's cheeks.

She examined herself more thoroughly. Nakedness never shocked Clío, but the countless small patches of black and pink that mottled her torso and limbs sent her pulse racing. She groaned at the effort needed to grasp the mirror from the bedside table. She looked with horrific antici-pation before relief flooded her. Apart from a single, minor blemish on her forehead, her face was untouched.

Shamed by her vanity, gingerly, Clío touched one of the blotches. It was dry, raised, and slightly abrasive. She looked down at the smooth ex-panse between her legs. Pre-dragon puberty, Clío was proud of her thick blonde bush, if only because it proved she did not get her blondeness from a bottle. She fondly remembered many sweaty nights of sex that began with, "Prove you're a natural blonde?" Serpent genetics gifted her zero pubic and body hair. At least that spared her the pain of waxing or the expense of the new electric razors.

"Fuck," she moaned.

A wave of guilt flooded Clío's cheeks with colour. Had karma and her rampant promiscuousness colluded to bring a contagion to taunt her? She mentally drew up a list of recent partners. The task was easy with her improved dragon memory. She foresaw inquisitions followed by painful retribution. She pommelled the bedclothes in frustration. Flakes of ash rose into the air. "I'm a dragon. I don't get the pox!"

"Not the pox, the plague." Ceara grimaced and threw off the sheet to show her own mottled body. "Thanks for infecting me."

Humiliated, embarrassed, and ashamed of her barefaced narcissism, more tears cascaded down Clío's face. *How can I possibly be a queen?* "I am so sorry," she whispered and reached out for Ceara. Comforted by the warmth of their bodies, they wept, kissed, and, exhausted, welcomed sleep's embrace.

\*\*\*

Several days later, they were awake when the bedroom door opened. Lazarus stepped in, carrying a breakfast tray. Clío's and Ceara's bellies rumbled at the smell of the fries. *Is there a better way to start the day anywhere in the world?* Both dragons looked at each other, and both wondered if their stomachs were up to the challenge.

Clío recalled the sage advice given by drinking mates and girlfriends. The best remedy for a hangover was to eat a greasy fry on the next morning. Clío's belly quailed but her mouth watered. "Dig in, Ceara," she said. "Trust me on this. Once you get past the first few mouthfuls, the world will look a lot better. Worst case, neither of us will throw up on an empty stomach."

She glanced up at Lazarus. "What? Why? How?"

"First, you owe Ceara your life. I injected the antibiotics, but without her inferno and transfer of life, you would be dead." Lazarus chuckled. "My apologies for your room but containing the fires of a dragon was a unique experience. I will be better prepared the next time." Ignoring Clío's stare, he said, "You can choose new furniture from Gillespie and Wilson when you are ready. I have already called our handyman.

"To answer your question: you were bitten by fleas carrying *Yersinia Pestis*—the plague. In turn, Ceara was infected by you. Hence, you are doubly in her debt."

"*Fleas!*" Clío glared at Lazarus and Ceara. "What makes you think that's better than syphilis?"

The dam burst. "*You did not just have fleas or the pox! You had the fucking Bubonic Plague!*" Fury and anguish filled Lazarus' voice; tears flowed down his cheeks. "How could I face Bráchthine if I lost you?" It was not lost on Clío that Lazarus spoke of her mother as if she still lived. Or that he had lapsed into using her swear words.

"I'm sorry, Grandpa." Clío patted the mattress and prayed it, and the bed, would not disintegrate. "Please sit beside me and explain what happened."

"You were infected by the final Nemed you exterminated…"

"Shite! I saw the evil bastard's grin in my dreams," said Clío.

"It was a memory, not a dream. Ceara will teach you how to glean even the smallest detail from your memories. In normal circumstances, and for future reference, the remedy is to increase your body temperature and fry the evil, disease-carrying creatures. However, you were already unconscious, and it was several days before we fully diagnosed your condition. You must never ignore even the most minor signs, Clíodhna.

"I injected you with antibiotics and Ceara wrapped you in an inferno." He signalled the state of the room. "Since your bedroom looks like a scene from Dante's Inferno, I propose we move to the Grand Central Hotel for a few weeks, until the renovations are finished."

Clío's eyes lit up at the thought of clean sheets and room service.

∗ ∗ ∗

When Lazarus visited on the following day, he perched gingerly on a bed that threatened to collapse under his weight. "You are long-lived, not immortal, Clíodhna. In the same vein, you are immensely powerful but not invulnerable. I call it the 'elephant and mouse' syndrome." Golden eyes flashed at Lazarus. "Hear me out."

Clío sensed Lazarus searching for an appropriate diplomatic analogy but was in no mood to help him out. "In dragon form, your scales will resist the most extreme forms of violence, whether ancient or modern— from arrows, spears, and swords to bombs and bullets. Nevertheless, they are like the slates forming the roof of this house. They overlap, otherwise you would be unable to move freely. Therein lies your vulnerability. Small organisms or small weapons, such as the edge of a poisoned blade, can slip under your armour. Among the Fomorians, a favoured weapon is the use of plagues." Lazarus looked directly at Clío and Ceara to emphasise his point. "We need to be more watchful."

Lazarus turned to exit the room but paused. "If you wish, you may use my bedroom tonight and we will move to a hotel tomorrow." He sniffed the air with undue deliberation. "You both stink. Get a bath. I will prepare the tub in my room." The down-filled pillow would have flown across the room had it not disintegrated a few inches after leaving Clío's hand.

*   *   *

Naively, and even with her long life observing other cultures, Clío never imagined a people so twisted they would turn another race into plague carriers. Did the Nemed know? *Should I feel sympathy for them?* After several baths and troubled naps with Ceara, Clío had no good answers. Her musings were interrupted by a soft tap on the door.

Lazarus entered, holding a silver tray, which he set on a side table. The platter held a sizeable glass bottle containing a pink liquid and several linen squares. "Now that you are well enough, I can relinquish my twice-daily chore of applying this lotion to your blemishes." Lazarus' blue eyes twinkled. "Be thorough. Maintain the application until the spots disappear. Not one can be missed."

The door closed with a soft click, and a frown settled on Clío's lips. She mused that her life had been rather good until her awakening—honey-sweet rather than sucking on lemons. Lazarus had protected her from the nastiness of life, but at what cost—being gullible? She visualised Bráchthine's disapproval. When she turned to face Ceara, her shield's face was a deep shade of red.

"The Hag! Are you ill, Ceara? What should I do?"

Ceara shook her head. "Do you realise the High King of the Tuatha Dé bathed and put lotion on *every* inch, crevice, and orifice of our naked bodies twice daily for the best part of a half-cycle of the moon?"

"I'm sure Lazarus was totally objective," said Clío, tamping down her rising discomfort.

"He's a man—more than a man, if the gossip about the Tuatha Dé is close to the truth."

"Fuck!" said Clío. "I don't know whether to feel appreciative, violated, or disappointed." Ceara's raised eyebrow demanded an explanation. "Think of all the orgasms we missed."

From the parlour came a loud peal of laughter.

# CHAPTER 21

The dark, musty cave did not bother Balora. She liked its earthiness, and the myriads of tiny creatures inhabiting the retreat were a constant source of entertainment. From her perch at the cavern's entrance, she appreciated the beauty of the vista before her, the meandering eastern coastline, and even the waters of Belfast Lough. The growl that escaped her lips caused those around the queen to glance nervously in her direction. Balora's prickly temperament was well-known.

The detachment of Fomorian warriors grumbled at the lack of action and their separation from the main army. Before they left their homes, rumours of war were rife. Still, none dared challenge Balora. The Nemed who occupied the sanctuary were agitated. Their demeanour was understandable as their roles were either to be cannon fodder or snacks for their masters.

Balora rubbed a scaley black hand across her forehead. It was an incredibly human gesture, and she hissed at what she perceived a contagion passed on by Nuadha. *I have no time for emotional entanglements or weakness. I must focus on my quest.* Success would justify all her actions. Yet, thoughts of Nuadha brought unforced memories of blissful days and steamy nights. *No, you bastard. You will not make me lose focus.*

She growled again and snorted contemptuously. Nuadha knew she was in Belfast. The Nemed had revealed her presence. Likely, the narcissistic arsehole believed she sought revenge for her father's death. True, originally Balora was furious with Nuadha and had ended their relationship. Later, she acknowledged it was a foolish decision. *My father, the heroic general, Balor, never wanted or loved me. He wanted a son to inherit his wealth and power. Nuadha loved me.*

Still, with one blade stroke, Nuadha guaranteed Balora's elevation to a Fomorian queen. *How can I be mad at him for that?* No, she was infuriated that Nuadha had never sought her out after the war. *The bastard abandoned me!*

Balora closed her eyes; the action helped order her thoughts. She encouraged family squabbles within the Fomorians. The tension kept her warriors alert and fractured until she needed them. Slowly she turned to face her command. Black leathery eyelids opened to expose fire-red eyes. Her gaze fell on the Fomorian who had led the attack on Nuadha's home. She would have blanched under Balora's stare if that were possible. Instead, she settled for a nervous shuffle and prayed for a quick death.

"Tell me of your failure," said Balora.

A torrent of words flowed from the terrified Fomorian as she attempted to recount the skirmish. In truth, Balora had expected nothing from the demon. She had been selected for the mission because she was inexperienced. Indeed, Balora was surprised she had not died. Thus, the queen's choice was to either reward the demon's initiative or devise a suitably painful punishment for her lack of success. The latter would send a message to her other warriors. Failure would not be tolerated.

When terms such as "The Mórrígan", "the Watcher", and "a second dragon" appeared in the spew of words, Balora's attention instantly sharpened. Long arms lashed out. She grabbed the demon by her throat, lifting her off the ground. Fomorian kings and queens were stronger and bigger than the general population. Balora placed a hand firmly on the Fomorian's head; red eyes commanded the underling's stare. "Thank you for your report, but I need a more in-depth analysis."

"No!" gasped the warrior. Her struggles were in vain.

The queen's jaw opened wide, revealing rows of razor-sharp, carnassial teeth set in blood-red gums. The victim's mouth opened as well, but she screamed in agony as Balora plundered her mind. As a process, it lasted only a few delightful seconds for Balora. It seemed a lifetime for the Fomorian warrior who was left a blubbering mass on the cave's dirt floor.

An almost total fish diet demanded an element of variety. Therefore, post their banishment to the ocean depths, Fomorian evolution developed cannibalistic peccadillos. Thus, the female's final demise would be neither painless nor swift. Her former comrades would happily consume her while she was alive and warm.

"Leave me!" shouted the queen. Only the foolish needed a second invitation.

\*\*\*

Back on her rock, Balora welcomed the silver light of the moon and its monochromatic shadows. She was more comfortable at night-time. It was unsurprising as sunlight rarely penetrated the depths of the oceans. She lifted a paw and peered through the diaphanous webbing between her digits. Was it a gift or a curse from Manannán?

Without the webs on their paws and the gills behind their ears, the Fomorian race would have drowned. Seafarers say it is not the worst way to die, but who had surveyed the dead? Balora cursed herself for the self-indulgence. She had a quest to complete. She pondered her minion's report, an account supported by the captured Nemed's final thoughts.

Life, and Balora's mission, had become more complex. Challenging Nuadha was inevitable, but their relationship gave her an edge. Nuadha had always been too compassionate, too sentimental. *Too soft.* It was improbable his nature had changed. The dragons were an unexpected complication. However, the presence of The Mórrígan sent shivers along Balora's spiked spine. No Fomorian king or queen had ever dared to confront two Womb-Born and two serpents. *I must bring my plans forward.*

Balora dismissed the Watcher as irrelevant to her quest. There would be no definitive answers on his mission until he was in her claws. She had heard strong rumours of a Sons of Mil community in the Land of Immensity. Given it was Daghdha who ruled the domain of the settlement, she could believe the absurdity. Daghdha's brains hung between his legs.

The queen knew the Sons of Mil were paid assassins. *Who is his prey? Probably Nuadha or his dragon ward.* If the dragons and Womb-Born knew why the Son of Mil was in Belfast, they would kill him. Balora's long, black tongue licked her lips, and she smiled. *I can use this.*

* * *

Deep in contemplation and having exhausted a bag of stale bread on the pond's ducks, Clío enjoyed a moment of peace as the waterfowl waddled back to the water. Since her awakening, life had moved too quickly and grown too complicated.

She yearned for the times of irresponsibility, blissful ignorance, and solitude. They were gone and soon she would have a kingdom to rule. Irritated, Clío exhaled until the last air left her lungs. Ever since the stakeout incident, Ceara had obstinately refused to allow Clío to travel anywhere alone. She loved Ceara but there were times when she wanted to be alone. She tried closing her mind to Ceara, depriving her of the knowledge of her intentions. However, the effort was wasted as Ceara proved to be a wily and tenacious tracker. They compromised on being out of one another's sight.

The wooden slats of the park bench protested, interrupting her serenity. She had sensed his presence from a long distance and amused herself by tracking his footfall as he approached. *Shall I dispose of him?* Clío smiled at Ceara's question but shook her head. She kept her eyes closed and prayed for privacy. Clío hoped, having rested briefly, he would quickly move on to find sanctuary at a vacant bench in the park. Minutes later, he had not budged.

"This is my refuge, Watcher. My one place of peace. Move on unless you wish me to consider you an enemy rather than a nuisance."

Ultán's laugh was pleasant and camouflaged his surprise. Clío sensed his demeanour. It conveyed confidence, with no hint of fear or malice. "My apologies. I understand the need for quietness and a sanctuary from life's tribulations."

"And yet, you invade my space. Perhaps I should have my shield remove you and resume my contemplations. She has asked permission and is already annoyed that I didn't allow her to dispose of you when she followed you to your accommodation the other night."

Clío sensed the Watcher's unhappiness at being bested at what he considered his skill set. He shook his head. "No. Such an act would only add to the turmoil that swirls around you and to the growing list of your enemies."

"Are there enough Sons of Mil remaining to be more than an irritant—a horsefly on a mare's arse?"

"Pray you never need to find out."

"An assassin's answer made from a position of weakness. Had you numbered in your thousands or tens of thousands, you would have led with a large, if boastful, number." Clío inclined her head and chuckled. "My shield has asked again if she can assist you to cross the veil." The melodic fluttering of Clío's spinal scales suggested there was no danger... yet. Could he be trusted? Was he an ally? Was he a friend?

"Yes, yes, and maybe more than."

"Fuck! Does everyone I meet read thoughts? As for the 'more than', join the long queue of the disappointed. Besides, I don't consort with ugly men, and Lazarus tells me the Sons of Mil are a disagreeable race."

The Watcher winced at the insult. "Someone as wise as a dragon should not judge by appearances."

"Who said I was wise or referred to your appearance?"

"Touché!" Ultán returned to safer ground. "I don't read minds. That said, I have been around a long time, although my race is not as long-lived as yours. I observe, and frankly, it doesn't take much detective work to discern your thoughts."

"Did you just call me a dumb bimbo?" Clío's temperature began to rise, and wisps of smoke curled from her nostrils.

"No, I did not," said Ultán. "I am excellent at reading body language. Please, reduce your temperature. I am not a fan of immolation." He hesitated before he spoke again, as if contemplating whether to reveal a confidence.

"I do, however, have exceptional hearing, which means I am enjoying the melody of your scales. That suggests that you're not entirely unhappy at my presence." His smile was genuine when he added, "Perhaps we could explore our taste in music later."

*He is a dead man. Now or later, but it will happen.*

Clío smiled at Ceara's interjection. *Is that jealousy I hear in your voice? Bitseach!*

Clío rolled her eyes, although the act was wasted on Ultán since hers were closed. However, no human could have avoided her backhanded slap and the potential decapitation which followed the Watcher's boldness. His evasion was too fast to be fully human. *Heightened eyesight, precognition, and rapid reflexes. Which is natural and which altered genes? What else might I discover should I indulge him?*

For the first time, Clío turned to face her companion. She was greeted with a broad smile. "Do you have a name?"

"Ultán."

"A 'Man from Ulster'. Well, that tells me nothing. Your parents should have simply translated 'Watcher' into Gaelic." It was an unkind retort and undeserved. She saw genuine hurt on Ultán's face. *He must be close to his parents. That is in his favour.* "Sorry. I can be a bitseach."

"Apology accepted."

Ultán's response was too quick and spoke of desperation. *Why?* "Do you ever remove that fedora? It never budged when I took a swing at you. Is it glued onto your head? Perhaps you are bald." The laugh and broad smile that swept over Ultán's face should have put anyone at their ease, including a dragon, but there was a caveat. A nervousness had crept into the melody when Clío's spine scales fluttered.

"I watch a lot of Humphrey Bogart movies," said Ultán before sweeping the hat from his head. Brown eyes sat nicely in a weather-tanned face crowned with short, dark hair. He was rugged rather than handsome. The eyes told Clío he knew her trust was not yet his. That, and the fact that the scales were no longer in harmony with his presence.

"What do you want?" Clío wondered what he looked like without the glamour.

"A meeting with Nuadha."

"I know of no one with that name," answered Clío. *I lie so easily and believably.*

Ultán tilted his head and smiled. "Apologies, I mean Lazarus."

"He is a busy man. How will I contact you?"

"We both know that dragons can communicate without requiring a physical presence." Ultán caught the fleeting grin on Clío's face and shook his head. "No, I did not give you permission to plunder my mind. Anyway, it is protected by generations of sophisticated engineering."

"Your faith in technology is touching… and misplaced." Clío stood and walked away. There was no "Goodbye", only a question.

"How much of you is real, Ultán?" Clío's scales quieted.

# CHAPTER 22

*Na h-Eileanan Beaga & the Island of Scáth*

As a warrior, Lady Scáthach rivalled The Mórrígan. This led many of the Tuatha Dé to believe they were doomed to become enemies. In the ancient era of heroes, battles, and wars, The Mórrígan would never suffer a rival or admit another had comparable fighting skills. Still, The Mórrígan had one critical advantage over Scáthach. She was Womb-Born, a position to which Scáthach could never aspire.

Following the war with the Sons of Mil, Scáthach departed the Land of Immensity and took up residence in the mist-shrouded islands of Na h-Eileanan Beaga of Northern Albu. There she lived in monastic solitude with only the winds, waves, and seabirds for company. Much to The Mórrígan's chagrin, Scáthach's legendary reputation as a warrior continued to attract the Tuatha Dé's elite. They sought her out as a mentor to learn from her battle skills and wisdom.

Scáthach changed. The solitude twisted her mind but worse, it made her vulnerable. It was reported by a few groups of her mentees and made noticeable by the stark change of colour in her choice of clothing. She cast aside her love of bright, primary tones for black. Those who knew Scáthach reported that she had the demeanour of one who grieved the loss of a partner. Perhaps she did. Scáthach also subjugated her love for battle strategies and tactics to focus on her suppressed talents as a sorceress—and dark magic.

Over time, the number of warriors making the pilgrimage to Na h-Eileanan Beaga diminished until no one sat at Scáthach's feet. On their return to the Land of Immensity, the final groups of Tuatha Dé heroes told tales of the presence of dark spirit which exerted its malign influence over the islands. Given the remoteness of Na h-Eileanan Beaga, who knew what ancient entities inhabited the lands and surrounding seas?

\* \* \*

A millennium passed, before a much-changed Scáthach and her daughter, Uathach, returned to the Land of Immensity. No one knew who, or what, impregnated Scáthach. Most preferred the convenient explanation that it was one of the heroes who visited her. Yet Uathach's eyes were silvered like a mirror. No one among the dragons, Fomorians, humans, or Tuatha Dé claimed the colour. The evidence pointed to an incubus, but few wanted to acknowledge that possibility or name the entity.

Excepting The Mórrígan, Scáthach was welcomed warmly by the Womb-Born. She requested a sanctuary for privacy, on the grounds that she had not lived among demigods or people for millennia and needed time to adjust to society. Few considered Scáthach's request as anything other than reasonable. The Womb-Born gave her an island off the north-western coast of the Land of Immensity, which she could transform to suit her needs.

A communal sigh of relief rose when, under Scáthach's guidance, the Island of Scáth became a lush paradise of green meadows replete with wildflowers, golden fields of corn, and fine, white, sandy beaches. The snow-capped mountain at its centre and the huge citadel of black basalt that squatted on its summit were conveniently ignored.

The Tuatha Dé adopted a laissez-faire attitude towards Scáthach, an oft-used strategy employed by the Womb-Born when they wished to avoid confrontation or not deal with a problem. How much of a threat could she be? For a millennium, they ignored Scáthach's dabbling in politics. When she embraced Bráchthine's son, Ciarán, and drew the black dragon into her sphere of influence, the Tuatha Dé belatedly took notice.

Scáthach had designs on the Dragon Throne and no one, not even Clíodhna, would be allowed to stand in her way. More alarm bells rang out when Scáthach regularly met with representatives of the Fomorians and the Sons of Mil. Neither were illegal, hence the Womb-Born had no grounds to reprimand, let alone punish her. Innumerable meetings with Daghdha, produced only disinterest, dismissal, or worthless promises to review Scáthach's tenure.

The unintended consequence of Scáthach's behaviour and Daghdha's inaction was a growing yearning for the return of Nuadha before events spun out of control. The rumour that the groundswell of opinion was perpetuated by the Queen of Whispers and Shadows was perfectly believable.

* * *

Ciarán Dubh was a dragon of the Clann Dubh, and therefore a member of an extended family of persistent troublemakers, conspiracy theorists, and would-be revolutionaries. Bráchthine's indiscriminate promiscuity coincided with a poor choice of lover and her time of peak ovulation. It was a scenario Serendipity could never resist. Clann Dubh had not had a royal dragon in aeons and all but a few eagerly adopted the warmling, Ciarán.

At first, Ciarán resolved to take up a position of service as his sister's protector. It was a laudable decision and by default, he was acclaimed as the true king of Clann Dubh. Tall, dark-skinned, and built like a brick shitehouse, Ciarán was handsome and could be charming. Moderately intelligent, he would never be a philosopher, inventor, or great leader, but in dragon society, he would never need to because he was the son of Bráchthine. He was wealthy by birth and would have his choice of female dragons.

Yes, he had a temper, although that was not unusual for the members of Clann Dubh. Like moths to the flame, Ciarán's looks drew many impressionable young female dragons to him. Too late, they discovered his dark, brutal side. Only his royal ties and the support of Clann Dubh's chieftains saved Ciarán from castration or death by irate fathers and siblings. Ciarán was a powerful dragon and a recognised warrior, if mostly in backstreet brawls, but many others were more formidable.

A simple conversation with Clíodhna and a promise to keep in touch might have resolved Ciarán's troubled mind. For that omission, Aodh and Lazarus would have to answer to Bráchthine. The absence of his sister gnawed at Ciarán's mind. He had never met Clíodhna, and as far as he was aware, she had never shown any interest in him.

Scáthach and her daughter, Uathach, took advantage of Ciarán's discontent. Furthermore, when drunk, Ciarán groused multiple times to any who would listen about the unfairness of the dragons' succession traditions. Thus, supported by Scáthach, he encouraged Clann Dubh's revolutionaries.

Ciarán had a hole in his life, and he griped continually about his disappointment with his sister. She was his only blood relative and the sole remaining link to Bráchthine. Was he so much of an ogre, that she had to be removed from his presence? He had heard of an ancient prophecy but knew nothing of its content and frankly did not care. All he desired was a sister who shared his blood. Was that too much to ask?

\*\*\*

On this day, Ciarán strode down the black marble floor of the Great Hall towards Scáthach. He smiled at his mentor. His mind was fuzzy on where, how, or why they met, but he submitted freely to her will. After centuries of drifting, Scáthach gave him purpose, and he was happy to be her protector. Uathach's sorcery convinced Ciarán that they should get rid of Clíodhna or delay her challenge until the Arena deadline had expired.

He would sit on the Dragon Throne with Scáthach as his counsellor. Convinced his sister did not care for him, in Ciarán's mind he owed her no fealty. Losing the Dragon Throne would serve the bitseach right for ignoring him. Ciarán noted Uathach standing to the side as he approached *Ríchathaoir Dubh*, the huge golden seat Scáthach referred to as her throne.

Both women were tall with raven-black tresses that brushed their arses. There the similarities ended. Scáthach was slender and softly contoured. Uathach was curvaceous with ample breasts, wide hips, a well-padded arse, and an intoxicating walk—the perfect body for a succubus.

He licked his lips. Uathach was the only female, apart from Scáthach, he had never brutalised before, during, or after sex. Her silver eyes sent shivers along his spine and something in them told Ciarán her retribution would be swift and dire. Close enough to gaze into Scáthach's eyes, Ciarán saw flames of fury. He shrugged; he would put up with the inevitable ranting. Afterwards, Uathach would open her thighs as compensation.

Scáthach's fury at Ciarán was held in check by several factors, not the least his temper. A single blast of dragon breath would put her beyond the healing powers of Daghdha's Cauldron. She had too much to accomplish. Therefore, she inhaled deeply and exhaled slowly until her eyes had recovered their natural grey colour. Still simmering, she smiled and beckoned Ciarán to sit beside her on the marble dais.

"Your sister, Clíodhna, recently visited the Island of Dragons and paid homage to her birthplace. I heard this from my informants, not you. Why?"

Ciarán looked troubled. It appeared to be a good sign... until he spoke. "Are you telling me the bitseach was here and did not pay me even a brief courtesy visit? What have I ever done to deserve such treatment?" The hurt in Ciarán's face was genuine, and that worried Scáthach. Her enchantments and Uathach's talents as a succubus had been unable to completely break Ciarán's familial attachment to his sister. He was hurt but did not hate Clíodhna. If she were to walk into the Hall, Ciarán's reaction would be to embrace her and sit at her feet.

Grinding her teeth, Scáthach said, "You must understand, Ciarán, your sister has never demonstrated any love for you. She visited the Island of Dragons to meet with the tribal and clann leaders to secure their support for her ascent to the Dragon Throne. When that happens, she will dispose of you… permanently. You must seize the throne before *you* are dead."

"I'm not stupid. I know dragon law and traditions. Clíodhna must challenge and defeat me in the Arena before sitting on the throne," snarled Ciarán. "The time for her to accomplish that draws near. If she misses the appointed time, her claim to the Dragon Throne becomes null and void."

Scáthach smiled. "You must train for battle, Ciarán. You have not fought to the death, or in a contest that was not predetermined, in centuries. Feed your anger by remembering how your sister persistently humiliates and ignores you. You deserve the Dragon Throne, not she." Scáthach inclined her head to Uathach. "Ciarán needs love and care. See to his every need, daughter."

The provocative sway of Uathach's hips kept Scáthach's attention until she and Ciarán exited the chamber. She smiled at a plan that was back on track. Still, Ciarán could not be trusted to dispose of Clíodhna, which was why it had always been Scáthach's contingency position. Her preference was to delay Clíodhna's appearance until it was too late for the challenge to be accepted.

"It is time I had an update from the Sons of Mil on the progress of their assassin," she murmured before joining Ciarán and Uathach.

# CHAPTER 23

*The Land of Immensity*

Ultán had not planned to return to the Land of Immensity and the city of the Sons of Mil until he completed his assignment. Each mission was allocated a limited number of Portal Passes. Daghdha issued a block of permits annually to the Council of Elders, of which the majority were allocated to the Watchers. In turn, the Watchers' commander dispensed them according to mission needs. Ultán used his frugally and saved those unused for unexpected situations. This was one of those times.

Like a burr on his arse, just beyond his reach to scratch, Ultán could not remove the suspicion of betrayal. Evidence and observation pointed to him having been set up to fail and likely lose his life. *Who is my enemy?* He intended to find out who was responsible and their motivation. Then he would mete out his form of justice—death. His Watcher code demanded it.

\*\*\*

Dawn broke. The seabirds awakened and the land smelled renewed as the waves crashed against the cave's entrance. Shortly, Ultán would stand before a disapproving Portal Keeper. The Keeper could not prevent Ultán from using the portal, but with subtle signals to the runes, he could make the journey unpleasant. His grin as Ultán dipped his head and walked through the portal was not reassuring.

As soon as Ultán's feet touched the dirt in the Land of Immensity, he fell to his knees and threw up. "Bastard!" he muttered. Still, he admired the man's unflinching loyalty to the portal and understood his disgust at what he perceived as its misuse. Ultán wiped fragments of sick from his lips, gargled a few mouthfuls of tepid water, and spat the liquid onto the earth. Life felt much better without the sour taste of puke.

A short jog later Ultán arrived at the gates of the Sons of Mil's city. The metropolis shimmered on the horizon, and beyond it was Daghdha's garish, hedonistic capital city, Muria. The city of the Sons of Mil did not have a name, not even a temporary one given by its builders or residents. None of the city elders wanted it named after them. *Why?* Did no one expect it to survive? The omens were not good.

Seemingly, the Sons of Mil were unimpressed by wealth and possessions. Hence, the city's construction was basic and defensive. The fortifications consisted of an inner wall about four yards thick and an outer wall two yards thick. Both were built of sundried, red mudbricks on stone foundations. In the corridor between the parallel walls were "rooms". Some were filled with soil or crushed limestone, some with weapons, and others with warriors or war dogs.

Ultán weaved his way through the dusty streets. They were busy, although not thronging. Artisans, farmers, and traders sold the fruits of their labour and grumbled at the lack of customers and the taxes levied by the Sons of Mil's council. The smell of baked bread made Ultán's stomach rumble. Food would wait until he visited his parents later.

The paucity of people signalled the poor state of the Sons of Mil's economy. *Will the race thrive?* Ultán had his doubts. He had observed similar sized communities in the Lands of the Humans sprout up, wither, and die. Unlike the Tuatha Dé or the dragons, the Sons of Mil were not demigods. *Surely the elders know the policy of racial purity is a failing strategy.* Not even the oppressive oversight and severe penalties stopped the drift of families away from what they perceived as a prison. Many paid the smugglers' price for freedom.

He stopped at the steps of the Watchers' headquarters. It was an anonymous, squat, two-storey, rectangular building with thick walls and slits for windows. It reminded Ultán of the stone keeps he had seen in the castles in Ireland. *Who is it meant to protect, and from which enemy?* He pushed against the heavy oak doors. They swung open smoothly and noiselessly.

The wooden stairway to the Commander's office was directly opposite the entranceway. Ultán negotiated two ranks of brawny Watchers to reach it. Camaraderie was not encouraged in the organisation. In a time of war, whose side would the Watchers take? Ultán ignored twenty sets of eyes, which said they would happily end him should he deviate from the narrow channel to the stairs. *Let them try.*

\* \* \*

"The Watchers were created to follow orders without question." The Council Leader's raspy voice was loathsome. "It is your job to see they do. If they do not, they are of no use to the council or the Sons of Míl. Choose whose side you are on very carefully, Commander."

"They are not mindless slaves!" growled the Commander. "Assassins who are unable to think for themselves will die on their first mission. Ultán is our best operative, with one hundred successful missions. He has earned the right to a certain level of freedom of thought." The Commander's voice was assertive but held a thread of fear. He knew that he was not the one with the real power in the room.

"Nonsense! My informants report Ultán has become infatuated with his prey. Bring him to heel or…"

\* \* \*

Ultán threw open the doors, abruptly ending the conversation, and took three long paces to stand at the Commander's desk. All three wore false smiles, although Ultán's was the more believable. The glint in his Commander's eyes told him he knew Ultán had heard the conversation. *Was it deliberate?*

"Does your presence mean you have successfully completed your mission, Ultán?" asked the Council Leader.

"You know I haven't. So why ask?" Ultán's tone was acidic. "Feel free to inform the cowards who spew lies to you that I know their names and their hiding places." He looked into the Commander's eyes. "You will not have the burden of their wages for much longer." Blood drained from the Leader's face. The Commander's hand covered his mouth to conceal a smile. He expected nothing less from Ultán.

Ultán pointed to the Leader, who recoiled as if touched by a red-hot branding iron. "*His* people would not pass the basic standards for a Watcher. However, I am curious. Did *you* know the Council spies on *your* Watchers? It indicates a lack of trust, but on whose part? Yours or the Council's? If it is you, I am truly disappointed, sir."

The Commander glared at the Leader but returned to Ultán. "That is a discussion for another time. Why are you here, Ultán, if not to report success and receive a new mission?"

"I am here for clarification."

"About what? You never needed an explanation before." The Leader's eyes narrowed. "Your orders are clear. Find and kill the one known as Clíodhna. The Council of Elders have declared her an existential threat to the Sons of Mil."

"That may be so, but I would like to know why you sent me to kill a dragon and, by implication, her shield?" The Commander's surprised reaction regained a small measure of Ultán's respect for his superior. *He did not know.*

"Nonsense! You are just making excuses for failure," snapped the Leader, who saw pain from the Queen of Scáth in his future.

"Please explain, Ultán," said the Commander.

"I was not informed my target was Clíodhna, Queen-in-Waiting of the Dragon People. She is accompanied by her shield, a serpent called Ceara Dearg, whose tracking abilities are superior to *any* Watcher. She is the daughter of Aodh Dearg, the dragons' battle commander. Is my mission to start a war with the serpents? If so, the Sons of Mil are well outmatched." The shock on the Commander's face was clear. He opened his mouth to speak, but Ultán had not finished.

"I was also not advised the third occupant of the dwelling where they reside was Nuadha, the Womb-Born and former High King of the Tuatha Dé. Or that, in recent times, Nuadha has been visited by his sister, The Mórrígan. She needs no introduction." Ultán paused to underline his accusation. "Again, why is my target the future Queen of the Dragons? Why do the Sons of Mil seek a war with the serpents and their Tuatha Dé allies? It is a war we cannot hope to win. We would be wiped out. That quartet alone could raze this city."

"Why do you care?" asked the Leader. "You are an assassin, a paid murderer. Politics is none of your business. Accept the mission or surrender and face execution for treason. The Council considers the wider picture, not just the small part you play." Beads of sweat glistened on the Leader's brow. "This is not just about your future. You risk the lives of your parents, too." The explicit threat surprised Ultán. Politicians rarely commit themselves to anything.

"Killing a Dragon Queen is never a 'small' component of any strategy," said Ultán. He turned to the Commander. "Is this what *you* want?" At the dip of his head, Ultán said, "So be it. You have signed the death warrant of the Sons of Mil." He bowed, turned, and exited the chamber. He heard the Leader's voice plainly as the door shut.

"I want his parents watched day and night. After this mission, that whole family must be executed for treason."

Ultán shook his head. "Foolish man. I hope I am there to watch when dragon breath burns the flesh from your bones."

\*\*\*

Later in the candlelit semi-darkness and solitude of his office, the Commander of the Watchers held his head in his hands. He had been unaware of the status of Ultán's target. Yet, he was guilty of not asking questions. By his omission, he had betrayed Ultán and now compounded this by affirming his orders. If Ultán carried out his mission successfully, the dragons and Womb-Born would massacre the Sons of

Mil to avenge their queen and former high king. If he failed, they would destroy the race as a lesson to others. There were no other options. *What were the Leader and Council thinking?*

The Commander reached for a papyrus scroll, a reed pen, and black ink and began to write. When he finished, he re-read and revised the text until he was happy. It was not a confession, blackmail targets, or a listing of others' sins and treasons. Scratched on the parchment were twelve names. Out of all the Watchers, excluding Ultán, these were the men and women he would trust with his life.

"I may not be able to help you now, but if you return, Ultán, you will need friends." He secured the scroll in the false bottom of a locked desk drawer and smiled feebly. "I hope I am around to give you the list."

***

The message from Scáthach arrived on the Leader's desk a few days after his meeting with the Watchers' Commander. The only optimistic component of the missive was he was neither Tuatha Dé nor dragon. Hence, the journey to the Island of Scáth would take a half-cycle of the moon. He would have plenty of time to perfect his story and who to blame.

Weeks later as he approached Scáthach's throne, all his plans, weasel words, and excuses fell apart. He heard her black nails beat a rhythm on the seat's golden arms. Uathach stood to the side; Ciarán was not in the Hall. Scáthach had decided his response to anything that focused on his sister would be irrational and disruptive. The Leader bowed deeply a few paces from the platform. As he straightened up, a great effort for one whose spine was so crooked, he opened his mouth. That was as far as he got.

"Why is Clíodhna not dead, badly injured, or even delayed? The first is preferred; the latter would at least ease my temper. You claim the Watchers are the best assassins in the Lands of Immensity and the Humans. I see no evidence to justify your boast. I only see reasons why you should die… painfully." Rivulets of sweat ran down the Leader's face.

Scáthach smiled at Uathach. "My daughter would love to practice reducing your mind to jelly. Ciarán can burn to ash what remains when she is finished. Who will miss you? You are not the only one on the Sons of Mil Council who is willing to sell the future of their nation to the highest bidder." Scáthach relished the Leader's terror. Black lips opened to reveal perfect white teeth.

"I was not informed the target was the Queen-in-Waiting of the Dragons," said the Leader, twisting his fingers before him. His use of words was worthy of the Tuatha Dé. "Or that there were two serpents—Clíodhna and her shield-maiden. The shield is reported to be the daughter of Aodh Dearg and a very accomplished warrior." Scáthach's eyes widened momentarily.

The Leader did not miss the sign. Despite his dread, his face remained neutral, and he played the only cards that might save him from an agonizing death. "Also, I was not told Clíodhna's guardian was the Womb-Born and former High King of the Tuatha Dé, Nuadha." Scáthach's lips pursed as she formed her next riposte. The Leader, who, while craven, remained a skilled politician, spoke first. "Yet that is not all *our* troubles. In recent days, Nuadha has had frequent visits from his sister, The Mórrígan. I believe you are acquainted with the lady."

"Be careful, *human*," spat Scáthach. The Leader flinched at the insult but wisely said nothing. "You are a small cog in my design and are replaceable."

"Am I? The time available to you is short." The Leader's confidence rose as his mind filled in the milestones until the Arena Challenge. "The Challenge for the Dragon Throne will soon be upon us. I will need to bring in additional resources, and that will require extra funds."

Scáthach settled back in her throne, an act the Leader perceived as surrender. She was in a bind, and he was her path out of it. "You will have your gold… and your final chance to please me. Do not spurn my benevolence." The Leader bowed, then backed away ten paces with his eyes firmly on Scáthach and her daughter. Whether he could do anything to protect himself if either of them decided the deal was off was debatable.

When the chamber doors closed, Scáthach turned to Uathach. "If Clíodhna is present for the Challenge, we will entertain ourselves by destroying his mind and body… slowly and painfully."

# CHAPTER 24

*Spring—Northern Ireland*

Ultán needed time and space to think. He chose the gardens of St. Matthew's Church because it was close to his target and, outside of mass times, the grounds were mostly deserted. The irony of a pagan seeking sanctuary in Christian grounds did not occur to him.

He needed to marshal his thoughts and construct new plans following the meeting with his Commander and the Leader. More than anything, he needed to pick a side before his growing list of enemies removed him from the game… permanently. Undoubtedly, the Leader had Watchers in his pay and had offered a bonus for Ultán's head.

Neither man had impressed Ultán, but, of the two, he felt some empathy for his Commander. Obviously, the Leader stood ready to plunge a dagger into his back. Likely, his parents, partner, and children were under threat to ensure his obedience. Ultán shook his head. His Commander should have known better than to put his future and his family's safety in the hands of that nest of vipers. *Still, do I not face the same quandary?*

Ultán's emotions were tightly controlled, leaving only room for two people—his mother and father. In the Watcher society even this level of bonding was frowned upon. Was it a weakness or had he risen above his genetic modifications to become a principled man? Ultán frowned. The Leader had threatened the only persons he loved and led him to two conclusions. First, his parents must be removed from the Sons of Mil's city and escorted to the Land of the Humans. Second, the Leader must die.

Ultán knew his mission to kill Clíodhna was impossible. From a practical perspective, none of his weapons could breach a dragon's armour before he was incinerated or torn apart by red hot claws. Any element of surprise was mitigated by Clíodhna's unique scales, physical size, and mental abilities. That she was guarded by a shield-maiden and a Womb-Born made the assignment wishful thinking, not a plan. *Am I the true target of the task? Is it a way to remove me? Why? I'm not important.* Ultán's ego bristled at this thought.

That said, Ultán also discerned that a successful completion of the mission would not satisfy the Leader or reverse the words overheard in the Commander's office. He and his family were marked for disposal. *Would I kill Clíodhna if I could?* He liked the young woman and had envisaged a much closer relationship. Ultán sighed. If it saved his parents, he would kill her and have no regrets. His dilemma was how to enlist the Womb-Born and serpents to his side, while concealing his duplicity.

*\*\*\**

In Bryson Street, Lazarus paced up and down the hallway's threadbare carpet. Given his long legs, it was the only place in the house that permitted this activity. "He cannot be trusted, Clíodhna. The Sons of Mil were enemies once and probably still are. They hate me for tricking them on the details of the Treaty and are probably bitter over the irreversible decline of the race. Why is he here—at this specific time? How many more are there? What part does he play? What will The Mórrígan say?"

The most interesting aspect of Lazarus' venting was his concern for The Mórrígan's opinion. The timing of the resurrected brother–sister relationship made Clío uneasy. *Am I jealous?* The past had shown Lazarus considered all options and opinions before choosing or aligning himself with one. On the other hand, by reputation, The Mórrígan had one loyalty—the Trinity—and one remedy—desolation. Still, like a phoenix, sisterly love had risen renewed from the ashes to embrace Lazarus.

*Why now and to what end? I need a long conversation with The Mórrígan.* Clío shivered at the thought. Then she snorted. How on earth would she arrange such a meeting? The Mórrígan appeared when she wanted, not at others' beckoning. "This is seriously fucked up. It must be the inbreeding," Clío muttered. When Lazarus stopped his pacing and stared at Clío, she realised she had spoken her thoughts aloud. The ensuing brief but awkward silence ended when her scales fluttered. The loud crash of brass on brass of the doorknocker followed on its heels.

"At least, one of his gifts appears to be excellent timing," said Lazarus as Clío pushed past him and opened the front door.

\* \* \*

Northern Irish hospitality and instincts took control of Clío's demeanour. Thus, Ultán found himself greeted with flawless teeth and a smile Dracula would be proud to claim. He inspected Lazarus warily and Clío thoughtfully. "Welcome," said Clío with as much sincerity as she could muster. It was followed by a quick sweep of her hand, indicating the parlour.

Ultán had enough sense to delay sitting until Clío and Lazarus' choice was obvious. Everyone has their favourite seat. When all were settled, Clío asked, "Would you like some tea?" She looked at Lazarus. "I think it's a chocolate biscuit day. Don't you?" He growled something about needing a whiskey and reached for a crystal tumbler and decanter.

If Ultán was surprised or annoyed the refreshments were brought by Ceara, or when she had served everyone, she set the tray on a small coffee table and perched on the arm of Clío's seat, he did not show it. However, he did recognise Ceara's smile as both false and threatening. In her mind, he was not to be trusted. If he gave her cause, the sanctity of the parlour would not prevent her attack. Ultán returned her smile, in genuine admiration for a fellow warrior.

None of the room's occupants were prone to small talk. Ultán chose flattery to start the conversation. "In hindsight, the Tuatha Dé's banishment to the Land of Immensity was a poor strategy by the Sons of Mil. The clause that gave you unfettered access to the Land of Humans was genius. We won the war, but you crafted the Treaty."

Ultán dipped his head towards Lazarus to acknowledge the architect of the Treaty between the Sons of Mil and the Tuatha Dé. "You kept your race's identity while ours became watered down to no more than a piss in the Irish Sea. It was a millennium, and almost too late, before we realized the danger of extinction. That sparked a frantic search to identify the purebloods and find a homeland."

Clío felt an urge to reach out and hug Ultán. The pain in his voice touched her, and her spinal scales' soft striking yielded a melancholic melody. She noted the satisfied smile on Lazarus' face. Once again, the mockers and disbelievers of the Tuatha Dé had underestimated his talents and foresight.

"Enough of this maudlin navel-gazing. The past is the past, and if we do not want to become part of it, the Fomorians must be destroyed." Lazarus held Ultán's gaze. "Maybe the Sons of Mil, as well." Clío gasped at Lazarus' lack of diplomacy and was stunned at Ultán's absence of protest. *He's hiding something, Lazarus.* Ceara shifted her posture imperceptibly for an optimum strike. The parlour had transformed into a deadly chess board.

Lazarus slapped a tumbler of amber liquid into Ultán's hand. "Tea and chocolate biscuits will not be enough today." It was not refused, and the room's tension eased as the decanter of single malt was drained. Lazarus snorted. "Maybe we should sip the *uisce beatha*—water of life— from this point. Drunks never make good choices."

Like a dog trying to catch its tail, the conversation eventually degenerated into the pointless posturing of tentative allies or potential enemies probing for information or advantage. Clío's eyes glowed gold with frustration at Ultán's evasions. The discordant clashing of her scales grew louder, and the temperature in the parlour steadily increased. *What is he holding back?*

Ultán sensed the conversation was going awry. He needed Clío and Lazarus on his side, and his usual strategy of giving nothing away would not gain their trust. Beads of sweat trickled down his back. The likeliest current outcome would be the dragons incinerating him. Ultán inhaled and took the only logical path. He committed treason, or he would have considered it sedition prior to his meeting with his Commander and the Leader. Dross had more value than his loyalty to the Watchers and the Sons of Mil. They had betrayed him and threatened his parents.

"The Sons of Mil have an informant in the Fomorian Council." The scepticism on Clío's face and Lazarus' laugh registered their disbelief. "Not all Fomorians are evil," he asserted. The looks became incredulous, but Ultán persisted. "A small group are tired of the eternal conflicts and would like a less bloody, less hostile existence. One influential family has been 'friends' with the Sons of Mil for millennia. They keep us informed of major developments."

The scepticism on Lazarus' and Clío's faces did not recede, until Ultán added, "Albeit, likely with the tacit approval of the current Fomorian High King." He looked pointedly at Lazarus. "What king does not want an escape route if events or plans go badly wrong?" Lazarus nodded, although whether in agreement or simply having imbibed too much whiskey was unclear.

"The Sons of Mil's elders think the human war and Balora's activities are diversions. None of the Fomorian Council, not even her strongest supporters, expects Balora to steal Daghdha's Cauldron from the Tuatha Dé." Ultán glanced at Lazarus. "Most support the theory she's looking to avenge her father. Personally, I think underestimating her would be a mistake. Balora is calculating and ruthless and sees herself as a future High Queen." Lazarus nodded again.

On a roll, Ultán said, "The war in Europe is the Fomorians doing what they have always done. They hate humans as much as they despise the Tuatha Dé or the Sons of Mil." Ultán shrugged his shoulders. "No one knows why. They also consider the Sons of Mil to be impotent. They may be correct." Raised eyebrows greeted Ultán's assertion.

"The Fomorians use hordes of Nemed to cause small- or

global-scale destruction. However, in the past thousand years, this became more of a game to avoid boredom and keep their warriors in line." Ultán added two fingers of single malt to his tumbler before looking at Lazarus. "Much like the internal squabbles of the Tuatha Dé."

"Is this conversation going somewhere?"

Ultán's last observation had rubbed Lazarus the wrong way. Clío sat up, surprised at Lazarus' intemperate interruption and the rise in tension. Tongues of fire flared in Ultán's eyes. It was an odd combination given their colour. And what was the almost imperceptible quiver of his body?

Lazarus chuckled. "It is difficult to maintain a perfect glamour when you are not Tuatha Dé. I congratulate you and wonder which of my siblings shared the gift with the Sons of Mil and to what purpose." He glanced at Clío. "Most, including my sister, lay the blame at my feet. They are misinformed."

Lazarus glanced at the whiskey decanter. "Another drink? After all, we are finally close to an honest discussion." Ultán offered a single nod. The king was as good as the gossip and rumours foretold. Genuinely sorry for his deception, Ultán smiled in apology to Clío, but the look in her eyes suggested a cooling of their relationship.

"The Fomorians hate the ocean depths and want dry land for their race. They would rather die than live another millennium with gills and webbed feet. They covet the Land of Immensity."

"An impossible fantasy!" snapped Lazarus.

"Are you so sure? Millennia have passed since the war between the Tuatha Dé and the Fomorians, but their blood still taints your tribe." Ultán clasped his glass with both hands and leaned forward. "As *you* know, Fomorian blood is powerful, and they can be very pleasing. The half-breed Bres failed because he was an impatient adolescent."

Ultán considered his next words carefully. "There are traitors among the Tuatha Dé. Eochaidh and Tuirill never forgave the Womb-Born for their exile beyond the four cities and kingdoms, although not beyond the Land of Immensity's borders. In my opinion, that was a grave mistake.

Mix in the Queen of Scáth who frequently entertains the Sons of Mil and the Fomorians *together*, and her dragon who is Clíodhna's brother. A potent brew is fermenting, with Scáthach the witch at its centre."

"No!" Lazarus' drink came near to sloshing over the rim of the glass.

Ultán pressed his argument. "Again, are you sure? Your abdication left the Land of Immensity with a weak High King. Daghdha is governed by gross appetites and lusts."

"My brother would not succumb to Fomorian wiles. True, he may often be ruled by his dissolute predilections, but he is still a Womb-Born. In his hands, the Land of Immensity will remain that of the Tuatha Dé."

There was a rare look of compassion in Ultán's eyes as he spoke, but it did not mitigate his words' bluntness. "The Sons of Mil city is located south of the city of Muria. The land was given to us by Daghdha in return for bribes and favours. He provides us with passes, allowing us to use the portals."

"Shite!" Clío's interruption aptly summed up the atmosphere in the parlour.

Lazarus' brow furrowed. "Does The Mórrígan know of these things?"

Ultán shrugged, "I don't think so... possibly." Then he added, "Who knows what The Mórrígan's true motives are, what information she holds, and whose ear she whispers into?"

"We need to know on whose side my sister stands. After millennia of not seeing each other, I welcome my sister's newfound love for me but also find it curious."

"The Hag's bony arse!" exclaimed Clío.

"What is your mission, Ultán?" queried Lazarus. "I doubt you are here by accident. The Watchers are assassins. Who is your target? You ask us to trust your word and information. Come clean. At worst, you will have a quick death." The atmosphere in the parlour shifted.

Ultán coughed to buy time. He was not fast enough to stop the briefest of glances at Clío or to prevent Ceara intercepting it. In a moment, his chair was upended, and he was on his back. Ceara's hand, talons extended, gripped his neck, and trails of smoke drifted from her nostrils. She looked fiercely at Clío. "I told you that he was not to be trusted. Now will you let me kill him?"

"I think we owe Ultán some grace." Lazarus' calm demeanour reduced the heat in the room, but the emotional undercurrents remained near the surface. "He may have an explanation, and I would prefer not to redecorate and refurnish another fire-damaged room. Please, Ceara, let him stand. We are three against one. He is not going anywhere."

Ultán lifted the armchair and restored it to its allotted place. The act recognised the parlour's position as the heart of the home and gave him time to order his thoughts. "My mission, sanctioned by the Council of Elders, was to kill Clíodhna. I was given no information on who or what she was, only that she was an existential threat to the Sons of Mil." Ultán reached for the glass and took a swallow of whiskey. "My investigations and tracking of all in this room pointed to a disturbing conclusion. I had been sent to kill the Queen-in-Waiting of the Dragons."

Ultán took another mouthful of Bushmills. "Recently, I returned to the Watchers' Command Centre to seek an explanation. Instead, I was told to complete the mission, or my parents would die, as would I, if I were to set foot in the domain of Sons of Mil." A wry smile fluttered on Ultán's lips. "Naturally, this placed me in a dilemma. The likelihood of me assassinating two dragons and a Womb-Born is infinitesimally low. Hence, my only choice was to come here and seek allies. I love my parents."

"I still vote we kill him," said Ceara.

"What would you or I do, if put in the same situation? If our loved ones were threatened?" asked Clío.

"Who do you think is coordinating this plot?" asked Lazarus.

"My guess would be Scáthach. She has the most to lose if Clíodhna ascends the Dragon Throne. To kill or delay her is a viable plan, if you ignore that we're talking about serpents," said Ultán.

"Why the frown?" asked Lazarus.

"The Fomorians. What part do they play in Scáthach's strategy?" asked Ultán.

"Perhaps the Lady is not as clever as she thinks and the Fomorians are playing her," said Clío.

"It would be pleasing to see her and that silver-eyed bitseach of a daughter get the comeuppance they deserve."

Ceara looked at Clío who was staring at Lazarus. His face looked like thunder, and his body had started to glow and tremble. *What did Ultán say to generate such anger?* Clío and she would compare notes later.

# CHAPTER 25

"You must go to Muria and speak with Daghdha. We need to know where he stands," said Clío.

Lazarus bristled at Clío's demand, but her motivation was founded on reason. Was Lazarus'? It had been millennia since he visited the cities of the Land of Immensity, and until recently he had no desire to set foot in the kingdom ever again. His brothers and sisters' betrayal and duplicity at best irritated him. The petty squabbles of the Tuatha Dé, even those he had sired, exasperated him.

He had a pleasant, uncomplicated life among the humans and no desire to relinquish it. *What has changed?* Was it a growing belief he should have fought rather than abdicated the throne? Or had it taken root following his sister's renewed bond? *Should I blame The Mórrígan? Am I strong enough to resist the seductive embrace of the High King's throne without being corrupted?* He did not know.

There was also An-Ársa. The Ancient Evil scattered clues in Lazarus' path, mocking him. Like breadcrumbs in a Brothers Grimm fairytale, only a few survived the scavengers, and calculatedly so. Lazarus sighed. Perhaps the simplest explanation was that he needed an excuse to avoid the obligation of duty in the Land of Immensity, and the malevolent phantom provided it. He swore under his breath. *What duty? They abandoned me. I owe them nothing.*

Nevertheless, unprompted, Ultán had described Uathach's silver eyes, immediately propelling An-Ársa from the ethereal to the substantial. Was it planned to ensure his interest or an error? Until that moment, Lazarus' dreams provided the sole glimpse of the entity and its signature mirror-like eyes. Lazarus thought of Scáthach and shivered. Th returning heroes knew evil had visited Scáthach on Na h-Eileanan Beaga and likely impregnated her. Uathach was the result of that union, but for what purpose? He looked across the room to Clíodhna. *Is this all about her?*

Travelling to the Land of Immensity was a test Lazarus preferred to decline or postpone indefinitely. He scowled peevishly at Clíodhna; the sinking feeling in the pit of his stomach affirmed she was correct. Stubborn and unwilling to concede, he put forward an alternate proposal. "We are overthinking the situation. The simplest explanation is the correct one. Balora wants revenge on me. Therefore, we should focus our efforts on finding the Fomorian nests and their Nemed thralls and destroying them. When that is accomplished, we will focus on disrupting Scáthach's plans to prevent Clíodhna ascending the Dragon Throne."

"This from a Womb-Born who once called Occam and his theory simplistic gibberish," said Clío.

Ultán could not prevent himself from chuckling at Clío's words, but a severe look from Lazarus drew a quick, "Apologies, but Clío is right." To salve Lazarus' feelings, he added, "If only from the perspective of eliminating one option."

"With the Tuatha Dé, no option is ever eliminated. They are put to the side until needed." Lazarus sighed and stood. "I need time to consider." With no further words, he left the parlour. A moment later, the front door slammed shut. Puzzled, Ultán looked at Clío for an explanation. She shrugged.

"It's his way. We'll not see him for a day or two."

\*\*\*

It was mid-week and mid-afternoon. Apart from the barman and a skeleton staff, Lazarus had McHugh's to himself. Situated on the city side of the Queen's Bridge, the pub lay in the shadow of the Albert Memorial Clock tower. It had been Lazarus' favourite bar ever since the establishment opened in 1711.

Proximity to the docks and shipyard guaranteed the bar a full house when the end-of-work sirens sounded. Lazarus dipped his head in acknowledgement of the original owner's sound investment. He sipped his Bushmills, occasionally adding a splash of water from a small, white porcelain jug. He smiled in appreciation of the amber liquid. McHugh's were neither miserly with their measures nor overpriced.

The staff were friendly and willing to engage in *craic*. At the same time, they were professional and remained unseen when he wanted peace and solitude. Belfast people were generous with their affections but were not great tippers. Everyone in McHugh's knew Lazarus was a generous man. Hence, the bar staff and bouncers would protect his privacy with their fists if warranted.

It grated on Lazarus that he was not the master of his actions. The reappearance of The Mórrígan, the Fomorians, the Sons of Mil, and An-Ársa exacerbated Lazarus' feeling of being a rudderless vessel. He was a cow before the drover and each incident seemed like a farmer's cane prodding or flicking his arse. All conspired to ensure he did not stray from a path he had neither chosen nor favoured.

Even the timing of Clíodhna's awakening was taken from him. He exhaled and took another sip of whiskey. It was tacit acknowledgement that a journey "home" to the Land of Immensity was in his near future. He must get control of the disparate and apparently unconnected parts of the game. A meeting with Daghdha in the city of Muria was as good a place as any to get his bearings.

*** 

The soft rustle of silk preceded a slight creak of the booth's wooden bench, prompting Lazarus to lift his eyes from his contemplations. He made sure his mind was veiled and glanced around before acknowledging his visitor.

The black velvet trench coat was unbuttoned. It revealed a scarlet gown with a plunging neckline, which left nothing to the imagination—Balora's breasts were the size of melons and as heavy. The dress complied with the war government's policy of simplicity in fashion and the minimal use of materials. It was undoubtedly backless. Memories of tracing her spine to the valley between her cheeks slipped uninvited but not unwelcomed into his thoughts. He sensed The Mórrígan's disapproval and muttered "Bitseach." It was unclear to which woman he referred.

Lazarus reflected that subtlety had never been Balora's strongest attribute. His eyes scanned over and beyond Balora's shoulder.

"I'm alone, Nuadha. Surely your senses informed you, or have they atrophied with millennia of neglect?" The mocking tone in Balora's voice drew a wry smile. The Mórrígan had said similar. She laid a hand on his heart, and he was loath to remove it.

"My name is Lazarus. Nuadha is long gone."

Lazarus inspected and took in all that Balora offered. Unquestionably, in human form, Balora was a beautiful woman and arrogant enough to know it. But then, if a glamour is chosen, why not make the best of the opportunity? The only item Balora had no control over was her skin's colour—that of dark, roasted coffee. Lipstick and eyeshadow perfectly accented her high cheekbones and garnet-coloured eyes. He knew from intimate experience that her body was perfectly proportioned. The few imperfections—battle scars she deliberately kept as mementos—added to her allure.

"You can have me again, Lazarus." The new name sounded strange on Balora's lips, but she would get used to it. "Bráchthine has moved on. There are no more rivals for your love... unless a misguided sense of duty counts. We managed to cope with that mistress before."

"Why are you here, Balora?"

"To fuck you. Now. On this table. You can make it so no one can see or hear us." Lazarus heard the dress rustle and knew the path to

Balora's *pit* had been cleared. The wafting fragrance from her dark triangle stirred his memories and stiffened his manhood.

Lazarus shook his head. "Always games. Does it not get tiresome for you?"

"As I remember, there was a time you sought and rarely protested my diversions—in or out of bed. Your manhood bears witness to that. I want you back. Can you not just accept it? We were good together and I was stupid to throw it away because of my father. In this age, there are no wars or lovers to drive us apart."

"That was aeons ago, Balora. Even demigods change. If they are fortunate, they become wiser." Lazarus lit a cigarette and took a long drag. "As for no wars, you are lying to me. Why are you plotting to steal Daghdha's Cauldron and your people scheming with the Sons of Mil?" Balora flinched at the verbal slap in the face.

"Whatever your game is, Balora. Please stop it. The odds are not in your or the Fomorians' favour and I do not want to see you hurt. Return to the deep waters before even they are taken from your race."

Balora's eyes flashed. Lazarus knew much more than she anticipated… or perhaps he was bluffing. She refused the bait.

"I promise to intercede on your behalf with my brother to stop the raids."

The spark of sexual tension evaporated. "As if you have any influence over Manannán," spat Balora. "He will refuse any intercession, if only to spite you." The veneer of calm on Balora's face cracked briefly before she regained control. She smiled broadly, a display of gleaming white teeth. "You always did know how to get under—or inside—me.

"I will love you forever, and my bed will always welcome you. For old times' sake, please stay out of my way. Be happy and enjoy your retirement… Lazarus." The name sounded hesitant and discordant, as if she had no right to use it and knew it. "My plans are of no interest to you… or Clíodhna."

Balora placed both hands on the table and stood. She bent and kissed Lazarus full on the lips. The action was pleasant. Then she glided elegantly to the door. Lazarus applauded the flawless accomplishment. Walking on a cracked stone floor while wearing stiletto heels is not for those who lack confidence. He savoured the rose-scented perfume that hung in the air and then called for one more Bushmills—a double.

"She has a great arse. Your girlfriend?" asked the barman as he set the Bushmills on the table.

"She was a long time ago," said Lazarus. *When I was young and foolish. Now, I'm old and foolish. Nothing changes.*

Lazarus scolded himself as he flung the liquid back in a single gulp. It was no way to treat an excellent single malt. He grimaced at the reality he confronted and which Balora's intervention had made unavoidable. Was it deliberate? He needed to travel to the Land of Immensity. He stood, gripped the high back on the wooden seat to steady himself, and dipped his head in the direction of the barman.

The rustle of bills slipped under the glass informed the man that payment and tip awaited. He smiled his thanks and touched his cloth hat. "Until the next time, sir."

\* \* \*

The shadow slipped between the open doors of McHugh's and followed until privacy was assured. The grip on Balora's shoulder twisted her around and sent a clear message. She was not going anywhere until the raven-haired beauty before her said her piece… or killed her. She was powerless to prevent either option.

"You are a clever woman, Balora, and under different circumstances would be a useful diversion for Lazarus. Whatever plans you have for my brother, my advice is to set them aside. This is not the time for reunions."

"Not even between an estranged brother and sister?"

"Impertinence will shorten your lifespan, Balora, and you are wise enough to know I can stop your heart with a thought. Thus, I wonder why you take the risk of baiting me. I will consider that later." Balora growled at her misjudgement. "I like you and at one time you were good for Lazarus. Now is not that time. Remove him from your plans."

"And if I choose not to?"

"Harm him in any way and I will destroy you, slowly and painfully. You are long-lived, but not as long as the Tuatha Dé or the dragons. I will not kill you, but I promise to make every day of your remaining life what the humans call 'a living hell'. There will be no mercy."

The demigod became the shadow and was no more. Balora rested against a bench on the riverbank to control her racing heart. The Mórrígan's advice was well-intentioned... and too late.

\*\*\*

Outside the bar, Lazarus inhaled. The smells of industrial Belfast, diesel spills, and rotting vegetation from the River Lagan flooded his senses. He smiled and glanced around to ensure he was alone before walking towards the Queen's Bridge.

Two cracks sounded as Lazarus passed the double streetlight at the centre of the bridge. The force of the bullets spun him around and propelled him over the bridge's low, stone railing. Intense pain was quickly followed by cold as the icy waters closed over him. Thankfully, it was high tide. At low tide, the foul-smelling mudflats of the Lagan were littered with humanity's debris and were no one's choice for a comfortable landing.

\*\*\*

"I hear you wish to speak with me." The Mórrígan's appearance at Clío's side in Victoria Park provoked surprise and anger.

"*Fuck!* My sanctuary is turning into McHugh's bar on a Saturday afternoon."

"Spare me the melodramatic, adolescence, Clíodhna. Lazarus may have indulged you. I will not and neither would Bráchthine. You are thousands of years old, and it is well past growing up time. In a few cycles of the moon and providing you successfully navigate the hurdles ahead of you, you will be queen of the most powerful race there ever has been or will be—the dragons."

Clío was shocked at The Mórrígan's diatribe. Trails of white smoke drifted upwards from her nostrils, her heartbeat increased, and… her scales were at peace. *What is going on?*

The Mórrígan chuckled. "I am not your enemy, Clíodhna. Whether you want me as a friend is entirely in your hands. You called this meeting. What is it you want?"

"Why the sudden appearance and sisterly affection after millennia? What do *you* want with Lazarus?"

"I want him on the High King's throne where he belongs. When Lazarus was birthed, Anúna saw in him something which was missing from the other Womb-Born—nobility, selflessness, and fairness. She rewarded him with dominion over the Womb-Born and we freely accepted his rule. Without Lazarus as our High King, the Tuatha Dé are doomed to fracture beyond repair and will fade away. Does that answer your questions?"

"I want Lazarus to be happy," said Clío. "Is that wrong?"

The Mórrígan shook her head. "No, it isn't. Unless you indulge him as much as he does you. He has responsibilities and you cannot connive with him to avoid them. I have lost much by not being close to my brother for such a long time and it will take me many centuries to have the same level of love and trust he has invested in you.

"Those are my goals. I want my brother back and to see him on the throne of the Tuatha Dé where he belongs, and I would like your help to achieve this."

Clío nodded. She was also shocked when she heard her scales harmonise with The Mórrígan's laughter. "Go on, Clíodhna. Ask me the question that has been on your lips since our first meeting."

"I saw fear in your eyes. Lazarus said it was because dragons can kill Tuatha Dé and they can never return. I don't believe him because I can't conceive of you being afraid in any circumstances."

"The dragons and I go back aeons, Clíodhna. Who knows who was first created? I fear the dragons' powers and they fear mine. It is a good balance and hopefully will never be tested in battle. Bráchthine was a great queen and maintained that equilibrium." The Mórrígan laughed. "Although deep in her soul, she thought the dragons had an edge over us."

The Queen of Desolation sighed. "Yes, I was afraid of you, although jealous is more accurate. I am at the beginning of my journey to get my brother back and become a proper sister. At the time I thought you were in my way, but I know you are not."

The Mórrígan's fingers closed over Clío's, and she whispered hoarsely, "Protect him, Clíodhna. It was your mother's wish, and it is mine." The Mórrígan stood. "I must go and whisper in more ears. I leave you to your sanctuary… and the ducks." Clío reluctantly disentangled from The Mórrígan's touch.

As she walked away, the Queen of Whispers and Shadows turned and laughed. "Do not be too hard on Ceara tonight. She is currently chasing shadows around Belfast Lough. I still have some tricks that even dragons cannot resist, and I wanted a meeting without eavesdroppers."

# CHAPTER 26

Tiled walls, white with two rows of blue at shoulder height, and faux mosaic floors comprised the décor of the Royal Victoria Hospital's surgical wards. All were scrubbed scrupulously clean. The ever-present smells of anaesthetic and disinfectant attested to this. Heavily starched uniforms crackled as nurses carried out their duties efficiently and without any sense of panic.

Lazarus awakened from a morphine-induced euphoria. He groaned and attempted to move. A spike of pain made him swear. Pain was manageable but only if it was expected. A torrent of curses in several ancient tongues prompted disapproving stares from the matron and senior ward sister but brought smiles to the worry-lined faces of those who stood at his bedside.

Clío and Ultán stood to either side of Lazarus' head; Ceara stood guard at the foot of the bed and glowered at any she judged unwelcome. Dark circles under Clío's eyes testified to a lack of sleep and deep concern. *How much morphine did they give me? How long have I been here?* His beard suggested several days. Had his glamour slipped? Were the Tuatha Dé revealed? *I must get out of here.*

A gaggle of constables hovered nearby, clearly disturbed at the role reversal of protecting rather than arresting Lazarus. Several Special Branch detectives vied for position with an unmoving Ceara at the end of the bed. A white-coated consultant, the most senior doctor in the hospital, testily overruled them all. He informed the officers that they were subject to his rules and would only have restricted access to his patient.

"You have lost your left arm from below the elbow." The Consultant addressed Lazarus in a tone that spoke more of rebuke than sympathy.

"Not again," sighed Lazarus.

"According to the police, two .303-calibre bullets were fired from a Lee-Enfield rifle and did a remarkably precise, almost surgical, job. I have recommended two weeks' rest in this intensive care ward to stabilise you. After that, we will transfer you to a recovery ward and can discuss prosthetics." The consultant scrawled illegible notes on a chart and handed the clipboard to the matron. He strode from the ward with a posse of interns in his wake. It was if he had just given a lecture and the patient was incidental.

The senior Special Branch detective bided his time until the matron and senior ward sister relinquished control to the staff nurses. These, he deemed, would be more amenable to intimidation. "It seems that you have elevated your status to victim." The detective shook his head and smiled. "Appearances can be deceptive, can't they?"

Lazarus nodded but kept a firm grip on Clío's hand. His ward was on the cusp of violence. She knew who was responsible because she had assigned Ceara to follow Lazarus. Clío's need to dispense retribution rose above impartiality. Since Balora was not available, and the arrogant doctor had departed, the Special Branch detective was looking good as a target of opportunity.

Oblivious of his impending immolation, the detective nodded to the uniformed constables. "For your safety, these constables will remain at the ward's entrance. I will return in several days for a longer chat. I may even bring flowers and grapes." The man chuckled at his joke, tipped his hat, and walked away.

\*\*\*

"What the Hag, Lazarus? Do you like losing parts of your body? Why did Balora sanction this?" asked Clío. The genuine concern in Clío's voice and her determination to hand out vengeance were gratifying.

Lazarus frowned. "You had me followed. How dare you," he said. His outrage was tempered by Clío's forlorn expression.

"Bráchthine made me promise to protect you. I failed you *and* my mother. You could have died." Golden tears streamed down Clío's cheeks.

A strong, gentle hand gripped Clío's. "First, I was never in mortal danger. Balora would never sanction my execution." Lazarus lifted his left hand to scratch the stubble on his chin and growled in disgust. There was no arm. "Dead, I am of no use to Balora. She needs me to lead her to the Cauldron." He inclined his head to the missing appendage. "This was a particularly subtle plan. Balora knows I have no choice but to go to Muria and meet with Daghdha." He smiled. "My former partner has grown a lot."

"You can admire and fantasise about her all you want. It will not prevent me from turning her to ash," said Clío.

"Not if I see her first." Ceara was furious at how Balora had duped her.

"We have other priorities." Lazarus shifted his head against the pillow and spoke softly. "I must get out of here before the Royal's excellent doctors, nurses, and biochemists discover I am not human." Lazarus looked at Ultán, Clío, and Ceara. "All records and blood samples must be destroyed. My bloodwork will prompt too many questions." The trio nodded. "Please avoid compromising other patients' samples and data. I have no wish to endanger anyone's treatments or recovery."

Lazarus' voice was heavy with resignation. "My return to the Land of Immensity can be avoided no longer. I need Daghdha's Cauldron, and I must know what my brother has been plotting."

* * *

Balora purred at the freedom of resuming her Fomorian shape. She stretched, flexed her wings, and took up her perch at the cave's entrance.

In her human form, she delighted in the admiring looks she received and the extended range of pleasurable activities in which she could indulge. Still, the drain on her powers to maintain the glamour was exhausting.

She gazed wistfully across the lough. The meeting with Lazarus had brought to the surface long-buried regrets and memories of missed opportunity. When they met, Balora had been young and wilful. Following her father's death, she came under tremendous social pressure to seek vengeance on Nuadha and the Tuatha Dé. It still grated on Balora that, for a short but critical period following her father's death, she had surrendered her path to others who cared little nothing her. They only wanted to fuck, manipulate, or subjugate her.

She would be High Queen of the Tuatha Dé if she had dispassionately considered all the options her relationship with Lazarus offered. Most certainly, she would never have allowed him to abdicate. *The foolish man needs me.* Balora's only consolation was that those who had given her such foolish counsel had met horrific deaths at her hand.

With the benefit of hindsight, she knew pragmatism and the betrayal of her nation would have led to much greater personal gain and power. The bitterness of unfulfilled ambitions and imprudent guidance soured Balora's belly. Even when crowned High Queen of Fomoria— and Balora had no doubts about this outcome—it would forever be a painful reminder of losing a much more powerful throne. For this, many more would suffer her wrath and enjoy lingering, painful deaths.

Balora genuinely regretted ordering Lazarus' injury. Yet how could she forego the fortune of discovering rifle bullets were steel—another word for iron? She rationalised the act as a temporary inconvenience for Lazarus. *Surely, The Mórrígan will see things as I do.* More importantly, it would place him exactly where she wanted him and reveal the Cauldron.

Yet had she created another problem? Undoubtedly, Clíodhna, and her shield, would seek revenge. Balora was certain that the serpents knew where her Nemed forces were camped. As a matter of practicality, she could not protect them. Her powers were not enough to conceal the entirety of her command.

Balora pondered which pieces to sacrifice. The Nemed were disposable and replaceable, but Clíodhna would sense a deception if no Fomorians fell to her wrath. That posed logistical and political issues. Some of her Fomorians had familial connections with the Fomorian Council, and Balora could not afford to snub that body... yet.

Balora's deep, throaty growl preceded her cursing Lazarus. He should have been the perfect lover, counsellor, and partner. Instead, she was alone and trusted none of the Fomorians within her command. Another thought caused her to snarl. What of Ultán? *How much should I care about the Watcher's presence?* Her knowledge of the Sons of Mil was limited to old wives' tales and gossip. Still, one characteristic made her wary—they were known to be excellent trackers. Perhaps she could use that to her advantage.

# CHAPTER 27

Ultán wondered what Clío and Lazarus would think of his mission, then shook his head. *They will be furious*. Eclipsed by his new allies' powers and status, Ultán's scientifically-enhanced ego had taken a beating. If the Watcher had a weakness, it was hubris, although that vice is common in men, ancient and modern. Thus, he felt compelled to justify his usefulness and participation in the group.

In doing so, Ultán demonstrated his lack of clarity on the concept of teamwork. Clío knew where the Nemed gathered but had been unable to uncover the veiled nests of Balora and her Fomorians. To prove himself, Ultán focused on discovering the Fomorian sanctuaries. Had he consulted Clío and Lazarus, they may have had reservations but also provided useful advice on tactics and support.

\*\*\*

Thousands of caves that could conceal an army populated the Glens of Antrim and coastal areas of Northern Ireland. In Belfast, where hills protected the city to the west, north, and south, the options were limited to a single rock formation. Overlooking a sparsely populated area, the Cavehill was a natural fortress with long sightlines over the city and the lough. Ultán's suspicions were raised when Clío said she had observed no Nemed activity in the crag, or its surroundings. It did not pass the smell test.

As they rose to meet the hill's plateau, the mountain's slopes were eminently scalable to a physically enhanced person. The incline, however, was made treacherous by the rain and slick from the winter's melting ice. Hues of yellow and purple, from the new growth of gorse and heather were released from winter snows and frosts. The thorns of hawthorn and wild blackberry bushes eagerly awaited the unwary.

Midway to the hill's crest, Ultán paused to calm his heartbeat and rest his strained lungs. He berated himself and resolved to achieve a better level of fitness. Tight spaces and darkness were Ultán's favourite battlegrounds. On the open grassy slopes of the Cavehill, he felt exposed. His nostrils flared as he passed a disused quarry. The breeze carried a scent he could not place, and his senses went on high alert. One thing was clear, neither Mother Nature nor humanity owned it.

Ultán observed that the smells were of two varieties and surrounded him. *Is it a trap? Have I stumbled into an enemy camp?* Taking a step sideways into a small copse of rowan, he unsheathed his knives and merged with the background. He took the presence of the mountain-ash, one of the five guardian trees of the ancient Celts and druids, as a good omen. Ultán mused that it was instinct, not engineering, that had led him to his enemy. Amid danger, Ultán gave himself a metaphorical pat on the back. His suspicions of the Fomorians making the hill their main encampment were well-founded. Still, that would prove to be scant solace if he died on the crag.

\*\*\*

"Find the intruder! Our queen will be furious if he escapes. She wants him alive." The hissing of the Nemed grew louder and the smell of decay became stronger.

The gruff Fomorian command made Ultán curse. *Shite! They know I'm on the mountain. How?* Ultán's pride in his tracking and concealment skills took another hammering. He had underestimated the Fomorians just as he had the dragons. He thought about praying, but to whom? Shadows closed on his left and right flanks. He took a deep calming breath, acknowledging that if he wanted to escape, he had no choice but to attack.

Emerging from cover, Ultán swept the larger of his knives in a semi-circle across the nearest, semi-corporeal Nemed. When the Fomorians corrupted and changed the Nemed, cruelly, they left the race able to experience pain and vulnerable to iron. Ultán eviscerated two and slashed a third's arm to the bone. He ignored their inhuman screams and cries of pain, roared, "*Lámh-derg abú!*"—the ancient battle-cry of the northern O'Neill clann—and charged.

\*\*\*

From her place of concealment, Ceara wondered what it would be like to have only knives or swords as weapons in battle. She would never know because her dragon breath, scales, and talons were stronger and sharper than any metal. Her skin was her armour, unlike Ultán's, which was his weakness.

A grudging respect for the Son of Mil crept into Ceara's head. He had led her to Balora's stronghold. Still, she did not fully trust Ultán, and from the timbre of Clío's scales, neither did she. Thus, Ceara did not enter the battle on his behalf. She would not let him fall into Balora's scaley grasp, but she had not decided whether she should let him die or rescue him.

\*\*\*

Many Nemed fell to Ultán's blade, confirming they were neither skilled fighters nor tacticians. Instead, they preyed on helpless victims or used overwhelming numbers to achieve their goals. That was not the case for the Fomorians. Ultán conceded that the demons appeared to be cognisant of the need for strategy and communications in battle. They tactically sacrificed groups of Nemed to drive Ultán onto their talons. *So much for the wisdom of my tutors who labelled the Fomorian race as brutes and dullards.*

Mother Nature is a fickle ally. The steep, slippery slope of the mountainside and his downwards momentum drove Ultán closer to the

Fomorians who blocked his escape. *They look much bigger in the daylight.* The smallest of the demons was half again Ultán's height. Without his glamour, Ultán was eight feet tall.

Sons of Mil lore claimed only dragons could best a Fomorian army. The knowledge was scant consolation in his present circumstance. Ultán clung to a faint hope. Perhaps the numbers before him did not constitute an army. How many were behind him or on his flanks? His musings proved academic as he crashed into the central Fomorian. Ultán's breath exploded from his lungs. *Like hitting a bloody stone wall!*

Instinct made Ultán stab with the shorter blade. He grunted as it met the resistance of the Fomorian's thick, thorny hide but heaved a sigh of relief as the dagger triumphed. He plunged it to the hilt into the demon's chest. The Fomorian's roar of agony confirmed that Ultán's choice of the weapon's poison was effective. Dark gore soaked Ultán's hand, making the hilt slick. He gripped the knife tighter, twisted and pulled it free, and then kicked the Fomorian aside.

"Queen Balora wants him alive!" roared the Fomorian chieftain again, prompting shouts of disapproval from the warband. Their intent was to tear Ultán limb from limb, roast him over a wood fire, and devour him.

With the Fomorian's words, Ultán's fortunes improved. Still, his long blade slashed at the demons' hides with little effect. Only a blow to their snouts caused them to pause, although that seemed more from annoyance than serious injury. He achieved better results with the short, stabbing dagger. However, the effort required to punch through his enemies' skin rapidly depleted his strength.

His demons' desire to bring him alive to Balora was Ultán's only advantage. Stubbornness kept him forging forward and momentum propelled him down the mountain slope. His face bled from razor-sharp talons, and he grimaced at the pain of another ripping blow to his back. His greatcoat, with its mail lining, was shredded, and its blood-soaked fabric made it heavier. *This was not my best-thought-out plan.* Grim determination to report to Clío kept Ultán focused and alive.

Mother Nature took pity on the Watcher. He tripped over the ex-posed root of a rowan tree, then tumbled over a rocky outcrop and down the hillside. Surprised at first, the Fomorians roared in fury. Helpless to intervene, the adversaries watched Ultán roll several times and plummet over the grassy ledge. Like a drunk after a weekend binge, Ultán was relaxed and mostly spared the unpleasantness of the rapid descent. When his head hit a rock, he experienced a merciful blackness.

*\*\**

Ceara considered grabbing Ultán and flying back to Bryson Street but disregarded the option. It was still daylight and the risk of being spotted while transporting the Watcher was too great. *His life is not that valuable.* She assessed his injuries as extensive but not fatal, lifted him, and laid him on the grassy ribbon that verged the public road. She waited. Several hours later, as dusk fell, Ultán regained his senses. Pain hit him like a truck, causing him to throw up and lapse again into unconsciousness.

Many nights out with Clío and her friends had acquainted Ceara with the concept of taxis. She knew there must be a taxicab office along the road. Her dress torn and exhibiting a good amount of breast, Ceara stumbled through the door of the decrepit vomit-, piss-, and tobac-co-stained office. "Accident! My boyfriend's badly injured," she cried, frantically pointing up the road.

The occupants ignored her. They had witnessed this scenario fre-quently on weekends. It usually meant they would never receive the promised fare, their cab would be stolen by joy-riders, or they would be beaten up. Ceara added one final touch. She wailed and puked. "Fuck!" exclaimed the older of the drivers. "I'll go, if only to get away from the smell in here."

"Thanks," sniffed Ceara, but the driver was gone. She slumped on the grimy bench and waited a short time before she whined, "I need to pee."

"Not in here. You can squat and piss outside," said the controller grumpily, pointing to the back door. "Then come back and clean up your mess." No one ever had, but it was always worth saying and he might get a better flash of her tits.

\*\*\*

On the hill, the Fomorian chieftain gathered his underlings. All remembered the fate of the last Fomorian who angered Balora. "No one speaks of this failure to Queen Balora. Kill the remaining Nemed who accompanied us. Kill and burn our wounded." None dissented, although a few grumbled at the waste of good food.

# CHAPTER 28

"We should get rid of that bloody door knocker and get one of those new ones that chime Mozart melodies." Clío's intemperate response to the untimely interruption of her traditional Friday night fish supper elicited a mutter of agreement from Lazarus. Oblivious to anything other than the battered pasties she was wolfing down, Ceara said nothing.

Clío unlocked the door and swung it open. Written on her face was the wrath of a woman deprived of one of life's greatest pleasures. The sun had set, and only the golden yellow glow of the streetlights softened the darkness. The smallish man before her jumped at the sound of the heavy door banging against the hallway's wall.

"Well?" She looked over his shoulder. "I did not order a taxi."

Caught off guard, the man slipped his worn, flat cap off. He pointed to the taxi. The vehicle was obviously in need of a paint job, although that might disturb the rust that was holding much of the body together. The engine idled, pumping oily fumes into the air. "Before he passed out, the gentleman in the back seat asked me to drop him off at this address."

With faux bravado, the taxi driver added, "He's lucky. A pretty, young lady came into the company's office and told us her boyfriend had an accident further up the road. He's bleeding like a stuck pig." The man scratched a head that sported a few clusters of lank hair. With a calmness he did not feel, the driver said, "She told me you'd pay the fare.

There'd better be a good tip, too. It'll take the rest of the night to clean up the blood and puke."

Golden eyes flared at the mention of a young woman. Clío glanced over her shoulder at Ceara, who vainly attempted to fade into the hallway's shadows. *We'll talk about this later.* Clío's gaze returned to the driver, putting him on the defensive. Yet his stance was more akin to a professional boxer readying to deliver a counter punch. He gave Clío a casual but thorough inspection. Years of picking up belligerent drunks from Belfast's clubs and drinking dens on weekend nights was not for the timorous. However, it was excellent training in assessing how dangerous a fare might be.

The man judged Clío was angry but not murderous… at least not yet. At that moment the smell of fish and chips, heavily doused with salt and vinegar, reached the doorway. Immediately, he understood and dipped his hat again. Smiling ruefully, he said, "Apologies for the interruption, ma'am. No one likes a cold, cod supper."

He pointed to the taxi. "Your friend's a big one and heavy, even for his height. I'll give you a hand to lift him from the car." A quick look at the one-armed Lazarus who had arrived at Clío's shoulder and the man gulped. "Sorry, sir, that was a poor choice of words. I meant no offence."

"None was taken," said a bemused Lazarus.

Clío pushed past the driver and swung open the car door. "Fuck!"

"I wanted to take him to Accident and Emergency at the Royal, but he insisted on coming here." He replaced his cap to free his hands and stepped closer. "I almost did my back in getting him into the car, but between the two of us, I'm sure we'll be able to carry him into the house." His jaw dropped as, in one smooth movement, Clío pulled Ultán from the car, effortlessly threw him over her shoulder, and strode into the house.

"She's stronger than she looks." Almost having forgotten about his fare, the man jumped at Lazarus' presence beside him.

"Thank you for your help. It is much appreciated. I hope this will cover the fare and your inconvenience." The driver mumbled his thanks as a thick roll of tenners and a bottle of Bushmills was placed in his hands.

He tipped his hat, again, and gave Lazarus a grimy business card. "Any time, sir." The remuneration was worth more than his car and he knew how to keep his mouth shut.

\*\*\*

In their bedroom, Clío glared at Ceara. "I asked you to follow Ultán to see if our suspicions were confirmed. Did I have to spell it out that I did not want him stabbed and beaten to within an inch of his life?" She looked from Ceara to Lazarus. "What was the eejit trying to do?"

"Ultán's a man—or close enough. He's intimidated by us and wanted to show you how he could contribute."

"By getting killed?" asked Clío.

"I doubt that was his intention. If he lives, my guess is we will know the location of Balora's nest."

Ceara coughed. Her face held a child's look of guilt after stealing a chocolate biscuit. "I know where it is. While I observed him, Ultán discovered Balora's main stronghold. The wounds are from his trying to escape…"

"You watched and did nothing?" Ceara blushed and Clío shook her head in disbelief. "It seems Ultán, and you have something in common. You have a lot to learn about how friends are supposed to be there for each other. I expected this of Ultán but am disappointed in you." The sob that caught in Ceara's throat went unnoticed.

Clío gasped as a glowing, knife-sized Blade of Light appeared in Lazarus' left hand. "We cannot use your dragon healing powers unless you want to give Ultán a fiery death." He looked at Ceara. "Which perhaps some of us do. I have some healing skills. Sadly, they have lain dormant for millennia, but do we have any choice?"

Lazarus turned his gaze to Clío and indicated his absent limb. "I am right-handed. Therefore, you will need to do the cutting—flesh and clothes. What is left of his clothing and armour will present no challenge to the blade. After that, you will need to clean and cauterise the major wounds using your talons."

He sighed. "There is one piece of information you should be aware of. The Blade of Light is attuned to me. Normally, it will destroy anyone else who grasps it."

"Fuck!" exclaimed Clío and Ceara.

"My hypothesis is that if I stand with my arms around you, my aura will protect you and the Blade will be happy. The alternative is for me to use the Blade to give Ultán a fast death."

"That's unacceptable. Let's do it," said Clío.

Lazarus looked at Ceara. "You will help Clío turn Ultán over when needed and hold him down while she cuts, trims, and seals his wounds. This will be agonising, and we have nothing to mitigate his pain. If the Goddess is merciful, he will remain unconscious. Minor tears can be sewn and dressed later; we have my healing powers and salves to reduce fevers, infections, and swelling." He gazed pointedly at them. "If we do not work as a team, Ultán will die."

\*\*\*

"Will he ever stop bleeding over our bed and sheets? Perhaps I should kill him. Do you know how expensive this bed linen is to replace? How many times do we need to redecorate and refurnish our room?" Clío was talking complete drivel, but it did not matter. She was building a bridge to mend a strained relationship.

Clío's use of "we" and "our" gave Ceara hope, and she tentatively reached out a hand to touch Clío's. "I'm sorry."

"You were right to be cautious. My scales are not completely at ease with Ultán, and I doubt they ever will be. Perhaps it is linked to what the Sons of Mil did to him. They made him neither human nor demigod, an outcast from both societies, and forced loneliness on him. To live in a place between both worlds must be awful."

She took both Ceara's hands and faced her. "Ultán is part of our group. If we judge him a liar who has betrayed us, we will kill him. Until then, he remains a friend." Ceara dipped her head and tilted it to meet Clío's impending kiss.

\*\*\*

The slab of raw meat and the widening crimson stain on her previously pristine white sheets pained Clío more than she cared to admit. Blood and serum continued to seep from the deeper slashes. Once the gore had been sponged away, they saw the woad-coloured, curling tattoos covering Ultán's body.

Celtic warriors believed in their painted spiritual armour, yet the blue extract also had a practical purpose. In battle, its medicinal and blood-clotting properties could be the difference between life and death. Clío hoped it was true. She wondered what the sigils meant. The Sons of Mil worshipped science. It was their god. How then could a soldier, a Watcher of their elite warriors, put his faith in mystical symbols? Ultán was a paradox. *Perhaps he is worth getting to know better.*

Clío inspected Ultán as he lay unconscious. Without his glamour, he was his full height and more muscled. He was not as ugly as Lazarus had suggested, and his features were craggily agreeable. She looked helplessly at Lazarus, hoping for wisdom. He shook his head. "My healing skills are rudimentary. Of the Tuatha Dé, Macha was the one with healing talents, and I never listened much to her. I could ask, but I have not spoken to Macha since the birth of our son." Lazarus mused that he did not do family well.

Clío's eyes demanded an explanation. Lazarus shrugged. "We were no different from most nascent civilisations. In the early days of the Tuatha Dé there were just nine—the Womb-Born. We needed to increase the population, so everybody rutted everybody, regardless of kinship." He blinked. "Macha and I were never close. I doubt she would have any interest in helping me keep a Son of Mil alive."

Tears streamed down Clío's face. Was the situation hopeless? What traditions did the Sons of Mil have in death? That she considered Ultán's death a disquieting possibility disturbed her. Whatever happened to the safety of isolation or avoiding closeness to humans—or proto-humans? "There must be something more we can do," said Clío.

Lazarus scratched the non-existent stubble on his chin. Should Ultán be allowed to die, if not in peace, then without the pain of consciousness, or fighting with desperate means? With a sigh of resignation, he said, "We can do no more, Clíodhna. His life or how he dies is in the Goddess' hands."

\*\*\*

After a half-cycle of the moon in merciful oblivion, Ultán's eyes awakened to the sight of Clío and Ceara in a passionate embrace. "All things come to him who waits. It's not exactly how I envisaged our first morning together, but I hadn't visualised a threesome, either. I'm not complaining."

"Dream on," said Clío. Ceara was not so dismissive of the idea. She felt sufficiently in Ultán's debt to owe him compensation for abandoning him to the Fomorians. Therefore, she considered a threesome as a not unpleasant way to redress the wrong. Ultán was naked and had been since Clío had cut and removed his blood-soaked clothes. Thus, both she and Clío had had more than sufficient time to assess Ultán's manhood. Both were impressed.

"Judging by your erection, you must be getting better," said Clío.

Ultán grinned, but immediately he fell to coughing harshly. He cursed the effect on his ravaged body and grimaced as newly sewn scars fought to reopen. The effort something simple needed made him swear. He glanced down and smiled thinly. "I see someone has been bathing me." He frowned. "Was shaving me for artistic impact or a delayed punishment?" He sighed and another bout of coughing splattered his hand with blood. "What a pity only you enjoyed it."

"You're not out of the woods yet, Ultán," said Clío. "Please do not strain your body unnecessarily. We will be angry if you die and waste the effort we put into saving you."

Ultán realised he had not thanked Clío and Ceara for tending to his wounds. He knew he must have been in very poor condition, and likely near death. Still, his Watcher training had not prepared him for such situations. Lone assassins tend to bleed out friendless in a back alley. He searched for the appropriate words.

"The expression you are struggling to find is 'Thanks.' No more is necessary, and it is pointless to utter it if you do not mean it," said Clío.

"Thank you. To both of you, and I mean it," said Ultán.

The room fell into an awkward silence until Clío spoke. "We must change your bedding and, unlike when you were unconscious, this time it will hurt when we move you." With a mischievous twist of her lips, Clío said, "However, if you behave, we will give you a sponge bath." Ultán's eyes lit up.

As Clío bent over the bed, she sniffed, rolled her eyes, and turned to Ceara, who was still in favour of a threesome as penance. She shook her head. "If you think I am going to suck or ride him before he has taken a full bath, can piss and shite by himself, *and* we have new bed clothes, you can think again." Ultán's outburst of laughter quickly turned into bloody coughing.

"Please be careful and don't die," whispered Ceara. "If you need an incentive, I'm a really good lay, and from personal experience and reputation, so is Clío."

# CHAPTER 29

*Late Spring—Northern Ireland*

The rambling discussion over dinner persistently circled back to the urgency of Clío ascending the Dragon Throne. "The dragons have no queen," said Lazarus. "It is not unusual for dragons to go for centuries, even millennia, without a queen. They are almost immortal, and most are solitary creatures or prefer to reside in small family-based communities. Most eschew pomp and circumstance. However, the time to crown a new queen draws near."

Not reading the room was the first of Lazarus' errors that evening. Clío's emotions were raw from Ultán's near death. Furthermore, she had not come to terms with assuming the responsibility for a people she had little personal knowledge of, and which was about to be laid on her shoulders. The idea that she might also have to kill a brother she had never met festered within her. Recent events had pushed her emotional turmoil to the recesses of her mind. On this evening, it rushed back.

Oblivious, and his mellow voice lubricated with whiskey, Lazarus continued his soliloquy. "With hindsight, I was wrong to withhold your bloodline and race. In my defence, I did it with the best of intentions. I am truly sorry and fully expect to be severely admonished by Bráchthine when she returns." His was an extraordinary, even valiant, admission. The Womb-Born never apologise, no matter the context or fault.

Committed to his elucidation but for the first time sensing all was not well, Lazarus had little choice other than to forge ahead. "The time is fast approaching when the dragons must choose a ruler. You must fight your brother, Ciarán, for the throne, and win… or die." Misreading Clío's unhappy expression, he smiled sympathetically.

"How did one lauded as the wisest of the Womb-Born and venerated as a strategic thinker and canny negotiator fuck up my ascension to the Dragon Throne quite so much? It does not say much for the intelligence of you, your siblings, or your race. Does it? Is it the in-breeding?"

Ceara put her hand to her mouth, barely stemming the gasp of shock following Clío's brutal words. Lazarus' darkening mien did not bode well. Neither did his golden aura beginning to overwhelm his glamour. Ceara put her hand over Clío's and squeezed, but the unspoken plea for caution was ignored.

"For millennia, *you* withheld knowledge of my mother and my race. You never hinted at my royal bloodline or that I was the Queen-in-Waiting of the Dragons. Instead, you sent me nightmares. Indeed, I learned of your training approach by accident.

"To cap everything, you have informed me that I must fight my brother, Ciarán—a sibling I have never met. Not only that but I may have to kill him for a throne of which I had no knowledge, to rule a people who are strangers to me. I am not well-acquainted with the Goddess, but it strikes me she would take a dim view of fratricide."

Clío glared at Lazarus. "Why does my brother hate me? He knows as much about me as I do about him. We have never met, never talked or argued. My human friends tell me that brothers and sisters fight all the time as part of growing up. None informed me that murder was part of adolescence. I can't hate Ciarán because I do not know who he is."

The final arrow plucked from Clío's quiver was nocked and shot. "The Mórrígan and you describe my brother as an unworthy person. How is that not a compliment given the information's source? Are his counsellors as poor as mine? I can understand Scáthach's motivation. What is yours? A belated apology to my ma or fear of the Tuatha Dé losing their protectors?"

Ceara muttered, "Shite!" as a smoking dragon faced off against a glowing Womb-Born. Still, she was furious at herself for not seeing Clío's internal struggle and angry at Lazarus for the same blindness. *What am I supposed to do?* Yet of those present in the parlour, Ceara was the only one who was clear about her duty. Above everything, she was Clío's shield-maiden. She pushed in front of Clío and faced Lazarus. "I *will* protect my queen to the death. Kill me or back off!" The Blade of Light appeared in Lazarus' hand. It was not a promising sign.

"No, Ceara, I can't lose you. This is my fight, not yours," said Clío.

"Then you should have considered the consequences of your words more carefully, my queen." Clío's face fell at the rebuke.

Lazarus shook his head. His voice trembled with anger, disappointment, and guilt. "Snap out of your adolescent whinging, Clíodhna. It does not suit a being whose years are counted in millennia. It is well past time for you to grow up. Life is not all parties and promiscuity. Your namesake and the famed Meadhbh realised that. Grow up!"

When he spoke again, Lazarus' voice sounded old and frail, echoing off the walls of an eerily silent house. "I did what I thought was best for you. Yes, I made mistakes, but who doesn't? If you don't like it, leave." He shook his head. "No! This is my home and I have my own life to live. I am done with you. Find another mentor and place to live." Lazarus turned on his heels and exited the parlour. Soon after, the front door opened and slammed shut.

"*Bastard!*" screamed Clío. Aghast, she turned to Ceara. Golden tears threatened to breach the dam behind her eyes. "What have I done?"

"On the positive side, we did not kill a Womb-Born, thereby averting a catastrophic war between the Tuatha Dé and the Dragons." Ceara took Clío's hands. "The ducks are calling. We need a long walk in the park."

\*\*\*

"Well, that turned out well." The Mórrígan slid noiselessly across the wooden seat in McHugh's snug to face Lazarus. Like her brother, she had black hair with blue undertones. Only the colour of their eyes was different. Lazarus' were blue. Unlike him, her tresses were long with several thin plaits on each side framing a smoky-white face. At the end of each braid was an emerald, which perfectly set off her green eyes.

Lazarus looked up from studying his single malt. Balora was seductively curvaceous, but The Mórrígan transcended all definitions of beauty. The blood-red lips and nails should have been garish but were a perfect touch for the Queen of Desolation. In her glamour she was tall, although diplomatically she chose to be fractionally shorter than Lazarus.

He smiled. The Mórrígan's apple-sized breasts would never need a bra, unless to protect her dress's gossamer fabric from her nipples. He would admire her small, round arse and the provocative sway of her hips later when she eventually departed. He sighed for lost times and smiled. It was a challenge to determine who was more impressive: The Mórrígan at war or the sensuous demigoddess before him.

"Shame on you, brother," murmured The Mórrígan. Her eyes said otherwise, and her cheeks had a hint of pink. "In this age, the Tuatha Dé are enlightened and our thoughts about each other are no longer carnal. The Goddess withdrew her approval and cursed us with infertility once we had bred our allotted number." A delicate tongue moistened The Mórrígan's lips until they glistened. These were the weapons the Queen of Whispers and Shadows used to seduce the foolish to war.

Lazarus shook his head to clear his thoughts. "I may have to change bars. First Balora and now you. At least you don't want to shoot me... I hope."

Slender fingers reached across the table and caressed Lazarus' hand. The physical contact shocked Lazarus. It was the second time in several months. Prior to that, it had been millennia since they had had any physical contact. His pulse quickened as he tried to resolve conflicting emotions. The Mórrígan giggled. Another contradiction? *She sounds "normal".*

"While the memory is as sweet as the first time, our time passed aeons ago and, in these times, I have rivals for your affections. As to killing you, that is unresolved, although I would be more subtle. Balora is so crude… in everything she does. Is that what attracts you to her?" Returning to the reason for her visit, The Mórrígan shook her head. "What were you thinking, Lazarus? Do you love Clíodhna?"

"You were watching?" The Mórrígan nodded. "Of course, I love Clíodhna and have done since she was a warmling." The Mórrígan's eyes narrowed. "*But never in that way.*" The flare of anger in Lazarus' tone reassured The Mórrígan and her breathing steadied.

"Good, stay with the 'grandpa–granddaughter' relationship. It is safer for both of you, and you have grown comfortable with it. However, the outcome of your indulgence is a very powerful and confused brat. It was good that you brought that to a head. The timing was awful, but things had to be said." Lazarus smiled wryly at his sister's support. He should have known better.

"But, what the fuck, Lazarus! When did your talents in diplomacy and carefully chosen words desert you?" Her words mirrored those of Clíodhna. Lazarus' mouth opened and he gave a good impression of a goldfish. He had never heard his sister curse, at least not in the human manner. "What happened to balancing a well-overdue scolding with understanding, comfort, counsel… and a loving grandpa hug?

"You messed up, Lazarus. This was not the time for a temper tantrum for either of you. There are too many moving pieces and players on the *fidchell* board… Balora, the Fomorians, the Sons of Mil, and at the centre of everything is that bitseach Scáthach and Clíodhna's brother."

"Scáthach may not be the driver or instigator of events. Her daughter, Uathach, has silvered eyes."

"The Hag, no!" gasped The Mórrígan. "How long have you known about An-Ársa? Did it never occur to you to share it with me?" She shook her head. "Never mind, now is not the time to deal with communications problems. The Tuatha Dé have a weak High King in Daghdha and the Womb-Born are apathetic." The Mórrígan's reprimanding tone made clear on whose shoulders she laid the fault.

"We must focus on the issues we can resolve—the first of which is Clíodhna because she is the queen on the game board. You have a well of care and goodwill working for you. Go to her. Be the grandpa she loves, but less of the easy-going one. She needs love and honest counsel from you. When her back is to the wall, she needs to know that you stand with her. Everything else she can get herself." The Mórrígan slid from her seat.

As his sister walked towards the exit, Lazarus smiled. *You do have a great arse.* Outside McHugh's, The Mórrígan laughed aloud.

Lazarus sipped his whiskey, sighed, and left his usual tip. As he exited the bar, for the first time in his long life, he felt uncertain and slightly nauseous about facing Clío. *Will she forgive me?*

***

The usual Belfast weather of cold, grey days, and constant rain showers would have matched the mood of the two sharing the park bench. However, on this day they were blessed with warmth, sunshine, and not a cloud in a blue sky. The day would never match their gloom. For an hour Clío cursed, railed against, and screamed at Lazarus, calling him every derogatory epithet she could think of. Still, her anger seeped away with each word and was finally washed away in a flood of regret. The sobbing eventually subsided apart from the occasional hiccup and snuffle.

Ceara smiled at the blonde hair plastered to her tear-soaked t-shirt and pulled Clío closer to rest her head against her breasts. Occasionally, she lifted Clío's face and kissed her. During the heat of Clío's rage they had shared furious, passionate kisses and Ceara wished they were home in bed. Yet this was not the time, or the place, for satisfying such desires. There would be other times. Her eyes lifted and she whispered, "Please," to the Goddess.

"What will I do, Ceara? My grandpa told me to piss off."

"Do you truly believe he meant it?" asked Ceara. She was glad Clío had started to think things through. "Do you believe either of you can walk away from many millennia of memories? It is not that simple or easy. Do you hate him?"

Clío lifted her head from Ceara's chest and shook her head. "How could I ever hate him? But he meant what he said. I felt it. Was it all due to the anger or something deeper? Have I held him back from doing what he wants?" She sat up, wiped her wet cheeks, and made a half-hearted attempt to straighten Ceara's shirt. "There was truth in what he said. I *am* the oldest adolescent brat in three kingdoms, but why did Lazarus have to be such an arsehole explaining it to me?"

"Would you have listened to a calm, patient Lazarus?"

"Probably not." She sobbed briefly again and pouted. "He didn't have to be so hurtful."

"Do you still love your grandpa?"

"Yes. I always will. I hope he feels the same way."

"I have known him for a short time, but I believe he will," said Ceara. "Is it so difficult for you to have faith?" She looked at the horizon. "Evening draws near and the ducks have gone. It's time to go home, my love."

* * *

Lazarus rose from his armchair when he heard the key in the front door's well-oiled lock and a "Shush" from Clío. He smiled. Clío was being especially careful to avoid disturbing him. *Perhaps a good night's sleep is what everyone needs. No, that is exactly what no one needs.* Procrastination was a curse afflicting dragons, demigods, and men.

He brushed his hesitancy aside, walked to the parlour door, and opened it. His timing was perfect. The soft golden glow of the hall chandelier framed Clío in the doorway.

"I've brewed some tea. Would you like some?" He gestured at the silver tray. "There's Cadbury's chocolate biscuits—the ones you like with the orange cream centre."

Clío looked beyond the peace offering into Lazarus' eyes. She saw his desire for reconciliation, and the pain and sadness she would cause if she rejected him. She wanted to cry; instead, with a scream of

"*Grandpa!*", she leapt into his arms. Only Lazarus' underlying strength prevented him from crashing into the tea and biscuits.

The embrace had such intensity Ceara thought they would merge. Instead, their combined auras became golden-red, enveloping their bodies. It was a beautiful vision Ceara would never forget. "I am sorry, dau… granddaughter. I said things I will always regret, but I have loved you since you were a warmling and I fear for you. My life would have no purpose if anything happened to you."

Clío pressed a finger against Lazarus' lips. "Shush, Grandpa. I am sure there will be more arguments between us because I *am* a brat, but there will never be regrets. You are my sanctuary and my stronghold." Clío sighed wistfully. "I do wish you were my da…" Her eyes lit up at a thought that slipped into her mind. "You could adopt me," she said. There was hope behind the grin. "Although, I'm not sure how that would work. Would we have to fill in paperwork in three worlds?"

Lazarus roared with laughter and tears streamed down his cheeks. "You would honour me by being my daughter. I agree. Daughter flows off the tongue much easier than granddaughter. Leave the formalities to me." He winked exaggeratedly. "I know people. "A troubled look settled on Clío's face, and he asked, "What is it?"

"You'll have to change your glamour. It will be too creepy having my da look as old as you do. Probably early forties would be better, and it will still give you gravitas when needed. You should adjust the next time we move."

Lazarus nodded. "Agreed. Besides, this glamour is not exactly attractive to females of any age." He chuckled at Clío's open mouth. "You're not the only one with *needs*."

\*\*\*

Ceara slipped, unnoticed, out of the room and house. When she returned, it was with a box filled with fish, battered sausage, and pastie suppers. The mouth-watering smells filled the air as she entered the room. She looked at the duo and rolled her eyes at the blank looks. "It's

Friday and it's our tradition. Did you think I was going to miss this just because you might still be fighting?" Ceara's broad smile measured her relief that harmony had returned to Bryson Street. She smiled wickedly and looked at Lazarus. "There's plenty of food for us... *and your sister.* Must the Womb-Born always make grand entrances?"

A hiss of annoyance accompanied the shadow as it became corporeal and emerged from the parlour wall. The Mórrígan stood in the middle of the room and inclined her head to Ceara. "You learn fast, dragon. Well spotted. I must brush up on my concealment skills." She looked at the steaming hot food and licked her lips. "Thank you, I am starving." She looked reproachfully at Lazarus. "You never treated me to such wonderful food. At least, not in several millennia."

Ceara's jaw dropped as she watched The Mórrígan lift a battered cod filet and swallow it in one gulp. "I bought extra but I may have to do a second run, if she gulps down food like a starving wolf," she murmured to Clío. The room dissolved into laughter. Abashed, The Mórrígan gracefully blushed and took smaller bites.

Greasy fingers were licked and burps expelled, heralding the end of the feast. "Now we're one big happy, dysfunctional family again, can we please focus on resolving the challenges that are racing towards us like a dragon shield-wall?" asked The Mórrígan.

"Are you always in our midst?" asked Clío.

"Not always. Lately, yes." At Clío's disapproving look, The Mórrígan tossed her hair dismissively. "I am the Queen of Whispers and Shadows. What do you expect?" She looked mischievously at Ceara and Clío. "May I make one observation. For both of you being so long-lived, and given Clío's long history of promiscuity, you are quite boring in bed. I can help. Let me be your dear, worldly grandma."

"The Hag, no!" exclaimed Clío and Ceara, while Lazarus laughed.

Ceara bent her head until close to Clío's ear and whispered, "Are we boring? Do I not satisfy you?"

"Of course you do. The bitseach is teasing us. We'll talk later in bed," said Clío huskily.

Having stirred the pot, The Morrigan moved on. "Let us consider one problem that has a clear solution. Urged by Scáthach, Clíodhna's brother has linked himself to a group of 'Progressives' in Clann Dubh. They think that dragon society needs 'rebalancing', a euphemism for policies that allow male dragons to become part of the succession." She looked at Clío. "There you have the answer to the urgency of anointing a new queen.

"They have persuasive arguments of equality and fairness, but Scáthach covets power and sees the Dragon Throne as providing it. Many believe Scáthach has returned to her roots as a powerful sorceress. Mentally, your brother is not strong enough to resist her or her daughter. Uathach is most certainly a succubus and a dark one at that. Once control rests in Scáthach's hands, she will never relinquish it. She will subjugate Clann Dubh and use them to quash all dissent."

"So, my brother wants to challenge my right to be queen because he is bewitched?" asked Clío.

"That and jealousy," said Lazarus. "Ciarán is a tool, and you are the roadblock to Scáthach and her daughter's ambitions. Dragon history and prophesy dictate he was always primed to challenge you."

"No pressure, then," said Clío. "Nevertheless, I will speak with my brother before fighting him. Perhaps I can break Scáthach's hold on him." Clío looked at Lazarus. "My mother would never want me to kill my brother, before I had tried to reason with him. That is my decision, and our plan needs to take my wishes into consideration. Agreed?"

# CHAPTER 30

"Information from the Watchers in Germany suggests the air raids will be extended to Northern Ireland soon." Ultán's tone was eager, much too eager. If he expected a positive reaction, he was disappointed. Not picking up on the warning signs from Clío and Lazarus, he blundered further down a cul-de-sac of his own making.

"This is an excellent opportunity for us. The bombing raids will provide Clío and Ceara with an excellent diversion when they attack the Fomorian camp. I will be on the ground to eliminate any injured Fomorian or Nemed stragglers." Ultán stopped at the sudden flare of anger in Clío's eyes and the rise in the room's temperature. *What am I missing?* "What?"

"Excuse me." Belying the rage building within her, Clío's voice remained cold and calm. The room, however, got steadily warmer. Lazarus' reassuring hand enfolding hers could not ameliorate the rise in temper or temperature. "You know that Belfast will be attacked. Hundreds, maybe thousands, will be killed. My friends may die. Yet you intend to do nothing, save to use it as a cloak for me to destroy the Fomorians and Nemed." Clío's lips thinned. "You disappoint me, Ultán."

Four words signalled the end of any hope Ultán may have had for a relationship, or even just sex, with Clío. Blind to her moral core, he shrugged and lifted his hands. "What else is there to do? The raid will happen. If I know this information, then so do the British Secret Service and the Armed Forces. It's up to them to alert and prepare their citizens, not us. We would be negligent if we didn't use the opportunity to our advantage."

Ultán's indifference to and lack of compassion for her girlfriends and neighbours, some of whom she had known for generations, dismayed Clío. The scales on her spine crashed discordantly. It was a sign Ultán could neither miss hearing nor misunderstand the meaning of. At that moment, he knew if he uttered one more insensitive word, open hostility and his demise would be the likely outcome.

"Where is your humanity?" asked Clío.

"I am not human. Neither are you, nor any in this room."

Ceara's backhanded slap across Ultán's cheek sounded like the report from a gun and made Lazarus recoil. The armchair Ultán sat on, and a side table, crashed against the wall. "Your education as it relates to females and dragons is flawed. Be thankful I interceded." Ceara inclined her head towards Clío. "*She* would have killed you."

Clío nodded her thanks to Ceara and then fixed her gaze on Lazarus. "What is your counsel?" Her demeanour shouted, *do not fight me on this*.

Deep blue eyes looked icily at Ultán, and the Watcher flinched under Lazarus' examination. "Ceara is right. You have a lot to learn about dragons. They have a black-and-white perspective when it comes to justice and vengeance." Lazarus turned to face Clío. "*You* must recognize the limitations and responsibilities placed on our kind. We are powerful, not omnipotent. We cannot stop human wars."

"So, you're on *his* side."

"Do not put words in my mouth," rebuked Lazarus. "We cannot walk into the local police station and say we have information that the Luftwaffe will attack. That will get us either locked up as spies or put in a straitjacket and escorted to Purdysburn Mental Hospital. Neither can we run up and down the Newtownards Road, shouting, 'The end is nigh!' Those hearty souls will dismiss us as drunks or newly converted evangelists." An uncomfortable silence descended on the room.

"Will the population suddenly become deaf, dumb, and blind?" asked Clío. "Are they not going to see the night sky lit up with dragon breath as Ceara and I destroy the Fomorians? Or hear the screams and thuds of demons falling to the earth?" Sarcasm dripped from Clío's lips. "For fuck's sake, unless they are in bomb shelters, many in Northern Ireland will already be looking up at the flights of German bombers!" Ultán and Lazarus had no response to Clío's logic and fell silent.

"Lazarus, you're a demigod with immense abilities." Clío stabbed the air with a finger. "Find a way to set off every fire alarm and air raid siren in Belfast *before* the air raid commences and *before* we attack Balora's Fomorians. That should have a knock-on effect across other towns. Make sure people have enough time to get to a shelter."

Clío's stare swung to Ultán. His attempt to match her gaze failed, and he shrugged broad shoulders, awaiting his orders. "You will leave immediately for the Causeway and Balora's camp. Secure a defensible hideaway and kill any Nemed or Fomorian that comes within your ground. Do not reveal yourself. Do not get captured. If you endanger the mission, *I* will kill you." Clío set her shoulders. "Now, get out of my sight. After the battle, it would be better if we did not meet... ever."

The front door slammed shut, and Clío turned to Lazarus. "Ceara and I will do what we must."

"You were harsh," said Lazarus.

"Ultán has no moral compass and cannot be trusted. It is horrific how his people have modified him. He sits betwixt two races but belongs to neither." She paused, considering. "His only hope may be his parents. If he asks, we will help extract them from the city of the Sons of Mil. Otherwise, my life will be perfectly fine without his presence."

\*\*\*

Clío fumed and her guts churned at the perpetual whistling of tens of thousands of falling bombs. The soft rustling of silk parachutes floating to the earth, each with a mine attached, scratched at her mind. She cursed the cloudless, moonlit sky for its complicity and uttered an enraged and impotent growl.

The rolling thunder of explosions and outbreaks of fires across the city made her scream in anger and frustration. Not even the alarms that had sounded well before the blitz began helped mitigate her wrath. People's lives and livelihoods were gone in a moment of barbarity. No matter what Lazarus advised, when she had finished with the Fomorians, she would return to the skies and bring death to any warplanes remaining.

*** 

Clío's flight resembled a great white shark swimming in the seas. Dragons consisted of a head, body, and tail. Where sharks had dorsal fins, serpents had spines and plates. Their massive heads were crested with feathers. Most dragons' plumage reflected the colour of their clann. Clío's shade changed according to her mood. Two long horns and two smaller ones protruded from above their eyes. Their great maws were populated with four fangs and incisors whose purpose was to hold, rip, and tear.

For a creature having the mass of a castle, Clío's flight was effortless and incredibly fast. She recalled Ceara and her father Aodh's words that her size was in her mind. It sounded like mumbo-jumbo or the words between mystic and follower. As she soared high in the night sky, Clío knew the truth.

Normally opalescent, Clío's scales became as dark as the night sky. Alongside her, Ceara's crimson plates deepened to match the blackness. As they circled the Cave Hill, the dragons were invisible to everyone but the Goddess. For the time being, she remained a spectator.

Clío convinced herself there was a plan. In phase one they would destroy the Nemed camps from the air. She had no idea how the Fomorians would react. Lazarus had warned her that, contrary to many stories, the higher demons were not stupid, and Balora was both a strategic and fierce opponent. She hoped, and prayed to the Goddess, that the Fomorians' curiosity would draw them out to investigate. When they emerged from cover, Ceara and she would slaughter them. If they did not cooperate, then she and Ceara would breathe dragon fire into every cave Ultán had located.

\*\*\*

The Nemed had no defence against the marauding dragons, and the napalm-like dragon breath spat at them. Their screams and cries for mercy were brief and unanswered as the dragons poured down their wrath. No god would hear or answer their prayers. When the last camp was ash, Clío and Ceara rose higher to circle and survey the hill.

It was April, which always brought with it wetter weather. The hillside steamed rather than smoked, obscuring the damage caused by dragon breath. Nevertheless, broad swaths of vegetation, glowing orange and red, were swept to a fiery end as the duo passed.

One thing perturbed Clío. *Why did I not see these Nemed during my playback of earlier interrogations?* Were the Nemed cloaked from her? That seemed unlikely given the Fomorians' disregard for any Nemed's life. *Stay alert, Ceara. Something stinks about this, and it's not just the Nemed.* She sensed Ceara at her shoulder before she saw her.

Had the Nemed been offered as a sacrifice to assuage the dragons' thirst for retribution? It was a plausible explanation. The Fomorians' customary tactics placed a heavy reliance on sacrificing the weak. That said, Clío suspected there was a link missing in her chain of logic. Her hunting instincts screamed warnings.

\*\*\*

The Fomorian chieftain considered himself a tactician underestimated by Balora. Given the length of his service in the Fomorian army, the clann leader knew surprisingly little about battles or death. He swore at the ease and speed with which the dragons exterminated the Nemed.

Although the most experienced of Balora's demons they had no experience fighting serpents. Few Fomorians had. The last war with the Dragons or Tuatha Dé was millennia in the past and only remembered by campfire tales or in whispered warnings to children of the consequences of disobedience. The stench of putrefaction and burnt flesh clogged his nostrils. Why did the Nemed not die like warriors: quietly, with dignity, and without smelling like a cesspit?

Nevertheless, the Fomorian had conceived a clever plan. His force contained one hundred demons. Of these, the best fifty remained in the cave alongside him. The remainder had taken wing before the dragons made their appearance and waited in the skies above to pounce. Common warriors' cloaking powers were not as strong as a queen's, but the captain gambled the dragons' attention would be focused on the Nemed. In this, his wager was well-founded. *Perhaps we can inflict damage on the serpents.* Yet that would be a bonus, not their purpose.

\*\*\*

The first tridents, a weapon long preferred by airborne demons, glanced off Clío's armour-plated skull. Hundreds more quickly followed, striking her scales along her length. Most bounced off her hide harmlessly, although a score slipped under the laminae, holding on because of their barbed tips. Clío snarled and thrashed to dislodge the spears. Her reaction was due to the inconvenience of the hooks rather than any pain.

Her gullibility and lack of tactical expertise made Clío angry. She made a note to talk to Aodh about advanced battle strategies for dragons on her next visit to the Island of Dragons. More immediately, she would make better use of Ceara's experience. She needed more mentoring and less sex. Learning "on the job" had few upsides.

*Keep rolling and use your tail to keep them at bay. Ignore the tridents. They're just an annoyance.*

The enemy's supply of tridents was soon exhausted. In their place, a thousand razor-edged talons clawed at Clío's scales as the Fomorians closed on her. It proved to be mostly trial and error for both opposing sides. These Fomorians had little idea of how to, or if they could, kill or incapacitate a dragon. Additionally, her ability to change size mitigated any attempt to swarm and overwhelm her.

Clío wondered whether she could breathe fire on herself without doing the enemy's job. *No!* shouted Ceara. *Remember how you singed your toes when you were learning how to use dragon breath and how it hurt?* She shook her massive head. *We need distance between us and the Fomorians to risk dragon breath. Watch me and follow.*

Ceara rolled over and over, swatting the demons' tough, black hides with her claws and tail. Both dragons' eyes were attuned to the night and the Fomorians' camouflage, and they uncovered each attacker's position quickly. The rapid rolling and twisting flung Fomorians from the serpents' bodies. Like great ships coming together in a harbour, the dragons crashed against each other, crushing any Fomorians caught between them. *Now, Clío!* Ceara flew horizontally and then vertically as Clío soared upwards. Then both dragons dived.

Long trails of dragon breath spewed from their mouths. Serpent glands produced a mixture akin to a corrosive napalm. Even a small patch of flame would stick and burn rapidly through most materials, especially if organic-based. If the citizens of Belfast watched the sky above the Cavehill, the fiery show would have been interpreted as an impressive meteor storm or another weapon. The screams of the Fomorians as they fell, burning, to earth would have been highly unpleasant. Still, most of the residents of Belfast had taken cover, and those who had not had other things on their minds.

\*\*\*

The Fomorian captain unleashed a round of swearing at those around him. Many were on edge after hearing the agonizing screams of former comrades and the thuds of their charred bodies striking the dirt around the cave entrance. Not wanting a rebellion on his hands, the Fomorian impaled the most vociferous protestor on his trident and roared, "This is a defensible position. One half will guard the entrance. The rest will remain with me and act as our reserve."

\*\*\*

Clío landed silently a few hundred paces from the cave's entrance. For a dragon of her current size, it was a remarkable feat, which made Ceara proud of her trainee. Unseen, Clío moved towards the opening. She smiled with satisfaction. "Good to see they've lined up nicely for me." She snarled at her artlessness. The Fomorian chieftain had a penchant for sacrifice. Why would he or she change now?

"This should keep the bastards occupied." A long burst of dragon breath struck the Fomorians at the cave's entrance, blackening the cavern's walls. By the time it had engulfed the demons, Clío had lifted into the air. As she circled the Cavehill, Clío scanned for hidden exits or slight movements. Her assault on the Nemed had denuded the area of trees and bushes, making the task less arduous. *Got you! He's all yours, my love.*

***

The Fomorian captain permitted himself a sigh of relief. The tunnel's exit emerged on the northwestern corner of the plateau. From there, his band would fly to their rendezvous with Queen Balora—albeit with a much-diminished force. That said, the queen was adept at using sacrificial lambs to preserve her life. She likely did not expect any to have survived.

Brushing off dirt and cobwebs from his armoured skin, the Fomorian looked around and shouted for the rest of his force to assemble. He screamed as Ceara plucked him from the ground. Luminous green eyes glowing in the night were his last memory.

"We learn, Fomorian. We learn."

# CHAPTER 31

Ceara remained on the Cavehill to reconnoitre the site for signs of Balora and the remaining demons, and for any injured who had escaped the dragons' claws and breath. She would ensure the charred bodies of dead Fomorians and Nemed crumbled to ash and, if needed, to help any wounded to join them. The corpses should have entirely disintegrated before breakfast. Early morning hikers would attribute any scorch marks on the hill to the air raids.

Meanwhile, Clío flew back to her home before dawn. The sun rose above the horizon when Clío, once more human, stood before her former home. The house on the corner of Bryson and Duke Streets was little more than a ruin. "No!" For a moment, Clío panicked. Her heart pounded and her head swam. *Where is Lazarus? Where will I live? Shite! I've never been alone.* Her knees buckled and tears flowed down her cheeks. Only memories of her home remained. She was not alone. Flattened by the nightlong blitz, half of East Belfast was devastated. Huge craters replaced potholes on its streets and roads.

The hand on her shoulder made her jump, and she swung around. "The Hag, Lazarus! Don't do that. I nearly had a heart attack." She hugged her grandpa, thankful he was uninjured. Despite their disagreements, Clío could and would not contemplate a life without Lazarus. Filled with hope, she looked into his eyes. "You've covered our home in a glamour, haven't you?"

Lazarus' crestfallen expression told Clío all she needed to know. He pointed to their neighbours' shattered homes. "How could I leave ours untouched in the midst of such tragedy and destruction?" His words were given emphasis by the poignant wailing of a woman in the next street. Her husband had scoffed at the air raid sirens and went drinking with his mates. All had died. All had left their families homeless and penniless.

"Ceara will return by midday. We should pitch in and help where we can. The churches have opened soup kitchens. I'm sure the nuns, and local doctors and nurses, will oversee the emergency first aid tents." Clío strove to keep her voice steady. "You could help with your healing talents without making it obvious. No miracles, just speed up their recovery."

He dipped his head and forced a smile. "What will you do?"

Clío thought for a moment. "Dragons are great at creating disasters but weak on aftercare. Ceara and I will use our strength to help search the rubble for survivors." She grimaced, "And the dead." At Lazarus' raised eyebrow, she added, "We will limit our strength… but not if there are children to save."

That evening and for many more, the three sat, red-eyed, hollow-cheeked, and silent around a brazier. A tarpaulin, nailed to the remaining vestiges of their gable wall, formed a makeshift shelter. All were scarred from the sights they had witnessed. Ceara spent her time sobbing and working furiously. If she did not, she would lose control and seek vengeance.

Clío and Lazarus had observed many wars, famines, plagues, and natural disasters. Yet they had never ended the day with their hands covered in victims' blood or their souls scarred by the memories of the last breath leaving a body. Belfast gifted the demigod and dragons something they had always evaded—humanity.

A howl broke through the tragedy. "It's Friday night, Lazarus. There are no fish and chips because the bastards bombed the chippie." Along the street resounded a chorus of, "You're fucking right, Clío! The devil take the bastards!"

Ceara and Clío snuggled up to Lazarus. "Where will we live?" Then Clío sat upright; remorse filled her voice. "I'm a selfish bitseach. What about our girlfriends? At first light, we must search for them." Ceara nodded and prayed that they were alive. She did not know if she could restrain her natural instincts to dispense vengeance and justice much longer.

# CHAPTER 32

*Summer—Northern Ireland*

It was mid-May and the Celtic festival of Bealtaine was behind them. Across Northern Ireland, Clío's and Ceara's dragon breath purged the last of the Nemed camps and the low-level Fomorians who oversaw them. There was no sign of Balora, or the several hundred Fomorian warriors who formed her personal guard.

Ultán remained absent, choosing prudence over confrontation. He hoped amassing good deeds would restore him to Clío's good graces. Hence, while in voluntary exile he remained in frequent contact with Clío and Lazarus. Mostly this was through couriers and notes slipped under the door in the dead of night. According to his latest report, the German raids on Belfast had concluded.

Over one thousand were dead, over one hundred thousand injured, and half of all the buildings and homes in Belfast were destroyed. The total of the missing remained unknown. For Belfast, a city of four hundred thousand, each blow was devastating and personal. Yet, while causing rivers of tears to flow, the destruction failed to break the people's resolve. More men volunteered to fight; the women took their places and jobs in the Yard and the city's many engineering factories and linen mills. Culture and society forever changed.

***

Clío looked around their new home—48A Castlereagh Street—a flat above a haberdashery. In the store's large backyard was a small wood-working shop and lumber yard. The rhythmic sound of wood saws and the smell of fresh sawdust drifted in the air. Clío found the activity comforting—an island of normality in a sea of destruction and heartbreak.

Ragged strips of wallpaper, the paste having long given up any pretence of adhesion, hung tenuously to damp walls slick with generations of glue. Mice scurried around bare wooden floors, scavenging crumbs while cheerfully avoiding traps baited with ancient cheese.

Patches of plaster on the canted ceilings, which followed the premises' rising roofline, had surrendered during the bombings, exposing wooden slats. When it rained, which was quite often, the roof leaked. The shop owner provided a range of buckets and pans, although her generosity was less about ameliorating her tenants' circumstances and more wanting to avoid water damage to her stock.

In a sea of ruination, it was remarkable the building remained largely intact. Lazarus steadfastly refused to use his Womb-Born powers to make life more comfortable. Clío reluctantly conceded his motivation was self-preservation and the need to keep a low profile. A building in pristine condition amid the surrounding desolation would have been suspicious and unpalatable to their neighbours, the police, and Special Branch.

Clío believed his actions were, in part, Lazarus' penance for being powerful yet helpless to intervene. All three did what they could to lessen the neighbourhood's burden without giving the appearance of being faerie godparents.

# CHAPTER 33

On clear days Balora watched the seagulls circle Rathlin Island and listened to their child-like cries. From the entrance of her new accommodation—a cave on the north Antrim coast—she surveyed her new home. Formed by centuries of an eternal battle between unforgiving seas and stubborn cliffs, the cavern smelled of dampness, salt, and rotting seaweed.

Its proximity to other similar, interconnected sanctuaries made it the perfect location to hide her remaining warriors. That it was also a short distance from the Giant's Causeway and its subterranean mysteries was no coincidence. Here, she could feel the throb of the Tuatha Dé's ancient power.

Balora knew of the Causeway's portal and its entrance, but the knowledge was useless. She had long set her mind to devising a strategy to outwit, blackmail, or bribe one of the Portal Keepers of the Tuatha Dé. Her lack of success increased her fanatical pursuit but to no avail. Indeed, a few of the Portal Keepers she had approached reported her and then resigned their posts. Furthermore, following Lazarus' injury, an order was broadcast to every portal, in every land, banning Balora from ever using them.

Frustrated, Balora sought alternatives. She gazed for days at the sea, while contemplating a diverse array of tactics. Her persistence eventually provided a solution. She grinned at the plan's ingenuity and simplicity. It was icing on the cake that it was also a punch to Manannán's nose.

Since their banishment, the Fomorians had hated the sea, perceiving it as a watery prison. Yet paradoxically Balora loved swimming and had done so long before the exile. She loved to explore the waters around her palace. Over the centuries she became an excellent swimmer and very knowledgeable about the oceans and their currents.

As she watched the tide ebb and flow, Balora finally solved the problem of her path to the Land of Immensity. The answer lay in the ocean's fluxes. Whether in the Land of the Humans or the Tuatha Dé, all oceans were connected. The common link was the currents. Balora deduced there must be a shared master current between the oceans of the Land of Immensity and the Land of the Humans.

How would she locate the master current's flow? Who controlled it? There were maps for all ocean currents but not this one. She had scoured thousands constructed by mapmakers and philosophers of ancient seafaring civilisations and had uncovered nothing—not even a hint. *Am I mistaken or deceived?* Balora refused to believe either.

"It must be here."

Many night swims went unrewarded until one evening Current reached out to seduce her, luring her with his flow, and wrapping her in his cold embrace. Balora loved it, but Current was a brutal lover, and only her strong nature and powerful body resisted its desire to hurt her. "Don't worry," she teased. "You can have me, very soon."

***

In the silver moonlight, Balora took stock. She had conquered her impatience and temper. Now she congratulated herself on the long game she had set in play. *Lazarus would be proud of me.* Inevitably, the Womb-Born would return to the Land of Immensity. Vanity would not allow him to remain a cripple for long, and the jaws of her snare would snap shut.

Balora had long admired the dragons' matriarchal society. *Only males would throw it aside.* She fully intended to be High Queen of the Fomorians and woe betide any man who got in her way. She felt a sisterly kinship with Clíodhna. *Perhaps we could be friends… if we don't kill each other.* Sharp teeth, more canine than human, tore a filet from the fish flapping in the basket by her side. She almost gagged. Why did everything remind her of the undersea exile imposed by Lazarus?

She drooled when she observed well-fed herds of cattle feasting on lush meadow grass just beyond the shoreline. In the absence of natural predators, a raid on the herds would succeed only in attracting the locals' attention, and quite possibly the Son of Mil and his dragon partners. She snarled and ripped another raw filet of pink flesh from the silver-skinned salmon.

Ruby-red eyes considered the remaining Nemed as potential snacks, but she had few of them. The dragons' purges had almost eliminated that food option. Balora could reasonably look forward to more Nemed conscripts soon. There were tens of thousands scattered throughout Europe, Africa, the Middle East, and the Americas fomenting trouble and dispensing diseases. But until reinforcements arrived, she must ration her meagre stock.

The same was not true for the Fomorians. Gone was the option to sink her incisors into Fomorian flesh. Balora ground her teeth. Clíodhna had proved surprisingly resourceful and ruthless in exterminating the Cavehill nests. That there were two dragons, not one, doubled the threat. *I must move my plan forward, speedily.*

The Fomorian nobility had always been sceptical of Balora's mission and motives. Hence, they were reluctant to augment her band with more of their progeny, no matter what she promised them from afar. The latter was also a problem. She was out of sight and out of mind. They could ignore her and the threat she posed. That she would take her revenge later did not help her now.

Not all was gloom and doom. Balora had sacrificed the less talented Fomorians. Thus, those who remained were her best and most experienced fighters. It was a formidable force. Balora smiled. *They will be my ultimate sacrifice.* As she observed her army, Balora wondered which of them were spies for the High King and the Council and how that could work to her advantage.

She stretched and inhaled deeply. The move was deliberately provocative. Simultaneously, she released a mist of mating pheromones into the cave. A frisson of pleasure surged through Balora's body at the open enjoyment of her form by the Fomorians. Always pragmatic, Balora knew passion loosened tongues. As was her habit, she would select four to satisfy her needs. She was agnostic about their sex, but she always included one pair, a male and a female, who were loyal and had consistently provided orgasmic experiences.

The use of her sexual allure would always be a primary and enjoyable weapon. Balora had seven days before the new moon and highest tide. Seven long days until the optimal time when Current would seek to violate her, and this time, she would not resist. Until then, she would interview her suspects. Soon she would know the identity of the High King's and Council's moles and meat would be on the menu.

\* \* \*

Ultán observed Balora's cave entrance and its surroundings from a deep hollow in one of the cliff-like dunes that edged the northeastern coastline. He ripped a piece of charred rabbit from the spit, enjoying the contrast between the crisp, burnt outer skin and the pink, blood-seeping inner flesh.

As with all Watchers, Ultán's senses—sight, smell, hearing, taste, and touch—had been heightened by practice, the environment, and genetic manipulation. The latter had been particularly painful, although obligatory to attain and sustain his position in the caste system, which defined the Sons of Mil's social structure and the elite Watcher community.

He scratched the two-week growth on his face. It was hardly stubble, but neither could it lay claim to the description of a beard. He idly wondered if Clío's preference was for smoothly shaved men. Instantly, Ultán spat a piece of gristle onto the marram grass. The action was unnecessary since the meat tasted good and was not particularly tough. It was Ultán's way of stopping a train of thought that could only end in painful reminiscing and wishful thinking.

Lazarus was right. He had a lot to learn about dragons, and particularly female serpents. He had not expected to find a principled backbone in one with a history of promiscuity and disregard for society's norms. Of greater significance was the realisation he must think beyond the confines of the Sons of Mil's cultural indoctrination. "*Enough!*" snarled Ultán. Without an audience, the exclamation was directed chiefly at his philosophical musings and the occasional seagull.

A flicker of movement at the edge of his vision caught Ultán's attention. The scent of Fomorians—a combination of fish, raw meat, and sea-salt-impregnated sweat—tickled his nostrils. Ultán congratulated himself. His instincts had been proven correct. More at home in the darkness, lower-ranking Fomorians had trouble maintaining their glamours during daylight. Thus, they presented as a series of jerky movements. It was as if they were walking through the beam of a strobe light. Balora appeared absent, and yet, it was apparent the twenty Fomorians were taking direction from someone.

Ultán smiled in admiration. The queen was very adept at maintaining her camouflage. Still, the direction of the Fomorian group drew a frown from Ultán. If they maintained their current bearing, they would be at the Giant's Causeway before midnight, which was worrisome. Ultán had arrived in the Land of the Humans via the Causeway's subterranean portal. At first puzzled by Balora's intent, Ultán's temperament quickly moved to concern. All Fomorians, including Balora, were barred from entering the portals.

"Who gave them Portal Passes?" Ultán answered his question with a mutter of, "Shite!" He mused that in the short time since he had known Clío, she had adversely influenced his language.

Caught between observing the Fomorian camps or travelling back to inform Lazarus of Balora's presence and apparent target destination, Ultán chose the latter. It would take him two days to get back to Belfast at a jog—hitching a ride would shorten the time. *Perhaps it's time I mastered the skill of driving a car.*

The blow to the back of Ultán's head took him by surprise. Before losing consciousness, he heard Balora's cruel taunt. "You're not as clever as you think, Son of Mil."

*** 

Ultán awoke to a throbbing headache and a sharp pain in his right hand. As his eyes became accustomed to the gloom, he looked down and swore. The Fomorians had severed his ring finger but had also neatly cauterised the stump.

"I wanted to send a believable message of your safety to Lazarus and Clíodhna," said Balora.

"You could have slipped the ring off."

"What would be the pleasure in that? A piece of jewellery is never sufficient evidence. It may have been stolen."

A glance around the cavern located his long coat and weapons belt on the stump of a broken stalagmite. It was as if they had been deliberately posed. He chuckled, and so did Balora. "I had to give you something to sustain hope and occupy your mind, in between torturing you."

"I won't tell you anything."

Balora's lips twisted into a crooked smile. "I know, but it will entertain my warriors for a few days. They are placing bets on how much skin they can peel before Lazarus and Clíodhna arrive to rescue what remains of you."

# CHAPTER 34

"Dancing to Balora's tune is not my favourite pastime." Sarcasm laced Lazarus' voice as he rolled Ultán's finger in the palm of his hand. A non-existent right hand clenched and unclenched in frustration. *If I travel to the Land of Immensity, can I break the links in Balora's plan?*

He snorted at the thought. If anything, events were likely to get more unpredictable and more dangerous should he return to his birthplace. He looked at Clíodhna, who sat motionless, unsettled by Balora's message. Ceara had already been dispatched to reconnoitre the area that Ultán's final message identified as Balora's new camp. *How can I protect Clíodhna in the Land of Immensity, if I cannot do it here?* Lazarus' rational pragmatism and invincibility were under attack.

"That's your concern, Lazarus. My safety." Clío smiled. It was rare for her to catch Lazarus with his thoughts unguarded. A flush of embarrassment made a brief appearance under Lazarus' sallow cheeks. It lasted no longer than a breath and was quickly followed by the iron doors guarding his mind slamming shut. Clío looked pointedly at his missing limb. "I am more anxious about your welfare. Your habit of losing arms is concerning."

"It was only twice," growled Lazarus.

"Surely, once is sufficient, even for a demigod." Clío inclined her head in the direction of Lazarus' missing arm. "For practical reasons, we have little choice other than to travel to Muria and a meeting with

Daghdha. Can we assume your brother will permit you access to the Cauldron?" Lazarus' grunt was anything but encouraging.

"However, our trip must be postponed," said Clío. "Our Watcher friend is an egotistic arsehole with an under-developed conscience, but his skills and network have been useful. We cannot leave him in Balora's grasp. The stubborn bastard will die before divulging information." Clío smirked. "When we rescue him, it will be a huge blow to his ego." The levity was short-lived. "We will meet Ceara at the Giant's Causeway and dispense retribution."

Lazarus smiled. Clíodhna sounded like Bráchthine.

\*\*\*

Ultán cursed and groaned. He could do little else since wet leather thongs bound him hand and foot to four stakes hammered into the cave's dirt floor. The thongs did not worry him. He was unlikely to survive long enough for them to dry out and cause more pain.

At dawn, Balora's warriors began a flaying game. Wagers were made as to who would cut the biggest strip of his skin. He wondered what they were betting. They had no gold. The Fomorians began with his torso, which Ultán thought was amateurish. When freed, his arms and legs would deliver his vengeance.

Unhappy at the small sizes of the pieces of flesh removed, the Fomorians swore in frustration. Ultán's genetic modifications caused his flesh to be tougher but less elastic. Hence, the Fomorians' efforts produced small fragments rather than strips. Ultán grimaced as talons carved deep, angry tracks in his torso.

Ultán wondered what Balora had planned. One thing was certain, her disinterest in his torture told him he was not the main attraction. *How many more blows can my ego take?* He coughed raggedly and spat a mouthful of blood at his current tormentor. In return, he received a swipe of talons across his chest. It was a fair trade for him being able to twist his limbs and stretch the bindings a little more.

\*\*\*

What do you see, Ceara?

*They're emerging from the cave and jogging east towards the cliffs. One hundred Fomorian chieftains and warriors flank Balora. There's a smaller number of Nemed, too. Balora in her natural form is an impressive lady. She dwarfs her warriors and will be a challenge to take down.* Ceara snorted. *That's not to say I can't.*

*Ultán?*

*I can't see him, Clío. They're keeping him hidden.* Ceara circled once again. *No, wait, I see him. He's obviously badly injured and held between two huge demons. They follow in Balora's footsteps.*

Fuming, Clío turned to Lazarus. "What is the bitseach planning and what part do we play in her drama?"

Lazarus stroked an imaginary goatee. "She has improved her skills in strategy and subterfuge. Also, she has one advantage over us. She is single-minded in completing her mission." He held Clío's gaze. "We should assume Ultán is dead. If he is not, Balora will sacrifice him the moment she needs her greatest distraction. Settle that in your mind and you can deal with what follows."

"She must get to the Land of Immensity if she wants to steal the Cauldron, but the portals are blocked to her. The runes and Portal Keepers will never let her pass. What is her plan, Lazarus?"

"It is something we have missed... or never considered."

\*\*\*

Balora's smile at a naked, bleeding Ultán drew a growl from him, and a fist to his belly from his guards. The evening sun glittered on the knife in her hand. Ultán recognised the weapon as his dagger by the blade's green sheen. "Bitch!" More blows were administered and would have bent him double, were he not held tightly.

"The cut I will make will be less painful than the many wounds my warriors have inflicted on you, but mine will be mortal. How quick or painful your death will be is a question only you can answer. It will, however, be a measure of the mercy shown to the many you killed with this blade." Near the cliff's edge, Balora grabbed Ultán's hand and held it high. She knew Clío and Lazarus were watching as she cut across Ultán's palm.

"No!" bellowed Lazarus.

"What do you offer as a trade for the antidote? Your bed? A shared throne? Wealth beyond comprehension?" Balora's voice was strong and as bitter as dandelion milk. "We had that and more once, but you tossed them aside for *her* and the humans. Make your offer or prepare to fight, my love." The Blade of Light was Lazarus' answer.

A single red tear rolled down Balora's cheek. "I must leave you." Only the sharp ears of her opponents heard Balora over the sound of crashing waves. "Choose. Chase me or search for the antidote and save him. No matter your choice, my warriors will fight to the last demon. Any delay will certainly bring his death closer. As the humans say, you are caught between the devil and the deep blue sea. In the circumstances, both are ironic.

"Protect your queen!" commanded Balora and then she turned, dashed to the cliff edge, and jumped. Moments later she laughed as she soared high. Silhouetted by the sunset sky, she flew eastward. Behind her she heard the swish of a dragon's tail as Ceara raced to catch her. There was no reason to conserve her reserves of energy and Balora expended them with a final burst of speed. All she needed was a few more seconds to complete her plan.

Ceara watched Balora hang in the evening sky for a moment before plunging into the sea like a diving bird. She barely made a splash as she broke the surface of the water and dove deep. Balora sacrificed herself to Current and he swept her to depths she had never experienced.

"Bitseach!" shouted Ceara. She had misjudged Balora's speed and misunderstood her intent.

\*\*\*

In the depths of the ocean, Balora resigned herself to death from the crushing pressures or drowning. *I have not finished with you.* The voice of Current was menacing and disturbing. Balora felt as if she wanted to scratch herself all over and needed a scorching hot shower.

Current mocked and battered her against innumerable reefs for his own pleasure. Finally, he took a sharp turn upwards and expelled Balora onto an idyllic white, sandy beach in the Land of Immensity. *Until the next time, my demon lover.*

Balora fell on her knees and puked. Her powerful legs barely held her weight as she stood and took stock of her surroundings. She smiled. The Sons of Mil city was directly north of her.

* * *

Ultán conceded Balora's judgment of him was entirely fitting. The Sons of Mil's weaponsmiths and scientists chose an evil poison and made it worse. They took the venom of the most poisonous viper known, guaranteeing an excruciatingly painful death. Not content, they also modified the toxin. Thus, while the victim was instantly immobilised, his agony extended for several hours. It was meant to send a clear message to the target and those who knew them.

There was an antidote. The small vial was sequestered in a pouch sewn into the lining of his overcoat. If the anti-venom was administered quickly, he would survive, although likely vital organs would be damaged. Still, Ultán knew he was past saving and was thankful. Living damaged and an object of pity held no attraction. He coughed raggedly and blood seeped from the side of his mouth.

The Watcher grimaced. One of the poison's side effects was massive internal and external bleeding. His flesh was already broken in many places, and he could feel his blood stream from a thousand open cuts. Not even what remained of his woad-painted sigils could help him. He shivered, juddered, and fought to stop the ever-more-violent tremors.

In the background, Ultán heard Clíodhna's rage as she called on Ceara and Lazarus to kill the Fomorians and Nemed. The smells of dragon breath and charred flesh tainted the salty coastal air. His eyes blinked painfully at the lightning flashes accompanying the Blade of Light. He would have enjoyed watching Lazarus wield it.

Above everything, Ultán wished he had met Clíodhna much earlier in his life. Perhaps she could have saved him from the Sons of Mil. Now, little more than a piece of bleeding meat, Ultán prayed to the Goddess for a weapon to end his life before those who fought to reach him succeeded. *I refuse to live as a cripple.*

Blackthorn spikes pierced Ultán's fingers as he scrabbled in the dirt next to him. *Was it there before?* He had not noticed it. He chose to believe the Goddess had heard and answered his supplication. "Thank you, Goddess." He smiled. That she answered gave Ultán hope of another life when he crossed the veil.

The broken branch was no more than a forearm's length, but the break was sharp, and his flesh was weak from torture and the poison. Ultán grunted at the effort needed to grasp and raise the wood. With his remaining strength, he plunged the blackthorn into his heart. It met with little resistance.

He smiled as Clío's face appeared above him and took the memory to the place the Goddess had prepared for him.

*** 

Ultán's death was unique among the Watchers because he had three who built a pyre in his memory and grieved for his passing.

"He did not deserve to die like this," said Clío as the flames rose high.

"Neither did those who died by his knife," said Lazarus.

Nothing more was said about Ultán.

# CHAPTER 35

*Land of Immensity*

The Mórrígan loved her raven form. The solitude it gave her allowed her to think without interruption, unless the Goddess was in a talkative mood. Soaring high above the lush terrain, she surveyed the four kingdoms and royal cities of the Land of Immensity. Each was unique in beauty and personality.

She knew Lazarus was more bitter than he would ever reveal regarding his forced abdication and the lack of support from his brothers and sisters. His public declarations that he had tired of the endless political bickering and backbiting among his Womb-Born siblings, and their sons and daughters, was a lie. Yet, as with all good deceptions, it had a kernel of truth which made it believable.

The Mórrígan had never agreed with her brother's flight to the Land of the Humans or his assertion that he had no other choice. Yet she was as guilty as her siblings. The High King's Throne was Lazarus' birthright given by Anúna. What had she done to support her brother, to defend him, or to go to war at his side to preserve his reign? *Nothing! I did nothing.* The Mórrígan's shame constantly reproved her.

Yet there was a glimmer of hope, albeit delivered by Balora. Lazarus must come to the Land of Immensity if he wanted to be made whole… and he did. Her plan to see Lazarus on the High King's throne, and reestablish Anúna's will, would restore order and purpose to the Womb-Born and Tuatha Dé. This time, she would go to war to accomplish her objective.

\*\*\*

The four domains reflected the temperament and personality of their Womb-Born king or queen. Even in his extended absence, Coria, the city of Lazarus, was a glowing symbol of compassion, enlightenment, and equity. The presence of Macha and Manannán's sister, Áine, lent the city a sense of mystery.

Meadhbh of the Friendly Thighs sat on the throne of Falia, a city that gave the warmest welcome to all. This included access to Meadhbh's bed and the lush, red triangle between her thighs. Her promiscuity, famed throughout the Lands of Immensity and the Humans, was matched only by her negotiation skills.

Meanwhile, laughter and fertility were the marks of the third city of Fania, whose king was Findbharr. For aeons, the fourth city, Muria, had been ruled by Áine, and in those days it reflected her joy for life, flair for art, and selflessness. Daghdha chose the city for his throne. That he selected Muria surprised and disappointed many, but the choice was his right as High King. Was it his revenge for having the crown foisted on him?

Muria quickly adapted to Daghdha's excesses, descending into a capital that encouraged and indulged the worst in men and women. Once known for its simple beauty and famed art and sculptures, Muria's architecture was tossed aside or crudely embellished. The Mórrígan looked down on Muria and saw a fat, gem-encrusted toad. The population of Áine's time had fled and were replaced by the depraved, the apathetic, and the indolent. Only the hills and meadows surrounding Muria retained their beauty because they were outside of Daghdha's purview.

Few, if any, knew where The Mórrígan rested. This was not unusual. The heroes, the fighting men and women of the Tuatha Dé, whether protagonist or antagonist, lived an itinerant existence, wandering the Land of Immensity, and occasionally the Land of the Humans, in search of causes, battles, and wars.

***

The Mórrígan transformed from a huge raven to a beautiful woman in the blink of an eye. Draped in a simple, sheer linen gown, held on her shoulders with emerald-studded gold pins, she stood at the entrance to Daghdha's palace. Her elegance drew a sharp contrast with the citadel's shabby demeanour and neglect.

The tasteless monstrosity made her grind her teeth. How could a member of the Tuatha Dé lack any concept of art, design, or style? In a land that encouraged and lauded artisans, how and why did such a demi-god exist? The Mórrígan muttered, "Perhaps, a better question is why do the rest of the Womb-Born and the nobility of the Tuatha Dé indulge Daghdha's excesses?"

Did they hope that, like puberty or adolescence, one day, a new, enlightened Daghdha would emerge from his obese chrysalis? "Some hope!" snorted The Mórrígan. A better probability was an uprising that ended in Daghdha's "death" and him spending several centuries in re-capithe to consider his lack of virtue. If her brother did not cede to her plan, it was a scenario she would encourage with a few well-placed whispers.

***

The Mórrígan approached Daghdha's chamber. The massive, gold doors were engraved with images of every conceivable sexual act and perversion. All featured Daghdha as the heroic lover with the perma-nently erect cock whose fame and exploits vied with Meadhbh's pit. The Mórrígan shook her head. "My sister may be unconventional, but she has class."

Quailing palace guards reluctantly moved to prevent The Mórrígan from entering the High King's private quarters. A wave of her hand and they were dispatched to their new island home. Another flourish and the doorway dissolved into a million glittering particles. The Mórrígan smiled as she walked through the shimmering, gold cloud.

"Welcome, sister."

Insincerity dripped from Daghdha's puffy lips. He chose neither to hide his irritation at the interruption of his perpetual pursuit of lust nor to ask the young woman riding his engorged manhood to dismount. Each time he thrust into her, she cried out and moaned with faux ecstasy. She played her part well and, like an orchestra's conductor, her orgasms were taken up and amplified by the sea of naked, writhing bodies surrounding the pair.

The Mórrígan inspected Daghdha's gross figure and the massive cock that mocked the concept of impotence. That she had once borne his child filled her with anger and self-loathing. His manhood was real, but the glamour was a mockery of his true form. *Why, brother?*

"Remove the sluts! Or I will... permanently."

Only the dim-witted did not instantly obey the Queen of Desolation. Before a reluctant Daghdha could give the order, the *striapacha*—whores—stampeded towards the chamber's remaining exits. Though not before grabbing their pouches of gold—business is business. Most left their clothes behind in their haste. It was a small pile. Raiment was optional in Daghdha's palace and city.

The Mórrígan shook her head. "Put some clothes on. We need to speak, and I do not wish for *any* distractions."

Daghdha laughed dismissively. The action made his belly quiver obscenely. "I am High King. No one can tell me what to do in my city."

A curved sacrificial dagger appeared in The Mórrígan's hand. "Your other option is that I slice that monstrosity off with this blade. Do you wish to pay the Cauldron's toll and experience the pains of regrowth?" The Mórrígan smiled wickedly, causing Daghdha to reconsider his bravado. The knife's hilt was polished blackthorn with an emerald pommel, but its blade was steel made by humans.

"We will have a discussion without distractions, or I will feed your meat to the wolfhounds, and you will be incapable of making any further penetrations... ever." The look in The Mórrígan's jade eyes confirmed his sister had no sense of humour and would execute her threat.

Likely with a great amount of pleasure. Daghdha dipped his head, and her dagger disappeared. The lines of her gown were not interrupted, and he wondered salaciously where she had sheathed the blade.

"Where is the Cauldron, Daghdha?"

"Safe," responded Daghdha. His expression held an insufferable "I know something you don't" smile. "*My* artefact is marvellous and can be any size from a thimble to the size of this palace. Hiding the relic is neither an arduous nor complicated task. Furthermore, it is visible only in times when its powers are required—and those tend to be private occasions. It was last used several millennia ago. For Nuadha, I believe."

"Do not ever think the Cauldron is *your* property. Behave or I will remove it from your oversight… forever," said The Mórrígan. "Our brother will arrive within the week. He needs to use the Cauldron."

Daghdha ignored his sister's threat but knew it held a promise. "He's hurt again! What happened? My brother hates the Land of Immensity."

"He does not," retorted The Mórrígan. "Rather than stand by him, we, his brothers and sisters, let him down. We gave him no choice other than to abdicate. Now, Lazarus simply prefers the life he has built with his ward Clíodhna and the humans. Who could blame him?"

"Lazarus? Who is Lazarus?"

"It is the name our brother has adopted and prefers."

Daghdha shrugged. "I don't care what he calls himself. It's his business." He looked askance at The Mórrígan. "Why are you here, sister? I do not recall you visiting Muria since my coronation and it's rare for the famed Queen of Desolation to be anyone's messenger, even if it is her *loving* brother." The wink was exaggerated and accompanied by a leer. All that was missing was drool flowing down Daghdha's chin. It was followed by a howl of pain when The Mórrígan grasped his long, red hair and jerked his head back. He gasped for air and his Adam's apple strained for release from his neck flesh. Bottomless obsidian eyes stared into Daghdha's.

Yet this was not why Daghdha cried out. The dagger that reappeared in The Mórrígan's right hand traced a slow and bloody path from under Daghdha's balls to his glans. The movement ended with a probing twist of the weapon's point and an agonising cut inside his peehole. "It's little more than a paper cut, but they can be irritating and painful. The next time I will not be so merciful," snarled The Mórrígan.

"Bitseach!"

\*\*\*

Later, brother and sister faced each other over a table laden with food and wine. Only the Goddess had no need of nourishment. The atmosphere had marginally improved.

"I am not a High King and was never meant to be one. You, and my other brothers and sisters, showed how little you valued the throne by forcing it upon me." Daghdha spread his arms wide and bowed. "I play an honest, if not a modest, fool to mock my siblings' apathy and cowardice." He laughed, glancing down at himself. "Do you think this corruption is the temple of a just High King?"

Daghdha observed The Mórrígan with amber eyes that showed no trace of his licentiousness. For a moment, she saw the man she had once loved. "He was the first of us, Mórrígan. He is our father and brother. Anúna bore him to rule over us, not to desert us."

"Pretty words, brother, which would sound genuine if *we* had not deserted him first. We forced him to find a new life… and he did. Now we bellyache that he deserted us and want him to rescue us. I was wrong not to support my brother and am willing to beg him to return. Are you? Are my siblings?"

No one likes being scolded, and Daghdha deftly avoided accepting responsibility. "The Land of Immensity is incomplete and unstable without Nuadha or Lazarus. After his injury, the Tuatha Dé would have lost the war with the Fomorians, if the dragons had not saved our skins. Today, the dragons are without a queen and are divided among themselves.

"If the war were fought today, who would save us? Whose side would the serpents take? Whose side would Lazarus choose? No matter which. Undoubtedly, we would experience a different and unpleasant outcome. I doubt the Goddess would intercede on our behalf. We have squandered any goodwill she may have had for us."

The Mórrígan was shocked. Daghdha had not spoken as eloquently and perceptively in a thousand years. Still, something in Daghdha's demeanour raised the fine hairs on The Mórrígan's nape, and her fingers moved closer to her dagger's sheath. "What are you not telling me, brother?"

"I have grown to like the throne of the High King. I can throw off this glamour of foolishness and debauchery as easily as I donned it. I could be a great High King if I wish. Who is better qualified than me?"

"That is not an option, Daghdha. Just as Anúna assigned Lazarus' role, so your nature was set for millennia before you ascended the throne. You cannot and will not change and need to be protected from yourself," said The Mórrígan.

"I will fight." Daghdha's jaw jutted defiantly.

"Then you will die the final death of no return." Daghdha's newfound backbone impressed The Mórrígan, but it was too late.

"Only a dragon can do that, and I have my serpent guards to protect me."

"Your guards can and will be withdrawn," said The Mórrígan. Daghdha's eyes opened wide at the statement. There was no hint his sister could not carry out her threat.

"What are *you* not telling *me*, sister?"

✳✳✳

"The Fomorian queen, Balora, engineered Lazarus' need for the Cauldron," said The Mórrígan.

"By the Anúna's tits! Why did the bitseach wait so long for revenge?"

"Revenge has little to do with Balora's machinations. She plans to steal the Cauldron."

"Never!" shouted Daghdha.

The Mórrígan raised an eyebrow. "Surely this cannot be a total surprise. Your informant from the Sons of Mil must have reported her intention to you?" The Mórrígan did not shrink from Daghdha's annoyance at her knowledge of his secretive dealings with the Sons of Mil. Yet he knew his day had worsened. Before he could deflect, The Mórrígan tossed another rock.

"Speaking of the Sons of Mil, why have you given sanctuary to our ancient enemy? Did the Council of the Womb-Born agree to this? Only a full Council can ratify such an agreement. I certainly did not receive my invitation." The Mórrígan's thunderous voice held real menace and Daghdha suddenly felt insecure in his claims to the High King's throne. The power of the Tuatha Dé's unholy Trinity struck fear into the hearts of all.

"As to the first question. Yes, he did report to me, but a single source of information can never be trusted." Daghdha rubbed one of his chins. "As to the second and third, that is the business of the High King. You have no right to know."

"I have every right to know, as do our brothers and sisters."

A rasp of exhaled breath and the reappearance of The Mórrígan's blade, this time at his throat, caused Daghdha to reconsider his position. Dinner had gone downhill. "I no longer consider the Sons of Mil as our enemy. The Tuatha Dé's treaty with them has held for millennia. Suffice it to say that the Sons of Mil provide a buffer and additional layer of protection." Belatedly, Daghdha tried to justify a decision that looked increasingly imprudent. "Their community is a small remnant of the original race. They are not a threat to us."

The Mórrígan pounced. "If they are that small, then they are no use to us either as a buffer or protection. They would be quickly overrun."

Daghdha rubbed sweat from his brow and changed the conversation. "If you insist, we can put it to a vote at the next Council meeting." Daghdha laughed. "If you think our siblings care, you are mistaken."

The Mórrígan's eyes glittered. "In the past, we befriended and welcomed a small number of Fomorians into our midst. That caused a war. Trust and mercy are misplaced virtues in the hands of the Tuatha Dé." The Mórrígan paused. Watching her adjust her posture reminded Daghdha of a scorpion getting ready to strike.

"Have the Sons of Mil's Elders informed you of the death of your informant?" Daghdha's mien transformed to one of uncertainty. Past decisions were returning to haunt him. "Balora tortured and killed Ultán in the Humans' land. How did he and they get passes to the portals, brother?" Daghdha blanched. The Mórrígan rubbed her chin, and her brow knitted as if in deep thought. "I know how. *You* gave the Sons of Mil passes for their assassins. *Your* informant, Ultán, had Lazarus as his target. Connect the dots, brother; you sanctioned the murder of one of the Womb-Born. Even my apathetic siblings will recognise that as treason."

"No," gasped Daghdha. In his head, he heard the squawking of chickens coming home to roost.

"The Sons of Mil gave Portal Passes to the Fomorians. Do you know how many?" asked The Mórrígan.

"How could I know?" Daghdha visibly shrank under The Mórrígan's interrogation. He prayed she was not in the mood to judge *and* sentence him.

"*You* are the High King. It is *your* job to know and to not make stupid decisions," snapped The Mórrígan. "Did your informant tell you a dragon will accompany Lazarus?"

"No, but why is that unusual? Many of us have serpent bodyguards."

The Mórrígan smiled at the bewildered look on Daghdha's face and struck again. "She is known as Clíodhna and is the daughter of Bráchthine. You will recall Lazarus was very fond of the queen. Clíodhna is the heir to the Dragon Throne and is Lazarus' ward. She is *very* protective of him." The Mórrígan's eyes glittered menacingly.

Daghdha's brow threatened to form a permanent furrow. He inhaled and exhaled to slow his pulse. He had a basket full of unexpected and unwanted problems to negotiate. "That will throw a spanner into the engine of the Progressives and that bastard who is the Isle of Scáth's guardian. Ciarán calls himself King of the Dragons, although it is likely that is the Lady Scáthach's and her daughter's plan. There is no way he has the brains to plot and execute a strategy to gain the Throne."

The High King regarded his sister and recalled her many titles, each of which represented facets of her character. The Queen of Whispers and Shadows had a deserved reputation for discerning weaknesses in others. "Ciarán Dubh remains a formidable dragon. He will be hard to defeat, and Clíodhna must beat him to rule."

It was the opening The Mórrígan awaited. "He is a brawler, has not fought a serious rival in centuries, and has grown fat and comfortable. *She* is battle-tested, and you would be ill-advised to add to your list of imprudent choices by wagering against her in *any* circumstance."

Daghdha looked at The Mórrígan. "Lazarus and an alliance with the Dragons' Queen-in-Waiting with a unified serpents' army would be a formidable force. Does Lazarus desire my throne?" Sweat beaded the High King's brow. The crown began to look like a millstone around his neck.

The Mórrígan smiled at Daghdha's discomfort. "Would that be such a bad thing, brother?"

There was no answer. Daghdha's mind had inevitably meandered back to considering the diverse talents of those waiting to serve his many vices. He knew of and had no qualms about their mercenary goals. Theirs was an honest and profitable business. The decent and the virtuous, male or female, had long fled Muria and he doubted there was a virgin to deflower in the kingdom. An imaginary rumble in his belly prompted Daghdha to reach out and grasp a fat turkey leg from the table.

The Mórrígan looked at Daghdha and shook her head. The gaze held sympathy for the role thrust upon her brother. It also held disgust at the lifestyle in which he chose to wallow like a pig. Would Daghdha have turned out different with Lazarus as High King? She shrugged. Probably not. Anúna made Daghdha subject to his nature, not it to him. Yet, in a less prominent role, he may cause less disruption.

# CHAPTER 36

Balora's feet sank into the beach's pristine, white sand. She blinked rapidly as her eyes adjusted to a cloudless, blue sky and the strong sunlight reflecting off the shingle. The queen paused to get her bearings before jogging northwards through lush green meadows and copses of hard- and softwoods. It was the perfect way to acclimatise to a life beyond the sea.

Moments of appreciation of the landscape's beauty were interspersed with curses aimed at Lazarus and the Tuatha Dé for her people's banishment to the depths. "Lazarus would have shown more mercy had he slaughtered the Fomorians to the last man, woman, and child," growled Balora.

Yet would she have done anything different had the Fomorians been victorious, and she reigned as High Queen? Balora's philosophy stated the victorious cannot show compassion. *With my foot on an opponent's neck, crushing his throat and snapping his spine are the only logical courses of action.* Nonetheless, Balora's emotions regarding Lazarus belied her pragmatic position. It was a weakness she could not, and perhaps did not want to, expunge.

The Fomorian queen's immediate destination was the Sons of Mil city to gather information and bribe her way to Muria. Her long, demon stride quickly covered the distance and soon she spotted the city. The description flattered the settlement, which shimmered on the horizon.

In the blink of an eye, Balora changed to her human form. She heaved a sigh of appreciation and relief at the ease of her transformation. Unlike the Land of the Humans, the sentient magic of the Land of Immensity lent its support to the use of all gifts and powers, irrespective of who wielded them.

Balora's less obvious abilities, which centred around her physique, including a chameleon-like ability to camouflage herself and basic mind-reading, received a welcome boost. In human form, however, her dark skin tone was immutable, setting her starkly apart from the Sons of Mil and other travellers on the broad avenue. To avoid becoming the subject of gossip and curiosity, she stole a cloak. Pulling its hood over her head, Balora quickened her pace.

Halting within a demon's stone throw of the city walls, Balora threw back her hood and opened her mouth to bellow a greeting to the occupants of the guard posts. Observing a quartet of men exit a smaller entrance adjacent to the main gateway, she stopped. Balora chuckled at the rapidity with which the heavy door slammed shut behind the delegation. *I'm only one Fomorian. How much trouble do they anticipate?* Her answer came quickly.

Like a wolf's, Balora's sensitive, pointed ears constantly rotated, even in her human form. She discerned the slap of boots with hobnailed soles on the stone floors of the ramparts and guard towers. It was followed by the scrape of wood on gravel, the squeal of skeins, and the slap of bolts settling into the ballistae's receiving grooves. *It's odd how the demigods and denizens of the Land of Immensity prefer primitive weapons. Humans are much more advanced in mass destruction.* She took several steps forward.

In their natural form, the Sons of Mil's similarity with modern-day humans was unmistakable. Nonetheless, Balora considered evolution had endowed humanity with a much more refined and pleasing countenance, albeit at the cost of diminished height and muscle. *Without a glamour, the Sons of Mil are unsightly.* It never dawned on Balora that her natural form might be considered unattractive, let alone frightening.

Balora glimpsed the men's heavily muscled torsos under loose, flowing robes as the delegation closed to within ten paces. Their footfalls were heavy. They did not walk; rather they stamped the dirt, crushing grass and wildflowers underfoot. On the surface, neither party carried weapons nor wore armour, although Fomorians always had their talons, teeth, and thick, armoured hides. If the Sons of Mil did not have concealed blades, Balora would be disappointed… and insulted.

The group's spokesman smiled and bowed. His mien radiated an assumed superiority. "You are welcome, if unexpected, Queen Balora. We have Watchers at each of the portals, day and night, but they appear to have missed your arrival. Their Commander will debrief them this evening when they return to their quarters." Balora could have felt compassion for the Watchers who would likely lose their rank. She did not. *Is it my fault these morons jump to incorrect conclusions?*

Balora said nothing, enjoying the man's alarm at the apparent security breach. She was, however, curious why the Sons of Mil knew her name and were monitoring the portals and Fomorians in particular. Her race was not banned from the Land of Immensity. Many among the Tuatha Dé had pre-war family connections and mixed-race offspring, dating back hundreds of generations. *Another example of the Tuatha Dé's insipid diplomacy. Enemies should be destroyed.*

Until her recent encounter with Lazarus, Balora could have walked the streets of any Tuatha Dé city. At the worst, she would be greeted by suspicious looks or offers to fuck. *What are the Sons of Mil hiding?* Balora's perfectly white teeth flashed. She loved having an edge, other than her body.

"Perhaps you would accompany us," said the spokesman. "This evening, the High Council will honour our Fomorian visitors and a few invited guests at a private dinner." Balora's ears twitched. *So, I'm not the only Fomorian.* "We will of course be honoured to have a Queen of Fomoria as our guest of honour. Rooms appropriate to your status are being prepared as we speak."

Smiling regally, Balora stretched out a hand. "Thank you. Your hospitality is appreciated." Balora was a stunning woman and knew it. From the looks on her welcome party's faces, it was not difficult to discern their thoughts. Underneath their accommodating demeanour was brutal lust. Like the Fomorians, the Sons of Mil society was patriarchal and she was a woman. Their body language screamed she was inferior and little better than chattel.

Balora knew at the conclusion of the evening's formalities, rank would dictate who, with or without her consent, bedded her first. As with Fomorian males of a similar rank, they perceived her first as a female to be used for their entertainment. Her title of queen came a distant second. All planned to take their turn or maybe they proposed to use her together. The only question to be answered was did they intend to slit her throat or detain her for future abuse?

She shook her head. *Amateurs!* These cretins had no idea of what an ambitious woman in Fomorian society had to overcome to become as powerful as she. Furthermore, they plainly had never seen a Fomorian queen in her natural form, otherwise they would have been much more circumspect in their lascivious ambitions.

That her visit appeared to be anticipated gave Balora pause. *Am I reading too much into the spokesman's words?* Who could have sent a message to the Sons of Mil? The most likely suspect was Ultán. He, likely, reported regularly to his Commander. The Mórrígan, and her whisperings, was another candidate. She sensed a chuckle in the air. A sudden cool breeze sent a chill up Balora's spine. The dagger strapped to her inner thigh gave her comfort. *I must be extra vigilant.*

From her hosts' obsequiousness, it was clear she would be the highest-ranking Fomorian at dinner. She wondered, briefly, who the other Fomorian guest was. She chuckled, imagining the look on his face when they sat down for dinner. Unless he was a complete fool, he would know he was a dead man.

***

Balora smiled with deep satisfaction at the looks of surprise and anxiety on the faces of the Fomorian guest, Scáthach, and her daughter when she entered the dining room. For her part she maintained a disinterested mien. She had three goals: to mine for information, to secure guides to Muria, and to cause mischief. She was dressed in a sheer Greek chiton pinned at her shoulders with ruby-headed pins that complemented her eyes. The gown left nothing to the imagination and her prominent nipples signalled an aggressive evening.

Twelve were seated around the table on elaborately carved wooden chairs. Balora noted the absence of the Sons of Mil's king—a man recognised for his political acumen—from the dinner. *He is a wise man.* Balora took his place at the head of the table. Apart from the Commander of the Watchers, who sat on her immediate left, the other guests were a miserable bunch of politicians and witches. The Leader of the Sons of Mil's Council sat opposite the Commander. From their body language it was obvious the men could barely tolerate each other, and that the Leader had leverage over the Commander.

The Commander of the Watchers' intense eyes rarely left Balora, and not because of her sexual allure. He obviously did not trust her and saw no reason to hide this. For that reason, Balora liked him and whispered in his ear, "I think you will find tonight's conversation highly entertaining and discover my loyalty to Fomoria is transactional."

Balora raised her voice, ensuring all present would hear her clearly, and dipped her head towards the other Fomorian. "If I was your Leader, I would be insulted at the presence of this low-level prince. He holds no power or influence. I doubt he has any substantial connections to the Fomorian hierarchy. He certainly has no authority to negotiate." She felt rather than saw the scowl on the Leader's face and laughed at the helpless fury of the Fomorian prince.

Placing her lips close to the Commander's ear, Balora murmured, "I require two guides to escort me to Muria. Can I trust you to deliver them to my room after the dinner?" She smiled at his nod. "Good. I suggest you grab a few bottles of wine and enjoy the theatre." She frowned briefly and inhaled. "This may arise in the conversation, but it is better that you should know first. Ultán is dead. He was on a spying mission for Clíodhna and Nuadha when my warriors intercepted him. He died a brave man and, at his funeral pyre, had friends to celebrate his life." The Commander's jaw stiffened, and he dipped his head.

Midway down the table and seated opposite each other were Scáthach and her daughter. Balora had never met the women before, but recognised them by dress, reputation, and in Uathach's case by her strange eyes. As she examined the duo, Balora felt a wave of dark magic reach out to her and immediately strengthened her defences.

Ruby eyes bored into the witches. "Dark magic is well known to my race and practiced by hundreds, if not thousands, of generations of Fomorians—*especially* the queens. Discontinue its use at this table. It is rude to your host." Balora paused. "Furthermore, your ability is so obvious and primitive you embarrass me with its use." Polished, black nails extended to finger-length talons and tapped the table. "Continue and I will skin you alive and eat your flesh as my entrée."

Scáthach refused to rise to Balora's bait. Her face switched instantly from fury to a mask of disinterest. She smiled slightly and inclined her head in Balora's direction. The queen laughed raucously at Scáthach's response and again at the bemused faces of the other guests. Garnet eyes stared at Uathach. *One day I will remove your eyes, abomination.* Balora braced herself in expectation of a challenge. Nothing happened. Scáthach whispered in her daughter's ear but was answered by a shake of her head. *Who is in charge? The mother or the daughter?*

Silence descended but was quickly replaced by the politicians reverting to habit. They ignored the problem in their midst and continued as if nothing had changed. Thus, as the dinner progressed, the Sons of Mil hierarchy feted Balora like royalty. Indeed, the snivelling obsequiousness of the council members turned Balora's stomach. Before she threw up, Balora changed the conversation's topic. "When does the war begin?"

It was asked in Balora's throatily best "I'm just a dumb female with big breasts" persona and accompanied by the release of several sprays of pheromones. In the small chamber, it was a potent catalyst.

Scáthach's black eyes sent furious messages to the Sons of Mil's Council members. Whether due to the alcohol or the pheromones, all but the Commander ignored Scáthach's warnings and stared infatuated at the dark beauty in their midst. The Watchers' Commander brought his hand to his mouth to hide the broad grin at Balora's audacity, and the Fomorian prince groaned, "No," before succumbing to Balora's chemical assault.

Balora needed to know the Fomorian council's plans, and these fools would tell her. The pheromone-impaired council members and Fomorian competed to gain Balora's favour. Through signals, hints, and boasts they gave Balora the information she wanted. The war would be triggered in the chaos following the defeat of Clíodhna by her brother. As she drew the intelligence from her audience, Balora appeared calm, bewitching, and accommodating.

Underneath the façade she seethed. The Fomorian High Council had excluded her from the planning of a major, although in her judgment, foolish, confrontation with the Tuatha Dé. Worse, according to the Fomorian Council, her goal to steal the Cauldron was no more than a distraction to deflect curious minds, including the Sons of Mil, and to keep her out of the way. *Why is it only me who recognises the Cauldron is a weapon of immense power?* As her hosts prattled on about cooperation and lust for long-lost strength, Balora's mind turned to thoughts of personal gain… and violence.

Suddenly, Balora's demeanour became awful. "Your designs and machinations are doomed to fail," she announced. "King Nuadha, or Lazarus as he is now known, will soon arrive in Muria to meet with his brother, Daghdha. Indeed, he may already be there." Scáthach and the Leader's sharp inhalations brought a smile to Balora's lips.

"I think I can say with some confidence that The Mórrígan

accompanies her brother—and she is not a friend of the Sons of Mil…or you, my lady." Balora gazed directly at Scáthach. "Lazarus is accompanied by his ward—a female dragon." The Leader's eyes rolled but Scáthach's burned like coal. "I agree a serpent accompanying a Womb-Born is not uncommon, unless she is Clíodhna, the Queen-in-Waiting of the Dragons. Her coronation will be in Muria, less than a day's march from this city." Balora smiled wickedly at Scáthach. "She will defeat her brother and your dupe in the Arena. I have seen Clíodhna fight, my lady. Believe me, your champion is well out-matched."

Balora observed the tremble in the Leader's hands and addressed him. "Even someone as slow-witted as you should grasp the implications of that event. Every dragon clann will attend the ceremony." Eyes glittering as she warmed to her topic, Balora held the Leader's gaze. "*You* sent an assassin to murder the Dragons' Queen-in-Waiting and the former High King of the Tuatha Dé. He failed. It was an impossible mission and only served to accelerate the march to Clíodhna's coronation.

"In my opinion, it is the toss of a coin as to who will destroy the Sons of Mil—The Tuatha Dé, the Dragons, or the Fomorians. Your lust for personal gain and power has ensured the extinction of your race. The Fomorians, because of their numbers, might survive a second battle with the Tuatha Dé. However, with the dragons united and looking for vengeance for the attempted assassination of their new queen, I think your confidence in your new allies is wishful thinking.

"You should have aligned with those who have the power and resources to ensure the Sons of Mil flourished. Instead, you betrayed your people to the Fomorians for personal gain." She pointed to the Fomorian prince. "Ask him how Fomorians treat their allies, or do you dare? Ask him about the Nemed. If you are lucky, my compatriots may simply kill you, but I think not. Slavery and painful deaths are in your future."

The Leader of the Council rose to protest. He looked at the Watchers' Commander, who feigned drunkenness and slumped back into his chair. "One thing is certain," said Balora. "From my experience as the partner of Lazarus, the Tuatha Dé will not take the betrayal of those to whom they gave sanctuary lightly. The Womb-Born and The Mórrígan are not known for being merciful to those who deceive them."

Losing any pretence of composure, the Leader shouted, "Lies! Bluff and lies. The Tuatha Dé and the dragons know nothing."

At that moment, the shadow on the tapestries moved and The Mórrígan stepped into the room.

"I would not be so sure of that," said The Mórrígan. She nodded to Balora and disappeared, leaving her laughter hanging in the air.

"I have long admired the Tuatha Dé's wonderfully timed entrances," said Balora. She inclined her head to the Commander, who dipped his head and slipped from the room. "I must go, but I leave you with this message and vision of things to come."

In a moment, Balora transformed into her natural state. The chandelier above the table was swept away and the table crashed to the floor under her weight when she jumped onto it. With a swipe of her talons, the Fomorian prince's head flew across the room. Gushing blood drenched the remaining guests.

# CHAPTER 37

*The Island of Dragons*

Ceara dumped Clío unceremoniously on her back, forcing the breath violently from her lungs. It was accompanied by an explosive grunt. This was not the first time the incident had happened that morning, or in the previous five days. Once again Clío was subjected to howls of laughter from Ceara and her dragon bodyguards.

"I am your queen," said Clío. She tried for anger, but the emotion refused to comply, forcing her to make do with a pout.

"I will repeat what my father once said to you. In this arena, we are equals." Ceara grinned mischievously. "And unless you drop pounds of that fat belly you drag along the dirt, you never will be queen."

"Bitseach!" shouted Clío. The dirt trembled as powerful legs stomped towards Ceara.

"Fighting weak Nemed and Fomorians is very different from fighting a serpent. Your brother's reputation is well-known. He is an able and dirty fighter and will not be a pushover. Furthermore, he *wants* the throne. *Do you?*" Ceara frowned and pointed to Clío's guards. "Our job is to ensure you are ready for the contest. Fight us like you mean it. Show us you want the Dragon Throne."

Ceara's words stalled Clío's momentum. *Do I want to be Queen of the Dragons?* The interruption allowed the shield-maiden to step aside, avoid the clumsy attack, and retaliate. A swipe of Ceara's tail and follow-up bash of her massive head against Clío's bowled her over and onto her back. She felt the weight of Ceara on her chest and hot sulphurous breath as her throat was trapped in the vice-like grip of Ceara's teeth.

"Ouch!" exclaimed Clío. "That hurts." Her lip trembled.

"*You are dead, bitseach!* You have no right to complain and no throne to ascend," said Ceara. Rolling off Clío's belly, she stormed away from the training circle. There were no hoots of laughter from the other dragons, only anxious looks.

Clío walked over to Aodh and Lazarus. Oblivious to all, they were in a furious argument.

\*\*\*

"What I see, Lazarus, is an enchanting, coddled young woman who, I am happy to say, is a good friend to my daughter. *But* she has no heart for this fight and exhibits no desire to be Queen of the Dragons. Bráchthine would be furious and disappointed… *in you.* You kept Clíodhna in the dark about her heritage and apart from her people far too long. I fear it may be too late for her."

"She will be ready when she is needed." Lazarus' hackles rose.

Aodh observed a hint of his golden aura permeating his glamour. *He is angry at himself and afraid for her.*

"Clíodhna is battle-ready. She fought the Fomorians and the Nemed in Belfast," retorted Lazarus.

"She fought bravely for her human friends, Lazarus, not a throne. And not for the responsibility of ruling the most powerful race of any known world. In the Land of the Humans, Clíodhna had the former High King of the Tuatha Dé, The Mórrígan, and my daughter to back her up. *Was she ever in mortal danger?*" Aodh sighed. He regretted the harshness of his tone, especially with one he considered closer than a brother, but he had a duty to the dragons.

"What are you saying, Aodh?"

"We are a cycle of the moon away from when Clíodhna must fight, possibly to the death, in the Arena. No one can stand with her. Are you willing to see her die? Because that is a real prospect. Her brother is not the best warrior among the dragons but, in my estimation, he is superior to Clíodhna." Aodh bristled with anger and the temperature of the air around the duo rose. "Clíodhna will die, and it will be your fault. There will be a civil war among the serpents. Bráchthine's legacy will turn to dust. How will you face her after her long sleep? If she is wise, she may choose never to awaken."

Aodh's demeanour softened. "My advice to an old friend is return to the Land of the Humans. Clíodhna and you can be happy there. There will be other battles for you to fight, and Clíodhna will stand at your side." Aodh cleared his throat. "I am not blind to my daughter's feelings for Clíodhna and have told Ceara she has my blessing to accompany Clíodhna, if she wishes."

"No. Clíodhna has a destiny to fulfil," said Lazarus.

"Again, are you willing to watch her die for that?" asked Aodh. Both men fell silent.

*** 

"With respect, the decision is neither Lazarus' nor yours to make, Aodh," said Clío. Both men jumped at the interruption.

Aodh blushed and bowed deeply. "I apologise, my queen." Clío's eyebrow lifted, and he smiled. "No matter my words or the outcome of the challenge, you will always be Bráchthine's daughter and my queen. Sadly, politics rarely reflects reality. The just do not always win."

"I wish to speak with my brother," said Clío. "Alone, with no interference from Scáthach… or yourselves. You, Neasán, and Lazarus are the most powerful men in several worlds. Make it happen." With that, Clío turned about and walked briskly after Ceara's retreating figure.

"At times like this, she reminds me of Bráchthine," said Aodh. "How do we make this meeting happen and where?"

"Perhaps it would be better for Clíodhna to renounce her claim to the Dragon Throne," said Neasán. "I doubt Scáthach's power is as formidable as ours. We can manage Ciarán's ascent or replace him with a more suitable candidate. Another female could be found." Neasán looked at Aodh. "Ceara would be the perfect choice."

"Never!" exclaimed Aodh.

"Weasel politician," said Lazarus. "Bráchthine never trusted you unreservedly and I see why." He turned and strode away.

\*\*\*

"I like Clíodhna, Lazarus, and can tilt the duel in her favour. Just say the word," said The Mórrígan. "Justice will be served. Bráchthine's legacy will be preserved, the dragons will avoid a civil war, and the Tuatha Dé will continue to have the protection of their strongest ally. Everyone wins."

Lazarus smiled at his sister's appearance but shook his head. "Thanks, but no, sister. If I have learned anything, it is that secrets are always uncovered, and good intentions are brittle. Whether she knew about it or not, when the cheating is uncovered, it will destroy Clío and tarnish anything she has accomplished. Your offer is well meant but it would be the wrong move."

"If only Scáthach and her daughter or Neasán had your principles, Lazarus." The Mórrígan frowned and then changed the subject. "At a dinner in the Sons of Mil city, I overheard Balora call Uathach an abomination and threaten to remove her eyes. I may have judged that woman too harshly. It would be a pity to kill her."

Lazarus' eyes reflected his disbelief. "I have complete trust in your ability to spike Scáthach's intrigues. As for Balora, she is a cunning adversary and not easy to catch, let alone kill. I assume she intends to travel to Muria."

The Mórrígan dipped her head but could not resist having the final word. "The Balora 'problem' would vanish if you bedded her. It is not much of a sacrifice to ask and would reduce the number of our enemies. I doubt it would be an unpleasant mission."

"Bitseach!"

"I am serious, Lazarus. You loved her once and she is a beautiful woman. It may be many centuries before Bráchthine decides whether to take a mortal form again and only the Goddess knows what memories she will retain. The Fomorians are not as long-lived as the dragons or Tuatha Dé. In all likelihood, Balora will be long dead before Bráchthine's resurrection. I highly doubt Bráchthine expects you to be celibate in her absence. Obviously, she was not. Ciarán is the evidence of that."

"Bitseach." Lazarus' riposte was in a much softer tone and The Mórrígan smiled.

\*\*\*

"Do you think I'm fat?" asked Clío. She lifted her head from Ceara's chest, leaving strands of blonde hair stuck to Ceara's breast, which was wet from sweat and tears. Clío looked around their bedroom and wondered if it was soundproofed. From the wreckage, it looked as if a fiery tornado had passed through. They had changed forms multiple times, thankfully synchronously. The sex had been passionate and violent, leaving them satisfied and covered in bruises and scratches.

Ceara closed her eyes, deliberately delaying her answer in the expectation and hope of Clío's response. She smiled as she felt Clío squeeze her breasts and a tongue as rough as a kitten's arouse her nipples. She held back a moan as Clío's fingers traced a path to her smooth, hairless mound but could not prevent her back from arching. She felt her pit opened. Her engorged lips were already well lubricated, as was the slippery, wet pearl captured within their folds. She felt its hood drawn back and Clío's mouth and tongue imprison it. Her back arched and lifted off the bed. "Enough!" she cried out without meaning it.

"That does not get you out of answering my question, but it does demand reciprocation," said Clío.

Ceara patted Clío's belly and chuckled. "Of course you're not fat, my love. I needed to get you mad."

"I didn't want to hurt you."

"That's the problem, Clío. I think you should have a new trainer."

Clío shook her head and kissed Ceara. "That is not an option. This is my problem to resolve... and I will." Clío grasped Ceara's hand and guided it over her belly to her pit. "Now, about your reciprocation."

"One thing, my love, before we forget about unimportant things like thrones and battle tactics. You are predictable."

"What!"

"I knew exactly how you would react when I didn't answer your question. I really enjoyed the attention, but I saw it coming. Just as I did your moves in training. You need to mix up your tactics on the battle-field. Add a touch of surprise." Ceara laughed. "Just like this." Clío eyes opened wide as she was brusquely rolled onto her belly, her arse cheeks were pulled open, and Ceara's tongue descended.

"*Oh fuck! Oh fuck!*" cried Clío. It was a lesson forever imprinted on her mind.

# CHAPTER 38

Clío looked around the cave and whispered, "Thank you," to Aodh and Lazarus. Curiously, Neasán had declined the invitation to accompany them. What could be a better meeting place than the home in which Ciarán and she were born? The ambience wrapped itself around Clío like a blanket. Yet she twisted her fingers, anxious and fearful about how her first contact and conversation with her brother would go.

"Help," she murmured.

*No matter what tradition these fools wish you to partake in, Clíodhna, remember two things. You are the daughter of Bráchthine and the true Queen of the Dragons. Also know whatever decision you make, you do it with my blessing. Above everything, you are my joy.*

"Thank you, Ma."

A deep breath filled Clío's lungs with the essence of Bráchthine's presence. She closed her eyes to imagine being wrapped in Bráchthine's long tail and feeling and hearing her great heart beating. A memory of suckling on her ma's nipple made a tear run down her cheek. She wondered if she would ever rest in her mother's arms.

A scuffling sound and a curse forced Clío from her memories. Framed by the cave's entrance, a tall man rubbed his forehead. "Bloody caves. I hate them." Ciarán's eyes settled on the shimmering figure at the centre of the home. A few moments and his gaze adapted to the half-light. "My loving sister, I presume. So, this is what the subterfuge was for."

Clío indicated he should come closer. Her brother was an attractive man, although his paunch surprised her. What did it say about him? There was no need for it. Only ancient dragons succumbed to expansive bellies, and he was the same age as she. His eyes disturbed her. They were black as charcoal and swirling with menace. Was it his natural colour or was it Scáthach's work?

"What is this place?" asked Ciarán. Suddenly nervous, he looked around, examining every inch of the cave. The temperature of the air rose.

"There are no assassins, brother. That is not *my* way." With a flourish of her hand, Clío said, "Do you not remember? This is our home, Ciarán. This is where our mother, Bráchthine, gave us life. Can you not feel her essence?"

"The bitseach took more away from me than she gave. A stupid prophecy presented her with an excuse to abandon and hand me over to the wet nurses of Clann Dubh. I was little more than a warmling and never suckled at her nipple. You, she fed and sent away to a life of hedonism with the former High King of the Tuatha Dé. Did he fuck you, sister? Was that part of the bargain?" The tone of the question rankled Clío more than its content.

"You are hurt, Ciarán, and that I can understand. I, too, was furious when Lazarus informed me that I had a brother. We have missed millennia of each other's company and support." Twin curls of white smoke escaped Clío's nostrils. "However, do not think I will tolerate insults to *our* mother or Lazarus of the Womb-Born."

Clío's severe tone startled Ciarán, and he examined her intensely—this time as an adversary. Her bearing had steel, the golden eyes were molten red, and the scars beneath the glamour told of someone well acquainted with battle. His marks were from knife cuts and carousing with whores. *Scáthach never warned me about this.*

"Scáthach, and her succubus daughter, see you as a doorway to power. Nothing more. They have bewitched you." Ciarán's eyes told Clío her intemperate remark was a mistake. *How would I feel if he said the same about Lazarus?* "I apologise, brother. My remark was rude and uncalled for."

"I wanted a sister… and a mother, once," said Ciarán. "Uathach is my sister and Scáthach is my mother. I did not know you before today, and I see no benefit in becoming better acquainted. You are a stranger to me and to the dragons. After the challenge, the serpents will hail me as their king and your Tuatha Dé friends will mourn your joining Bráchthine."

"We could have begun a great journey today, together, Ciarán. It saddens me, and our mother, that you have chosen instead to antagonise me. You are misled and misinformed by those who do not love you and who seek to use you." Ciarán turned about. "A word of advice, brother. Never turn your back on me again. No matter what Scáthach and her sycophants have informed you, a fat street brawler is no match for me."

"Bitch!" Still, Ciarán wondered at the iron in Clío's words. Were they matched by her talons?

In the cave, Clío sat down, cross-legged on the dirt floor. "Well, I fucked that up, Ma."

*You tried, Clíodhna, and that is all I could hope for. Try not to kill him in the Arena. He is my son and your brother. Neither of us want to live with that shadow.*

# CHAPTER 39

The high, sandstone mountains of the Island of Dragons shimmered as a merciless sun beat down. Perhaps it was a reminder to the serpents, who called the peaks home, that there was a power mightier than theirs. The deep canyon's floor, chosen as Clío's training ground, repelled anything resembling "normal" flesh. It was a brutal location, chosen deliberately by Aodh to test Clío's resolve as much as her strength.

Dragons do not sweat. Yet as Clío rested against the canyon wall to catch her breath, she envisioned millions of open pores and rivers of saltwater flowing from them. She refused to believe her eyes that the dirt showed no hint of dampness. It was midday and she had already drunk hundreds of gallons of cool water from the underground lake nearby. Indeed, she found it challenging to drag herself back up the stone steps to face the sun and her too-eager opponents once again.

"Fuck!" she mouthed as she stepped from darkness to blistering sunlight. Voicing the word was hard and adjusting her eyes to the brightness was painful. Giggling around her made Clío growl. Her huge head turned to Ceara. "You and your bitseacha are worse than my girlfriends after a night on the town." At Ceara's glum face she said, "Sorry, *our* girlfriends."

Clío glowered at her protectors. "I'm in pain and you're primping and flexing as if you were in the gym and a group of hard-bodied men walked in." At their blank faces, she laughed. A metaphor is only appropriate if its recipients comprehend it. "If we get through this, I promise you a night out dancing in Belfast. Then you'll understand." The offer prompted a round of excited chatter. It also increased the resolve of Clío's guards to make sure she won the upcoming duel.

Ceara opened her mouth, but Clío's palm forestalled her words. "I know. I know. It's for my own good. I need to know how to fight in an inferno." Some activities need fingers, not talons. In a blur of movement, Ceara transformed into her human persona and ran her hand through Clío's soft, feathery crest. No words were spoken. None were needed.

Yet Ceara's glamour could not shield her from the scorching heat of the sun. "Turn back, my love," said Clío. "An evening of smearing your burnt and blistered skin in aloe vera, while you cry with the pain, is not what I had in mind for après battle training."

* * *

Aodh was happy, although it was difficult to tell on a weather-beaten face that could adopt benign neutrality in an instant. Pride was written on his ancient visage. The end of Clío's half-cycle of the moon training approached. He turned to Lazarus as he watched Bráchthine's daughter attack a ten-dragon shield-wall without fear or mercy.

"Before today, I feared for a delightful young woman, who through no fault of hers was out of her depth. Today, I see the future Queen of the Dragons. Not long ago, the bruises mostly covered Clíodhna's body. Today, the welts and cuts are shared equally between Clíodhna and her dragon guards. Another few days to sharpen tricks and tactics and I will have no fear of wagering my wealth on her in the Arena." The great dragon chuckled. "The Goddess help her brother, he doesn't know what is coming."

Neasán received Aodh's report with a nervousness that was difficult to hide from Aodh and Lazarus. Operating in the background and shadows, the wily politician had done everything within his power to prepare a path to the Arena—but for which contestant? Surprises were an anathema to Neasán. As he watched Clíodhna train, he frowned at the newfound fervour evident in her and sighed. He had chosen badly. Could he plot an exit from his ambitions?

* * *

As The Mórrígan expounded on the dark arts of fighting, Ceara and her bodyguards listened to the fearsome Womb-Born with bated breath and wide eyes. Clíodhna's reproachful looks were dismissed. "Lazarus has forbidden me to interfere with the Arena contest. Thus, I can only provide counsel. There is only one thing you need to know. Break Ciarán's mind and you will have broken his body."

# CHAPTER 40

*The Land of Immensity*

Smiling broadly, Daghdha stood and opened his arms wide as Lazarus and The Mórrígan entered. The visit was expected as Lazarus insisted on adherence to the diplomatic niceties and protocols. The respect shown pleased Daghdha. He was less thrilled when Lazarus scrutinised him with an intensity that made him squirm.

"You are High King of the Tuatha Dé, brother," said Lazarus, standing five paces away from Daghdha. "It is long past the time for you to get over your millennia-old sulk. Why have you chosen this repulsive glamour? Why have you despoiled Muria, a city founded by our sister, Áine? Once it shone as an example of beauty of mind and spirit in the Land of Immensity. Áine has wept and lamented for thousands of years over its desecration. What harm did she ever do to you that you should inflict such pain?"

"You said it, brother, *I* am High King, appointed by the Womb-Born. I can do whatever I want. Look." Daghdha sniggered, gesturing to his surroundings with soft, pudgy hands. "It is *my* right; I nurtured Muria according to my character and desires. Ask The Mórrígan. She knows the city and its people mirror my nature."

A malevolent hiss from The Mórrígan rocked Daghdha back on his heels. He stumbled against the granite plinth and fell heavily onto the cushioned throne. Daghdha's brain shouted, *Stay silent, fool!* Instead, he said, "What is your excuse for the old man glamour, brother? Is the missing arm part of the act? How much will you bribe me for the use of the Cauldron?"

The snarl was worthy of a massive wolfhound and the grip of Lazarus' hand around Daghdha's throat that of its unforgiving jaws. Daghdha squeezed his eyes shut to protect them from the aura radiating from the tall, golden figure inches away from his face. He would have shrunk deep into the cushioned throne were he not paralysed with fear.

"Like Clíodhna, my glamour is a camouflage and a consideration for our friends and neighbours in the Land of the Humans. Never compare mine to yours. Also, the Cauldron is free to all Tuatha Dé. You are its guardian, not its owner. Do I need to add profiting from the Womb-Born's artefacts to your list of sins? Where are the Staff and the Harp?" Lazarus sighed with exasperation and released Daghdha. "I hope the brother I once knew and admired remains within this corpulence. I will soon find out." He turned to The Mórrígan. "Has Clíodhna arrived?"

"She waits outside the chamber with her shield-maiden." The Mórrígan put her hand on Lazarus' forearm. "Whispers tell me that Balora is in the city. She has Watchers with her. I do not know their purpose, but we know hers."

Lazarus dipped his head and turned to face Daghdha. "You are a demigod. That is your nature. When I return whole, I'd better see changes in this city. Raise yourself and take me to the Cauldron."

"I am the High King. You cannot chastise me as a child."

With a firm arm across his shoulder, Lazarus guided Daghdha towards the exit. Before the doors opened, he said, "I, not you, was chosen by Anúna to lead the Womb-Born. That will never change. Do you want to test your strength against mine?" Lazarus smiled. "That would be a very foolish act, brother." Muting further protest by Daghdha, Lazarus said, "When I return, you will explain to me your part in the negotiations between Lady Scáthach, the Sons of Mil, and the Fomorians. I wish to know if treason should be added to your foolishness."

\*\*\*

The Cauldron's chamber was reached by descending six flights of carved stone steps. The room was dark and smelled of earth, mildew, and rancid vegetable oil from the rushlights. As with most smells, it resurrected memories of Lazarus' previous visit. Held in iron sconces, several torches threw fluttering shadows onto the rough oak beams and wooden roof. The variable light gave the ceiling the appearance of being alive, which, allowing for the probable infestations of mice, rats, and spiders, added to the gloomy atmosphere.

A more apt description of the room was a dungeon. Each of its walls were constructed of tightly laid blocks of carved rock. Various implements of torture—or, depending on personal predilections, erotic delight—hung on wooden pegs. Lazarus shook his head. Was the chamber another facet of Daghdha's lifestyle? Perhaps, although his brother was not usually this private.

"Don't be so judgmental, brother. We all have our peccadillos. Even you, I suspect." A chuckle rumbled deep in Daghdha's chest. Lazarus chastised himself for leaving his thoughts unguarded, inhaled and exhaled several times to gain control, and stepped towards the plinth.

An unhappy and irritated Daghdha grunted and tilted his head in the direction of the large vessel perched on a slab of black basalt at the centre of the room. It had appeared as the first member of the Tuatha Dé entered the chamber. "This is not your first time, so I presume you know what to do, Nuadha. Apologies, Lazarus."

"Wow!" exclaimed Clío. "I was not expecting this." Ceara nodded, open-mouthed. Both had assumed the shape of the vessel to be a larger version of the domestic cauldron. To be faced with a half-skull was a shock.

The Mórrígan laughed. "The Womb-Born have our secrets."

Lazarus turned around. He peered at Clío, Ceara, and The Mórrígan as if struggling with a decision. The Blade of Light appeared in his left hand. Its brightness made the chamber seem uglier and Clío wished she could turn it off or douse it like a torch. Lazarus indicated for her to come forward and placed the sword into her hands. "You have held the Blade before without harm. Please keep it safe for me."

Without further words, Lazarus let his robe drop to the dirt floor and climbed a set of rickety wooden steps. Unbalanced by his missing limb, there was a moment of awkwardness and Clío took a step forward to help him.

The Mórrígan's hand stopped her. "Unless crippled beyond movement, supplicants must enter the Cauldron unaided," she whispered. She heaved a sisterly sigh of relief as Lazarus swung his leg over the rim and lowered himself into the waters. The liquid glowed gold and its surface became mirror-like as the ripples ceased.

"It seems our brother does not trust his siblings," Daghdha remarked as Lazarus sank below the waters. "But then he has no reason to, does he, sister?" In the torchlight, The Mórrígan looked unhappy. Did Lazarus still suspect her motives or was she annoyed because she was his sister, and it was a sister's duty to protect?

Daghdha turned to Clío. "In the scheme of things, his injury is minor." His tone suggested he wished the wound were more severe. White steam curled from Clío's nostrils, and she growled. Startled, Daghdha retreated several paces and held his hands up to placate her.

The Mórrígan laughed. "Forgive him, Clíodhna. His ears are still ringing from Lazarus' scolding."

"Thanks, sister. It is just after sunrise. We will return this time tomorrow." Daghdha nodded to several chairs and a small table with fruit and a jug of water. "If you need rest and refreshment from your watch."

Clío smiled. "We have stood lookout for much longer than a day. We will be fine. Thanks for your concern."

Daghdha turned away and then, as if recalling something, placed a hand on Clío's shoulder. She flinched and he quickly withdrew his hand. "A word of warning. Treat the blade with care. *Any* wound from it is fatal... possibly even to a dragon."

As Daghdha scurried away, Clío turned to The Mórrígan, who

lingered and stood with her hand pressed against the Cauldron. "Lazarus means no ill by his choice. He can be awkward around his true family."

"Thank you, Clíodhna. For one so young, your diplomacy is admirable. Like your mother, you will make a great Queen of the Dragons. Yet you do yourself a great disservice if you exclude yourself from the description of 'true family'. You have been at his side for millennia, whereas I have rarely visited him in that time. That is my mistake and my regret."

The Mórrígan smiled, kissed Clío's cheek, and whispered, "I will be close… just in case."

* * *

"Do you think she's gone or is she one of the shadows?" asked Ceara.

Clío laughed. "I find her presence strangely comforting, so I don't mind."

# CHAPTER 41

The Commander of the Watchers kept his word and assigned two men to guide Balora. The pair were taciturn and efficient. Keeping the spires of Daghdha's palace in their sights, they navigated Muria's narrow backstreets and alleyways. One assassin strode ahead of Balora while the second protected her back.

Balora assumed they planned to execute her. She had killed Ultán. There was scant camaraderie among the Watchers, but its code required an eye for an eye. The question was when, and how? *Probably a poison-coated dagger.* The slim blade was the one weapon that could punch through her armoured skin. She tensed her arse muscles and smiled. Balora had discovered Ultán's antidote when he was captured and replaced it with a vial of coloured water. The original was safe in a place few would dare to search.

The single trait Balora could count on was the Sons of Mil's contempt for women. Thus, for miles Balora exchanged mindless tittle-tattle with the Watchers. Every word she spoke confirmed she was witless and clueless as to where they were or where they were going. She even threw in that she was available to fuck, individually or as a threesome, any time they wanted to stop. Apparently, killing her had a higher priority than using her body. *Their loss.*

As they walked and jogged along Muria's streets, Balora drew on old memories of the city. Unfortunately, she and Lazarus had spent most of their time in Coria and made infrequent visits to Muria. Her memory was not as detailed as a dragon's. Nonetheless, some knowledge was better than none and, while Daghdha had done his best to ruin the city, its major landmarks and buildings remained.

To Balora's way of thinking, Daghdha personified the Womb-Born. Under him, Muria had become a place of villainy and debauchery with few saving graces. She was no stranger to using sex as a tactic in her stratagems, yet Balora cringed at the crudity and corruption surrounding her. Still, tonight, the city's venality would work in her favour. When she killed the Watchers, the gold and gemstones she had hidden on and in her would be more than sufficient to buy confirmation of the Cauldron's location. Her wealth—she had let their approximate, if false, location in Muria slip during her ramblings—ensured her protectors would take her close to her destination before striking.

Balora sighed. Was Lazarus the only honest being in the Lands of Immensity and Fomoria? Perhaps the young dragon, Clíodhna, too, although she was inexperienced. Without wise heads to counsel her, she was a prime target for corruption, sorcery, or trickery.

\*\*\*

Balora's instincts screamed, "Danger!" when the torches and lamps in the alley were mysteriously snuffed out and her protectors faded into the shadows. She read the warning signs several streets ago when she unequivocally knew they were going in the wrong direction. She smiled. Darkness was her friend. Balora instantly transformed into her natural form, concealed herself in the shadows, and waited. Her patience was rewarded.

Her protectors were not in the same class as Ultán, and momentarily Balora regretted his death. Sadly, it had been necessary for her escape. These Watchers' tactics were crude and obvious. The Watcher Commander had not sent his first team to kill her. Balora was insulted, pleased—and overconfident. Even the stupid can get a lucky strike with a bored Serendipity at their side.

Knife in hand, the forward Watcher retraced his steps in the pitch blackness to where he expected to find a helpless and confused Balora. Hot breath on his nape told him he had gone too far and the shadow on the wall was alive. He had never seen or confronted a Fomorian queen. Thus, he had no comprehension of her natural form or her size, power, and speed.

He never did. Razor-sharp talons sliced through inferior chainmail like a knife through winter butter. His chest was opened to the bone and his belly slashed horizontally. Guts spilt onto the cobblestoned entry to mix with the dog piss and shite. The young man's hands automatically went to his stomach and without thinking he looked up at his killer. In doing so, he exposed his neck to Balora's other paw. Claws slashed across the fragile flesh. The Watcher was dead before his brain acknowledged it.

Balora contemptuously pushed the corpse away. Arrogance fostered her mistake. She should have killed the first Watcher swiftly and immediately turned to face the second. Instead, she gifted her enemy precious seconds. Older and more experienced than his companion, he grasped them. The sharp pain in her back drew a gasp of agony. His mistake, like Balora's, was to celebrate a victory not yet his. The demon queen swung about and grasped him by the throat. The fool had not bothered to unsheathe his second knife. As he dangled before her massive demonic face, all he had was bare hands to attack or defend. His struggles were ineffectual against her armour-plated Fomorian skin.

Unlike his comrade, the second Watcher had wounded Balora. Foolishly, vindictively, she took her time to carve deep tears into his flesh. Needle-sharp teeth ripped the flesh from his face. His nightmare continued with the sound of her rough tongue licking his blood. Balora crushed his skull in her massive jaws as a final mercy. She would have spent much longer torturing him, but she felt the poison in her veins, and she had one task to complete.

\*\*\*

There were no windows to give them guidance. Hence, Clío and Ceara lost track of time soon after they entered the Cauldron chamber. Clío reckoned it was midday, but Ceara insisted it was late evening. A combination of curiosity and worry forced Clío to stand, stretch, and then gingerly climb the wooden steps. She peered into the Cauldron. Its surface, still as glass, reflected her face.

Her concern for Lazarus intensified and a spider's web of worry lines radiated out from the corners of each golden eye. Lazarus was fully submerged and although the water was shallow—enough to take a bath in—Clío could not see him. Neither could she sense him nor gauge how the healing process progressed. *Is he in the Cauldron or is it a portal? Has he been transported to another place?* Her sense of being cut off from Lazarus supported the portal theory. She imagined a pulsating glow in the water's depths, but that could be the reflection of burning torches or an echo of the Blade of Light gripped in her right hand.

The faintest of sounds, a soft scuffling outside the chamber's door, set Clío's scales off. Their music was well beyond human hearing, even that of the Tuatha Dé, although not the Womb-Born. Lazarus had enemies beyond these groups. Could a Fomorian queen hear her melody? She hissed at Ceara and, after snuffing out the torches, both assumed their dragon forms. With their laminae the colour of night, Clío waited in one corner and Ceara in another diagonally opposite her.

\*\*\*

Splashes of blood marked Balora's steps as she staggered into the room. Her breathing was ragged, and her eyes were pinpricks of red in the darkness as she swept the chamber. Only dragons rivalled Fomorians' night vision. Balora proceeded cautiously, feeling each step on the cold, rough stone slabs with padded paws. Traps were a distinct possibility. She was vulnerable as the poison flowed through her veins, depleting her defences.

Sniffing the air for unwelcome scents, she growled softly at the fragrance of recently extinguished torches. Who guarded the Cauldron? It was unlikely Lazarus would be left alone. When she finally reached the

Cauldron, she reached out and touched the vessel. Like Clío, she could not sense Lazarus within its depths. *How will I know if I died by your side, my love?*

Balora's thought stunned Clío but before she could process it, her mouth moved faster than her brain. "I doubt the vessel is portable enough for you to steal." The remark was mean and sarcastic at best. She swore at her indelicacy.

The Fomorian queen whirled around at Clío's mocking voice. She gasped and winced at the burning pain generated by the movement. "The legend is true; the Cauldron is a skull… or half of one," said Balora. Anúna must have been huge to have that size of a head, but lore tells that she birthed nine Womb-Born whole."

"What do you mean?" asked Clío.

Curiosity overruled Clío's impulse to attack. Balora must have known if an alarm was sounded, the chamber and floor would be flooded with dragons and Tuatha Dé warriors. The Fomorian coughed to clear her throat, dislodging clots of blood, which she spat on the floor. "Legend has it that after the Womb-Born were birthed, the sons and daughters of Anúna had their first nourishment from her breasts. After receiving her blessings, the siblings dismembered and ate her. They fed Daghdha using half of her skull as a bowl… and here it is." Balora laughed. "He must have been a pig even then."

Balora scanned the room unsuccessfully. The dragon's abilities had grown considerably, whereas she weakened with every drop of spilt blood. She placed a bloody hand on the ivory vessel. To Clío it seemed as if she were trying to draw strength from it. "How is Lazarus?"

"He is healing." Clío spoke with the conviction of her heart, not her mind. "Why are you here? If it's to steal the Cauldron, its size restricts your options." A wrathful tone entered her voice as an alternate explanation surfaced in Clío's head. "If it's to finish the job you began in Belfast, you will not leave this room alive." The Blade of Light appeared, lighting up the small chamber.

"That is a revelation. Lazarus never trusted others with his sword—not even a Womb-Born." As Balora spoke, she coughed and spat up more blood. She felt her senses reel and struggled to stay on her feet. "I have accomplished one, and perhaps the more important, of my tasks. Lazarus is recovering, and is safe, and protected." She chuckled, although it came out more of a gurgle with the blood in her maw. "And *my* Cauldron is secure… for the moment."

White teeth stained with blood flashed in the half-light. Confident neither dragon would leave Lazarus unguarded she said, "I will go," and took a step in the direction of the door. A sharp pain in her back took her breath away and she stumbled, going down on one knee. Clío spotted the trail of blood into the chamber, and the fresher splashes close to Balora.

"You're wounded," said Clío, not knowing whether to be pleased or sympathetic. This was Lazarus' enemy. Yet, by Balora's admission, she had also been his love. Clío's previous suspicions had become facts, and she was uncertain how to resolve the conflicts in her mind.

"Let her die," said Ceara emerging from concealment.

"Ah, someone who is loyal and does not overthink situations. Keep her at your side, Clíodhna. She strengthens you with the balance she offers." Balora coughed again and cried out at the pain.

"What happened? Can we help?" asked Clío. Ceara looked at her partner incredulously. "She was Lazarus' partner in the days before the war with Fomoria. In a fight or war, our duty would be to challenge and kill her, but, unlike the Watchers, we are not killers who strike in the darkness. Only Lazarus has the right to judge her."

"Thank you," whispered Balora. "I was betrayed by the two Watchers who acted as my guides. Their act was predictable, but one stabbed me in the back while I finished off his comrade." She shrugged and smiled grimly. "My error was pride. As fate would have it, he used a poisoned dagger, like Ultán's." She laughed. "I have the antidote. There's irony for you."

"The Hag! Why haven't you used it?"

"In my natural form, I have no need for protective clothes or armour. My skin fulfils that requirement. The antidote is hidden *within* me. The wound's position and the spreading poison make it impossible for me to retrieve it."

"Again, let her die. Ultán died because of that poison. The Goddess would judge it a fitting end for her," said Ceara.

"Ultán was not blameless. He should never have had such a terrible weapon. I blame the Sons of Mil. He would have been a good man without their interference." She looked at Ceara, but the shield-maiden shook her head vigorously.

"Oh no. What your eyes are asking goes well beyond my oath and the duties of a shield-maiden… or a lover. You are on your own, my queen. I am not retrieving a small vial from her large arse." Balora growled weakly at the insult. Ceara thought for a moment. "And I am not holding the Blade of Light. Lazarus gave you a special dispensation, not me. I will stand ready to defend you, like a good shield."

Ceara's words were unsurprising. Clío dipped her head. "I will have your word that none of this goes beyond this chamber, especially what I will do next. Agreed?" Ceara's offended look gave Clío her answer.

"Can we please leave the lovers' chat for later? I am dying," rasped Balora.

Ceara's and Clío's faces turned towards her in the half-light. Clío's riposte sat on her lips, but one look at the ghastly sweating face of Balora and she mumbled, "Sorry." She inspected Balora. "We will need to reposition you for better access. I'm sorry but it will hurt." She smiled, hoping to give an impression of confidence. "I watched a vet do something similar on a farm a year ago."

"Did you just compare me to a cow?"

"Don't get prissy with me," said Clío. She looked at Ceara. "Help me roll her over… please." Clío frowned. "The vet had long gloves. I hope the vial has not migrated to the depths. Here goes…" The rejoinder on

Balora's lips was stemmed by a scream of pain, a shudder, and an ominous silence. "Got it," said Clío, holding up a small vial.

She looked at Ceara, whose face had taken on a glimmer of anxiety. "What?"

"Let's hope you didn't kill her getting it. She looks awfully still. Thump her chest until she moves. I've seen my father do that for dragons."

"I'm holding a vial in one hand and the Blade of Light in the other. *You* thump her. We need some sign of life before we pour the antidote down her throat."

Ceara sighed and rolled Balora onto her back. "The Hag, she's heavy!" She straddled the queen's massive chest and beat on it hard until Balora's lungs and heart sprang into action. Relieved, Ceara said, "Great. Empty the vial down her throat. After that, our business is done."

"Not quite," said Clío. "She is badly injured and cannot stay here. Daghdha and The Mórrígan will be back at dawn to retrieve Lazarus from the Cauldron. One of us should remain here and the other must take Balora to somewhere safe. Luckily, we're dragons or we'd never have the strength to carry her weight. Hopefully, her Fomorian constitution includes faster-than-normal healing." Clío bit her lip. "I should stay with Lazarus."

A resigned Ceara nodded. A few moments later, a mischievous glint appeared in her eyes. "I know just the place to hide her. Trust me."

# CHAPTER 42

Clío exhaled sharply as the surface of the water broke and Lazarus' face appeared. Relief flooded her as first one, and then a second hand gripped the sides of the Cauldron, and he emerged from the water. The descent of the wooden steps proceeded cautiously, although that had more to do with their state of disrepair. Lazarus looked at Daghdha.

"You should provide a better ladder for the Cauldron. It is not as if you cannot afford it."

"Your first words are to scold me," said Daghdha.

"When you do something to deserve praise, I will be the first to declare it abroad. When I walk from this chamber to my quarters, will I see the improvements I commanded?" Daghdha shuffled his feet. He looked both angry and ashamed. "Shall I order Áine to return and re-claim *her* city?"

"No!" spat Daghdha. "I will start the refurbishments, immediately. I was waiting until you emerged from the Cauldron. Will you not allow some latitude for a brother's concern?" The siblings stared at each other until Daghdha averted his gaze. "Obviously not," he muttered and exit-ed the chamber.

The Mórrígan tossed a robe to Lazarus. "Are you going to stand na-ked in front of Clío and Ceara? Admittedly, the Cauldron does amplify your aura and other things, but do the girls need to be subjected to your manhood?" The hint of blushing in his golden cheeks was gratifying.

"You will be weak from the Cauldron because it uses a tithe of your strength to heal you. That is its toll." She turned to Clío and Ceara. "We will assist my brother back to his rooms. There, he can rest until his full vigour is restored."

Ceara muttered a soft, "Shite!" and tugged Clío's hand. "Can we talk… in private?" The duo stepped aside. "Can you keep our conversation from The Mórrígan?" Clío nodded and although it was unnecessary, Ceara whispered into Clío's ear.

"You put her where?" exclaimed Clío.

"So much for a private conversation," said Ceara. The Mórrígan's expression changed from mystified to amused. "It seemed like a good, if mischievous, idea at the time. Who would think to look for *her* in *his* quarters?" Once Clío recovered from the shock, she had to admit, while Ceara's motivation was suspect, her judgment was right.

"May we speak, privately, my lady?" asked Clío of The Mórrígan.

"Will someone tell me what is going on?" Weariness and irritation threaded Lazarus' voice. "I am getting very tired, much more than the previous time I used the Cauldron. I will be displeased if I need to be carried to my bed."

"Sit on one of the chairs," said The Mórrígan. "This will not take long." One eyebrow raised, she looked at Clío. "Will it?"

Clío shook her head and motioned Ceara to join them. "There is a situation to resolve." She gave The Mórrígan a summary of what had transpired during the night, including Ceara's choice of refuge for Balora. The raucous peal of laughter from The Mórrígan echoed off the room's stone walls. It was unexpected, and, to Clío, worrisome.

"Oh, that is perfect," said The Mórrígan. "The Goddess has a wonderful sense of humour." Adopting a more severe demeanour, she said, "Our priority is Lazarus. We will take him to his suite." Ceara gasped. "Don't worry. By the time we get there, he will be sound asleep, and we will be carrying him. Everyone pays a toll for the use of the Cauldron. We will make him comfortable in one of the rooms and depart."

"What of Balora?" asked Clío.

"A word of advice, Clíodhna. Never take sides in a relationship between lovers, whether it is current or in the past. You will always be the loser."

\*\*\*

"Are you sure she's still alive?" asked Ceara. After settling Lazarus in one of his rooms, the trio checked on Balora. "The room smells like a rotting corpse that can still piss." The description was apt. Balora had retained her natural form. Unconscious and motionless, she overflowed the huge bed. The Tuatha Dé are ten feet tall but Fomorians are much bigger. The bedclothes were soaked and stiff, fouled with blood and other bodily fluids and excretions.

"This is unsanitary and a breeding ground for infections. We should change her bedding," said Clío.

"How do you propose we do that?" asked Ceara. Both dragons looked at The Mórrígan.

"Don't look at me. I am neither slave nor servant," said The Mórrígan. "We have done enough. I will, however, disguise the revolting smell and hold any diseases at bay. When Balora and Lazarus awake, they can call for new bed linen and take a long soak in the bath… a scented one."

\*\*\*

Days later, Balora and Lazarus awakened in separate rooms, at roughly the same time and with the same craving—they were starving. Lazarus sniffed and was repelled by the noxious fragrances in the apartment. The Mórrígan's cosmetic application of fragrances could only do so much. "Surely I cannot smell this bad."

He attempted to stand, but his brain refused to communicate with his legs. Nausea and weakness made him immediately stumble back onto the bed. After several stubborn attempts, he eventually made it to the bedroom door. Worse smells emanated from another bedchamber, and Lazarus decided to investigate. He padded across to the other room and opened the door. A wall of disgusting odours hit him. "Fuck! Who died?"

"You're a demigod. Do something about it, and enough of the coarse language. That's human talk. Clíodhna is a bad influence on you." Balora had transformed to her glamour, but the effort had depleted her remaining reserve of strength. She struggled to stand without falling on her face or throwing up. Her nostrils flared. "You stink, too," she accused.

"We need a bath, food, and new bedding, and in that order. Then we can talk," said Lazarus.

"Food while we bathe would be good. I have no strength and have gone through enough without drowning in filthy, tepid bathwater."

Lazarus nodded. "Everything has been ordered." He chuckled. "It is one of the benefits of being a demigod." He held out a hand. "May I assist you to your bath?"

"Fuck assisting me!" She ignored Lazarus' raised eyebrow. "I was stabbed and poisoned. You just had a soak. I deserve to be carried"—Balora's voice took on a husky tone—"and soaped and sponged, *personally*. Look on it as a test of your new limb's functionality."

* * *

Bathed, fed, and satisfied, the Queen of Fomoria and King of the Womb-Born cuddled on a soft leather love seat. "Rumour has it you impregnated a dragon. I am aggrieved, but also impressed and jealous. You never made my belly swell." Balora chuckled. "Maybe this time we will be successful. I lost count of the number of times you filled me. There's nothing wrong with your manhood or your stamina."

"It is only a rumour, Balora," said Lazarus.

"I do not care. I like Clíodhna. She is untainted by politics. She could have let me die, and in her place, I probably would have. In my opinion, if she survives the ridiculous tests the dragons demand of her, she will make a great queen." Balora smiled at Lazarus' stunned look. "Have you told her the Arena is only the first of her trials?" His expression gave her the answer.

"That is foolish of you, Lazarus. You endanger your relationship with her, and if that is much more than a mentor to a ward, it will be devastating for both of you. My advice is to be honest with her… *now*." A peeved grunt was Lazarus' answer. Balora shrugged. "As for me, I am in Clíodhna's debt. I will kill anyone who seeks to harm her until my obligation is repaid." Balora chuckled. "I wonder how she will feel about having a demon as her shield."

"Are we enemies, Balora? You desire the Cauldron, and no matter the cost, you know I cannot let you take it."

"That makes me a thief, not an enemy."

"That depends on how you intend to use the Cauldron," responded Lazarus.

"Why make a mountain out of worm crap? Once I have it in my hands, we can negotiate the price. You will have the right of first refusal."

Lazarus exhaled and shook his head. "You are exasperating."

"True, but I'm also the best ride you've ever had." Balora stood, bent over, and kissed Lazarus. "I must go. I am a queen, and the matriarch of my clann. It is my duty to persuade our imbecilic Fomorian generals that a war between our races would be insane. I will fail because men are obdurate and mentally inflexible. Possibly I will die, but I must make the effort." Balora looked towards the quarters' exit. "Will I be arrested if I step beyond the door? Yours was only a minor and temporary disability, after all."

"No, I rescinded the arrest orders. Do you need a Portal Pass?"

Balora laughed. "If you are trying to get me to tell you why I no longer need the portals, you will be disappointed. On this occasion, I need a long swim in the ocean to reach my people. You can escort me to the beach, if you wish. I have some titbits of information from a meeting in the Sons of Mil city. It will make the journey worth your while." She giggled. "And I have not been fucked on a beach in a long time."

"Language, Balora."

"See how quickly you infect me."

# CHAPTER 43

The menacing public entrance of Clío's brother accompanied by a guard of six Clann Dubh dragons should have sparked alarm throughout Muria. In human terms, the dragons represented an army that could devastate large swathes of the land with relative impunity. The three Womb-Borns' reaction was to raise their collective eyebrows at the blatant attempt at intimidation.

Lazarus stood at the centre of the three Womb-Born. His voice boomed across the cavernous reception room. "You have neither an invitation nor the grace to petition for a meeting. Get out! Or we will remove you... permanently." A sneer formed on Ciarán's lips but froze when four sets of double doors swung open and ten warriors from Clanns Dearg, Foruaine, Ór, and Umhaí marched in. They were commanded by Aodh.

"A surprise entrance is rarely a shock if half the population of Muria knows about it," mocked Lazarus. "The discipline of Clann Dubh leaves much to be desired, as does its propensity for alcohol and bribery." The insult raised growls from Ciarán's guards, but a dog's whimper held more threat. Ciarán looked behind him in desperation for direction and guidance. He was disappointed. Lady Scáthach and Uathach were absent.

Lazarus smiled. The enchantress and succubus were blocked by Ceara and her ten dragons. The Womb-Born stood, radiating a golden aura and looking every inch his full ten feet. As if that were not enough, the Blade of Light appeared in his right hand. "You will bow to the High King, turnabout, and exit this chamber in an orderly manner. Or you will not leave this room alive." He pointed to Ciarán. "*You*, I do not wish to see until the Arena Challenge. Those who accompany you will be killed on sight if they ever enter the Land of Immensity again. *Go!*" Humiliated, the black dragons exited the room, muttering threats and curses. They were aimed, not at the Womb-Born, but at Ciarán.

"Ceara, please allow Lady Scáthach to enter this chamber," roared Lazarus. "I will deal with her daughter another day. If Uathach tries to accompany her mother, introduce the silver-eyed bitseach to dragon breath."

"Did the arrogant bastards think they could intimidate us? I am insulted." The Mórrígan's aura glowed a menacing red-gold as she watched the receding backs of the Clann Dubh cohort. Red snakes of anger fought for the freedom to attack the dragons. She held them back, but only with a promise they would feed another time.

As for Daghdha, his musings centred on one subject. *Do I want the throne?*

* * *

*What made the black dragons so full of hubris they challenged three Womb-Born?* The question, barely formed in Lazarus' mind, was answered as, head held high, Scáthach strode forward. The solemnly dressed Queen of Scáth paused and acknowledged the Womb-Born with the briefest of bows.

"Things are beginning to make sense, Brother and Sister." Lazarus' words took the wind from Scáthach's sails, forestalling the well-rehearsed and imperious words with which she intended to bless her audience. She glowered at The Mórrígan with unveiled animosity. The hint of a black aura became more definite.

"We should ask Clíodhna to join us. I suspect some of this conversation will concern her," said Lazarus. Lazarus turned to The Mórrígan. "Have you, as I have, wondered what event—*or entity*—in the lady's past turned her from a role model and a person fondly remembered to one who will be quickly forgotten? Was it your rivalry that spawned her darkness?" Sensing things were not going as she had planned, Scáthach opened her mouth to speak, only to be outmanoeuvred by The Mórrígan.

"Her theatre is a tad dramatic, which is usually the sign of a weak position and not knowing what intelligence the other side is privy to. Both are mistakes the Scáthach I once knew would never have made." Clío savoured the venom permeating The Mórrígan's words. A flourish of an imperious hand dismissed the unwelcome guest. "I refer, of course, to both the entrance *and* her dress.

"Did someone die, my lady? Perhaps it is a foretelling of death. If yes, then please accept my condolences for *your* loss. Surely you know the Gothic ensemble and make-up does nothing for your complexion except to make you resemble a corpse. Do you have a death wish, Scáthach?" Long talons tapped the marble throne. "I can help with that."

"Fuck!" murmured Clío. "Can she teach me how to do that?"

Dragons and Tuatha Dé have excellent hearing. Thus, Clío's words, although muttered under her breath, were heard by all present. The Mórrígan smiled inwardly, and Daghdha, aroused from his internal deliberations, laughed aloud. The latter almost blew out the jewelled windows of the palace. Scáthach's level of hate for those before her grew exponentially.

Lazarus nodded in approval and turned back to Scáthach. "Perhaps, you have something on which you wish to elaborate? An apology or entreaty for forbearance?" It was the perfect slap across Scáthach's ashen face. "It is only fair we are all on the same page. Human judges and barristers call this process 'discovery'." Lazarus stared at Scáthach. "I will start. Balora, Queen of Fomoria, informed us about your meetings with the Fomorians and the Sons of Mil. The word 'treason' comes to mind, but I am sure you have a reasonable explanation. *Do you?*"

Unnerved but finally permitted to speak, Scáthach said, "There are no laws forbidding meetings with either the Sons of Mil or the Fomorians…"

"But there are for inciting a war," snapped Daghdha. "And in Muria there are laws about taking advantage of my good nature."

Scáthach chose to ignore the last few threats but, if it were possible, her smoky white complexion appeared even paler. "Thank you, King Nuadha…"

"My name is Lazarus," hissed the king.

"Apologies, I was unaware of the change." Scáthach cleared her throat to give her a moment to reassemble her words. "It is well past time to choose a ruler of the dragons. On behalf of Clann Dubh, I invoke the right of combat to settle the succession of either Ciarán or Clíodhna."

"Yes, yes, we know. Why else do you think we are here? The other Womb-Born and dragon clanns will arrive during this coming week. The Arena is being prepared." Lazarus leaned forward. Clío thought he looked like a buzzard eyeing a cadaver. "Perhaps *you* did not get the message, or your thrall is illiterate." Lazarus' response was that of a parent chastising a petulant child. "The Womb-Born and the Dragons expect to attend Queen Clíodhna's coronation. My advice to you is withdraw Ciarán's challenge and release him from your dark magic."

Scáthach ground her teeth. "The Arena will settle the succession to the Dragon Throne."

"The succession is from mother to daughter; the brother was born to protect, not kill, his sister. It will pain me to watch Clíodhna kill her brother, but I know who to blame and I will seek justice after the contest."

"My party and I will remain in the palace until the coronation of the dragon *king*. Please prepare rooms for us." Anxiety had taken hold of Scáthach's vocal cords, and her words reached no further than her breath.

"You will not, and I will not," growled Daghdha. "You are not welcome, are uninvited, and have treated the position of the High King of the Land of Immensity with manners a street whore would be ashamed to own. Since you are so fond of them, you can camp outside the walls of Muria with your black serpents." He stood in his Womb-Born guise, appearing less a shameless sloth and more a huge rock of granite. He turned to Clío and dipped his head. "My apologies, Princess, I meant no disrespect to you."

"None was taken." Clío smiled and bowed. Daghdha was beginning to grow on her.

# CHAPTER 44

Clío and Ciarán tossed a coin to decide the order of the practice sessions. Clío lost, which was disappointing because she would not get a day's rest prior to the contest. Her brother's jubilation at the minor win caused Clío and Ceara to roll their eyes. "He'll have a heart attack if he wins," said Clío.

Ceara shook her head. "His reign would be the shortest in dragon history when I turn him into ashes."

"You can't do that. They'll kill you."

"Well, that will make the two of us dead," said Ceara. "Enough of this maudlin shite. You're going to win and afterwards we're going to get falling down drunk. Now let's inspect the Arena."

Clío's eyes widened as she entered the Arena and marvelled at the immense amphitheatre the Tuatha Dé had created for the duel. The ancient Circus Maximus in Rome could have been dropped several times into it, and there would have been enough space for a few more. Unlike the circuses, this stadium enclosed the combatants using invisible barriers. There would be no flight beyond the circle's perimeter or the agreed ceiling.

Clío walked around the stadium, gazing with the wonderment of a child and taking in every inch of the edifice. Enthralled, she did not notice Ceara exit the stadium. Only when she was tossed into the air and landed in the dirt with a bruising thud on her arse did she realise

Ceara had returned. More surprised than angry, she looked around to find Ceara and her bodyguards grinning broadly.

"What?" asked Ceara. "Did you think this was a day for sightseeing? We have more bruises for you and a few dirty moves not even The Mórrígan knows."

\*\*\*

Several days later, the atmosphere in the Arena reminded Clío of the gladiatorial contests in ancient Rome she and Lazarus had attended. The festivals were bloody, sadistic, and cruel in the extreme, but few disputed the spectacle. To mark the occasion, Daghdha dressed in a purple toga and sported a laurel wreath crown.

Clío thought the other Womb-Born were a glum lot. Lazarus had introduced his siblings before she entered the long tunnel to the battleground. Perhaps the pampered kings and queens realised the jeopardy they would face should Clío lose the duel. Clann Dubh were in a celebratory mood. They could not conceive of a scenario where Ciarán would lose to a young woman. Clío looked at Lazarus. *A bit premature, don't you think?* He smiled and dipped his head.

Muria's population had swollen to an incredible level in anticipation of the spectacle. It had been millennia since the Land of Immensity hosted such an event and those present were not about to let a party go to waste. Clío's lips pursed in a wry smile. Mysteriously, the city never appeared crowded.

Artisans relished the opportunity to display their works and enhance their reputations. Whores flocked to the celebration, knowing they could retire on the earnings. Still, most were addicted to the orgiastic, if ephemeral, pleasures and would not. They brought numerous salves to relieve overworked *piteanna* and arses and soothe bruised flesh. The more entrepreneurial spirits among the Tuatha Dé initiated a thriving system of betting. Given money was not required in the Land of Immensity, Clío wondered what would be lost or gained but concluded she was better off not knowing.

The Arena shimmered with the colours of the rainbow in the afternoon sun. Around the Arena, crowds of Tuatha Dé and dragons mingled freely in tiered crystal seating. It was an illusion, of course, but a solid one and quite comfortable for those who chose to deposit their arses. Aodh explained to Clío that most would rise when the fight began and stay on their feet until it ended. The exception were the black dragons who, along with Scáthach, sat separate on the curve of the circle farthest from Muria's walls.

The stadium was within sight of Muria's southern-facing walls, which became prime viewing galleries for those uncomfortable with mixing with the crowds. Banners and flags flapped in non-existent winds. Every type of musical instrument sounded out with impossible harmonies, but above all, one dominated—the throbbing heartbeat of the *bodhran*.

The dragons were an impressive and colourful sight and a revelation to Clío. *I'm the odd one out.* Clío's mouth dropped with sudden realization she had no clann. A reassuring hand squeezed her shoulder. "Bráchthine was unique among the dragons and so are you."

She smiled at Lazarus. "No pressure then."

Lazarus laughed. It was a good sound and a sign of his improved health after his time in the Cauldron. Clío watched him absentmindedly scratch at his "new" arm. According to Lazarus, it was fully functioning, but it would take time for the limb to become truly part of him. Palace gossip said Balora had played a major part in his rehabilitation.

Near the end of the long, gloomy tunnel leading to the Arena, Lazarus stood in front of Clío, held her shoulders, and smiled. "Be yourself, Clíodhna. Fight in your style. Your brother has no answer to that. You are battle-tested, and he is a street brawler."

\*\*\*

Clío paused to settle her nerves before crossing the entrance to the battlefield. *How did I ever get into this? I was happy in the Land of the Humans, and content in Belfast with my friends. Now, I must kill my brother.*

*That is my fault, and perhaps Lazarus', too.* The new name still felt strange on Bráchthine's lips. The glow before Clío seemed a hint more solid and the outline more definite. Hope welled up in her heart. Bráchthine shook her head. *I, too, yearn for my return and to hold my daughter. It is not the Goddess' time. Even if it was, I can never be the Dragon Queen again. It is not our way. You cannot avoid this day, Clíodhna.*

*I have no wish to see my son die and I know neither do you wish death for your brother. He is foolishly led.* Bráchthine's voice grew harsh. *Punish the bitseach, Scáthach, and her daughter.* The tone softened and Clío felt ethereal arms around her. *Always know, I am with you, my daughter. Everywhere.*

The spirit of Bráchthine faded and Clío walked forward towards the light. One word, and the emphasis her ma placed on it, was uppermost in her mind. *Everywhere! Am I ever alone?*

"Shite!"

\*\*\*

Clío transformed into her dragon form the moment she entered the Arena, although she kept her height to about ten feet. She made a somewhat nervous appearance but avoided the embarrassment of tripping over her tail. All sections of the crowds, except for Clann Dubh and Scáthach's coterie, erupted in cheering. The ordinarily conservative serpents roared their approval for one who bore the scales of their former, revered queen.

"No pressure," muttered Clío. An even greater bout of laughter and applause ensued. *Fuck! I'm surrounded by creatures and demigods with acute hearing and mind-reading talents.* She let that thought ripple outward to an appreciative crowd, before bringing down the veils on her mind.

In comparison, muted clapping and loud ridicule accompanied her brother's arrival at the challenger's entrance across the stadium. The Queen of Scáth and a relatively small congregation of Progressives had few friends or supporters. Insulted and belittled before his clann, Ciarán's face grew angrier and darker. The latter was a significant feat, given his black scales.

Clío ignored her brother. Instead, she took aim at Scáthach and Uathach. "The pair of you should add colour to your livery," she bellowed. "If you had any friends, they would tell you the monochromatic fashion does not work for you." The crowd erupted with loud cheering and laughter once more at Clío's comment and the impotent fury of Scáthach and her dragon. Uathach's silvered eyes glittered vividly.

\*\*\*

There was no official start to the combat. No flag dropped or arrow shot high into the sky. As with all contests, there were rules. However, this information was absent from Clío's education. The Mórrígan looked at Aodh and Lazarus. "Well played, gentlemen. I approve."

The crowd noise dropped from a deafening roar to silence. Clío took it as a signal, promptly changed in size to that of a small palace, and barrelled across the Arena with the momentum of a steam train and the effortless grace of a prehistoric shark. The force bounced her brother off the stadium's protective shield and into the centre of the battlefield. His involuntary backwards somersault demonstrated a surprising agility and would have garnered a perfect ten in the Olympic Games.

Clío hovered above the tip of her opponent's long tail and spat a gout of dragon breath. The rules frowned on, although they did not specifically ban, the use of fire. Ciarán's scream of agony and the disapproving silence of the spectators alerted Clío to her error. She sighed. *I'll ask for forgiveness later. His tail will grow back… eventually.* A handspring using curvature of her brother's spine planted Clío's powerful back legs just below her brother's neck scales. Steam curled upwards from her nostrils as long, razor-sharp talons dug in. Ciarán screamed again, shocked by his sister's tactics.

To give him his due, Ciarán was a stubborn brute. Growing to twice Clío's size, he rose higher, twisting and turning as he attempted to dislodge her and gain control. Remembering her fights with the winged Fomorian demons, Clío hung on for grim death. Slammed frequently against the stadium's invisible barriers, Clío emitted a series of

"Oooooffs!" *I'll be black and blue tomorrow… if I'm still alive.*

Her brother's mind was not well shielded, so Clío knew he had every intention of killing her. However, she could not make gross changes to her size without releasing her grip on her rival. Unwilling to give up that advantage, she sought for a plan and clarity before her ribs cracked.

\*\*\*

Uathach had few qualms about the dark abilities she possessed. At the same time, she struggled against the entity who had violated Scáthach and now shared Uathach's body. Gradually, An-Ársa had weakened her defences. She knew he intended to remove any sliver of free will remaining, and that she was too late to prevent this.

On this day, An-Ársa sensed Clío had the upper hand and, through Uathach's eyes, watched her relentlessly press her advantage, thus thwarting his embryonic plans for the Land of Immensity. The entity overwhelmed Uathach and forced her to look directly into the sun.

A flare of intense light reflected off Uathach's eyes and struck Clío in hers. Startled, she lost her grip and fell heavily onto the hard-packed dirt ground. If there was one thing Ciarán was an expert in, it was how to kick a victim when he or she was down and helpless. Blows rained down like iron rods on Clío's body.

Silence, apart from the thuds of Ciarán pommelling Clío, descended on the stadium, but soon, whispers of "Cheat" rose to a great roar. Those in the black dragon section looked nervously at each other and glowered at Uathach and her mother. The Clann's honour was under attack, and Scáthach feared for their lives.

The Mórrígan muttered an unqueenly, "Shite!" An awful silence descended on the Arena as everyone saw Lazarus appear before Uathach, brandishing the Blade of Light. "The abomination in you will never use your eyes again, witch!" shouted Lazarus and brought the sword down. Uathach screamed, Scáthach shrieked, and both collapsed. An-Ársa fled back to the blackness.

\*\*\*

"Ma, I can't see." Uathach's pitiful whimpering reached Ciarán's ears. He paused his battering of Clíodhna, looked up, and saw Uathach's scorched, eyeless sockets. The Blade of Light had cleansed the entity from her at the cost of her sight.

"*My sister?*" roared Ciarán.

"I'm your sister, arsehole. She's a witch and a whore," snarled Clío, landing a tear-inducing blow on her brother's snout.

*Rip the scales off from below his skull. They protect his neck.* Startled at the clarity of The Mórrígan's words, Clío wondered if this was considered cheating. The Mórrígan's answer came quickly. *They cheated first. Consider it filling a gap in your anatomical education. No one among the Tuatha Dé or the Dragons wants that arsehole to be victorious.*

Once again, Clío launched herself into the air and onto Ciarán's back. However, rage at Uathach's injury boosted Ciarán's strength. Another series of furious loops and batterings against the Arena walls made Clío nauseous. She spat mouthfuls of blood onto the dirt but fought her desire to puke. *I need a time-out.* Her single advantage in this contest was the element of surprise. Ciarán had underestimated her, and she would make him pay… eventually.

With grim determination, Clío extended the talons anchoring her paws to Ciarán's spine and fed fire into them. The smell of cauterised flesh tainted the air. The black dragon screamed as the lengthening spikes came perilously close to vital organs. He redoubled his efforts to dislodge the unwelcome parasite. Breathing raggedly, Clío grasped the first scale in her paws and twisted. It fought as if sentient and conscious of her intent, but Clío persevered. With a wrench, she pulled the plate free.

Ciarán shrieked. The crowd's raucous cheering dropped to a hush of disbelief as the great black lamina glided downwards to land on the Arena floor. Scáthach clutched her throat, realising Clío's intent but knowing she was helpless to intercede. Lazarus' Blade would remove her head at the merest hint of sorcery. She watched a second and a third scale fall. The black dragon screeched, thrashing and rolling as he fever-ishly tried to free himself from his sister's talons.

Clío dropped her mind-veils. *I know your intent, brother, but I will give you a choice. Land and kneel before me. Acknowledge me as your queen. Refuse and I will sever your neck and burn your body to ash.*

"Bitseach!" snarled the black dragon. Yet, Ciarán knew the choice Clío gave him was between life and true death. A mortal wound at his sister's hand would never allow him to return. Hope that he could over-come her at a future time made the sourness in his belly more palatable.

"Agreed," he spat.

*** 

The Arena's crowds of Tuatha Dé and dragons erupted in raucous cheers, chanting, "Clíodhna! Clíodhna!" That is, all except the black dragons, whose faces held a mix of anger, disappointment, and fear. The latter became uppermost when Clío strode across the stadium and stood before them. At her side was Ceara and at her back were her red-scaled bodyguards.

Clío pointed to the dirt. "Your king is defeated. I want your chief-tains on their knees before me. *Now!* My guards will drag you out, if nec-essary." The Clann Dubh section shuffled as their leaders pushed a way through to kneel before Clío. "I am Clíodhna, Queen of the Dragons. Clann Dubh's millennia of rebellion and insurrection and bowing to foolish witches ends now."

She pointed to the dozen chieftains. "These men have led Clann Dubh foolishly. Their lives are forfeit. They do not deserve any mercy, but I will let them choose their death and say goodbye to their families." She looked at the leaders. "Try to flee and I will hunt you and your fami-lies down. I will slay everyone and wipe your houses from the Annals of the Dragons.

"As for the future of Clann Dubh. I will give you one chance to redeem your tribe. When I call on you, you will come and fight in the front ranks of *my* army. Fail me and I will destroy Clann Dubh to the last dragon, whether man, woman, or child. *Have I made myself clear?*"

\*\*\*

"I was wrong, Lazarus," said The Mórrígan.

"About what?"

"I thought you brought Clíodhna up to be a pampered, promiscuous child. Instead, you have raised a real badarsed woman. Well done. Bráchthine will be proud of you."

Lazarus shook his head. "No, I did many things wrong. It was Clíodhna who discovered the woman and the queen."

\*\*\*

The silence after Clío's speech ended when a huge black dragon leapt into the Arena. He stood before Clío and laughed in her face. "Pretty words and threats to cower snivelling chieftains. They mean nothing to me. *I* am Conn Dubh—the true King of Clann Dubh."

The serpent pointed to Aodh, whose anger matched the colour of his scales. "The Black Clann swore fealty to me millennia before your wastrel brother was foisted on us by Bráchthine and Aodh." Scorn dripped from black lips. "You have my congratulations on vanquishing the whore Scáthach's champion. The fight was passably entertaining, and you demonstrated some skills, if against a backstreet brawler whose fame is founded on the bedding of whores and deflowering naïve virgins."

The king pointed to Scáthach. "Clann Dubh is happy to be rid of him and the witches." Conn bowed. "For that I thank you. A true dragon, however, would know the Arena is the first of several trials. Dragon law states the Queen-in-Waiting must have the consensus of all the clanns. You do not have my, or Clann Dubh's, support. Your celebration is premature.

"You are not Clíodhna, Queen of the Dragons. You are a foolish girl betrayed by those you trusted. Take my advice. Go back to the Land of the Humans where you belong. You are a stranger among the dragons and not wanted here."

# CHAPTER 45

The line in Daghdha's chamber consisted of Aodh, Ceara, Lazarus, Neasán, and The Mórrígan. Bráchthine was naturally (or unnaturally) missing, although her anger hung like a cloud over the room. Clío sat on Daghdha's throne. Crushed by the loneliness of betrayal, her shoulders slumped, and her heart was broken. The High King graciously ceded to Clío's use of his throne and stood on her right side. Not the subject of Clío's inevitable wrath, Daghdha was happy to side-step the imminent maelstrom.

Clío stood and paced the raised marble plinth. She gritted her teeth but was unable to prevent a painful groan due to the numerous weeping cuts and bruises that mottled her body. "Each and every one of you, including my mother, betrayed me. You lied to me and fed me fantasies of being Queen of the Dragons. Yet, I blame myself because I believed you. I trusted you and in return you humiliated me before the Dragon People and the Tuatha Dé. In the homes of Clann Dubh, I am openly mocked. Throughout the kingdoms of the dragons and the Tuatha Dé, I am pitied.

"My friends in Belfast have words for what I am: an *eejit*—a foolish wee girl. A stupid bitseach." Clío's bitterness matched the bile of her anger. "After a few days of rest, I will return to *my* home—the Land of the Humans—where I am welcome. During that time, I do not wish to see or speak to any here. Indeed, I never want to see you again. Please do me the courtesy of abiding by my wishes."

She turned to Daghdha. "Can I rely on you to provide a Portal Pass?"

"Of course you can. Will you accept a piece of advice from a reprobate?"

Clío nodded.

"Don't burn bridges unnecessarily."

Clío pointed to the small group standing before her. "There are no bridges, Daghdha. *They* burned them to ash."

*** 

Finely attuned ears alerted Clío to the soft knock on her quarters' outer door. When she ignored the tapping, moments later she heard the door open. Clío groaned and made a mental note to admonish the guards and servants Daghdha assigned to her. Her body was a mass of purple and black bruises and her tightness of breath pointed to broken ribs. Supernatural healing came with a price. On this morning, she had enjoyed the privacy of a long recuperating soak and the pleasant scents of jasmine and rose oil... until now.

The polite cough outside the bathroom snapped Clío back to the present. It assured her this was not an assassination attempt and identified her visitor as female. *Who could it be? The scent is not one I recognise.* Stiffly and painfully, she rose from the water, stood, and stepped gingerly out of the porcelain tub.

Clío grabbed a large towel, although not to hide her nakedness. Now was not the time to drip water on the marble, slip, and fall on her arse. That part of her anatomy had enough bruises already. Clío's visitor made a graceful bow without averting her eyes. The unabashedly admiring inspection from her visitor unsettled Clío and brought a blush to her cheeks.

"Queen Clíodhna."

"My lady Scáthach. Your visit is unexpected. I see you have changed your wardrobe. Autumn colours suit you much better."

"Thank you, my queen." Scáthach curtsied and her smile was a valiant attempt at friendliness and perhaps a new start for a relationship with Clío. Clío's scales fluttered and to her surprise, the sound held no hint of conflict.

"My lady, I am not your queen. As the King of Clann Dubh made clear, I am nobody's queen." Clío's smile could not disguise her anger and disappointment. Scáthach was surprised. Clío was a dragon, yet she demonstrated no desire for vengeance.

Scáthach had not been on the defensive in millennia. All her experience and teaching on battle tactics and sorcery focused on attack. Whether she meant to or not, this girl continued to confuse her. Yet, it was hard not to admire Clíodhna. She inhaled deeply, causing the top buttons of her blouse to open and show a significant amount of cleavage. She smiled seductively. "Our relationship started on the wrong footing. I was hoping we could discuss a new beginning."

Clío raised an eyebrow, perfectly summing up her scepticism. "I thought Uathach was the succubus, my lady." Scáthach twisted her fingers. "You promoted an insurrection among the dragons, used dark magic on my brother, and set him on a path to kill me. Now you wish to be friends." Scáthach nodded nervously. The attitude seemed incompatible with what Clío knew about the woman, yet Clío sensed she was genuine. "My lady, what part of dragon culture and lore makes you think your strategy has the slightest chance of success?"

"Many of the Tuatha Dé were once bitter enemies, but with time they overcame their challenges and now live together in harmony. All I ask is for time and a chance to erase the taint of enmity from our relationship." Scáthach's lips tightened. Effecting a sea change in demeanour was challenging, and she was in danger of lapsing into her comfort zone of assertiveness and imperiousness.

Clío's discomfort with the discussion prodded her to dominate. She grew taller, until she towered over Scáthach. Her skin took on an opalescent sheen, although no scales appeared—apart from those along her spine. Golden-red eyes, which Scáthach found it impossible to wrench her eyes from, commanded Scáthach's stare. A change of tack was needed.

"Clíodhna, the Goddess does not exempt any of us, whether demigod, dragon, or human, from setbacks, disappointments, and tragedy. How we deal with them is the test of our character. I was once celebrated among the Tuatha Dé. Jealousy of a dear friend, The Mórrígan, made me flee to a foreign isle. There I was raped by one known as An-Ársa. I gave birth to Uathach, but she and I were infected by evil. Lazarus' Blade of Light cured us of that misery, although Uathach is now blind and has lost her abilities.

"What would you recommend I do? Wallow in self-pity? How would that help my daughter, restore my reputation, or repair friendships? You may not be queen by acclamation, but you have four dragon clanns on your side and the Womb-Born of the Tuatha Dé. I see before me the most powerful woman in the Land of Immensity, the Island of Dragons, and likely the Land of Humans." Scáthach chuckled. "Only The Mórrígan might object to my assertion, though no one knows how powerful she truly is or wishes to test her.

"I would like to be your friend, but I won't beg—unless it will help Uathach. What will you do? Run away to the Land of the Humans? Perhaps, you should first ask yourself why An-Ársa followed *you* from one world to another and wants to prevent you from becoming Queen of the Dragons. I am here to help, if you ask, my queen." Scáthach bowed deeply and exited the chamber.

"Shite!" muttered Clío. "Daghdha was right. I hope the bridges were fireproofed."

\*\*\*

The shadow smiled, detached from the tapestries, and left in the wake of Scáthach. Had she, The Mórrígan, burned their bridge of friendship thoughtlessly? Could they be friends again?

\*\*\*

The recriminations and "I told you so's" began almost immediately following Clío slamming the double doors as she exited Daghdha's throne room. Ceara was the exception. She sobbed inconsolably.

The first arrow was shot by The Mórrígan and aimed at her brother. "I said this before, but in what world did you think you would get away with this? Keeping Clío in the dark about needing the full consent of every dragon clann before she ascended the Dragon Throne was a fool's judgment."

"I agree and said as much to Aodh," said Neasán. "If this was Bráchthine we would be dead already. As it stands, we have an irate, unstable dragon who will soon realise she is a hero to eighty percent of the Dragon People. Most, if not all, will take her side against us, especially when it becomes known she had no idea about the second criterion." Neasán paused. "Our lives hang by a very fine thread. You can be sure someone will spread this around. Lazarus should persuade her to follow her instincts and go home... to the Land of the Humans."

"Weasel!" snapped Lazarus.

"I observed the Lady Scáthach enter Clío's chambers and depart unscathed," said The Mórrígan. "Since you blinded Uathach, she has no love for any of us. Rumours will spread like wildfire without any help from me." She glared at Lazarus. "You should consider using the Cauldron to heal Uathach. It may give us some leverage." Lazarus said nothing, and the only sign he was perturbed was the throb and red tint of his aura. "The Hag, Lazarus! Say something. We stand on the precipice of a dragon civil war, unless we can mend bridges with Clíodhna."

Lazarus held Aodh and Neasán's gaze. "*You* told me with Ciarán defeated and Scáthach's hold on the black dragons broken, the clann would be amenable to Clío ascending the Dragon Throne." "I trusted you, and now I am estranged from my daughter. You have more problems than a humiliated Queen-in-Waiting." Lazarus turned to The Mórrígan and Daghdha. "As for you, choose whose side you are on, Brother and Sister. The Fomorians may not start the first war." The throne room doors disintegrated into a thousand fragments as Lazarus strode from the room.

"Well, that settles the question of who Clíodhna's father is. It also confirms the Womb-Born and Wind-Born came from the same root—Anúna," said Daghdha.

\* \* \*

*Daughter, you have every right to be angry, and vengeful, but you must rise above your emotions. The dragons will descend into a civil war over you or without you. Lazarus will lead the Womb-Born and Tuatha Dé against our people in retaliation over you. And the Fomorians will get revenge against their ancient enemy.*

"You cannot put this on me, bitseach! You betrayed me as much as the others. What wisdom advised you to keep secrets from me?"

*I am your mother Clíodhna. You may not agree with me, but you will respect me if only for breathing life into you. I trusted the man I love. He was misled, if not intentionally. How can I blame him? Who among us is perfect?* The golden tear that splashed Clío's hand shocked her. It was real.

"No, Ma. No more tears. The price is too much to pay—for both of us." Clío's shoulders slumped. "But what can I do?"

*Be the Queen of the Dragons. Knock their heads together.*

\* \* \*

Ceara opened the bedroom door as quietly as possible and padded across the marble floor to the massive bed. Inhaling deeply, she gently lifted the covers and slipped in beside Clío. There was no movement. *Is she ignoring me? Is that better or worse than hating me?* Another deep breath to settle her thudding heart and Ceara snuggled up closer. Arms surrounded Clío and pulled her tight against her body. Clío's scales fluttered happily, and Ceara's heartbeat steadied.

"I didn't betray you." Tears soaked Clío's back until she turned around.

"I know you didn't, and I could never hate you." Two pair of arms locked the embrace. Neither would break it; neither wanted to. The shadow moved from the wall, smiled, and exited the room silently.

"Is she still here?" asked Ceara.

"No, she just left."

"I don't mind her being around. It's quite comforting, and those tips she gave us improved the intensity and frequency of our orgasms. I wonder what else she can teach us."

"Go to sleep, my love. There are hard decisions to be made tomorrow."

"Spoilsport."

"Did I mention, sex makes you sleep better?"

# CHAPTER 46

Daghdha's throne room was an intimate chamber with a grand name. Still, given the size of the participants, whether Tuatha Dé or dragon, small was all things to all people and subject to Daghdha's whims. At Daghdha's request, Clío again sat on his ornate chair. The Tuatha Dé and dragons rarely sat, so he stood to her right. Ceara took up a position on Clío's left and glowered at anyone who dared to hold her gaze—including her father, Aodh.

Apart from the trio on the plinth, the composition of those in attendance was curious. Still, none refused the meeting. Only a fool, defies a summons delivered by envoys of the High King of the Tuatha Dé, no matter their opinion of the current occupant. Before Clío stood the four kings of the red, green, gold, and bronze dragon clanns, plus Aodh and Neasán. Representing the Womb-Born were Daghdha, Lazarus, and The Mórrígan. Seated nearby were Lady Scáthach and her daughter.

As Clío stood, the dragons dropped to one knee in acknowledgment of their queen, although Neasán appeared unenthusiastic. The Tuatha Dé bowed respectfully, which was as good as anyone could expect.

"My advisors…" Clío inclined her head to Ceara, Daghdha, and Scáthach. The latter brought a wry smile to Lazarus' face and a chuckle from The Mórrígan. "And one whose company and wisdom the Goddess enjoys." Clío's voice cracked momentarily, and she smiled. "I hope for not too much longer. I never knew my mother, but I miss her."

Clío's demeanour swiftly turned darker than thunder clouds. "I was betrayed…" The silence was profound, and thoughts of looming retribution rippled through those assembled. Some were delighted; one was terrified. "…as I believe were most of you." Relief flooded minds. It was short-lived. "Given your longevity, I am surprised at how easily such paragons of wisdom were walked by their snouts into a trap. Only your hearts and the Goddess know your reasoning. On my mother's advice, I will assume it was well-intentioned."

Clío looked at Lazarus. The sadness on both of their faces spoke of faith and trust that would need a long time to rebuild. Their eyes misted, signalling their prayers that such perseverance would be rewarded. "I have been at your side for millennia, Lazarus, and yet I am not sure who you are. You keep too many secrets. Therefore, you are doomed to disappoint those you have vowed to protect.

"In colloquial parlance, An-Ársa played you like a fiddle."

The Mórrígan grabbed her brother's hand and squeezed tightly. "She is hurting terribly, as are you, Lazarus. Hear her out, before your ego makes you do or say something you will regret… again."

"Still, by blinding Uathach you set her, and her mother, free of that evil. You also inadvertently thwarted the Ancient One's mission when he followed *me* to the Land of Immensity. I expect you to dispense justice by consenting to Uathach's use of the Cauldron. I have talked with Daghdha, and he awaits your agreement. Do not disappoint me."

Clío drew a long breath. She hoped the next items on her agenda would not be as painful… to her. "The deception that led to my betrayal by those I trusted was devised by a very clever man, well-attuned to politics and moving pieces around the fidchell board. Why he chose to betray me, his family, his clann, and his race, I do not know, and I do not care. I have weightier things to resolve." Clío's eyes held Neasán's. "Have you anything to say, Neasán Ór?"

"It's a lie!" shouted Neasán. The outrage was forced; the fear was genuine.

"The Mórrígan can prove me wrong and without much pain or injury to you," said Clío. "Will you give your consent?" Slumping shoulders gave Neasán's answer. "Leave this chamber. A guard of Clann Ór awaits to escort you to your new home."

Daghdha leaned over and whispered in Clío's ear. "That's very magnanimous of you, Queen Clíodhna."

Clío's laugh sent chills down the High King's spine. "At sundown, in the Island of Dragons, his ashes will be scattered from the highest peak in Clann Ór's domain. His family will not suffer for Neasán's treason— that is my generosity."

Clío turned to her congregation. "Daghdha has arranged for food and drink to be served in the adjoining room Let us eat, drink, stretch our legs, and refresh ourselves. Afterwards, I will tell you what is to be done about Clann Dubh."

***

Two stiff-necked strangers remained in the room after the others filed out. One needed forgiveness; both needed to be loved. "What name should I call you?" asked Clío.

"Father or Da would be appropriate... and truthful. I'm sorry, Clíodhna. I should have told you a long time ago."

"There are many things you should have told me a long time ago. It wasn't years. It was millennia."

"I intended to tell you much earlier. The centuries slipped by, we became comfortable with our lifestyle, and I became afraid to spoil what we had. It was an error of judgement—a terrible mistake compounded with a lack of common sense." Deep blue eyes gazed into golden ones. "If you hate me, I will understand. All I ask is please don't ignore me."

A hand gripped Lazarus' and squeezed it. Perhaps a bit more strongly than necessary, but she was a dragon. "Don't be silly, Da. We survived my puberty. I'm sure we will adjust to being father and daughter."

# CHAPTER 47

Conn Dubh was a tall, burly man, confident in his status. He was also arrogant and narcissistic, a common shortcoming in powerful beings. The king contemplated ignoring Daghdha's request to meet with Clíodhna. *Why should I give her any legitimacy?* Reminded by his advisors of The Mórrígan's support for Clíodhna, he changed his mind. The Queen of Whispers and Shadows would ensure rumours of him being afraid to meet Clíodhna would circulate like wildfires throughout the Land of Immensity and the Island of Dragons. A black serpent could survive many character flaws; cowardice was not one of them.

The king was not stupid. He brought a bodyguard of ten dragons with him, taking full advantage of his rank. The instant he stepped across the room's threshold, his blunder became obvious. Conn had underestimated Clíodhna. A growl rumbled in his throat, but he cut it off. *I will not give her supporters an excuse to end me.* His path to the plinth was flanked on either side by ten warriors from each of the other clanns. Unlike his guard, each one was a champion of their clann. Jaws clenched and teeth grinding, the king strode forward.

Aodh and Ceara stood on the plinth alongside Clíodhna. Where was Neasán? Daghdha, Lazarus, Scáthach, and The Mórrígan were nearby. Wisps of smoke betrayed Conn's anger as he closed on the platform. He had lost the first round of whatever game the bitseach played. His ire climbed further when he saw that his adversary—belatedly he honoured her with the title—would always look down on him, and not because of the plinth. Her glamour was six inches taller than his. *How did she know?* The Mórrígan's eloquent smirk gave him his answer. Conn stopped five paces from the marble base; Clíodhna walked to its edge.

Everything about Clíodhna's bearing screamed "Queen!" *Where is the creature I humiliated? Why did she not run home to the humans?* Her gossamer robe perfectly matched the colour of her natural, opalescent scales. Tresses of long blonde hair were piled up on her head like a crest. The king ground his teeth again. The style gave her more height. Yet it was Clíodhna's face, a mask of small scales, that troubled the monarch. It was clearly animated. How did she control her glamour so finely and effortlessly? He glanced at Lazarus. Was the gossip true?

"A disgraced and humiliated pretender to the Dragon Throne who had any dignity would have fled home to the Land of Humans for her safety. Why are you still here?" Conn decided attack was his only choice.

"And yet, you are here at *my* command." Clío's smile was benign. Her eyes promised pain. "As to your question"—Clío smiled at Lazarus—"this is my home as much as the Land of Humans or the Island of Dragons." The king opened his mouth, a caustic retort perched on his tongue, but Clío's raised palm ensured it would never be spoken. "I will, however, admit to naivety regarding Clann Dubh's honour. I also should have been more diligent in my research before I entered the Arena. They are mistakes I will never make again.

"To wit, I would have discovered that you, like many of Clann Dubh, have no honour." Again, the rumble in Conn's throat stopped short of a growl. "You attempted to trick me by citing an arcane clause buried deep in the tomes of dragon law. It originated in the dark, chaotic days of *our* history before the Reign of Queens brought peace and order. As well you know." Eyes more red than gold glared at Conn. Every fibre of his body wanted to shrink back, but he held steady. "My friend, Lady Scáthach, and I had a long chat about how you, and your coterie of chieftains, who are obviously not scholars, used dark magic to uncover the clause.

"What do you say, Conn, King of Clann Dubh—or should I call you traitor?"

"I am no traitor, and you are not the Queen of the Dragons. Clann Dubh will never support you. They are my people and follow me." Conn's voice gathered strength and momentum. "Your presence will bring civil war within the dragons and with the Tuatha Dé. When this news spreads, your support will disappear like a stream in a summer drought…"

"Are you willing to bet your life on that?" Clío pounced and the jaws of the trap snapped shut.

Conn glanced around and swore. His bodyguards looked impressive but were chosen for appearance, not for fighting a rearguard battle out of Daghdha's palace. "The law is the law regardless of time or circumstance. You are not the Queen of the Dragons."

"Are you willing to bet the lives of your children on that?"

A cold sweat broke out on the black dragon's face. "What do you mean?"

"While you and the hundreds of 'brave' warriors who accompanied you to the Arena celebrated my demise by getting drunk, rutting, and plotting revolution, *I acted*. Your lands, women, and children are surrounded by *my* army drawn from the other clanns." Fear and panic knotted Conn's and his guards' guts. "The Womb-Born can open a window to let you observe, if you do not believe me."

"Bitseach!"

"You have no idea. I am Bráchthine's daughter. A wise king would have met with me prior to the contest to take the measure of his enemy," said Clío. "One command from me and I will have every black dragon egg and warmling destroyed. Clann Dubh will wither on the vine of its king's foolishness."

"What do you want? My support?" Resignation replaced defiance in Conn's voice.

Clío laughed. "You expect me to trust your word. That would truly be naïve of me." She shook her head. "I want your ashes and those of every Clann Dubh chieftain and civil leader." Clío's voice chilled everyone in the room. The king thought of his warmling son and daughter and ground his teeth.

"I am, however, not without mercy," said Clío. The black dragons sighed in relief. They should have known better. "The Arena has been prepared and the people of our races notified. In two days, you and the chieftains of Clann Dubh will fight me and a similar number of warriors drawn from the other clanns. It will be a fight to the death. You should say your goodbyes to your families."

Clío looked Conn in the eyes. "We will see if the bullies and drunkards of Clann Dubh have any honour. I am not hopeful. Any who choose to flee will be hunted down and executed… along with their families."

"And you?" asked the king.

"I will be the one who kills you."

\*\*\*

The crowd was tense with expectation but met the entrance of Conn and fifty of his black dragons with loud boos and shouts of derision. There were no other Clann Dubh serpents in the stadium to cheer their comrades. In fear of reprisals and the safety of their families, they had fled Muria immediately following their king's meeting with Queen Clíodhna.

Conn did not blame them. He had dispatched close friends to protect his family in the Island of Dragons. He had underestimated Clíodhna and had a newfound respect for the queen's brutal pragmatism. She had informed him that, in a likely war with the Fomorians, the remaining black dragon warriors would be put in the front lines. Was it an undeserved honour or did the queen intend to castrate Clann Dubh? Only he could prevent the latter. The leader wondered which side the Goddess would choose and prayed to her for mercy.

\* \* \*

"Here I go again," muttered Clío. She stood, together with her dragons, in the long tunnel leading to the Arena.

"No, my queen," said Ceara. "Today, you do not fight alone. You have friends at your back and the best dragon warriors at your side."

"Thanks," Clío whispered. "The Hag! I would kill for a beer, a fish supper, and hot peas in vinegar after this."

"That may be possible, but would the delicate womanhood of Belfast survive fifty horny male and female dragons rampaging through the streets and bars?"

Clío snorted. "Knowing our friends, I'd be more concerned for the safety of the dragons."

She felt a hand on her shoulder and a whispered, "A word, please." Ceara bowed as Lazarus guided Clío to an alcove. "You have spoken with Lady Scáthach and my sister on battle strategy." Clío nodded. Scáthach had instructed her to take out the weak first. The Mórrígan had winked at her friend and assured Clío that many of the black dragons would be weak before they got near the Arena. She shook her head. *Is that cheating?*

A cough drew her back to Lazarus. He smiled. "My sister has become fond of you, Clíodhna, and that has its good and bad points. To her, you are family. Thus, mostly the bad will be directed at those she considers a threat to you."

"Mostly?"

Lazarus laughed. "Traditional weapons are not considered cheating. I want you to take this with you." He took the Blade of Light from the folds of his cloak and placed it in Clío's hand. Further down the tunnel, she heard Ceara's explosive gasp of "*Shite!*"

"This is considered 'traditional'?" Clío shook her head. "I can't, Da. What if I drop it?"

"That's your main concern?" A broad smile captured Lazarus' face. "The Blade is sentient and is more than capable of taking care of itself. It will also sense the proper form and size in any given situation. Your role is to mark the enemy and avoid getting killed." Strong arms embraced Clío. "When you step onto the Arena, you will be in the Goddess's hands. Most times, she is a just god." Clío's eyebrow lifted and Lazarus shrugged. "None of us is perfect."

He drew a long breath. "There are other challenges to face, Clíodhna. You will need all your dragons for the war with the Fomorians. Use the Blade to tilt the balance in your favour and end the contest quickly. Daghdha's Cauldron and Macha's healers await the injured."

* * *

In contrast to the entrance of the black dragons, Clío's chevron of serpents were cheered raucously as they stepped into the Arena. Loud chants of "Clíodhna!" were interspersed with "*Dragán go Brách!—* Dragons forever!" Clío glanced up at the royal seats and a smiling Daghdha. He waved to the crowd and then threw weighted bronze, green, gold, red, and opalescent ribbons into the centre of the Arena.

"No prisoners!" roared Clío and raised the Blade of Light. The crowd went eerily silent and then the thunderous drumming of a thousand *bodhráin* filled the air. The dragons transformed to mansion size and the formation charged forward: a score took to the air, and another twenty hurtled along the dirt to confront their opponents. Clío, Ceara, and her flight of protectors ignored the melee and stormed forward to confront Conn.

Conn shook his head as Clíodhna brandished the Blade of Light. *How is this possible?* He swore at himself. *Fool! The rumours are true.* He had misread Clíodhna, and his tribe would pay a terrible price. Yet the king was a brave and skilled warrior. He knew the battle would be painfully short if he did not kill the queen, and bellowed, "To me!" Together with his best warriors, Conn charged to meet Clíodhna's wedge.

* * *

The aerial ballet was tragically beautiful. Smells of brimstone and burning flesh, and screams of agony, assaulted the senses of the spectators in the Arena. Many wished to avert their eyes from the awful battles in the air and on the ground but found they did not have the willpower. The pageant was horrifying and breathtaking. Dragons and demigods screamed for more blood.

The Goddess soared high above the Arena in the guise of a great eagle. She shook her head. The Womb-Born and their progeny were infected by hubris and immorality, as were the Humans. Both races' survival teetered in the scales. Thus, her hopes resided in the Wind-Born—the dragons she created, and Anúna birthed. Of all the nations, their balance of justice and vengeance most resembled the Goddess. She could not let corruption's seeds germinate in that rich soil. *The spectacle must end quickly.* Thus, the Goddess put her hopes in an imperfect tool—Clíodhna.

Huge bodies, some in flames, fell from the sky; the Arena's dirt trembled with each thud. Many were injured, some mortally. The fighting circle became a slop of dragon blood, gore, and earth. Clann Dubh's wounded were dragged aside. Ignoring pleas for mercy, they were incinerated by dragon breath on the queen's orders. Loyal serpents were gathered up by friends, conveyed to the exits, and placed into the hands of those who waited to heal bodies or build funeral pyres. It was a taste, a microcosm of what a civil war among the dragons would resemble.

At the centre of the field, Clío and her red-scaled protectors fought grimly and inched closer to Clann Dubh's king. She looked around and raged at the loss of dragon lives—fathers, sons, mothers, and daughters. Her eyes, red with wrath, caught Conn's. She screamed, "*Bastard!* Look what you have made me do."

Like the Goddess, Clío knew it had to end, and so did the Blade of Light. Sword clasped in her talons, she strode forward. As she crossed the Arena, each step brought increasing gasps. "What is she?" asked every member of the Dragons and Tuatha Dé.

The Mórrígan rounded on Lazarus. "Did you know this would happen? Is she Dragon or Tuatha Dé?"

"I did not, sister," said Lazarus. "As for your next questions, I don't know what her transformation means and, yes, I am concerned. If this is the Goddess's work, I hope she knows what she is doing."

"Whatever the meaning, when this concludes, you must reclaim the Blade and purify it. When you cleansed Uathach of An-Ársa, the abomination may have contaminated the sword." Lazarus nodded.

As Clío drew closer to Conn, the crowd became silent in awe and terror. With each step, Clío lost her dragon form, although not her scales, and she glowed like one of the Tuatha Dé. She walked upright, ten foot tall, naked, and gripping the Blade. Any who, out of a misplaced sense of loyalty to the king, confronted her, the Blade contemptuously swept aside.

"What creature stands before me?" bellowed Conn.

His tail began to move before he finished. Clío jumped to avoid a crushing blow. Without thinking, her hand swept downwards. She heard a roar of pain and saw several feet of tail lying on the dirt. "I am a dragon, and my hand will deliver your death." Only then did Clío glance down at the hand that held the Blade and then her body. "*Fuck!*" She looked to Lazarus with beseeching eyes. *What am I?* His raised hands gave her no answer.

She barely avoided the gout of dragon breath that scorched the ground she had stood on but could not evade the swipe of the leader's long stump of a tail. Clío smashed against the Arena wall with a loud, "Oooooff!"

"You're a piss-poor dragon if you can't breathe fire or swing a tail," roared Conn. "A Queen of the Dragons must know who she is and her limitations. Learn quickly, Clíodhna, or your people and those who love you will suffer." Conn charged. When he was a few paces from Clío, she leapt upwards, spun around, and landed behind the black dragon's crest. He laughed loudly. Clío wondered why until she hit the Arena wall and felt ribs break.

"You are predictable, my queen. It will be your downfall."

"It is a bit late to acknowledge me as your queen. Do you hope to bargain for your life?"

Conn shook his great head, and his long, black plumage rustled. "I ask one favour."

"If I say no, what then?"

"Then we fight on. I have more tricks and will fight to the last breath. Do you want an end to our contest that will embarrass our audience and make them cringe? Or an honourable one, worthy of a Dragon Queen and a King of Clann Dubh?"

"Your request?"

"Publicly declare there will be no reprisals against Clann Dubh. They are an unruly tribe and have been badly led by me and others. Show them you are a different type of leader. Understand them and they will give their loyalty freely. Kill any leaders who remain. They, like me, have failed their subjects." The king laughed. "Treat them fairly but do not indulge their ancient fantasies. Well?" The dragon's head turned, and his eyes looked deep into Clío's.

"You have my word."

Conn sighed. At least he had done something good for his people. "If the Goddess allows, we will meet in the future. I will tell Bráchthine she has a daughter to be proud of." The serpent paused and dipped his head. "Do it!"

The Blade cut through the dragon's neck as if it were winter butter and his great, crested head tumbled onto the dirt. Clío's voice resounded across the Arena. "Build a funeral pyre fit for a king who loved his people. Conn Dubh will cross the veil with honour. There will be no reprisals for Clann Dubh. There will also be no place for foolish leaders and those who follow them."

Chants of "Queen Clíodhna!" reverberated across the stadium as Clío strode across to Lazarus and The Mórrígan. She held out the Blade of Light, reverberating in Clío's head was the Blade's sigh of satisfaction as it took Conn's head. "Take this evil thing. I never want to hold it again."

"I understand," said Lazarus.

"I hope you do." Clío walked past the duo and into the arms of Ceara. "I want a long bath, lots to drink, and a visit to a chippy in Belfast. There must be one left unscathed."

# CHAPTER 48

Baoth, King of the Sons of Míl, repeatedly adjusted his well-padded arse on the chair's deep cushion. His nervousness was understandable. While Baoth had a reputation as an astute leader, he was lax at tracking his Council's operations.

Before him sat the Womb-Born and the recently crowned Queen of the Dragons. Even the estranged sea god, Manannán, attended and sat beside a brother he had not spoken to in many thousands of years. On Daghdha's right were Lazarus and The Mórrígan. Prior to the meeting, Baoth had hoped his relationship with Daghdha would shield him from the others and ameliorate any reprimands. Given Daghdha's demeanour appeared less a High King and more a second-in-command, Baoth's disquiet did not diminish.

The dispositions of all present foretold of devastation to the city and people of the Sons of Míl. As terrible as their countenances appeared, the one who sat on Daghdha's left troubled Baoth most. Clíodhna, Queen of the Dragons, gave the impression she was at best bored with the proceedings. In this, Baoth was mistaken. Clío was mad because Lazarus had curtailed the dragons partying in Belfast.

Thus, Clío radiated an aura that gave every indication that she wanted the Womb-Born's sanction to send her serpents to administer justice so that she could return to her carousing. If her manner was a pretence, Baoth thought it an exceptionally good one. In an attempt to exert some control over the proceedings, Baoth pre-empted the predictable questions from his hosts.

"I had no knowledge of my Council's plottings and would never have sanctioned such folly." The other members of the Sons of Mil's Council of Elders, seated to the king's left and right, glared at him. Blinded by misguided hubris, they saw no reason to beg for forgiveness or mercy or even provide a rationale for their actions. Their eyes foretold Baoth's imminent death. The Sons of Mil did not need a weakling as their king.

"You are either disingenuous or a poor king. Which is it?" Lazarus' tone caused consternation for the king and a few of the seated Womb-Born. Had he supplanted the always agreeable Daghdha? Was he High King in all but name? And with whose support? Eyes drifted to The Mórrígan, but her face and body language held an exasperating neutrality.

"Baoth is weak. He does not speak for us or the people," interjected the Leader of the Sons of Mil's Council.

"Obviously," said Lazarus.

A vain man, the Council's Leader failed to consider his position was perilous and his options limited. His short-sightedness, founded on Fomorian promises of power and wealth, produced a false sense of security. He puffed his chest like a preening bird. "We have the strength of Fomoria's armies behind us. They almost defeated the Tuatha Dé once. Today, their armies are greater, and they have the Sons of Mil as an ally."

"Almost is not a victory," said The Mórrígan. "Still, I am sure your impressive divisions will give great comfort to the Fomorian generals, many of whom I know. How many thousands stand in your army?" She paused as if hunting for a nugget of information hidden in the folds of her mind. "You have not quite reached a thousand, have you?" The Council Leader blanched. Stripped of its flowery promises, the substance of the Sons of Mil's treaty with the Fomorians was tenuous at best.

"Please," said Baoth, his arms outstretched in hope, "let us discuss an equitable treaty between the Tuatha Dé, the Sons of Mil, and the Fomorians. The Land of Immensity is big enough for all to dwell peaceably."

The flicker of optimism quickly died, snuffed out as a pinched candle flame. "Enough of this charade. It is not even good entertainment!" The Mórrígan glared at Daghdha. "At best, you were foolish to cede land to this race without consulting your siblings. At worst, you had nefarious motives. Which is it, brother? Either way, the Tuatha Dé and the Dragon People have been deceived and betrayed. War is at our door." Daghdha slumped in the huge throne. Previously, the seat had seemed too small for his vast frame. Now it seemed to dwarf him.

"That is a conversation for the Womb-Born and the Dragon Queen, not our enemies." Lazarus's rebuke left the position of the Sons of Mil in no doubt and produced pale faces and sweaty brows. The Mórrígan looked to Lazarus. He inclined his head, and she addressed the Sons of Mil's delegation.

"Leave Muria and return to your homes. No one in this room or of the Tuatha Dé will harm you. I doubt you will receive the same consideration from the Fomorians."

The omission of Clíodhna caused a ripple of anxiety among the delegation. Baoth nervously asked, "And the Queen of the Dragons?"

Clío's lessons from The Mórrígan proved effective. She smiled menacingly and Baoth trembled. "You are beneath my concern. My dragons will not interfere… unless you give me cause."

Relief proved short-lived for Baoth and his Council. "The Tuatha Dé and the Dragons will not have to destroy the Sons of Mil," said Lazarus. "The Fomorians do not have allies—only thralls. Look at the example of the Nemed whose numbers were vastly greater than your race. The Fomorians' first act will be to either annihilate your tribe or enthral you. Either way, the Sons of Mil will be erased from history, and we will not come to your defence.

"Get out of my sight."

\*\*\*

Lazarus turned to Manannán as the Sons of Mil's delegation scurried from the chamber. "I wronged you in the past, brother, and for that, I am sorry. As an apology, you are free to destroy the Fomorian settlements and cities that infest the depths. Withdraw the ability of the Fomorians to breathe underwater. There can be no retreat to the seas. I would, however, ask you to wait until their armies are on our lands."

Never one for long speeches, Manannán nodded, and his countenance lightened.

\*\*\*

As the chamber cleared, Lazarus looked at Clío. He could not hide the pride in his eyes. "You played your part well." Clío shrugged. "What will be asked of you next will be more difficult. Are your dragons ready... and united?" Clío dipped her head. "Good. For the first time, I think we are a move ahead of our enemies."

"Balora?"

"She did not achieve her mission. The Cauldron is safe."

"Do you still maintain that stealing the Cauldron was her sole objective?"

Lazarus looked curiously at Clío. "You are not of that opinion?"

Clío shook her head. "On the one hand, yes she was here to confirm the existence and power of the artefact, and she accomplished that. Its form and size were a surprise to her, ruling out an opportunistic theft. I doubt she knows that the Cauldron can change size, yet, but that will not stop future attempts to steal it."

The Dragon Queen hesitated, unsure if she should speak openly. "On the other, like you, Balora is conflicted. Her actions showed her primary mission was not to steal the Cauldron but to ensure her lover's wounds had healed. After spending several days with you, I presume she confirmed your full recovery."

Lazarus ran agitated fingers through long charcoal-black hair. In the Land of Immensity, the tresses rested on his shoulders. "She says she is a thief, not an enemy." Exasperated, he looked at Clío. "Should I believe her?"

"Balora is clever and pragmatic, and perhaps thief is the best description. What is obvious is that she feels belittled and betrayed by the Fomorian nobility. She is not committed to the Fomorian war because she sees no profit in it. If I were to guess, I'd say she knows her future lies neither in the Land of Immensity nor Fomoria."

"Will she return to Ireland?"

"Why not? Apparently, she has no need of the portals to traverse worlds." Clío inhaled deeply. "The imminent war between the Tuatha Dé and Fomoria needs to be settled quickly and decisively, and we must return to the Land of the Humans. What is your plan?"

# CHAPTER 49

Balora woke up screaming from a sleep filled with terrifying visions. Sweat lathered her thick, black hide, and the whites of her eyes were bloodshot from salty tears. In the latest dream her injury had burst open, poison raged through her body, and her lifeblood gushed until she was no more than an empty husk. She gingerly touched the puckered edges of the knife wound and felt her bed linen. Reassured her sheets were wet from perspiration not blood, her heartbeat subsided.

Nightmares had persistently invaded Balora's sleep after she departed the Land of Immensity. Underlying their physical nature came the realisation she was strong but not immortal. In recent days, the dreams' nature had changed to prophetic visions. The wailing of hundreds of thousands—old and young, men, women, and children—haunted Balora. The sounds of a nation struggling for air tormented her ears. The crashing of great waves against failing walls and defences filled Balora with horror and anguish. *No, it cannot be. Surely, Lazarus would not allow it. Have the Fomorian hierarchy and nobility overplayed their hand?*

"*Fools!*" she roared.

＊＊＊

"Pompous, incompetent clowns!" thundered Balora, striding into the beachhead pavilion. In her fury, she tossed aside tables laden with food, drink, maps, and stratagems. Insulted, the Fomorian High King glared at her. In contrast, the generals and members of the High Council scoffed at what they perceived as her impotence. How could a mere female understand the complexities of war? Still, none dared to remove the queen. Her savagery was well known. Some of them would die.

This was the second time she had interrupted their discussion of the upcoming battle with the Tuatha Dé and the anticipated glorious victory. Five days earlier, Balora had bulldozed her way into their strategy meeting and ranted incoherently about the destruction of Fomorian cities and dwellings in the depths.

Asked for evidence, Balora cited nightmares and visions. At first, they doubted her sanity, but, in honour of her father, they nodded paternally and thanked her for her insights. They recommended that a counsellor should attend her and she should rest until her mind settled. Only the veteran Fomorian commander-in-chief looked at Balora with anything other than amusement and pity. Still, it was unclear whether he was evaluating her as an addition to his concubines. She was, after all, a beautiful demon.

"It was I who asked *Queen* Balora to attend this gathering," said the General. His emphasis on Balora's status served as a sharp reminder of propriety to those in attendance. It elicited grunts of acquiescence from some and mutterings of, "Scheming whore," from others. He dipped his broad head to Balora.

"Perhaps you would, with more control and less emotion, describe your recent mission *and* visions." The latter prompted a round of eye-rolling and derisory snorts of, "He wants to fuck her." Glares from Balora and the General brought the malcontents to order.

The retelling, although delivered calmly, made little difference. The Council's minds were made up and sides taken. Future glories were inevitable. The truth and contrary opinions were not what they wanted to hear. The General shrugged broad shoulders and looked at Balora. "Did you expect anything else?"

Balora shook her head and, for the briefest of moments, she felt a deep despondency before anger established dominance. The army's generals returned to squabbling over the spoils of a battle not yet fought, much less won. They jostled for the position of their clann, not for battle strategy but to maximise the opportunities for glory, pillage, and political advantage.

Only Balora observed the shimmering, translucent shade that moved within their midst, whispering into the ears and minds of the Fomorian hierarchy. The Mórrígan, the Queen of Whispers and Shadows, was already at war. Balora shrugged broad shoulders. She could have warned the king and his generals of The Mórrígan's presence, but they would neither have listened to nor believed her.

*** 

"*Outside!*" Several days later, the order barked by the General left no room for refusal. Dutifully, if grudgingly, the Fomorian king, council, and generals fell into line and followed. Their pavilion sat on a high mound, which had long sightlines, south to the coast and north to the smouldering ruins of the Sons of Mil city. Beyond that, mirage-like, the capital of Muria hovered on the horizon. None commented on the sky's colour change from its normal vibrant blue to tones of grey and purple. In the firmament, the sun held its apex position, casting no shadow and giving advantage to neither side.

By any measure, the Fomorian army, forty thousand strong and supported by a hundred thousand Nemed, was impressive. The demons had hulking, naturally armoured physiques. Needing space for their wingspans, they stood in relaxed rows with each clann distinguished by its banners and flags. Black wings furled and unfurled, although this was partly to avert cramps and relieve the monotony.

The front rows towered over those further back. These were the descendants of those who had thwarted the Tuatha Dé army at the Battle of Mag Tuired. Few among them entertained any doubt they would do so again. They carried giant axes, clubs, and tridents, but their primary weapons remained their brute strength, talons, and teeth.

The Fomorian army appeared a dark mass of mindless brutes, but appearances are deceptive. True, the Fomorians' capacity for brutality was unmatched—except perhaps by humans. In both instances, intelligence made the trait more deadly and horrific. Further back, in the army's tents, intermittent screams rose from broken and enslaved men, women, and children. Once a proud people, the Sons of Mil were now cruelly abused by the resentful dregs of Fomorian society.

"Glorious. Irresistible. A fighting force beyond all others." The High King beamed at his commander-in-chief as if looking for consent. The troubled look on the General's face provided no comfort, and there was no relief from the insistent whispering in the king's mind. The others preened and puffed up their chests. Balora observed and shook her head. She caught glimpses of ethereal flashes of light and shadow. She put that down to the spikes of pain in her head and her unrelenting visions. *Maybe I am mad.*

The General pointed to the gathered army. His voice was deep and sonorous, perfectly matching his girth. "What you see before you is what remains of the Fomorian nation. There will be no reinforcements. We have no reserve. We will not be resupplied. We stand alone."

"Preposterous!" exclaimed the king. He was loudly supported by the High Council's civic members and generals. "We have at least this number in reserve, and our supply logistics are secure. Our population, men, women, and children, are numbered in the millions." The king glared at his general. "Disloyalty is unacceptable. Should I replace you?"

The ancient general bowed. "You can replace me and execute me if you wish. It will not change what I said, but you will lose your most experienced commander. First, answer one question. Where are your gills and webbed paws?" He pointed to the ocean. "Go for a swim and test how long you can stay underwater." The soldier's matter-of-fact delivery sent a chill up the king's back.

The king and generals frantically felt behind their ears for the gills and held paws up to see the webbing. Neither existed. "What does this mean?" asked the king. The silencing of the king and his sycophants brought a grim smile to Balora's lips.

The General pointed to Balora. "Everything you mocked her for is confirmed. We have no home and no families. Their bodies will wash up on these beaches long after we are dead. Vultures will feast on their flesh, and the sun will bleach their bones." Gasps of shock and disbelief reverberated within the group. The shade that moved undetected among them and whispered in their ears kept their minds blind, chaotic, and focused on war.

When they returned to the pavilion, Balora looked contemptuously at the group. "You underestimated King Lazarus, The Mórrígan, and even the fat Daghdha. You learned nothing from the Battle of Mag Tuired. Centuries of exile served only to multiply and reinforce your delusions."

Balora's voice rose. "You believed that after millennia, the Womb-Born were weak and had no stomach for a war. Your delusions said they would tremble at your army and cede land and power to you. *Fools!* With a single command to his brother—the sea god, Manannán—Lazarus drowned our nation, our children, and our future." Resentment flared in Balora's garnet eyes. "Worse, you ignored my plan—the one option for negotiation."

"Now who is confused? Your search for a mythical Cauldron is nothing but an over-indulged child's faerie tale," snarled the High King.

Balora dipped her head to the General. "I rest my case. They are idiots and do not deserve or merit your loyalty. I pity you. Watch your back, General."

At Balora's stinging rebuke, the Fomorian High King roared, "We have many queens in our army who will breed a new nation. Our army outnumbers the Tuatha Dé. We prevailed before. It is well-known that the Tuatha Dé can never grow beyond forty-four thousand. Each death inflicted on them sentences them to centuries of recapithe, if not the final death. When they reawaken, they will be our slaves."

The king pointed to his general. "*You* will order the army to assault Muria. A fast, aggressive attack will decapitate the leadership. Their army is little more than undisciplined bands of wandering heroes seeking glory for themselves. How many of them will gather to face us?"

The king's confidence grew as he spoke and while the raven shadow perched on his shoulder whispered in his ear. When he looked at Balora, the Fomorian ruler felt unease. *What did she know? What did she see?* "You will fight alongside us. Perhaps you can prove you are more than a whore who dreams and schemes."

Balora shook her head. "No. My place is with the remnant of my command, and they are in the Land of the Humans."

Outraged at Balora's disobedience, foam flecked the lips of the king as he shouted, "I can have you executed!"

"Yes, you could, and I would respect you for that, but you would not be alive to witness it." Balora smiled, revealing rows of pointed teeth. As her tail swished the dirt, she raised her paws, showing sharp talons. "You are a coward." She gestured scornfully at those gathered. "And these fat pretenders have not fought in centuries. I have. How many of your generals do you wish to lose *before* the battle, my king?"

Balora smiled at the General. "I do not include you in my observation. Please walk with me."

\*\*\*

Accompanied by the General, Balora walked away from the agitated group surrounding the king. She nodded to a row of tall spikes. Impaled on each were the heads of the Sons of Mil's king and his council. "They never told you what they knew or saw, did they?" asked Balora. "Nor did any of their Watchers or civilians, even under torture." The General shook his head.

"Will you?" he asked.

Balora shook her head. "They were a proud, stubborn people who, like the Fomorians, deserved better leaders. They took their knowledge to the grave. I respect that and will not betray them."

The General smiled. "You would be a great battle queen, Balora. Better than your father. We might confound your pessimism. We do not need to win the war. We just need to secure a negotiating position… like the last time."

The demon queen laughed. "Where is the profit for me?" Balora placed curling talons on the General's arm. "My advice. No matter what the king orders, proceed cautiously. Measure your steps and any counsel offered." A movement at the edge of her sight drew Balora's attention, and she watched a black raven soar high in the sky. She dipped her head to the bird.

"One last piece of counsel. Disregard the whisperings in your head. The Mórrígan started the Second Fomorian War many weeks ago. By assembling the Fomorian army on this beach, you lost the first battle." The General scowled, but any riposte was quenched by Balora's next words. "In the discussions, I heard no talk of the dragons."

The General rolled his eyes, and Balora shook her head. "You are badly, and I suspect deliberately, misinformed. The Fomorian plan to place Ciarán on the Dragon Throne and foment a black dragon rebellion failed. Instead, the serpents are united under a new queen—Clíodhna, daughter of Bráchthine. She is also Lazarus' ward and his daughter."

"No."

# CHAPTER 50

"Were you successful?" asked Lazarus.

"Of course." The Mórrígan smiled. Her brother always underestimated her talent for mischief-making, although his inflexion suggested amusement rather than judgment. "Did you doubt me, Brother?"

Lazarus laughed. "Perhaps my assumption that you have not had much practice in fostering mass strife during the past few thousand years was ill-founded."

On the periphery of the discussion was Daghdha. The High King had made an impressive start to cleaning up Muria's infrastructure and removing its less-than-savoury elements. That said, a high percentage of the previous denizens were whores, who now lived in tents beyond the city walls. In their profession, war was excellent business, and they refused to be bullied from taking advantage of the opportunity. Indeed, many would face down a Fomorian demon than confront an angry striapach brandishing a blade.

Daghdha coughed. "Am I to have a part in the war? No one has asked." He held Lazarus' gaze without breaking and his amber eyes were crystal clear.

"Do you have the Staff?" asked Lazarus. "It is a weapon that could give us a significant advantage."

A frown accompanied Daghdha's answer. "No. I did not think it safe or wise to keep all the artefacts together in Muria, so I sent it and the Harp away… far away." Frustration and hurt rang clear in Daghdha's voice.

"Where?"

"The Land of the Humans. I thought since you were there, it would be secure. Not in my wildest dreams did I think *he* would rise again, or we would be at war with the Fomorians. I am sorry, Lazarus."

"You did the right thing, Daghdha. We will discuss the safekeeping of the artefacts after the war." Daghdha's eyes shone at the praise. "As for *him*, he is gathering strength but is weak and without form. Uathach was his eyes. When I blinded her, An-Ársa fled." Lazarus paused. "We four will consider Uathach's future later. Do we permit her to use the Cauldron? Technically, she was possessed and any evil she did was not her fault. Like Clíodhna, I favour clemency."

He turned to Clío. "Are your dragons ready?"

Clío nodded. "As agreed, we will remain out of sight behind the city until called upon to attack the Fomorian army. It was challenging to limit the numbers. My main force is two hundred, of which half are Clann Dubh." Lazarus' eyebrow twitched. "They are led by their new queen. She was Conn's wife and is a fearsome lady." Clío chuckled. "I may have a rival." Lazarus' brow became deeply furrowed.

"They know the consequences of disobedience, Da. More than that, they know I will not shrink from slaughtering their families." Sharp intakes of breath followed in the wake of Clío's cold words. "I also have a reserve of four hundred from the other clanns, just in case."

In a more sombre tenor, Clío said, "This will not be a walkover. The Tuatha Dé and my dragons have not fought a no-holds-barred, full-scale war since Mag Tuired. That outcome proved neither satisfactory nor decisive." Clío's scolding tone did not go unmarked. The fledgeling queen had become increasingly comfortable with her new position and the accumulated knowledge of the dragons she inherited.

Lazarus stroked his non-existent beard, causing The Mórrígan to round on him. "The Hag, Lazarus! Grow a beard. Then your affectation will be less annoying." Clío giggled at The Mórrígan's scolding. Yet, both women sensed Lazarus' unease.

"I agree with Clíodhna," said Lazarus. "The Fomorians are ferocious, well-disciplined warriors. With their homeland devastated, they have no place and no families to return to. I think I may have made a rash judgment. Unlike us, they have nothing to lose."

The Mórrígan stared with disbelief at her brother. "Of course we have something to lose—The Land of Immensity. You should reconsider your words. Anúna appointed *you* to be the leader of the Tuatha Dé. You cannot be divorced from *your* people. It is commendable that you care for and love humanity, but you are not one of them. You are and always will be Tuatha Dé."

***

The Fomorian commander scratched his snout and, with a grunt, plucked a clump of irritating, long nose hairs. It was not the coarse, ticklish hairs that bothered the General. The Fomorian army drew closer to Muria, halting no more than half a mile from the city's gates. So far, they marched unopposed, except for blades of grass. The demigods had transformed forests into plains, depriving his army of any cover. This alone was enough to raise the General's concern.

They encountered no skirmishing groups, not even random bands of heroes seeking to burnish their reputations. No envoys emerged from Muria, seeking to negotiate peace or surrender. Indeed, the Tuatha Dé gave every appearance of ignoring the Fomorian army. Only glinting helmets and spearheads along the entire length of the city's walls gave the lie to that perception.

"What am I missing? Do they want a siege?" mused the General. It was a tactic to which he had given little consideration. His aides gave no hint that they understood their commander's question or that they cared. Once again, the General's eyes scoured the city's walls. He glanced upwards. In the ominous, grey sky, a magnificent black raven with the wingspan of an albatross circled, swooped, and rose on warm updrafts.

"*Bitseach!*" snarled the General, knowing full well it was The Mórrígan. Her laugh was even more terrible because of its childish tone. He consoled himself that at least, while the Queen of Whispers and Shadows flew, she could not encourage more foolish behaviour among the Fomorian hierarchy. His confidence was misplaced because The Mórrígan was the Tuatha Dé's Holy Trinity.

A cough from his second-in-command drew the General out of his contemplations. Moments later, Balora's final words, before she padded away across the lush meadow towards the sea, surfaced in his thoughts. *Where are the dragons?* A few seconds later, he heard shouts of "Dragons!"

The General smiled and thanked Balora. Half of this army was already in the air.

\* \* \*

"It seems the good general has regained his wits," said Clío.

Lazarus turned to her. "Without meaning to pre-empt the advice of Aodh and your clann leaders, may I suggest that the Queen of the Dragons puts half of her dragons in the air and uses the other half to attack the Fomorian flanks?" Clío gave him a look of pity which made The Mórrígan and Daghdha roar with laughter.

Deflated, Lazarus chuckled. "Your shield-maiden is not shadowing you as normal. I assume she is already in the air."

Clío nodded. "Ceara is unhappy at what she sees is a dereliction of duty. Even the presence of my flight of guards at my side did not improve her temper." Clío sighed. "We eventually compromised. That said, it's not actually me that is directing the dragons' battle tactics." She turned to Aodh. "I take advice from my general."

"You are most assuredly in command, my queen." Aodh's eyes twinkled.

Lazarus laughed and turned to The Mórrígan. "Are you ready to switch roles to the Queen of Desolation? Are the Tuatha Dé ready to get bloody? We would not want the dragons to claim all the glory. They are already insufferably arrogant without having their egos puffed up more."

***

One hundred huge, brightly-coloured dragons in full flight, and without camouflage, is a terrifying sight. Clío watched from the ground with rising jealousy. Still, she recognised that most of the dragons with Ceara had many centuries of experience in battle. Hence, she placed the aerial fight in the hands of wiser heads. As Clío watched from the city walls, a densely packed chevron of one hundred serpents flew at an incredible speed towards the massive cloud of winged Fomorians. The effect was like that of a well-placed cue ball on a snooker table—only this ball was on fire.

Seconds before impact, Ceara bellowed, "*Fire!*" The layered flanks of the dragons spewed gouts of dragon breath at the Fomorians. Tradition and lust for glory dictated that Fomorian chieftains and kings fought in the front ranks. In an instant, the serpents incinerated the majority of the demons' leaders and crippled thousands of others. Drifts of ash fell like black snow on the Fomorian ground troops. In the purple-grey expanse, the remaining Fomorians, like snooker balls, scattered into smaller clusters across the battlefield.

The thrill of the assault almost made Ceara forgive Clío for ordering her to take command of the aerial battle. This was Ceara's stage and the opening of the sky war was a well-choreographed ballet. Reeling from the dragons' momentum, those in the shattered Fomorian formation searched feverishly for new leaders to assume command. Nerves needed steadying and orders communicated.

Having seized the advantage, the dragons sought to sustain it. Ceara divided her serpents into five smaller chevrons to attack the smaller but denser clumps of Fomorians. Dragon breath spouted as the leading dragons head-butted and burned the remaining demon chieftains and low-status demons under their control.

***

"Rounds one and two to us," muttered Clío. More charred flesh, demon

300

corpses, and limbs rained from the skies. Injured Fomorians with shredded wings tumbled to the earth, hoping to land softly and safely behind their comrades. Instead, uncontrolled impacts with hard-packed dirt shattered bones.

The spears of the Tuatha Dé dispatched those falling within sight of Muria's walls. In the first attacks, Clío estimated one-third of the Fomorians died or were too severely wounded to fight. "That makes it only seventy to one," she snorted. The odds had narrowed, but Clío knew it would be a long day of bloody attrition before either side could claim victory.

Clío's relationship with the Goddess was tenuous, yet she prayed for Ceara's safety as she strode along the parapet to join her dragons, who were assembled before Muria's main gateway. Her nose wrinkled, and she twisted her face in a grimace of disgust. "What is that stench?" She spat a glob of saliva over the parapet. Ignoring The Mórrígan's chastising expression, she spat again. "And the awful taste?"

Lazarus chuckled, which did nothing to dampen Clío's growing nausea but caused her golden eyes to flare red at her da. "It is the Fomorians. In battle, they produce and exude a range of foul-smelling and -tasting chemicals from their sweat glands. It is a common tactic employed by many land and marine animals to knock enemies off their balance. With the numbers the demons have, it can smell rank."

"And you neglected to tell me this because? The Nemed already roil my stomach and now this." Piqued, Clío stomped from the battlements and took her position at the head of her dragons.

The Mórrígan looked on Lazarus with disapproval. "It seems *I* must spend much more time with Clío. She needs to learn the art and brutality of war. That is my area of wisdom." Lazarus grunted and muttered peevishly under his breath.

\*\*\*

"Let's do this." As speeches go, Clío's was neither inspiring nor comforting. However, dragons tend towards a hermit-like existence of isolation from large groups or communities. Therefore, they are less prone to verbosity, and Clío's brevity found favour.

"Any advice?" Clío looked at the red-scaled Aodh on her right and Clann Dubh's queen on her left. Clann Dubh aimed to redeem its pride and valour and had the place of honour at the front of the assault.

"Stay behind us," was both dragons' gruff reply. "We have no wish to go through a millennium of searching for a new queen." Both mouths opened, revealing rows of enormous white teeth. They arranged their maws in a fashion Clío recognised as a serpent's smile.

"Tuili, bitseach!" growled Clío as she attempted and failed to rearrange her jaws into a smile.

"From what I have heard and witnessed when you fought my husband in the Arena, you have inherited your mother's aptitude for battle and"—the Clann Dubh queen's smile widened—"unconventional tactics. Let that guide you. Now is not the time to try new tactics."

Aodh grunted his agreement. "Nevertheless, your unique colouring makes you an obvious target." He nodded to the black dragon. "We will guard you but also have our clanns to command. Your usual guard of ten red dragons are behind you. Their sole job is to die before you do. Ceara will join them when she thinks the aerial battle is won." The general stymied Clío's impulse to protest. "You should know by now this is not up for debate." Clío's eyes widened, and, somewhat embarrassed, she turned around to acknowledge the members of her shield.

"Hi girls," said Clío. She wondered what their names were and blushed at her lack of such basic knowledge. *I'll treat them to a night out after the battle and get to know them better.* Serendipity laughed.

"Oorah!" shouted the dragon squad, adopting the shout from the U.S. Marines, because it was short and easy for a dragon mouth to bellow.

Aodh chuckled. "No one protects better and fights more viciously than females. My choice is pragmatic." Having reached the limits of his loquaciousness, the red serpent brought the conversation to an end. "I suggest we get on with the fight. Your subjects are impatient for battle."

The rumble of assent from the queen of the black dragons spread along the serpent ranks like a peal of thunder.

\*\*\*

The earth trembled under the pounding of heavy Fomorian paws as twenty thousand demons, accompanied by one hundred thousand Nemed, crossed the fertile meadow. *It will not be long before we assault their walls.* Wings spread, the General leapt ahead of his army. At the end of each of his long arms, a great trident and mace were grasped in his talons.

The General cursed and swatted away the black flakes that drifted to the ground. The grass was dark and greasy with charred Fomorian skin and blood. The warriors behind him swore as they were splattered by a variety of body parts and liquids from their airborne comrades. *I doubt it is going well above, but that is beyond my control. This is not.*

Another sound, a deep bass to his baritone, resonated in the General's ears. The ground before him rippled as if a great beast burrowed beneath its surface. To the Fomorians, it seemed an avalanche of huge boulders tumbled towards their front flank. The demons, arrayed in their standard phalanx formation—twenty ranks of one thousand—roared defiance and charged to meet the ancient enemy. Shouts of "Avenge our families!" increased and the General smiled. His warriors did not need him to motivate them.

Clío's dragons, formed up in two ranks of one hundred, matched the span of the enemy's front line. With perfect timing and before the opponents clashed, the forward row of dragons spewed dragon breath. Man or beast, all have a common fear of fire. No claw or blade slash can match its agony. Burning throats cried out until silenced by the firestorm.

Unrelenting, the forward dragons continued to immerse the demons in flames. The air stank of brimstone and burning flesh. The momentum of the serpents carried the front rank into the midst of the Fomorian formation. At a bellowed order from Aodh, the dragons' rear row divided, spreading out to attack the left and right flanks of the enemy. Dragon breath remained the dragons' primary weapon until the likelihood of "friendly fire" became too great a risk.

An atmosphere filled with smoke and blackened demon debris choked nostrils and throats. Many on both sides wanted to stop and throw up or slake dry throats, but close-quarter fighting left no time for such luxuries. Claws shredded skin and tails lashed out. Clío heard the deep *barrr-ewww* of ancient Celtic battle-horns and thumping of bodhráin and smiled. The Womb-Born and Tuatha Dé had taken the field.

With a cry of "*Ní ghéillfimid, ná ní chúlaímid. Ní thaispeánfaimid aon Trócaire*"—"We will not surrender, nor will we back down. We will show no mercy!" Clío led her dragons into the centre of the battle. A rustle of red, crest feathers and a scent she would never forget told her Ceara had arrived.

"Follow the queen!" roared Ceara. It was unnecessary, Clío's lungs were bursting from attempting to stay abreast of her dragon shield-wall.

\*\*\*

In the skies, the battle became one of flapping wings and swishing tails, slashing talons and snapping jaws. After the initial shock of the dragon attack, a surviving Fomorian queen took control and changed tactics. Small swarms were formed to attack and bring down isolated and wounded dragons.

The greatest damage to the Fomorians was the death of their veterans in the early clashes. Consequently, the queen was left with younger warriors who, although brave and strong, had a lower level of battle intelligence. To the Fomorian queen's chagrin, the dragons reorganised their battle plan to fight in pairs, with each partner protecting the other from snapping demons. Vastly outnumbered, experience reigned as the dragons contemptuously swatted the Fomorians like clouds of fat horseflies.

Nevertheless, neither demon nor dragon possess unlimited strength, and few creatures can maintain the rigours of an extended aerial battle without breaks for rest and nourishment. On both sides, the toll from extreme fatigue and screaming muscles, spasming for rest and relief, grew. Fomorian wings flapped slower and were shredded by dragon claws. Dragon tails swished more slowly.

On both sides, reflexes dulled, and necks were clamped and snapped in massive jaws. Some Fomorians took comfort in small groups isolated from the main battle, but that strategy left them open to the enemy's dragon breath. The Fomorian numbers dwindled, and their strength waned.

The dragons were not immune from injury or death. Battle weariness diminished the effectiveness of the great bellows in their chests and hence the supply of dragon breath. The serpents also had a unique disadvantage. Sustaining their colossal size in the sky was an immense drain on their physical and mental fortitude. The weak were swarmed and ripped asunder in increasing numbers. For the dismembered serpents, there would be glory but no recovery.

On the ground, the earth reverberated with falling dragons and demons. Great scales in multiple colours and glistening with blood glided to the ground. The Clann Dearg chieftain in charge of the dragon reserve counted the death toll. Over one-third of the serpents were dead or severely injured. Of the Fomorians, two-thirds of their force was mortally wounded or burnt shells.

The dragon reserve's commander turned to his second-in-command. "Finish this before we lose more comrades." The aide nodded and shouted orders. Two hundred fresh black and red dragons launched their colossal bodies into the sky.

"*No!*" shrieked the Fomorian queen. The force was greater than that which had commenced the fight. Despair overwhelmed Fomorian minds. If they lost, where would they go? The Fomorians had fought well and bloodied the haughty serpents. The task before them, tough when they were fresh and had overwhelming numbers, now seemed impossible. Apart from a few Fomorian queens, the leaders were dead.

Waves of pheromones flooded the air, broadcasting a new command to the demons.

"Retreat, survive, and build new nests or join the ground battle." Most of the remnant chose survival.

\*\*\*

In the chaos of battle, Ceara took a moment to assess Clío. The queen showed no hint of allowing her seven remaining guards—three had fallen to save her life—to steer her away from the fight. Indeed, Clío showed every intention of battering her way to the heart of the Fomorian formation. Any thoughts of ring-fencing the queen to protect her from the fight were sharply rebuffed with threats of violence. Yet, there was no way Ceara was going to lose a queen. So, with three dragons protecting the queen's back and two on each side, Ceara strode ahead of the formation as they slashed and burned a path forward.

The scene reminded Ceara of the few times she had clumsily attempted ice skating in Belfast. The mass of skaters circled the rink's perimeter, but once passage had been negotiated, they discovered an island of calm at its centre. Reaching the middle of the demons' formation was the safest place for the queen. Fomorians traditionally put the most formidable warriors on the flanks and the weakest in the centre. Fire and brute force created cracks in the demons' formation, allowing the dragons to carve a path to its core.

"Let them through!" roared the wily Fomorian General. "Encircle the serpents, reinforce the perimeter, wear the bastards down. Our hides are as tough as their scales." The General's statement was bravado. Still, he needed his soldiers angry, confident, and willing to sacrifice themselves. Had he been successful, it would have been a remarkable achievement since Fomorians had a propensity to martyr others but not themselves.

Two hundred palace-sized dragons formed a constantly rotating circle with Clío, her guard, and her shield-maiden positioned at its centre. They were covered with a sludge of foul-smelling demon gore and charred flesh. Surrounding them, the Fomorians hurled hate and slashed with a hedge of claws. A few Fomorians took wing, but they proved easy targets for dragon breath and discouraged others from following their example. A mist of spit and blood hovered above the heaving mass. Dark ichor flowed from demon wounds, turning the pleasant meadow into a nightmarish marshland.

The sight saddened Clío, who wanted to find some good in others. She smiled grimly as she recalled Balora. Even that dark, selfish demon had saving graces. Clío wondered if they would meet again. She thought it likely given the band of Fomorians who remained in Ireland. "Do they not deserve some measure of compassion?" Spoken aloud, if softly, Clío's rhetorical question touched Ceara's ears.

"Mercy of a kind was shown once, but that did not end well for the Land of Immensity… and your homeland. Give the order, my queen."

Clío nodded, rose above the fray, and opened her great maw.

\*\*\*

Too late, the General sensed the trap. He remonstrated with himself and congratulated the new Queen of the Dragons. "The bitseach has a natural affinity for battle and mayhem." He roared desperate orders to his aides and messengers. "Retreat! Abandon the circle! Form up in clanns and warbands. Attack and overwhelm the beasts when they give chase."

\*\*\*

Lazarus' Blade of Light perpetually caught the sun, even when slicing through Fomorian flesh or the Nemed's wraithlike bodies. The Nemed's talents were better suited to the darkness, to back alleys, and to whisperings in the night. Although heavily outnumbering the Tuatha Dé, the thralls had no defence against demigods. Still, the clash in full daylight delayed and distracted the Tuatha Dé from joining their ally in the battle. Perhaps it was what their Fomorian masters wanted. The Nemed fell in their tens of thousands until only a remnant remained. Neither Fomorian nor Tuatha Dé cared.

Above the battleground, The Mórrígan, in giant raven form,

swooped and soared. She watched the slaughter of the Nemed with unhidden satisfaction. "Loathsome creatures. Vermin." There was no pity in her voice. To The Mórrígan, the Nemed's leaders had walked their people into a disastrous relationship with the Fomorians. Yet, perhaps fatally, what dammed the Nemed was that they did not revolt against the Fomorian agreement or ask for help. Thus, in The Mórrígan's eyes, they had no place in the Land of Immensity or the human domains.

The Mórrígan looked down upon Lazarus with sisterly pride as he took his rightful position, leading and marshalling the Tuatha Dé army. She observed the golden horde stride closer towards the clash of the dragons and Fomorians. As the battering ram of the Tuatha Dé column touched the Fomorians' outer circle, the demigods divided.

It appeared Lazarus intended to corral the demons while the dragons fought at the centre of the circle. Alarm bells pealed loudly in her mind. *Why and for what?* What disturbed her? A sickening realisation dawned on The Mórrígan as she watched Clío rise above the fight and saw her great mouth open to shout one command: "Dragon breath!"

"No!" The Mórrígan swooped downwards screaming, "Retreat! Retreat!" But in her guise, her words were the cries of a bird.

Clío's order bellowed out before she spotted the enormous black raven and heard a scream that made no sense. Victory was within the dragons' grasp. *What made The Mórrígan shriek? What did she see?* A bright sword flashed on the periphery of her vision, and Clío's eyes widened. "Lazarus!" Had no one alerted the Tuatha Dé to the strategy?

Once the order was given, Clío could not rescind it. The sound of huge lungs filling with air was followed by great gouts of fire spouting from the circle of dragons. To avoid the risk of harming their comrades, the serpents faced outward, towards the Fomorians. Thus, none held back on the ferocity of the burning and corrosive flames. In an instant, several ranks of demons disintegrated into black ash. With another deep breath and exhalation, the fire penetrated deeper into the Fomorians' rear ranks.

To stem the dragon breath, many rushed forward. The demons pushed aside burning comrades to close in on the serpents. Most were incinerated. The few who reached the dragon circle were felled by scaley tails and sharp claws or impaled on twin pairs of horns.

\*\*\*

The rising stench of burnt flesh filled Lazarus' nostrils. Added to this, the incoherent screeching of the raven circling above increased his level of concern. *Is Clíodhna in trouble?* That thought increased his heart rate substantially, but he was helpless to render assistance.

The Mórrígan, having decided she would not let her brother face a painful and true death, alone, swooped down and landed beside him. "Retreat, you stupid bastard! Sound the retreat!" Wild-eyed, The Mórrígan gripped Lazarus' shoulders, held his gaze, and uttered two words: "Dragon breath."

"*Shite!*"

# CHAPTER 51

*The Island of Dragons*

The war was over and Lazarus and Clío were impatient to return to Northern Ireland. However, the mourning season for the fallen dragons had just begun. There was little need for grieving among the demigods of the Tuatha Dé. Even if the wound was mortal, it might simply be a longer process to full health. They had the Cauldron and the long sleep of recapithe.

The dragons did not. A powerful, yet small, race, the dragons could ill afford to lose one serpent, let alone scores. The memories would always be fresh, but it would take millennia to replace the dead. Thus, the Island of Dragons was awash in tears for the fallen from the Second Fomorian War. Funeral pyres burnt fiercely on the mountain tops celebrating and mourning the dead.

Clío, Daghdha, Lazarus, and The Mórrígan walked together past the blazing fires, along with hundreds of others. They paused respectfully at each one to sympathise with the families and ask the Goddess for journeying mercies. Dragon lore was vague about the serpents' afterlife. Clío knew Lazarus fully expected to see Bráchthine again, so reincarnation was a good bet. But under what conditions? Only the Goddess knew who would be chosen to rise like the phoenix from the ashes—and why.

The group were not obligated to pay homage. The gesture was appreciated by all, but one—Ceara. She had been sullen and withdrawn since the battle and had refused to talk to Clío. Neither would she accept her love's embrace nor share her bed. When the group stopped at the pyres for Clío's fallen guards, Ceara turned to Clío. "Name them." The tone was confrontational.

"What?"

"Your protectors died for you. Name them. Is it so difficult?"

Ceara's aggressive tone startled Clío. A worried Aodh stepped forward to chide his daughter, but Clío held a hand up and shook her head. Still, no matter how hard she tried, she could not recall her guards' names. She remembered her unspoken promise to get to know her guards after the war. Her cheeks blazed with shame. That she was a dragon multiplied Clío's omission hundreds of times.

Humiliated and close to tears, Clío asked, "Why are you doing this to me, Ceara?"

"You had your protectors and trainers for many months. They trained with you and fought at your side, yet you cannot put a name to any of them." Ceara paused at one pyre where her father and mother stood. A cold chill ran up Clío's spine when Ceara pointed to the bonfire. "She was called Mór and was my sister."

\*\*\*

"This is dangerous, Lazarus," whispered The Mórrígan. "This could rent the dragons in two. The Tuatha Dé cannot afford a war within the dragons. Aodh and you need to stop whatever this is, *now*."

Lazarus shook his head. "No. Clío is the Queen of the Dragons. Ceara is her subject as well as her friend. It is Clío's problem to resolve. We cannot interfere between lovers, or we will be enemies when they make up. Patience, sister. I have faith in Clío… and you should have faith in me, regarding Balora."

\*\*\*

Mystified, Clío asked, "How can that be, Ceara? Dragon mothers only have two eggs. I know you have a brother. How do you have a sister?" The low but unambiguous growls emanating from Aodh and his partner were directed at Ceara. Both demonstrated their unhappiness at having private family matters exposed in public—more so at a time when their focus should be on grieving for Mór.

Clío's genuine question and her parents' ire unsettled Ceara's tirade and committed her to an explanation. "My brother and I are from my father's second partner. Mór's mother died in childbirth." Ceara looked at her father and mother's devastated faces, and her lip trembled. "Forgive me. This is my fault. I recommended Mór for Clío's guard. If I hadn't, she would be alive." A torrent of tears pooled on the scorched dirt before Mór's pyre. Desolated, Ceara fell to her knees, beating the red soil with her hands.

"No, Ceara. *I* selected Mór because she was a brave, skilled warrior, not because of your recommendation. Surely, you know I would never appoint someone to such an important position based on family. Only the Fomorians are to blame for Mór's death. Not you and certainly not Queen Clíodhna. You owe your friend an apology."

Ceara could not be consoled. Her chest heaved with sobbing, and her heart was cleaved by guilt. Aodh looked to Clío. His eyes begged her to intervene. She ran to Ceara and dropped to her knees. Whispering a prayer for wisdom to the Goddess, she put an arm around Ceara's shoulders. Clío heaved a sigh of relief when she was not rejected. She held Ceara close to her.

"I have no sister, Ceara," said Clío. "Hence, I cannot comprehend the pain of your loss. I may not know each of my guards' names, but I remember each of their faces. I promise I will find out their names and those of the others who died in battle. Nevertheless, I do not need their names to know that I bear the responsibility for their deaths. I will grieve for each of them until I cross the veil."

Queen and shield-maiden sobbed in each other's arms until the fires of the pyres became cold ash. As the sun rose, Ceara turned to Clío. "Would you mind if I took time away from being your shield-maiden? I need some time on my own."

Clío looked away so Ceara would not see the sorrow on her face.

When she turned back, she smiled and brushed a tress of red hair away from Ceara's face. "Take as much time as you need. I will wait for you." As Ceara's back disappeared into the distance, Clío's tears cascaded first onto the dirt and then over Lazarus' shirt as he knelt beside her and comforted his daughter.

The Mórrígan watched Ceara until she disappeared in the half-light of dusk and then she turned and walked over to the duo. As she listened to the cries of Clío and the soothing words of Lazarus, The Mórrígan's eyes glittered obsidian and she did what her nature demanded. The Queen of Desolation swore Clío and Lazarus' pain would be visited a hundred-fold on Ceara.

# CHAPTER 52

*The Land of Immensity*

A pensive Daghdha, aware that he was High King of the Tuatha Dé in name only, sat at the centre of the table and pondered what his future held. On his right sat Lazarus, and on his left, The Mórrígan. The rest of his brothers and sisters, the Womb-Born, filled the remaining places except one. That was where Clíodhna, Queen of the Dragons, squirmed.

Dejected about Ceara's absence, Clío had regressed and behaved like an adolescent. At the meeting of the Womb-Born, she was in perpetual motion as she constantly shifted on the cushion. For good measure, she also scratched her arse. She and the dragons had fulfilled their duty and Clío saw no reason for her presence in the Land of Immensity. Furthermore, she needed to be far from places that reminded her of Ceara.

Was her attendance punishment for singeing the egos of the Tuatha Dé? Most had escaped her dragons' flames with little more than minor burns, and the Cauldron's waters healed those with the severest injuries. Still, there was no ignoring the angry glances and annoyance of their embarrassment. *Spoilt brats.* In serpent fashion, Clío hissed and growled at her accusers while daring them to meet her angry gaze.

"For all that is wonderful, Clíodhna, sit at peace. The day will be long enough without the distraction of your constant fidgeting…" Lazarus paused before adding, "…and deliberately unguarded thoughts." The chastisement was a breath of fresh air to Clío. This sounded more like *her* Lazarus, and she smiled at his return. Control was within Clío's grasp when a giggle escaped her lips. Lazarus rolled his eyes, and more admonishing stares were turned her way.

Clío's guard, made up to ten again by Aodh, refused to leave her side. They also took every slight personally and deflected criticisms with unveiled threats of retaliation. Undoubtedly, Clío had much to learn about diplomacy and politics, but she was their queen, and they would brook no more Tuatha Dé slights. Unguarded thoughts reminded the Womb-Born their presence and continued sovereignty over the Land of Immensity were due to the dragons.

There had been no sign of Ceara since the night of the funerals. Therefore, Clío had no shield-maiden. It was a situation Aodh could not allow to continue. It reflected badly on him, his family, his clann, and the dragon nation. Yet, despite his entreaties, Clío steadfastly refused to consider even temporary solutions.

✻ ✻ ✻

Lazarus' cough brought focus and sobriety back to the room. The Fomorian General and the surviving members of the nation's High Council stood before the long table. "What fate awaits the Fomorian people?" asked the General. "I plead for mercy since only a few thousand survived the battle. My people present no threat to the Tuatha Dé or the Dragons."

The Mórrígan spoke. "The thorns on a rose's stem are few and small but can still draw blood and infect flesh. We know several queens fled the battle with significant numbers of warriors. And there is Balora." Obsidian eyes held the General's ruby gaze. He saw no compassion in them, and his shoulders slumped in resignation. Were the roles reversed, the Fomorians would show their enemies no mercy. None of the warring nations held the moral high ground. This was real life, not philosophy.

The Mórrígan turned to Lazarus and whispered in his ear. He sighed. "There can be no leniency. That will only encourage future confrontations."

"Many of the Tuatha Dé's offspring have Fomorian blood. Will you not foment discontent?" asked the General.

"That is a problem for another day and for the Tuatha Dé to resolve," said Lazarus.

"Procrastination is a politicians' strategy and is rarely successful. I never expected it of you," replied the General. "I request quick deaths for my warriors."

"For your men and women, yes. For you and your leaders, no." There was intense sadness in Lazarus' voice. The burden of past decisions sat heavily on his shoulders, and by nature, he was not vindictive. He turned to Clío. "May we prevail upon Queen Clíodhna to administer the executions?"

Clío smiled benignly at Lazarus, The Mórrígan, Daghdha, and the remaining Womb-Born. "No." A stunned silence fell upon the Tuatha Dé. The Fomorian General and Daghdha guffawed. "Dragons serve justice and retribution. We are not executioners."

Clío stood and stared at the Womb-Born. "My people fought and died willingly to recover a situation that was of the Womb-Born's making. I concur with the judgment pronounced by Lazarus, but it is past time for the Tuatha Dé to do their own dirty work. My dragons and I will return to our homes after this evening's banquet." With that, Clío and her guard marched from the room.

Lazarus turned to The Mórrígan and smiled. "Bráchthine would be proud of her, as I am."

The Mórrígan nodded and placed a hand on her brother's. "After we have concluded our other business, you should take her home, Lazarus. She is in pain and deserves it."

"Where is home for either of us?"

\*\*\*

The Womb-Born's troubles did not end with Clío's departure. Later, the Mórrígan stood before the Womb-Born and pointed at Lazarus. "You are the reason for our troubles because you abdicated the office of High King without a fight. Did you value the position so little?" Lazarus squirmed, but then few would not under his sister's glare.

It was the first time any of the Womb-Born had dared confront him on the issue. Was it a measure of their indifference or respect? Had they expected him to break the Law and refuse to give up the throne? Their traditional strategy to resolve weighty issues was to hope the problem would simply disappear like early mists in a warming sun. Lazarus remembered the Fomorian General's words and smiled. Endless compromise and procrastination were no substitute for taking difficult decisions. The recent war was a case in point.

His brothers and sisters seated around the table nodded sagely in agreement with The Mórrígan. They also chose to ignore their guilt and complicity. Their ancient, yet fragile, egos would not allow it. The Mórrígan's tongue was in no mood to be merciful. She ignored Daghdha, who sat forlornly at the heart of the gathering. Daghdha had learned harsh lessons, but was it enough? Long, artistic fingers pointed to each of The Mórrígan's remaining siblings. "*You* let Lazarus abdicate and did nothing to support or stand by him. None of you are without guilt. Worse, you connived to anoint Daghdha High King and then turned your back on him."

The Mórrígan fastened her gaze on Daghdha. Sympathy momentarily crept into her eyes, only to be replaced with anger as she held the others accountable. "There are those among us worthy of the crown, yet *we* selfishly washed our hands of the duty."

A rumble of rebellion rose from the Womb-Born. "Who are you to lecture us, sister?" said Áine. "You speak honeyed words of strife into weak minds. You cause mayhem and then fly away to wherever your bed resides while rivers of blood are spilt."

The Mórrígan looked at Áine with gleaming eyes. "I am the Trinity of goddesses, sister. Do you wish to bear that burden? Take it. It is yours." Áine recoiled and averted her eyes. "I include myself among a dishonourable group." The Mórrígan turned her gaze on Lazarus. "It is time to set things right. Will you sit on the High King's throne?"

"No."

The answer shocked The Mórrígan. She thought she had done enough to convince Lazarus. It also left the Womb-Born with their jaws slack. Who, if not Lazarus, would come to their rescue? Daghdha laughed at their confusion.

*Where did I fail? What sign did I misread?*

"You did not fail, sister, but you misread the signs in the Land of Immensity and the domains of the dragons and humans. All are interconnected. Balora showed us that when she by-passed the portals." Lazarus smiled at his siblings. "Anúna gave me leadership over you. It is a role I have neglected, and I shall make amends."

Green shoots of hope sprang up in the breasts of the demigods. It was quickly extinguished. "This does not mean I should be High King of the Tuatha Dé. That is a responsibility for one who resides in the Land of Immensity. The Goddess, and our mother, Anúna, gave me an obligation that goes beyond the borders of one kingdom."

"Then who, brother?" asked The Mórrígan.

Lazarus' eyes turned flinty, and his mien became severe. The Womb-Born shrank from his gaze. His brothers and sisters gazed at him, dismayed that he might turn his face from them—again. When their self-centred angst dissipated, looks of helplessness and a need for direction replaced it. The moment was poignant, given the power each of the demigods held.

"Áine…"

"No!" exclaimed Áine. "I will not be High Queen."

Lazarus smiled, which softened his sombre demeanour. "It appears that the Womb-Born need lessons on self-sacrifice. However, please let me finish, sister." Áine blushed and muttered apologies. "Áine will be restored as Queen of Muria." He looked at Daghdha. "Our brother has gone some way to reverse the changes made during his reign. I look to you, sister, to make Muria better than it was before." The beam on Áine's face told Lazarus it was a good decision, for she loved the city.

"In my absence, Macha will continue to reign as Queen of Coria."

"Shite! I'm homeless," said Daghdha, to titters around the table.

"Not quite, brother. Your siblings will build you a city in the Valley of Summer worthy of a High King."

"No! He cannot be High King," came the chorus from the Womb-Born. The Mórrígan and Daghdha looked bemused.

"Stand up, the brother or sister who wishes to be High King or Queen? It must be one of you." barked Lazarus. No one moved. "Who among you is better qualified? Daghdha did the job badly for several millennia, but whose fault was that? It was yours. Daghdha has acknowledged his mistakes, taken steps to make amends, and knows the job. His second season as High King will be much better…"

An icy look in Lazarus' gaze, and the sudden appearance of the Blade of Light, sent chills along Daghdha's spine. "It will not go well for you, brother, if I am called upon in the future to deal with you." With a flourish, Lazarus indicated the remaining brothers and sisters.

"You will cease squabbling among yourselves and accept full responsibility for the people in your kingdoms. The Goddess made you demigods, kings, and queens. From this day, you will accept that duty—fully. If you want to bask in the people's adoration, then put effort into understanding their needs, not just your own." He paused. "Only in the gravest of circumstances will you shift that burden onto Daghdha's shoulders."

"What of the Cauldron?" asked Daghdha.

"We have ignored for too long the possibility of the Cauldron as a weapon of more potency than either my Blade of Light or Lugh's spear. Balora is set on making it hers, but there will be others, too." Lazarus paused and said, "The Cauldron and the artefacts will become Clíodhna's and my responsibility."

"What if we need their powers?" asked Daghdha.

Lazarus laughed. "We are powerful demigods. Distance and time place few constraints on where and when we can travel."

"Anything else?" The Mórrígan's tone was dry.

"Yes. The Sons of Mil and the Fomorians are destroyed, apart from small remnants of both tribes. Hunt down the remaining Fomorian queens and keep a close watch on the borders of the Land of Immensity. The portals will remain in place as the sole means of journeying back and forth. Simultaneously, I will investigate how Balora does not need the portals. We need to either destroy the phenomenon or control it."

As the meeting broke up to prepare for the evening's banquet, The Mórrígan took Lazarus aside. "Well done, brother. Perhaps I should take lessons on intrigue from you." Lazarus smiled, shook his head, and kissed his sister. "Not quite a lover's kiss, but we are well past that season."

∗∗∗

"When do we go home to Belfast, Da?" asked Clío.

"Just as soon as you speak with the Dragon Council. Serpents are used to living far apart, more so than the Tuatha Dé. You residing beyond the Island of Dragons should cause few problems."

"This sounds like something my friends would say about *having your cake and eating it*."

"However…"

"There's always a 'however'," muttered Clío.

"Don't pout. It's unqueenly. You are the Queen of the Dragons. Aodh will always be concerned for your security. The Dragon Council will wish to assign you a permanent, *expanded* guard." Lazarus lifted his hand to forestall the inevitable protest. "Do not challenge them on this. We have the Cauldron to protect, and the other artefacts to find. Also, there's Balora's force to contend with. Additional firepower will be useful even if not the intent of the Dragon Council."

# CHAPTER 53

*1942—Spring—Northern Ireland*

Clío stood on the opposite side of Castlereagh Street in Belfast and inspected the crumbling, second-floor flat. She turned to Lazarus. It was strange to see him as the elderly Lazarus and not the tall, muscular Womb-Born colossus. In Belfast, he looked like a real person, not a powerful Tuatha Dé king. His transformation to her da would come later when they inevitably departed Ireland. The thought of leaving her home brought a tear to Clío's eye.

"Our flat has served its purpose well, Lazarus, but we will soon have additional guests to accommodate and feed. Where are we going to live?" Lazarus grunted non-committedly. It was his "Things will sort themselves out" response.

"Bloody men!" snorted Clío. Lazarus laughed. It felt good to have the "old" Clíodhna back.

The Dragon Council had conceded, albeit reluctantly, to Clío's request for a guard that was less obvious than the ten previously assigned to her. However, Aodh flat out refused when Clío insisted one bodyguard was sufficient. She was the queen and there were protocols to maintain.

The agreed compromise was five dragons—one from each of the dragon clanns. The four females and one male would arrive in two days. Clío chuckled. It would be the largest group of serpents to visit Ireland, if not the world, in several millennia. *Eat your heart out, St. Patrick.* The male, a dragon from Clann Dubh, caused Clío some soul-searching, but she conceded that it was an olive branch and honour. The recently confirmed black dragon queen valued the gesture and Clío's support.

The other consideration was the Cauldron. The half-skull gathered dust on the mantelpiece, looking like a leftover from Halloween. Indeed, a thief would think it odd but not give it a second look. Clío stared pointedly at Lazarus. "What is your plan for the Cauldron?"

* * *

Shifting to human form, Balora sat on the grassy cliff edge and looked seaward to the verdant rock that was Rathlin Island. She enjoyed the sound of crashing waves and the smell of salt and seaweed. She rubbed salves into her body and moaned. Current had deliberately battered and bruised her. The entity took a sadistic pleasure in hurting her. *Why? Is it just me or does Current hate women in general?*

Familial ties held little importance to Balora. Thus, mourning the death of her mother and siblings seemed hypocritical. Ironically, the only person whom Balora deeply missed or admitted to having any depth of feelings for was Lazarus. She sighed at the memory of their few nights together in Muria. They had a relationship, but it defeated Balora to describe it or its boundaries.

Clíodhna was a key part in her future with Lazarus. She sensed the dragon, if not her shield-maiden, was not antagonistic, unless she tried to hurt Lazarus again. *But why would I? It is not in my best interest.* She patted her belly and smiled.

The Fomorian High Queen… Balora snorted loudly at the elevation. *As if the title means anything now.* With a shrug, she turned to inspect what was probably the largest Fomorian army remaining in any world. She had heard rumours of several queens fleeing the Second Fomorian War, but with no access to the portals they were stranded in the Land of Immensity. She assessed their chances of surviving the inevitable search and destroy missions of the dragons as negligible. As for any goal to propagate the Fomorian race, that bordered on the delusional.

Balora's force numbered one hundred demons and a similar number of Nemed. She saw no sense in hiding the tragic demise of Fomoria from her warband. Upon hearing of the Fomorian defeat, despair came first, then in-fighting and accusations of blame, and then more despondency. She was their only hope. Both she and they knew it. The Nemed's reaction seemed increasingly rebellious, but she dismissed any threat.

Of more import to Balora, her band might be a reasonable sacrifice in her pursuit of the Cauldron. How would she determine the location of the vessel? Where were Lazarus and Clíodhna? Balora's ruby eyes glowed in anticipation of the hunt and an embryonic plan formed in her head.

\*\*\*

Clío thought their new home had more to do with Lazarus' liking for Bushmills whiskey than strategic planning. Yet, his choice did have clear advantages.

Located at the northern edge of the tiny village of Bushmills, close to several glens, and only a few miles from the Giant's Causeway, the Bushmills Coaching Inn had fallen on hard times. Each attempt to revive its fortunes had been unsuccessful, and the ongoing war and air raids had done nothing to help its cause. Apart from a skeleton staff, the inn was deserted. Yet, the building was structurally sound, its setting, aspect, and surroundings were exceptionally pleasing, and the bedrooms were kept scrupulously clean—a testament to its current owners.

Unsurprisingly, the middle-aged couple who managed the inn were delighted the day Clío and Lazarus appeared on their doorstep. They gratefully accepted Lazarus' offer to rent the building for six months, with an option to extend. That he offered payment in advance and with gold coin put both icing and marzipan on the cake.

\*\*\*

The discussion took place in the inn's common room, where everyone found a deeply cushioned leather armchair or couch to sink into. "We have two tasks. Find a safe place to hide the Cauldron and search for and destroy the last Fomorian nest," said Lazarus. "The second will follow the first as Balora is sure to uncover the Cauldron's refuge, especially as we will leave breadcrumbs for her to follow."

"Bury the Cauldron in the Glens. You could hide several armies in the crags and valleys," said Clío. The dragon nodded to her cohort. "We will reconnoitre the area and find suitable options." The whispering among the dragon guards piqued Clío's curiosity. "Feel free to add anything to the discussion. We are easy-going here."

One of the guards dipped her head to Clío and Lazarus. "We have already surveyed the region. It would have been negligent of us not to have done so. From here, it is about ten miles to the glens, and five to the coast, so it's not a large area for five dragons to cover." She grinned. "Also, there's not much to do at night in the village unless you like much older men." The serpent glanced anxiously at Lazarus, and blushed. "Sorry, your majesty."

Lazarus laughed. "No offence was taken, and here, I am simply Lazarus. Please finish your report."

The dragon smiled and dipped her head. "Our night vision is excellent and cloaked we can travel quickly and unseen." She reached for a large sheet of paper. "We have charted a map of the area." The serpent took a deep breath and held Clío's gaze. "To be clear, my queen, we are not simply hired muscle. The Dragon Council chose us and our skills to support you by whatever means in whatever activities you choose to involve yourself. That includes taking the initiative." She tapped her head and smiled. "Brains and brawn." A murmur from the other dragons prompted another grin. She rolled her eyes. "And beauty."

Lazarus almost split his pants, laughing at a disconcerted Clío. Her response was a growl, which sounded more like a peeved kitten than a lion. "What is your name?" asked Clío and then slapped her forehead. "Fuck! I'm doing it again. Have I not learned anything from Ceara?" Five puzzled serpents stared at Clío. "Please humour me. I am still learning on the job. I would like to know your names. For those who do not know me, I answer to Clío or Clíodhna." She looked at the red-haired dragon and smiled. "I suspect you are Clann Dearg."

The dragon smiled and dipped her head. "I am Íde and yes, I am Clann Dearg." One by one the other dragons gave their name and clann.

"I propose that Íde determines the best location for the Cauldron and takes it there without delay," said Clío. "Take a backup, just in case. Then, your team should guard the vessel around the clock. Three shifts of eight hours should accomplish that and not place too much of a burden on the members. I will take my turn in the rotation." Murmurs of dissent rippled through the dragons. "You will do nothing I would not. There will be times when I will crack the whip but now is not one of those." Clío grinned at the surprise on her guards' faces. "We can all read and converse through our minds should an emergency arise."

Lazarus stood. "Now for our immediate priority—Balora's Fomorians."

\*\*\*

Balora knew she was outgunned. Stalemate was not an option, and winning was improbable. Therefore she had one chance: to upend the board. After previous orders to conceal their camp, Balora now commanded her Fomorian captains to form small parties and forage for food and supplies. Albeit this only took place when darkness fell.

Several nights later, she chose a handful of demons and exited the cave. Those left behind thought she was setting an example and doing her part of the scavenging mission. If they survived the night, Balora would kill them because of their naivety. Balora had sensed the presence of dragons, and she put her plan into motion.

Íde and another dragon followed the trail of one foraging group back to the main camp. Too late, the Fomorians realised Balora had duped and betrayed them. By then, it was too late, and they could do little as the serpents filled the cave with dragon breath until the demons were ash.

\*\*\*

Balora had engineered her diversion but was unprepared for what she found. "The bastard!" screamed Balora in frustration. Before her lay not one but one hundred small half-skulls. All were the same colour and dimensions, making it impossible to choose the genuine Cauldron without first examining all the candidates. Perversely, Balora knew the Cauldron was among the group. She could sense its presence.

A chuckle came from above the cave's entrance. "It is an excellent deception, is it not?" At Íde's mocking voice, Balora's teeth ground against each other like a pair of quern stones.

"I am your match, dragon, and I will have the Cauldron."

"Even if I were alone, your assertion would be debatable, but I am not. Feel free to examine each of the skulls. I am in no rush." Íde's great maw opened to reveal her fangs and rows of razor-sharp teeth. Long talons extended from her hands and feet. "Or you could kneel before me. I will make your death swift, if not painless."

Caught off-balance, Balora glanced around to identify who accompanied Íde. The five Fomorians who escorted the queen stomped the ground in anger. They were the biggest demons in her force. Balora had chosen them purely for their brawn and she was confident the quintet could keep Íde's dragons distracted while she escaped. Her nose twitched at a familiar scent, and she smiled before muttering, "Bastard."

"Whatever happened to that nimble brain, Balora? You have become predictable. I do not have to read your mind to know what you are thinking: send the brutes in as a diversion, steal the Cauldron, and escape in the chaos." Balora swore at the voice of Lazarus and the insult. The glow of golden light that appeared to the right of Íde resolved itself into the shape of her former lover. In his right hand, he held the Blade of Light.

A patch of inky blackness on either side of Lazarus moved fractionally, suggesting more dragons. Defeating or distracting one dragon would be a challenge; more than two plus a Womb-Born was a near impossibility. Balora methodically and quickly assessed the scenarios available to her. None were to her liking, and all resulted in her death.

"*Attack!*" shouted Balora. With little thought or analysis, the bodyguards lumbered forward, wings outstretched, and claws extended. It was no surprise to anyone, including Balora, that the five Fomorians became ash. Likewise, it was no surprise to Lazarus that as her minions advanced, the Fomorian queen flew swiftly in the opposite direction. The brief period of their sacrifice proved enough for her escape.

\*\*\*

"You could have stopped or pursued her," accused Clío.

"So could you," retorted Lazarus. "We are both conflicted over Balora. You saw her as an enemy yet saved her life in the Cauldron Room."

"She told you."

"No. The Cauldron teases, or tortures, its supplicants with awareness without being able to do anything to intercede. I heard."

"She was yours to deal with. I had no right to execute her."

"She asked me if I considered her an enemy or a thief. I prefer to think of her as the latter. Balora also sees herself as your protector. Does that bother you?"

Clío shook her head. "No, but she is a dangerous, intelligent, and focused woman. We should hope that her attention is diverted by other treasures."

*The End*

# BACKGROUND NOTES

I treasure the memories of East Belfast and the many friends I made during my formative first forty years. Yet, I never fully appreciated how growing up in East Belfast influenced my development as a person, until I crossed the Atlantic, first to Canada and then Texas, USA. Now like Clío, I reminisce about fish suppers and Ulster Fries. *Dragons, Demons & Demigods* is perhaps, partly, homage to where I came from.

My great-grandfather was called Lazarus and as much as I can recall, physically looked like the character in this book, smoked like a train, and drank like a fish. I lived on the corner of Bryson and Duke Streets for about five years when I was eight years old, attended Beechfield Street Primary School, and played piano in Pitt Street Mission Hall—I was not very good. I also lived for a spell in the apartment on Castlereagh Street. Victoria Park and the ducks were a twenty-minute walk away. I can still taste the fish, pastie, and sausage suppers from The Star chippie and nothing beats an Ulster Fry for breakfast.

Lazarus' favourite bar, McHugh's, remains my drinking place in Belfast, and I share his love for Bushmills Single Malt.

For those who have never visited Northern Ireland, if you can, treat yourself. You will never regret the journey.

✳✳✳

*Wingless dragons. Who heard of such a peculiarity?* Well possibly Eve in the Garden of Eden. In Genesis, after the Fall of Adam and Eve, God cursed the serpent and said, "Upon your belly you shall go," (*Genesis 3:14*). This appears to imply that, prior to the Fall, the serpent had legs which sounds much more like a dragon than an ordinary snake. It was also thought to be a beautiful or magnificent beast. In Revelation, St. John equates a dragon to the serpent of the Garden.

Pliny the Elder, the Roman author, describes the Indian drakōn as a big constricting snake, similar to the Indian python. The Lernaean Hydra, a multiple-headed serpentine swamp monster killed by Heracles, is said to have been a dragon. In Ancient Greece and Rome, dragons were typically depicted as large, wingless serpents or lizards. Dragons from East Asian cultures are typically serpentine, legless, lack wings, and are often considered benevolent or wise creatures.

The Celtic dragon may have developed from a horned and poisonous or fire-breathing snake. In Celtic art, the dragon design is known in diverse styles and may have derived from a serpent-like creature in ancient folklore of the Middle East and Greece. Western Celtic peoples were familiar with dragons in the pre-Christian age, and the native people of Britain are said to have worn Celtic decorations with motifs of dragons on them during the Roman invasion. Archaeological evidence points to the continental Celts using brooches and pins in the form of a dragon during the La Tène period from 500 B.C. to 1 A.D.

So, where did the wings come from? Winged, four-legged dragons became common in European folklore and Medieval art, during the Middle Ages (5th to 15th century). More recently the imagery has inspired movies, such as *Reign of Fire*, *The Hobbit: The Desolation of Smaug*, and *Dragonslayer*.

In modern times, dragons are usually shown with the body of a huge lizard (or snake) with two pairs of lizard-type legs, bat-like wings, and breathing fire from their mouths. The shift was likely influenced by factors such as artistic evolution, culture, and the conflation of different mythical creatures.

# GLOSSARY

**ANIMAL ALTER-EGOS**
Irish Wolfhound (Lazarus)
Raven (The Mórrígan)

**PHRASES**
Ard Righ (High King)
Bitseach/Bitseacha (Bitch/s)
Bodhran/Bodhráin (Drum/s)
Caomhnóirí (Personal guard)
Céili (Dance/party)
Craic (Pleasant conversation)
Dragán go Brách! (Dragons forever.)
Fidchell (Strategy game)
Pit/Piteanna (Vagina/s)
Ríchathaoir Dubh (Scáthach's Throne)
Seanchaí (Storyteller)
Sláinte Mhaith (Good Health)
Striapach/Striapacha (Whore/s)
Tuilí (Bastard)
Uisce beatha (Water of life, i.e., whiskey)

# RACES/CLANNS

## Dragons (Wind-Born)
Clann Dearg (red)
Clann Dubh (black)
Clann Foruaine (green)
Clann Ór (gold)
Clann Umhaí (copper-bronze)

## Fomorians (Demons)
## Nemed
## Sons of Mil

**Tuatha Dé Danann** (People of the Goddess Danu)
Womb-Born

## TUATHA DÉ ARTEFACTS
*Claímh Solais*—the Blade of Light
*Coire Ansic*—Daghdha's Undry Cauldron

# DRAMATIS PERSONAE

Áine (Womb-Born, Queen of Muria)

An Ársa (Father of the Womb-Born)

Anúna (Mother of the Wind- & Womb-Born)

Aodh Dearg (General of the Dragons' Armies, Red Dragon)

Badhbh (Part of the Trinity of Goddesses)

Balor (Fomorian General killed by Nuadhu)

Balora (Queen of Fomoria, daughter of Balor)

Baoth (King of the Sons of Míl)

Bráchthine (Former Queen of the Dragons, Clíodhna's mother)

Bres (Ériu and Elatha's son)

Ceara Dearg (Red Dragon, Clíodhna's Shield-Maiden, Aodh's daughter)

Clíodhna (Queen of the Dragons *aka* Clío)

Conn Dubh (Black Dragon, King of Clann Dubh)

Current (Master of Ocean Currents)

Daghdha (Womb-Born, High King of the Tuatha Dé)

Elatha (Fomorian prince, married Ériu)

Eochaidh Breas (Tuatha Dé noble, led rebellion against the Tuatha Dé)

Ériu (Daghdha and Meadhbh's daughter)

Fate

Íde (Red Dragon)

Lugh (Tuatha Dé, warrior with a magical spear and skilled in all arts)

Macha (Queen of Coria, Part of the Trinity of Goddesses)

Manannán mac Lir (Womb-Born, God of the Sea)

Meadhbh (Womb-Born, Tuatha Dé Queen)

Midhir (Daghdha and The Mórrígan's son)

Mór (Red Dragon, Ceara's sister)

Nuadha (Womb-Born, Former High King of the Tuatha Dé, *aka* Lazarus)

Neasán Ór (Gold Dragon, Civil leader)

Scáthach (Tuatha Dé, Queen of Scáth, a Sorceress & expert in battle tactics)

Serendipity (Goddess)

The Goddess

The Mórrígan (Womb-Born, Tuatha Dé Queen, Queen of Whispers & Shadows, Queen of Desolation)

Tuirill (Tuatha Dé Rebel)

Uathach (Scáthach's Daughter & a Succubus)

Ultán (Son of Mil, Watcher/Assassin)

# LOCATIONS

**ISLAND OF DRAGONS**

**LAND OF IMMENSITY (THE MOUNDS)**
Coria
Muria
Falia
Fania
Fomoria
The Island of Scáth

**LAND OF THE HUMANS**

**Northern Ireland**
Antrim (County in N. Ireland)
Belfast (Capital City of N. Ireland)
Belfast Lough
Bushmills (Small town on east coast; home of Bushmills Distillery)
Cavehill (Hill north of Belfast)
Giant's Causeway (Famous rock formation on north-eastern coast)
Glens of Antrim
Irish Sea
Rathlin Island (Island of the northern coast)

**Northern Albu (Scotland)**
Na h-Eileanan Beaga (The Small Isles—the Inner Hebrides)

# ABOUT THE AUTHOR

Award-winning author David H. Millar was born in Belfast, Northern Ireland. David writes historical and urban fantasy influenced by Celtic mythology. He is the author of the five-volume, *Conall* series, which is set in 400 B.C. Europe, and the series spin-offs: *The Dog Roses* and *The Blood Queen Chronicles*.

*Dragons, Demons & Demigods* is the first novel in a new Tuatha Dé Chronicles series.

David settled in Houston, Texas, in 2011. An avid reader, armchair sportsman, and Liverpool Football Club fan, Millar lives with his family, and two tuxedo cats, Beau and Stiletto.

## Contact David:

Website:
www.david-h-millar.com

Facebook:
facebook.com/aweepubco

Instagram:
@author.davidhmillar

X (Twitter):
@DavidHMillar

CLÍODHNA, QUEEN OF THE DRAGONS